A

Lifelong romance a[...]
Zealand. Writing f[...]
happy endings and t[...]
can follow her a[...]
jcharroway, instagram.com/jcharroway and twitter.com/
jcharroway

Sherelle Green is a Chicago native with a dynamic imagination and a passion for reading and writing. Her love for romance developed in high school after stumbling across a hot and steamy Mills & Boon novel. She instantly became an avid romance reader and decided to pursue an education in English and Journalism. A true romantic, she believes in predestined romances, love at first sight and fairytale endings.

As a child, books took **Robyn Donald** to places far away from her village in Northland, New Zealand. Then, as well as becoming a teacher, marrying and raising two children, she discovered romances and read them voraciously. So much she decided to write one. When her first book was accepted by Mills & Boon she felt she'd arrived home. Robyn still lives in Northland, using the landscape as a setting for her work. Her life is enriched by friends she's made among writers and readers.

One Night...

One Night...
to Forever

JC HARROWAY

SHERELLE GREEN

ROBYN DONALD

MILLS & BOON

All rights reserved including the right of reproduction in whole or in part in any form. This edition is published by arrangement with Harlequin Enterprises ULC.

This is a work of fiction. Names, characters, places, locations and incidents are purely fictional and bear no relationship to any real life individuals, living or dead, or to any actual places, business establishments, locations, events or incidents. Any resemblance is entirely coincidental.

This book is sold subject to the condition that it shall not, by way of trade or otherwise, be lent, resold, hired out or otherwise circulated without the prior consent of the publisher in any form of binding or cover other than that in which it is published and without a similar condition including this condition being imposed on the subsequent purchaser.

® and TM are trademarks owned and used by the trademark owner and/or its licensee. Trademarks marked with ® are registered with the United Kingdom Patent Office and/or the Office for Harmonisation in the Internal Market and in other countries.

First Published in Great Britain 2022
By Mills & Boon, an imprint of HarperCollins*Publishers*, Ltd
1 London Bridge Street, London, SE1 9GF

www.harpercollins.co.uk

HarperCollins*Publishers*
1st Floor, Watermarque Building,
Ringsend Road, Dublin 4, Ireland

ONE NIGHT...TO FOREVER © 2022 Harlequin Enterprises ULC.

One Night Only © 2018 JC Harroway
If Only for Tonight © 2014 Sherelle Green
Stepping out of the Shadows © 2012 Robyn Donald Kingston

ISBN: 978-0-263-30489-3

MIX
Paper from
responsible sources
FSC® C007454

This book is produced from independently certified FSC™ paper
to ensure responsible forest management.

For more information visit: www.harpercollins.co.uk/green

Printed and Bound in Spain using 100% Renewable electricity at
CPI Black Print, Barcelona

ONE NIGHT ONLY

JC HARROWAY

To E

for inspiring the fun, bubbly, caring Essie. X

CHAPTER ONE

IF THIS SETTING, so far from the wreckage he'd left behind in New York, couldn't provide ballast, nowhere could. Ash Jacob closed his eyes, sucked in a deep breath and focussed on the sun warming his back, the hypnotic chatter of English birdsong and the continuous distant hum of London traffic.

'Shit!'

The violent exclamation pulled him up short. So he wasn't the only one having a bad day. His vision hazed as the bright July sunlight hit his retinas once more, his surroundings sharpening into focus. He stretched one arm along the back of the park bench, the wooden slats of which dug into his fatigued muscles—a reminder that he'd spent twelve hours on a plane yesterday, largely bent like a pretzel despite his first-class seat.

'Bloody, buggering, shit.'

What a charming turn of phrase.

His mouth twitched and his mood lightened. She stood a short distance away from his secluded spot in St James's Park, her short, flowery dress revealing bare, shapely legs; golden hair streaked with enough russet to turn her long ponytail to fire in the right light; a small denim backpack slung over one shoulder, which made her appear younger than what he estimated as mid-twenties.

A student? A tourist? A fellow soul, far from home?

One delicate finger jabbed at the screen of her phone, as if she could poke it back to life by dogged persistence alone.

Intrigue and a flicker of lust made Ash sit up straighter. Her quirky English accent and endearing choice of expletives reminded him that New York was a long way away. And yes, the women in his exclusive, affluent circle had the kind of polish and poise that this beguiling stranger seemed, at first glance, to lack, but the effect of the jut of her pert breasts and the cut of her fine-boned features in profile on his jet-lagged libido equalled, if not surpassed, his usual level of interest in the opposite sex. An interest that circumstances had shaped into two simple rules: one—on his terms; and two—one night only.

He shifted on the hard seat, his jeans becoming skintight, at least around the groin. The beauty dropped the hand holding the offending device to her side and cast her wide eyes around their corner of the park.

Ash slammed his own stare closed again, pretending to enjoy the formerly relaxing ambience. He'd come to London to work on a joint business venture with his oldest friend, not to rescue an English damsel, no matter how long her legs or how curvaceous her ass. And more importantly, he'd come to get away from public drama and get his life back under control. Control that couldn't come soon enough.

'Um, excuse me…'

Damn.

She'd moved that delectable derrière of hers closer. There were few people around, mainly joggers and the odd parent pushing a stroller. She *must* be talking to him. Ash relaxed his eyelids and slowed his breathing. Perhaps if she thought he was asleep, she'd leave him alone. Find someone else to rectify her technology issues.

Her footfalls scuffed the gravel of the path.

There was an embarrassed tinkle of laughter.

Right in front of him now.

Close enough for her scent to tickle his nose— light, floral and mixed with the unmistakable smell of sunscreen.

His libido roared anew. Man, would he love to see those curves and that milky skin clad in a bikini and sprawled on a lounger at his holiday place in the Hamptons.

The sexy intruder delicately cleared her throat.

The sweet sound rolled over his out-of-sync senses. Physically, she embodied the epitome of his type. Under other circumstances, he'd turn on the charm, get to know her enough to assess if her persuasion for no-strings sex aligned with his, and pass a satisfactory afternoon between her thighs.

But the last thing he needed right now was an encounter with a woman *that* beautiful, especially one who awoke his interest to the degree currently rendering him momentarily trapped on the park bench by his tight jeans.

He'd been played in the past—the old, female-inflicted wound recently reopened in the most humiliating and public way being the main reason for his rather hasty departure from New York.

For now, women were categorically off the agenda.

And really, who talked to complete strangers in a city centre park? His appearance today could only be described as dressed down compared to his usual attire of bespoke tailored suits. He'd wanted an escape from the cloying, air-conditioned hotel he'd booked for his first couple of nights in London until the Jacob Holdings apartment had been spring-cleaned. Some fresh air. Green spaces. Anything that helped to reprogram his brain from its current gut-churning cycle of guilt and bile-inducing self-loathing.

So he'd thrown on a T-shirt and his comfortable jeans, both the worse for wear having spent forty-eight hours in a suitcase, forgone shaving off the three days' worth of scruff and headed outdoors. The casual look was a visual cue that his move to London represented a major change from the norm; a shift from everything he'd lived, breathed and strived for these past ten years: his role in the family business, which was fraught with dysfunctional politics in the hands of his ruthless, manipulative and, as he'd bitterly discovered in the most degrading way, cheating father.

'Excuse me, are you…okay?'

Ash surrendered to the soothing voice with a sigh that dragged his mind back from the edge of a dark abyss. She wasn't going to give up. Perhaps she was lost. He didn't know London that well, but he'd spent enough time here over the years to have a vague sense of direction. Better to hear what she wanted and send her gorgeous ass on its way.

He opened his eyes, forcing his face to exhibit a tight, inquisitive smile instead of the frustration that put his teeth on edge at having the embodiment of feminine temptation literally thrown into his path.

'Of course. Just enjoying the sun.'

Her answering beam had two opposing effects on his overwrought body: the fullness of her pouty lips direct-messaged his groin with a slug of not wholly un-welcome blood-pounding heat, and her open, friendly stare twitched his shoulders up several notches until his muscles cramped. Were all English women this naive? This trusting? For a man who trusted no one, she was a complete mystery.

'Oh, good. I don't suppose I could ask for a fa-vour…?' She waggled her dead phone in front of his face. 'My phone just died.'

'Okay… Are you lost?'

Give her some damn directions and watch her groan-worthy legs walk away.

But then his view would be far less appealing.

Another megawatt smile warmed his insides and made him think of childhood trips to Coney Island.

'No. I wondered if you could take a picture for me.' She pointed at the view of the London Eye in the distance. 'On your phone…and perhaps…send it to me?' Her voice wavered and she curled some escaped strands of hair at her nape around her index finger.

His expression must have been comical. Had he woken up in some parallel universe or was her friend-liness some sort of ancient British ritual? Did he care if it meant a few more seconds surreptitiously eyeing her glorious body and fantasising about her naked under him?

Ash shifted, discreetly readjusting himself in his pants as he allowed his gaze to properly take in every inch of porcelain beauty. Up close, she was stunning. Flawless creamy skin, enormous sky-blue eyes and a charming dusting of copper freckles across her slightly upturned nose. And on first impressions— the embodiment of a sunny disposition.

And if she wanted a photo, she was clearly a tourist. Perhaps this was her last day in London?

Another point to his libido.

As if matching his interest, she flicked her stare over him from head to toe, skimming over his creased tee and well-worn jeans and flooding his body with heat to rival the summer sun. Was she flirting?

'Sure,' he said.

Why not? He could surely oblige her with a photo and perhaps anything else she might want. He lifted one eyebrow as her eyes returned to his face. Bright spots of red appeared on her high cheekbones as she straightened the charming little head tilt she'd employed while checking him out. Yes, perhaps she was exactly what he needed… A little help with his current hard-on predicament. She seemed to share his physical interest. Perhaps that would cure his mind-numbing restlessness and get his usual focus back on track.

The tension snapped with her tinkling laughter. Ash grinned back. At least she owned her flagrant sexual curiosity in him—how refreshing. He reassessed her age—perhaps she wasn't as sweet as she looked. She flicked her ponytail, sunny smile back in place.

He shifted on the bench, fishing his phone from his back pocket. The angle of the sun meant her dress was practically see-through from his position. Should he tell her? Or just enjoy her shapely silhouette? Imagine those long legs wrapped around his waist…

No.

His mind zapped to ancient history come back to haunt him. His recent discovery of the lengths his ex had gone to in order to deceive him, and the depth of that lie, only confirmed his stand on the opposite sex. He was done with women, unless they, like him, wanted one thing only and understood the rules.

The weathered wooden rungs of the bench creaked as she sat next to him. 'You're American, aren't you?'

He nodded and then looked away from her open, earnest face. At least this woman couldn't be interested in the prestige and power of his family name or his considerable personal fortune, dressed the way he was. She couldn't know his family owned half of Manhattan and a sizeable chunk of London. She couldn't guess he'd come to London to distance himself from his 'real estate tycoon' reputation—as well as from the ruthless deception by one family member in particular. Not unless she read the society pages of the *New York Times*.

He tasted bile. How could his father do that to him? To his own son? Making a mockery of the years of professional loyalty Ash had given the family business? Fuck—did he have 'trusting schmuck' stamped across his forehead?

The sexy stranger didn't seem aware of his inner turmoil. She turned her body to face him so her bare knees bumped his denim-clad thigh, eyes alight. 'London is an amazing city, isn't it? Have you seen Buckingham Palace? It's just over there.' She pointed over her shoulder, warming to her change of subject and speaking with dizzying speed in her excitement about the tourist attractions the city had to offer.

'And do you know about the Seven Noses of Soho? I'm scouting them out today. Fun fact…' She pointed towards the small lake in the park. 'Did you know the pelicans were a gift from a Russian ambassador to King Charles the second in 1664?'

She talked so quickly, her charming accent distorting the English until she might as well have been speaking Mandarin. Noses? Pelicans? Perhaps the impotence coiled inside him was steadily infecting and destroying his brain cells. Perhaps he was more jet-lagged than he'd assumed. Perhaps testosterone had fried his usual laser-sharp mind.

'So, you wanted a picture?' He unlocked his phone and leaned forward, preparing to stand. Do a good deed for the beautiful English rose so he could get on with trying to cobble his shit back together. He could no longer pretend that his sole motivation for coming to London was for a new business opportunity. Other factors had made him flee across the Atlantic—his guilt at forcing his mother to face her sham of a marriage, and the shameful publicity that had followed his bust-up with his father. Belonging to a high-profile family had its distinct downsides.

But he'd left all that behind.

Focus on the here and now.

London, the rich culture and vibrancy of the city, provided abundant distractions, though none quite as appealing as the distraction warming the sliver of space between her body and his and momentarily taking his mind from his troubles.

'How long have you been here?' Another head tilt, her tongue peeking out to swipe her lower lip.

A silent groan rattled his skull.

So not fair.

'A day or two.' How could he ignore such delicious temptation right in front of him? Surely he'd read her signals correctly. The perfect diversion sat before him looking at him as if he were a tasty snack—what could be more temporary than two travellers making a connection and enjoying one lost night in London?

No need to confess his real identity—one of New York's top corporate attorneys, a real estate mogul and heir to the Jacob fortune. Not that he wanted to publicise any association with his bastard father right now. Hal Jacob's ruthless streak had long made Ash wince. But even he hadn't seen the train wreck approaching, hadn't anticipated the far-reaching, closer-to-home consequences.

He scrubbed his hand over his face, forcing his dark thoughts to take a sharp left turn, and focussed on the enticing, quirky and sexy woman in front of him. She smelled fantastic. Just the thing to settle the out-of-control spiralling of his thoughts,

Yes, she was a little greener than most of the women who passed briefly through his life, but just as striking. Practically the polar opposite of the sophisticated women he usually invited into his bed, her bubbly personality was as intoxicating as a breath of fresh and fragrant summer air. The flicker of interest in his groin built, stirring his limbs with urgent energy.

Ash covertly checked her ring finger—bare.

But in his experience, women who looked like her—

peaches and cream complexion, whimsical ponytail—
wanted more than he was willing to offer. Wanted a
relationship. And he never went there, no matter how
appealing the inducement.

Not since his ex-fiancée…

Ash stood in an attempt to banish the jitters in his
legs. He'd take her damn snap and put an end to this
weird Transatlantic lesson in charming, but eccen-
tric, cultural differences. Remove himself far from
temptation.

He stepped into the centre of the path and raised
his phone to the distant iconic view of one of London's most popular tourist attractions. With a click
he'd completed his obligation, his intentions still wavering between polite dismissal and revealing some
of his cards in case he'd been wrong about her and
she shared his philosophies on casual sex.

'Have you taken the ride?' She appeared at his side,
her eyes focussed on the giant wheel, its half-glass
pods glinting in the sun.

'Not yet.' He held out his phone for her inspection, his mind flitting to a different kind of ride as
she leaned close to stare at the screen and the tips of
her silky hair glided over his wrist.

Fuck! No amount of English fresh air was going to
shift this…urge. And, away from the negotiation table,
Ash was never more in control than in the bedroom.

Yes, a little summer loving would both banish his
restlessness and put his head straight. Hopefully, the
control he demanded in the bedroom would re-infect
the rest of him and shunt him back onto an even keel
in time for the first day of his new business venture
tomorrow.

The captivating stranger smiled, and his heart rate accelerated again.

'Thanks so much. You're a lifesaver.' She rattled off her number and he typed in the digits, sending the photo via text.

'My name's Essie, by the way.' She held out her hand—delicate; smooth-skinned; short nails painted purple.

He shook it, the brief slide of palm-to-palm grating in its formality after the mild flirtatious banter bouncing between them.

'Ash.'

She grinned as if he'd confessed his name began with HRH and he'd come to invite her back to the palace for afternoon tea.

'So, Ash the American tourist…' She had her photo, but she wasn't leaving. In fact, she was twirling that hair again, her eyes glinting with an unmistakable interest—one matched in him. No, his instincts were spot on.

'So, Essie, English fun facts expert…'

Another laugh that shot straight to his balls. 'Wanna grab lunch?' she said. 'I don't know this part of London well, but there's a cute deli not far from here and I have tons more facts about the city…' Her pretty blue eyes gleamed.

Heat soared in his chest. She *was* coming on to him in a subtle, fetching way he found way more enticing than the overt advances of his usual hook-ups. Absolutely, he'd be up for a no-strings one-time with this beautiful stranger. And as a tourist, he needn't spin his usual spiel about *having a good time*, *keeping things casual*, *hooking up* and other euphemisms that let the women he bedded know exactly where they stood. Where *he* stood.

She'd leave London to go back to whatever charming part of the UK she came from and, as far as she'd know, he'd go back to America.

He held out his arm, indicating she take the path ahead of them before tucking both his hands in the front pockets of his jeans. She smiled, swung her hair over her shoulder and set off at his side. For a few beats they walked in silence, the warm summer air heavy with possibility and an insistent flicker of sexual chemistry.

Something stirred in his gut—that delicious coil of excitement that the anonymity of meeting a stranger in a foreign place brought. Today he could be anyone. There were endless possibilities to reinvent himself and shake off the recently acquired shackles that held him down as if his feet were entombed in concrete.

Not Ash the duped, who'd not only been cheated on but also lied to by the two people in his life who should have had his back. *Yeah, fuck that guy.* He was Ash the American tourist, killing time with the interesting, beautiful breath of fresh air that was Essie.

'So…' he flashed his first genuine smile her way, enjoying the telling pink flush of her cheeks '…tell me about these noses.'

Essie Newbold laughed and bumped shoulders with the sexy American she'd spent the afternoon and evening with. Well, she would have bumped shoulders with him if he weren't so tall—instead, her shoulder bumped his arm. But the effect was the same.

Contact.

Those delicious little trembles of static electricity zinged to all her highly attuned erogenous zones as they'd been doing all day, every time their arms had brushed as they'd hunted the Seven Noses of Soho or when they were squeezed together, chest to chest, on the standing-room-only Tube. She'd never been more grateful for the crowding of London's underground.

Instead of allowing the momentum of her flirty little shoulder bump to ping her away from him, Ash scooped his arm around her waist and grinned down at her.

Her head swam.

She was really going to do this—sleep with the dreamy man she'd met in the park this morning? Her first one-night stand.

Essie slipped her hand into the back pocket of his jeans, her fingers pressing into his tightly toned backside. Where had her uncharacteristic bravery come from? The desire for something more than the dribs and drabs she'd tolerated from her no-good ex?

Her ex's idea of foreplay had been a mandatory squeeze of the boob. And to her shame, she'd accepted such lazy, shoddy attention.

All the more reason to explore a one-night stand with the drool-worthy, confident American. She'd gain some much-needed experience in the one-night-stand stakes, and hopefully score herself the kind of orgasm that only existed in her world as a mythical will-o'-the-wisp, and afterwards they'd move on having both had a good time. Unless Ash was a serial killer, it was a win-win situation. She absorbed the foreign, heady thrill of his big warm body next to hers. Not that it was cold—her shivers originated purely from anticipation.

The best kind of shivers.

She sucked in a stuttering breath—she'd never felt more reckless. And, if she was honest, she also felt a little embarrassed. There was no law that stated that, before her twenty-fifth birthday, she should have experienced at least one night of no-strings sex, but, as she touted herself as something of a relationship expert, didn't she owe it to the readers of her relationship psychology blog to experience what all the fuss was about?

Ash's hand looped around her shoulder. She reached up and clasped his fingers. They grinned at each other, Essie's belly jolting in time with her excitable pulse.

No serious scientist could rely solely on academic theory. She could finally verify her years of extensive research with some cold, hard, scientific data.

Surely he must be able to hear the blood whooshing through her head?

Because in practical terms, what did she really know about relationships, especially the functional kind?

Her face fell at the momentary wobble. Her one serious boyfriend during uni had left her practically swearing off the opposite sex for good on the grounds she clearly couldn't spot a decent relationship candidate if he was stark naked in front of her wearing a *pick me, I'm a safer than houses bet* hat.

A trait she'd inherited from her mother perhaps… The woman had, after all, procreated with Essie's lying, cheating, deserting father and spent many years playing second fiddle to his actual wife, his *real* family.

Not that Essie had known all that back then. She'd simply been a girl who desperately missed her beloved father while he'd worked overseas for long stretches of time. Clearly she and her mother shared a desperate-for-love vibe that usually sent men running.

But Ash wasn't running.

And she wasn't looking for a relationship. Just sex. She'd gleaned from Ash's subtext that, like her, he was only interested in a one-night thing. She shoved the buzzkill thoughts from her mind, focussing on the specimen of manly perfection beside her. Exotic Ash. A gentleman. Funny, intelligent and interested in what she had to say.

So different from her ex, and she'd wasted two years in that flawed relationship.

Her throat tightened.

Perhaps she was ready for a change. It was, after all, the eve of a brand-new chapter of her life—her new job working for her until-recently estranged half-brother began tomorrow. Or perhaps it was just charming, sophisticated, sexy-as-sin Ash with his crinkle-eyed smile, his quick wit and his tales of New York that earned him a place at the top of Essie's bucket list.

Nothing at all to do with his muscular physique and his dark good looks, which were enough to attract smiles and stares everywhere they'd gone today. And she instinctively knew, as if it were stamped on her overworked ovaries, that Ash would be phenomenal between the sheets. High-calibre screaming orgasms—another experience sadly lacking from her rather pathetic repertoire.

But she could still back out of this. Thank Ash for

his company and bid his sexy American butt fare-well. Her insides twisted while her indecision ping-ponged inside her skull, releasing an uncharacteristic verbal catharsis.

'I've never done this before.' She nibbled her lip, ignored the heat almost suffocating her and raised her eyes to Ash's.

Now he'd think her some sort of ingénue when re-ally she'd simply tolerated mediocre for far too long.

He turned to face her, drawing her closer with the arm banded around her waist while his glittering blue stare danced over her features. 'Okay...'

No judgment. Only the heat she'd seen in his eyes most of the afternoon.

The sizzle and spark over lunch at the funky deli had turned into flirting around Piccadilly Circus and Trafalgar Square, where Essie had provided a 'how to' tutorial on travelling the Tube. Flirting had turned to inhibition-lowering drinking at a typical Victorian Soho pub, where Ash had insisted they sample pints of tepid real ale, which was strong enough to make Essie both giggly and bold. Which was probably how they'd come to their current location—on the pave-ment outside his hotel, with his arms around her and her lips tingling to kiss him.

Still she wavered, caught between lust and caution.

She wanted to slap herself. Her doubts, her des-peration to get it right where her parents had got it wrong, hadn't helped her avoid heartache. She'd just had one bad experience...

Ash didn't have to be the perfect man—he could be perfect for now, this one night. Then she'd never

see him again. And she could try out her sexually sophisticated legs.

Ash smiled, his blue eyes sparkling with promise and his yummy mouth stretching in a sexy, lopsided way.

Full lips so close.

Warm breath laced with hops.

Shrugging off the last reservation, Essie stood on
tiptoes and kissed him, right there in the street where
people walked around them. For a second he seemed
frozen, his stubble chafing her chin and his lips
slightly parted as she feathered the lightest of kisses
on his beautiful mouth. And then his hand found the
small of her back, pressing her close as he took control, angling his head and orchestrating the slide and
thrust of lips and tongues, a thrilling concerto that
left her head light and her legs weak.

Wow. The easy-going, considerate gentleman
she'd spent the day with had a demanding side. She
wanted more. The street snog was so good, her stomach clenched like the final seconds of a free fall, and
her heart ricocheted against her ribs.

Ash groaned and pulled back from her kiss, his
erection a hard length against her belly. He looked
down as if trying to dissect her inner secrets from
her irises. 'Not that I'm bothered…' he pushed back a
stray wisp of hair from her face '…but I'm intrigued.
Why not?'

Essie captured her lip with her teeth, her insecurities rising like bile. What did she want this sexy tourist
to know about her poor track record with the opposite
sex? Despite her psychology degree and her PhD in
human relationships, her own love life, and most of

her non-romantic personal relationships, relied heavily
on the theory she pored over for her studies and for
her beloved blog, one she'd started as an undergraduate as a way to purge her own feelings of abandonment and constant rejection at the hands of her father.

Ash wanted her; the evidence was crystal clear.
Why burst the bubble? Yes, she normally avoided
picking up hunky strangers in parks. But once he'd
cracked his first genuine smile, Ash had relaxed into
a fun, smart and entertaining guy. She hadn't confessed she lived in South East London and was soon
to graduate from her PhD. She'd merely gone along
with his wrong assumption—that she, like him, was a
tourist. It added to the mystique, the risqué recklessness currently pounding through her blood and fanning her libido to a blaze.

But they'd never see each other again after tonight.
Who better to take off her training wheels with than
a sexy stranger, a temporary tourist, soon to be on a
plane to a whole other continent?

While Ash fingered the end of her ponytail, waiting, Essie shrugged. 'My male role model growing
up was an unreliable, lying shit. It kind of put me off
men.' Oversimplified, but true. She'd spent years trying to fit her subpar relationship with her ex into a
perfect mould, desperate to have the opposite of her
parents' dysfunctional union and determined to flex
her psychology muscles and prove she could practise
what she preached. But when she'd finally conceded
that the emotionally abusive relationship she'd pinned
all her hopes on was over, she'd given up on her own
happily-ever-after and shelved finding love, preferring

instead to focus on helping others with their relationships through her blog.

'I'm a man.'

Wasn't he just? She nodded, stopping short of rolling her eyes back at the solid hard bulk of him pressed
against her. 'You are.'

She knew enough about human interactions to
know there was more to Ash than the charming back-
packer, despite appearances. For a start, he was older
than the typical traveller, she guessed early thirties.
Although casually dressed in slightly rumpled clothing, he carried himself with that air of command,
confidence and authority that was such a turn-on—
she practically had drool on her chin. That he was
bothering to explore the reasons behind her hesitancy
instead of ramming his tongue down her throat or hurrying her inside faster than he could say 'God Save the
Queen' was another astounding point in his favour.

But the less she knew about him, the easier it would
be to walk away. When she left in the morning, she'd
feel satisfied no boundaries had been crossed, no mis-
understandings had been created and no feelings had
had time to develop.

Mustering every ounce of confidence and female
allure, she gripped his biceps and pressed her body
closer. 'Are we on the same page?' Her limbs twitched
while she waited for his confirmation. What if she'd
read him all wrong? What if, like her ex, Ash thought
her too clingy? Surely he could appreciate the merits
of this—they'd never see each other again.

Ash dipped his head, pressing his mouth to hers
once more. 'Totally.' The word buzzed over her tingling lips and then the tip of his tongue dipped inside.

With a surge of lust Essie embraced the kiss, scooping her arms around his neck with renewed enthusiasm.

Please let her be right about his sexual talents.

When she pulled back, breathless, she registered her surroundings. They'd come to a stop outside a rather upmarket hotel in St James's. She looked up at Ash, her eyes round.

'Is this where you're staying?' She'd guessed that he was more than he'd seemed in the park, but wealthy...?

He shrugged, a playful twitch on his lips.

Yes, Ash had offered to pay for her sandwich at lunch, but after she'd insisted on paying for herself, he'd accepted they'd be going Dutch for the rest of the day. He hadn't flashed money around—a definite turn-off for Essie, who had what her flatmate called *money issues.*

He released his grip on her waist and Essie missed his touch instantly. 'I know the owner. I'm only here tonight.' He placed his index finger under her chin and tilted her face up to his. 'Changed your mind? It's okay if you have.'

So considerate.

Her body was still fully on board with spending the night with this ruggedly handsome stranger. And did it matter if he had rich, hotel-owning friends? She wouldn't know him long enough to confess her monetary hang-ups, ones that originated with her absent father, who used affluent bribes and constant gifts as a substitute for investing quality time in his only daughter's life.

A shudder snaked down her spine.

One of the reasons she'd taken a job working for

her half-brother, which began tomorrow, was to start earning some money. Finally, after five years of full-time study, she'd actually be able to support herself rather than take more student loans. Because she'd rather be in debt for the rest of her life than take one penny from her scheming father. She'd never once cashed one of the regular cheques he sent towards her tuition fees. It felt like hush money, and by accepting it she would be condoning what he'd done, to her, to her mother, to his wife and to Ben. She'd rather live on a park bench.

Ash, perhaps interpreting her silence as a change of heart, stepped back half a pace, ending the delicious contact between them and leaving Essie more bereft than the dark turn of her thoughts had done.

'I'm happy to walk you home…or put you in a cab.' He shrugged as if it was no big deal but his stare darkened as he looked down at her, waiting. A stare of longing, one that matched the well of sizzling heat rising up inside her.

Don't spoil what promises to be the best night of your life with your hang-ups.

Essie moved closer, her fingers finding the belt loop of his jeans. She tugged, bringing his chest into contact with hers, scraping her nipples to exquisite, nerve-tingling awareness.

No way would she back out now.

'Are you sure?'

Yes, yes, yes…

At her silent nod, he took her hand, laced his fingers through hers and led her inside the glass and chrome rotating door of the swanky hotel.

Essie hurried after him, his longer strides swiftly

guiding her across the elegant foyer that she was too
turned on to appreciate. Her last thought—how nice
it must be to know someone who owned such a well-
appointed and convenient establishment—fled the
minute the lift door closed and Ash pinned her against
one wall with the stealth and predatory instincts of
a jungle cat.

Essie surrendered to the reckless impulses, so foreign but urgently addictive. She climbed him, her own
instincts set free as her hands tugged his hair and her
mouth found his while her legs encircled his thighs
and she clung to him for dear life.

Every taut inch of him was hard. She knew, under
his slouchy clothes, he'd be sleek and toned and bulg-
ing in all the right places. They broke apart long
enough to hurry from the lift to his room, although she
was so turned on that Essie was certain she'd floated.

He took a key card from his pocket, swiped it
through the reader and stood back so she could enter
first. Essie turned to welcome him as he followed
her inside, her pent-up libido and the fizz of adrenaline in her blood making her embarrassingly eager.
She gave him no time to activate the lights or even
wait until the door had fully closed before she leapt
at him, the air leaving her in a whoosh as he caught
her around the waist and hauled her up to his equally
insatiable mouth.

The chemistry between them practically melted her
body to his as if they'd been welded together.

The kissing, unlike anything she'd known, was so
voracious she whimpered out her pleasure. With dizzying speed, Ash deposited her on the bed, whipped
off her underwear and produced a condom.

Essie panted while he tore at his fly and covered himself, a look of desperate concentration on his face, barely visible in the gloom. This was wild, audacious and thrilling. But then Ash's mouth was back on hers, his fingers stroking her nipple to a peak through her clothing while he pushed slowly inside her, and she lost herself to what she was certain would turn out to be the single best sexual experience of her life to date.

She wasn't wrong. Ash pulled his mouth from hers, yanked his T-shirt over his head and reared back. With her hips gripped in his large hands and her stare locked with the white-hot one he bore down on her, Ash pounded into her again and again.

He was a god—ripped torso, a smattering of dark hair trailing down to his magnificent manhood, which she couldn't see, but which was currently rendering her a speechless bag of raging female hormones. When he scooped her hips with one arm, not losing his rhythm, and slipped his free hand between them and located her clit, her world fractured and a broken cry left her throat as she came, shortly followed by Ash.

Yep—best sex ever.

Go, Essie.

CHAPTER TWO

ESSIE EXITED THE Piccadilly Circus Tube station into glaring sunlight and joined the mass of people heading towards the start of their work week. Stifling a yawn with the back of her hand, she dragged her sunglasses from the top of her head and scoped out another coffee fix. Of course, if she'd had more than three hours' sleep last night, she wouldn't need another dose of caffeine. But she always worked on her blog first thing in the morning when the words flowed freely and the ideas were fresh, and this morning, the morning after the best sex of her life, had been no different.

Ash had kept her up into the early hours with his impressive stamina. After a second round of high calibre, sheet-clawing sex, another life-redefining orgasm, she'd sneaked out of his hotel room, like a sexually enlightened Cinderella, in the early hours while Prince Charming had slept.

She sniggered, scuffing the toe of her Converse on the tiled floor. Yes, it hadn't been her proudest moment—leaving without so much as a 'nice to meet you, thanks for the orgasms'—but that had been the unspoken deal, right? The casual sex secret code. One of the pros. No awkward swapping of numbers, no obsessively checking her phone for his call and no stalking him on social media to confirm his single status.

Of course, in practical terms, she was no expert. But she'd been right—what had occurred with Ash last night far surpassed the commonplace.

Good thing he was leaving the country soon. Sex that good should come with a health warning.

Hazard! You are ten times more likely to develop feelings for this man. Avoid sexual contact at all costs. Danger! Disappointment ahead.

And she'd had enough of that to last a lifetime.

Essie accepted her coffee from the barista, wincing as she set off at a quicker pace into Soho—starting her new job for her brother on a few hours of sleep was not her wisest move.

She sipped her latte and checked her phone for directions, cursing at the time displayed as she hurried along unfamiliar streets to meet Ben at the basement-style club and cocktail bar he'd recently purchased and had just completed renovating.

Of course, she wouldn't have needed the map if she'd scouted the route to her new job yesterday as she'd planned. But the sun had been shining and she'd disembarked the Tube a few stations early to indulge in a pleasant walk in the park. Meeting a sexy stranger hadn't been part of the plan. But she couldn't tell Ben why she'd got…sidetracked.

Essie quickened her pace, holding her coffee out in front of her. Of all the days to be late. And for Ben, too. Her older half-brother, seven years her senior, had taken a chance, offering her a job at his new club. Yes, she'd done some bar work throughout uni, but she'd never held a managerial position. All the same, she had assured him she was capable—she had a PhD, for goodness' sake, well almost, the conferment ceremony only a few weeks away—and she was determined to make the best of the chance to work for her brother.

This was more than a job. Working with him would hopefully lead to a closer relationship than the cordial but unemotional one they currently shared. Not that she blamed Ben for the distance—she had been equally hesitant. Their father had kept *her* existence a secret from his only son, too. They both had some making up for lost time to do.

That was why Essie had grasped at his request to help out, when his current manager had quit unexpectedly, with both eager hands. If she had a career plan, bar work would have no place in it, but the job comprised predominantly night shifts, which protected her dedicated blog-writing time during the day. And until she decided if she was cut out for a stuffy academic position, it provided a perfect stopgap. And the pay Ben had offered was great.

Essie rounded the corner, dodging a steady stream of smartly dressed office workers and frantic stallholders setting up their fresh produce and delicious-smelling street food for Soho's famous, three-hundred-year-old Berwick Street Market.

She stepped off the kerb to dodge a fruit and veg vendor carrying a precarious tower of produce-laden boxes six high, narrowly avoiding a delivery van that screeched to a halt. The coffee sloshed inside the takeaway cup with a violent lurch. A spout of scalding liquid jettisoned from the sip hole in the plastic lid and sprayed the front of Essie's favourite dress, deliberately chosen for her first day at work.

She cursed while a trail of coffee dripped down her cleavage and soaked into her bra. Her eyes stung as she dabbed at the brown stain with her fingers and stepped back onto the pavement, pushing her way back into the hustle of the commuter crowds.

She breathed through her disappointment over the dress, her face forcing a bright smile. Ben wouldn't care how she dressed. Only that she turned up, offered him as much help as she could and became someone he could rely on. And if she hurried, perhaps she could beat Ben and his business partner there and she could clean up before making a good impression.

This part of Soho housed an array of trendy bars, eclectic restaurants and small, elegant hotels. The innocuous, black-painted street frontage of The Yard—sandwiched between a designer menswear store and an Italian deli—meant Essie almost walked straight past. If it hadn't been for a van parked on half of the pavement and the sign writer blocking the other half with his ladder while he worked on the shiny new nameplate, she might have missed her destination completely.

Essie followed the harassed sign writer's directions to the narrow alleyway between the deli and the club that led to the rear entrance of The Yard. Yanking open the ancient, squeaky door, she entered the cool gloom of the darkened interior.

'Ben?'

She made her way along a maze of dimly lit corridors, following the sounds of activity, her insides a flurry of twisting energy, one she couldn't blame on the barely tasted coffee.

The bar area swarmed with electricians rigging reams and reams of neon lights into every available nook and cranny. The sharp chemical tang of new paint filled the air and a very harassed-looking Ben paced near the front entrance door with his mobile phone glued to the side of his head. When he saw Essie, he visibly sagged and quickly ended his call.

'I am *so* glad to see you.' He gripped her elbows and kissed her cheek, a gesture that felt far from natural. She forced her breathing to deepen so she didn't pass out from excitement.

Baby steps.

Although they'd known of each other's existence for some years, their sibling relationship held a new and fragile quality. Recalling the first time Ben had made contact still held the power to suffocate her with emotions; the date, time and what she'd been wearing when his call had come in engraved on her memory as if it were yesterday.

Twelve months ago, he'd relocated full-time to London, which had taken their contact from the occasional awkward video call to an actual face-to-face meeting. From that moment Essie had been secretly and cautiously smitten, because all they'd really shared to date was a genetic bond with their devious and unscrupulous father, a string of hesitant emails and a few quick, stilted coffee dates. If they were going to have a lasting relationship in the future, using this opportunity to get to know each other better was crucial.

Essie shrugged off her doubts by rummaging in her backpack for her notebook and a pen. She was here to lighten Ben's burden. To show him who *she* was. To build on their sibling status, having been denied that opportunity all their lives by their father.

She bit down hard on her lip—she wouldn't spoil her first day by thinking of Frank Newbold. She flipped open the notebook, pen poised, a picture, she hoped, of cool, unfrazzled competence. The coffee stain notwithstanding.

'Tell me what you need. You look stressed.' And so much like their father, a man whose face she could no longer bear to look at.

Ben scrubbed his fingers through his already messy hair.

'The shit's hit the fan with one of my New York clubs…' He winced.

As well as renovating The Yard in Soho, Ben owned and managed a string of clubs in New York, where he'd grown up.

'You don't need to hear my work woes.' His wince turned into a hesitant smile. 'But I am going to have to leave you to things here—I have to fly to the States tonight and sort shit out.'

Essie rolled her shoulders back. That he would trust her with his shiny new cocktail bar and nightclub gave her shivers that bubbled up at the back of her throat, threatening to close off her windpipe.

'Of course.' She swallowed, eager for another of his grateful smiles. 'That's why I'm here.' She could pull a pint from her years of working the uni bar, and the rest she'd learn on the job while her own career path loitered in an uncertain slump. Her motivations were more about personal bridge-building than flex-ing her managerial muscles in the hospitality industry. But looking at the furrows in Ben's brow and the dark circles around his tired eyes, she knew she'd walk a path of hot coals to help, even if it took her away from developing her relationship blog full-time, one of the ideas she'd considered now that she'd finished her PhD.

A small frown settled between his brows. 'Are you sure you can spare the time? Shouldn't you be job-hunting or schmoozing professors?'

Essie snorted a nervous laugh. Now that she'd finished her PhD, an academic position held far less appeal than it should. She'd considered a university teaching post but was way too intimidated to believe she had anything useful to teach others. She'd love to focus full-time on promoting her blog to wider audiences, but part of her secretly baulked at dedicating all her energy to making it a success—the 'lost little girl' part of her who missed her dad and couldn't understand why he spent so much time away. After all, what did she know about healthy human relationships? Everyone would see through her, know she was a fraud.

'I'll be fine until you can replace me with someone better qualified.' She had plenty of time to build her own career, whatever that looked like. She only had one brother. And, for now, he needed her.

He cracked a wide smile. 'Great.'

Essie flicked through her notebook to hide the attack of rapid blinking. She'd be the best bloody bar manager he'd ever seen. He wouldn't be able to resist falling deeply in sibling love with her.

'So, to recap on our previous conversation...' She tapped the pen on the page, tempted to push it behind her ear to inspire greater confidence. Perhaps she should have bought a clipboard. 'My predecessor has already hired waitstaff, bulk ordered the beverages and organised a cleaning crew...'

Ben nodded. 'All you have to do is be around to supervise things here.' He squeezed her arm. 'You are awesome.'

Warm treacle flooded her veins but she shrugged off his praise with a small shake of her head. She wished she'd recorded the moment so she could play it back to herself in the privacy of her flat later or every time her bones rattled with insecurities.

'The decorators have finished downstairs in the basement, and the interior designer will be here in—' he checked his Rolex '—thirty minutes. Can you make sure they install the leather seats in the VIP area and remind them we decided on the black privacy curtains for the booths instead of the white?'

Essie nodded, scribbling a quick note as they walked. Ben ushered her out of the path of a man in paint-speckled overalls hefting a ladder on one shoulder and offered a tight, apologetic smile.

'Oh, and can you remind the electricians before they leave to install the string lights upstairs on the roof garden?' He sighed. 'Sorry. It's a lot.'

Essie shook her head. 'Not at all. I have a list.' She brandished her notebook with a reassuring grin.

A small nod. 'Have you...had any contact from... Frank?' Ben shot Essie a cautious look, tinged with the usual flash of guilt. He felt somehow responsible for their father's actions, but they'd both been victims of the lies.

She shook her head. The last thing she wanted to discuss was their father and the endless sob story he'd

made of her young life. How he'd decimated her childhood adoration of him, a daughter-father rite of passage, through cowardly evasion and cruel deceit. Essie
had learned early on, by the amount of time he'd spent
in London, that she'd ranked pretty low on her father's
list of priorities. But to discover, on her fifteenth birthday, that her whole life, her very existence, had been
a lie, that she hadn't mattered enough, that she had a
half-brother…

She swallowed back the familiar burn in her throat
and shoved her father from her mind. Today was the
start of something new, something positive—she
wouldn't let him tarnish it the way he'd managed to
tarnish every other significant moment in her life.
Birthdays, school awards ceremonies, her first prom
night—he'd been conspicuously absent.

Ben led the way to a door beside the bar. 'Come
and meet my buddy.'

Her mouth twitched with a small, indulgent smile.
Despite growing up in Manhattan, his mother's hometown, he'd lived in London for a year. His accent and
his choice of slang wavered wildly between the two,
something else about her big brother Essie found endlessly endearing.

How could this amazing man be related to Frank?
Not that she was the best judge of character. She'd
idolised their father growing up, but he'd used his
frequent business travel to successfully navigate his
deceptions and conduct two separate lives on two separate continents; conceal two separate families.

Essie tossed her coffee cup in a black bag and
ducked through the door Ben held open for her.

'Although he's supposed to be a silent partner, he's

up to speed with everything so, between the two of you, you should have most things covered. I'll be back in a few days—plenty of time for us to put the finishing touches to the launch party.'

'I promise, your club is in good hands.'

They'd chosen the perfect trendy and glamorous location—this part of London was always buzzing with young, beautiful people. And now she'd seen the club's interior, which was tasteful, chic and oozing sophistication, that she could participate in her brother's venture filled her with pride and renewed hope. And something less tangible…a small bud, blooming open, affording a glimpse of the full beauty to come.

Belonging.

Something she'd craved for as long as she could remember.

As the door from the bar closed behind them the noise levels dropped as if they'd entered a vacuum. Ben grinned at her impressed expression.

'State-of-the-art soundproofing. Costs a bloody fortune but worth it.' He took a left turn, pointing out the salient landmarks as he strode ahead.

'Kitchen here and staff break room. Staff toilets on the right.' Another left turn. 'You can use this office.' He paused outside a room where the furniture had been sited but still wore its protective Bubble Wrap clothing. He flashed his handsome, lopsided smile and Essie nodded, eyeing the sparse space.

They'd arrived at the last room. Ben rapped lightly on the door.

'Come in,' a voice said.

If she hadn't been so dazzled by the warmth and camaraderie of her brother's welcome and the affec-

tionate bonding moment of him sharing his shiny new
club with her, she might have clued on sooner. But she
followed him into the room, blind to everything but
Ben and blissfully oblivious to the impending cata-
strophic confrontation.

And came face-to-face with Ash.

The smile she held on her face morphed into a frozen grimace. Her cheeks twitched with the effort of
keeping it there, like a painted-on clown smirk.

She scoured her gaze over his height and breadth,
seeking confirmation. But, no, it was definitely him.

The verification came, a breath-stealing blow to
the solar plexus.

'Essie, this is Ash Jacob, my oldest friend and now
business partner. Ash, my little sister, Essie Newbold.'

Essie wanted to run a lap of honour at hearing
Ben's description of her, but her stiff skeleton could
barely manage a small chin tilt in Ash's general direction as her neck muscles seized like a rusty gate.

Confident, commanding Ash stood, smoothing
down his graphite tie as he rounded the sleek, modern desk and strode into her personal space with his
hand outstretched in greeting as if he had not a care
in the world. Saliva pooled in her mouth, her throat
too tight to allow it passage. Her mind ping-ponged
inside her skull, playing catch-up.

His gorgeous face, now clean-shaven to reveal a
chiselled jaw and sinful creases that bracketed his
full mouth, was relaxed, a small, polite smile on his
lips as if he welcomed a total stranger, not the woman
he'd come inside last night with a yell she heard every
time she closed her eyes.

The memory of his now absent stubble scraping

across her nipples gave her an acute pang of longing to see the relaxed, playful Ash of last night. Tourist Ash. Not this tie-wearing, professional version with distant, accusatory eyes and a tense jaw. But for the embers flickering in his navy stare, she'd almost have believed she'd concocted last night's torrid one-night stand. But her hips and thighs still bore the ghostly imprints of his fingertips as he'd held her tight and drilled into her with fierce determination.

'Nice to meet you.' The rich, dark rumble of his voice scraped her eardrums. Her coffee soured in her stomach. How could he maintain such a poker face? Why didn't he suffer the same jaw-dropping disbelief currently rendering *her* speechless? And why, oh, why out of all the men in the universe had she chosen her half-brother's best friend and business partner for her first one-night stand?

Ash's warm hand enclosed hers, reminding her of last night's touches. Touches that should have been more intimate but paled against this simple handshake, because this time all pretence was stripped away.

Ash Jacob was The Yard's co-investor.

Ben's silent business partner.

Ben's billionaire friend from uni. A man she'd wrongly assumed was a tourist and picked up in St James's Park. A man she'd had sex with, twice, whose bed she'd only left mere hours ago. A man to whom she'd confessed her pathetic lack of sexual experience, and thought she'd never see again.

Molten heat engulfed Essie's throat. She swallowed it down with a sour chaser of you've-only-got-yourself-to-blame. But her stomach rebelled the dose of self-inflicted medicine.

Pulling herself up, she levelled her best cold stare on his sinful good looks and returned his handshake with an overly firm one of her own, ignoring the delicious glide of his callused palm.

Social pleasantries complete, she yanked her hand from his as if he were a live wire, connected to the mains.

He'd lied to her.

Deceived her.

Pried into her sordid hang-ups about her crappy father figure.

Why had she told him such personal information? Why hadn't she asked more about him? She really was a one-night-stand rookie. Her burning eyes darted away, but not before his image branded her retinas.

She'd wanted to experience the casual sex hype, desperate to lend an air of real experience and authority to the relationship advice she touted on her blog. All because, despite her qualifications, despite years of academic research, despite actually having had a long-term relationship, she feared herself an imposter.

Of course, the fact she'd been starved of earth-shattering orgasms during that relationship and that Ash was…easy on the eye had helped…

She snatched another scan of his sublime body. Unlike the relaxed, slightly crumpled hottie she'd met yesterday, today Ash wore a crisp white shirt with the sleeves rolled up to the elbows and sharply tailored suit trousers that complemented the silver-grey tie and highlighted the intense blue of his eyes.

Gorgeous. Mouth-watering. A duplicitous scumbag...

As hot as he'd looked dressed down in jeans and

a T-shirt, he wore this sharp, professional outfit like a second skin, as he wore the power that oozed from him. As he lived and breathed the air of command and authority that immaculate tailoring afforded. Her breath caught. She could have slapped her own forehead. Another piece of the puzzle slotted home—Ben's new business partner was a top New York attorney… like a character from that TV show, only a hundred times hotter and a thousand times more untouchable.

But she *had* touched.

The seconds stretched.

Awkward seconds. Seconds absent of the expected social niceties. To compensate, Essie blurted the first inane thing to pop into her head.

'So you're Ben's business partner?' *Duh…*

Ash nodded. Slow. Easy. His stare glittering. As if he recognised the turmoil rendering her tongue-tied. And not one hint of regret or embarrassment. Unlike her, who was practically molten with shame.

'Guilty as charged.' His voice carried a bite that had been missing from the deep, hypnotic rumble of the easy-going sightseer. As if he was used to being in control?

And lawyer humour… Really?

'Ben has been talking about you all morning,' he said. 'Of course, he mentioned a while ago he'd recently united with his half-sister, but I'd failed to pay attention to your very pretty name.' His eyes flicked down the front of her dress. To the coffee stain…

Perfect.

Essie fought the temptation to fold her arms across her chest and keep on folding herself into a tiny origami Essie. Had Ash told Ben about last night? About how she'd thrown herself at him? How she'd blurted out her inexperience and then eagerly climbed his ripped body? Had he laughed at her? And why was *he* pissed? She'd been the one deceived, duped. Dazzled by his confident charm and his promise of a string-free night to remember. It wasn't as if she'd stalked him here for a repeat performance…

And how much of her sad little tale, her pathetic past, did he know? Had Ben told him all about her sorry past? Had Ash linked the woman confessing her daddy issues before fleeing his bed with Ben's sister?

As if he'd heard her thoughts, he said, 'Imagine my surprise when I heard Ben's sister was to be our new bar manager.'

The trembles turned into jolts. Surely Ben would have said something if he knew. She tensed her muscles to hold herself still. It wouldn't do to show a man like Ash, the real Ash, any weakness. Last night, she'd have run a mile from this powerful, controlled man. She *should* run now. Leave with what was left of her self-esteem intact before Ben clued on and her embarrassment became full-blown.

But leaving her brother in the lurch…? When he needed her help more than ever? Not an option. Not if they were to have a chance at a deep and lasting sibling relationship.

Ben snorted, flicking Ash a friendly but distracted grin.

'Leave it, Jacob. Essie's been a lifesaver, stepping in at the last minute.' Ben rounded the desk and flopped down into the chair Ash had vacated, leaving the two of them alone on the other side of the impressive block of wood.

Essie levelled her stare on Ash. She narrowed her

eyes but kept her voice free of the sarcasm fighting to break free. 'Tell me, have you been in London long? Had a chance to do a little sightseeing perhaps?'

For Ben's sake, she kept the acid from her tone, but Ash shrugged, seemingly indifferent, and Ben looked too engrossed in the screen of his phone to have even heard the vague barb.

Ash moved to an informal seating area in one corner of the office, which was decked out like something from an exclusive gentlemen's club. He held out his arm to offer her a seat and then, when she declined, sank down into the leather, all the while assessing her with his narrowed stare.

'I have managed a tour of the more…exciting highlights the city has to offer.' He quirked a brow, his mouth twisted. He reclined, one arm stretched out along the back of the sofa, thighs spread in that confident, manly way that screamed, *Look at my junk! Oh, wait, you've already experienced it.*

Heat slammed through her, pulsing between her legs with every lurid memory of him inside her last night: his hips slamming into her; his gruff voice commanding her pleasure; his uncompromising control brooking no arguments, even though she'd been one hundred per cent complicit.

Her cheeks warmed. She'd fully embraced the *wham-bam, thank you, ma'am*. She dragged her gaze from his crotch, pressing her lips together so she couldn't lick them. This morning, one night had been enough.

But now, with him looking at her as if he wanted a repeat performance, her body hummed with need, in traitorous, clit-throbbing agreement.

One night *hadn't* been enough.

Not of this man, who she suspected would be twice the lover of relaxed, tourist Ash. Was that even possible? No. She didn't want to know.

'So you have managerial experience? Hospitality experience?' Ash flicked his eyes over her from head to toe as if they were alone, his tone grating and transforming her buzz of arousal to one of irritation. It was the way he asked, as if he already knew the answer and found her…lacking.

Another lawyer trait? Or pure, unadulterated arsehole?

Essie changed her mind. Selecting the chair opposite him, she faced him, forcing her body into as relaxed a demeanour as he displayed. She was, after all, an expert at body language.

'I'm a graduate.' She lifted her chin. 'I've just completed a PhD and I have lots of hospitality experience.' So she didn't have a Harvard law degree, but she wasn't an imbecile. She could work a till and wipe down tables. 'Would you like to see my CV?' She pursed her lips in a tight, sickly smile.

'What's with the third degree?' Ben joined them, taking the second armchair. He shot Ash a curious glare and then turned to Essie. 'Forgive my friend. He's not long arrived from New York. He's not used to your English customs and manners yet.'

Ben turned back to a smiling, completely unfazed Ash.

'Look, it sucks balls that I have to leave today, but I expect you to look out for my sister, Jacob. Employ a dash of that charm that gets you endlessly laid.' Ben's grin dropped. A frown lodged between his brows. 'But keep your hands off my sister.'

A titter of hysterical laughter clogged Essie's throat

while her cheeks flamed. She'd already sampled his friend's goods. She lifted her chin, her stare honed on Ash. She might not be able to control her flush response, but she could certainly control her misguided libido.

'I can manage anything your friend can dish out, Ben. Don't worry.'

Both men looked at her as if inspecting her for the first time. Their faces were unreadable and likely concealed very different thoughts. Essie examined her fingernails and tried to keep her feet still.

Although certain she lacked the sophistication of the New York babes Ash probably usually bedded, Essie wasn't a pushover. And this job was about her and Ben. Not her and Ash. So she'd let some personal baggage escape last night, been indiscreet about her track record—that ended right here, right now. Arrogant Ash had seen all he was going to see of unguarded, easy-going Essie.

She returned Ash's stare, the standoff a game of wills.

'Good,' said Ben. 'Because Ash here has a bit of a reputation with the ladies…if you know what I mean.' He winked at Essie, who tried to catalogue the sparse contents of her fridge to stop another telltale blush giving her away.

'Don't worry.' Ash's lip curled. 'Little sisters aren't my type.'

Essie concealed her indrawn gasp with a nervous chuckle. Was he daring her? Goading her to out them to a clueless Ben? White-hot fire replaced her blood—she'd been his type less than twelve hours ago when he hadn't even bothered to fully strip either of them

before he'd lowered her to the bed and pushed his delicious dick inside her.

No.

*Not delicious. Wrong. Forbidden. And probably as
devious as the rest of him.*

She cringed, her fatigue-weakened body veering
towards kissing the smirk from Ash Jacob's handsome
face one minute and coming clean to Ben the next.

Day one on the job, and already locking horns with
the co-owner, who now knew more about her than
most people...as well as sneaking round behind her
brother's back?

Well, from now on she'd be the consummate professional and just get the job done. She couldn't risk
disappointing Ben or she'd be back to square one.

Alone.

Rejected.

No relationship with her father to speak of, and no
relationship with Ben.

Her whole life, she'd felt somehow responsible for
the choices her father had made, as if she were the
reason he'd stayed away. And now she was responsible for the mess she'd made of this, too.

But she refused to play into Ash's sexy hands. Her
sister status meant more to her than point scoring
over Ash. She could ignore him at work, pretend she'd
never met him, try to forget how he'd expertly shunted
her into not one, but the two best orgasms of her life.
She could pretend just looking at him radiating the
kind of self-assurance born of supreme confidence
wasn't a real fucking turn-on...

Ben's phone chirruped a text alert and he pulled it
from his pocket with a sigh.

'My car's here. I have to go.' He stood, and Essie and Ash followed. He stooped to kiss Essie's cheek again and turned to shake hands and shoulder bump with Ash.

'Play nice.' Ben levelled an index finger at his friend, who shrugged, his expression all laid-back charm and cocksure nonchalance.

Ben turned back to Essie.

'And if you need me, email.'

Essie nodded, more than half tempted to fling herself at her brother's Oxford-clad feet, wrap her arms around his knees and beg him to stay. To mediate between her and Ash. To stop Essie from orchestrating a rerun of last night's recklessness. To see that underneath the stained dress and the bad decisions, she was a worthy sister.

But instead she stood and watched him leave while her stomach flopped to her coffee-speckled shoes.

Get a grip. You're a grown-ass woman. Soon to be Dr Essie Newbold, psychologist and relationship guru. Not some insecure sad sack ruled by her hormones.

She straightened her spine and prepared to follow Ben's lead and leave the room that shrank the minute she and Ash were alone, compressing the available oxygen.

'Well, you failed to mention this last night...'

She yanked her stare back to Ash.

Every minute hair on her body stood to attention. Ben seemed to have taken the sun with him, too, because the room's temperature plummeted as Essie and Ash faced off.

'Me?' Was he for real? 'What about you?' Playing

the charming tourist and allowing her to believe he'd
be leaving town in a few days. Laughing at her London anecdotes and listening intently when she'd offered top tips for surviving the capital, when all the
time he probably knew the city better than her. If she'd
known last night that he owned a sizeable chunk of
St James's, she might have put two and two together
and kept her knees and her mouth shut.

And now she and Mr Moneybags had to survive
an intolerable working relationship, where every time
they crossed paths she'd blush beet red at her folly.

Her phone vibrated in her bag, a reminder it was
time to publish the blog post she'd drafted that morning. Oh, the irony. She'd waxed lyrical about casual
sex, clutching her shiny new members' badge to the
one-night-stand club. Now the pieces of that newfound
air of authority lay scattered around her two left feet.

Perhaps she could quickly pen an alternative piece:
How to work with people you want to...jump.

No.

Not jump. Ignore.

Ash stepped close, his big manly body producing enough heat to scorch her bare arms, lobster red.
Flicks of blue flame danced in his eyes.

'I didn't conceal anything. I just didn't mention
anything personal.'

The unspoken hovered in the air... *Unlike you.*

Essie wanted to curl in on herself, but she held her
head high. Being eager to take off her casual sex training wheels was nothing to be ashamed of.

'If you made wrong assumptions, that's your problem,' he bit out. 'And what was with the *"My phone*

died. Please take a photo for me..." Why were you playing the tourist? You live here.'

She'd wanted the photo for a future blog post, the wheel symbolic of the spectrum of human emotions and the sun catching the Eye a reflection of hope—a new day. But she couldn't tell him that, couldn't tell him about the blog. Not when her reckless, mind-blowing one night with him was the focus of today's post. When she published it later, this new element of fucked-upness, would give the subject matter even more credence—a cautionary tale of how people concealed what they really were to get what they wanted. To get laid.

The perils of casual sex...

'You're the one who lied. Ash the tourist? From what Ben told me, you own half of London.' *Typical.* She'd inherited her bad taste in men from her mother...

She bit the inside of her cheek, scalding heat flooding her body. Her mum was a good person who'd raised Essie virtually single-handedly. No, she only had herself to blame for her foolhardy behaviour last night and its humiliating consequences this morning.

Where were all the honest, dependable, upfront men? And why was she a magnet for the opposite type? The ones who evaded the truth, like Ash. The ones who claimed they wanted a relationship but took more than they gave, like her ex. The ones who made promises and then broke them and threw money at the situation so they avoided dealing with real life, like her unreliable, phoney father...

Ash's stare raked over her features. 'So?' He lifted his chin, looking down his nose with a lazy smirk on his face. 'You didn't seem to care who I was last night. In fact, all you seemed concerned about was marking your one-night-stand card—or was that part of the act, too?' He inched into her personal space, invading until the breadth of his chest eclipsed her field of vision.

Essie placed the flat of her hand between his well-developed pecs, ignoring the burn of his body heat and the clean male scent wafting up from his expensive shirt.

'I'm not the only one who made wrong assumptions. And I rocked your world last night, counsellor.' Her fingers wanted to curl, to dig, to tug. But she forced them to stay flat. Time to put some boundaries in place. No matter how fantastic their brief, steamy interlude, the after shame currently making her hot and twitchy rendered the high worthless. Another important post–casual sex lesson she could impart to her readers.

His mouth kicked up on one side, and he snorted a soft gust of air.

'Funny, I thought I'd rocked *your* world?'

Her internal muscles clenched at the memories of his spectacular manhood. She laughed, stepping away from toe-tingling temptation and heading for the door with a shake of her head. There was no chance of damaging this man's ego, but she didn't trust her voice to emerge without the breathiness that made her light-headed.

'No?' His hurled question stopped her in her tracks. 'We could rectify that situation, right now.' He flicked his stare to the uncluttered slab of a desk, his sinful mouth twisted, but his eyes hot.

Challenging?

Essie imagined herself spread there with Ash, determined to prove something, between her thighs. Thighs that loved the idea if the tremble between them was any indication. She instinctively knew that sex with hot lawyer Ash would be twice as intense as sex with hot tourist Ash. No mean feat.

Tempting.

Lying made sense, serving a dual purpose of bringing him down a peg or two and fortifying her own wobbly defences.

'There won't be anything more between us. I'm here for Ben, my *brother*. And, as you'll remember from last night, I don't trust your type.'

His cocky, lopsided smirk lifted her shoulders until they threatened to dislocate.

'You're right, there won't be.' He closed the distance between them, his dismissive stare dipping down the length of her body. 'Ben is my friend, this is my business and I don't trust anyone.'

'Good. So we agree on one thing.' That didn't mean she couldn't toy with him as he toyed with her. Make him crave a repeat performance. One he'd never get to experience. It was childish and vengeful and filled her with white-hot shame. But she longed to cut the arrogant jerk down to size. To claw back some of the dignity her poor choice and shabby vetting had decimated.

He nodded. 'It seems so. I made it clear yesterday— one shot is all you get from me.'

Her back teeth ached as she ground them together. 'What a gent you are. Ladies must be lined up around the block.' She forced his spicy scent from her nose with a short snort.

He raised his dark brows. 'I've never had any complaints. And you didn't walk away unsatisfied.'

She wanted to deny his prowess. To tell him he'd been a lousy lay, but that was one lie too far. Instead she stepped closer, fighting the urge to rub her body against his like a cat. 'As you're so…experienced in the casual sex department, I'm sure you know this.' She looked up at him from beneath her lashes. 'There's a world of difference between mindless fucking and the ultimate connection found during a real, honest human interaction.'

She dropped her head back with a prolonged sigh, feigning a look of utter ecstasy while she ran her fingertips slowly down the length of her exposed throat. She released a breathy moan, her hand coming to rest at the top of her cleavage.

And then she snapped her head up and dropped her arm to her side. Her expression returned to one of mild scorn while power blazed through her nervous system at the sight of lust glittering in his eyes and the tent in the front of his trousers.

'If you've never experienced the latter—' a shrug '—I feel sorry for you.' She smiled her brightest beam. 'Have a good day.'

She turned on her heel and left his office with her burning back ramrod-straight and her belly quivering in time to the soundtrack of *When Harry Met Sally*.

CHAPTER THREE

ESSIE SPENT THE rest of the day holed up in Ben's office answering phone calls, sending emails and hiding from Ash. For all her bravado, her encounter had left her shaken to the core. Not because his confirmation there would be no more sex in their future left her reliving their one night together, over and over until her erogenous zones ached and clamoured for a rerun, but because, burning with righteous indignation, she'd rashly clicked *publish* on that morning's blog post, retitling it *The OMG Pros and One-Night Cons of Casual Sex*, while still reeling from their verbal and sexually charged spat. And now her tongue-in-cheek cautionary tale of her first one-night stand winged its way through cyberspace to land in the inboxes of the thousands-strong audience her relationship blog attracted.

Stupid.

Reckless.

But providing a belly-warming kick of satisfaction.

Her small, naughty smile turned into a lip nibble.

Thinking about her blog should have brought her a sense of pride. Her usual posts were heavily theoretical and science based, calling on the latest psychological research on relationships, love and the complexities of all forms of human interaction.

But crammed full of shame, betrayal and an overwhelming head spin of good sex hormones, she'd thrown caution to the wind and edited her earlier draft with personal details of her explosive but reckless night with Ash, detailing a pared-down version of the sheet-clawing sexploits and their disastrous morning-after fallout as reasons for prudence.

She'd kept it totally anonymous, only referring to Ash as *Illegally Hot*, but she shouldn't have mentioned him at all. She was a professional with a serious academic reputation to consider, not some kiss-and-tell reality blogger.

Her belly twisted even as her breathing accelerated, a sickening swirl of opposing emotions. The added personal anecdotes afforded her writing an air of authority she'd never before believed she possessed. As if, overnight, she'd become a true expert, at least on her chosen topic.

Heady stuff.

She grinned, dragging her lip back under her teeth as the first comment came in, lighting up her phone with a ping.

Well, BatS*#tCrazy liked it. They'd even asked where they could find *Illegally Hot*…

Bugger—it was too late now for regrets.

She slammed her laptop shut with screen-cracking force. Ash didn't strike her as an avid pop psychology reader—he'd never know.

As the triumphant head rush dwindled, the lip-gnawing insecurity returned, full-blown. She'd begun her blog, *Relationships and Other Science Experi-*

ments, as a first-year psychology undergraduate. Still struggling with the knowledge of her father's betrayal, emotionally and geographically isolated from a half-brother she'd never met and angry with her father's desertion and the lies he'd spun to cover it up, she'd taken to putting her own complex and often overwhelming feelings and thoughts into a sort of online diary. Shortly after, she'd made the mistake of falling in what she'd assumed was love. Two tumultuous years later, the ex she'd pinned all her happily-ever-afters on had left her with her self-esteem in tatters, and her heart seriously doubtful that honest, dependable men—let alone love—actually existed.

Around the same time, she'd fallen in academic love with social psychology and her fascination with the intricacies of human relationships began, guiding both her writing and her choice of PhD study.

Initially, she'd been amazed to acquire a handful of keen followers who had warmed to her quirky, often humorous take on the complexities of interpersonal dealings. No subject was taboo. From the rude man on the Tube to the day-to-day social minefield of undergraduate life, she tackled the full gamut of complex interactions humans faced and presented the science behind them.

And now she had a whole heap more fodder for her writing in the guise of her sexy but arrogant boss, her one night of orgasmic bliss and the awkward, self-inflicted quagmire her temporary job had become.

Essie reopened her laptop, determined to end the day leaving no stone unturned when it came to her responsibilities towards Ben. With tomorrow's to-do list stuck on a virtual sticky note on her desktop, she performed one last check of her emails before heading home.

There was one from Ben's interior designer and another from his PA, asking for her bank account details for payroll. But it was the one from her brother, entitled *A Favour*, that she pounced upon.

Essie

I left some documents in the safe for Ash to sign. I can't get hold of him—suspect he's still jet-lagged and has fallen asleep. Can you please take them around to him and then scan the signatures through to the bank before six p.m.?

PS A spare set of keys to Ash's apartment is also in the safe, in case he's out of it and doesn't hear you knock.

A combination number and address accompanied the request.

Essie dropped her head into her hands, tempted to headbutt the laptop screen and pretend she hadn't read the urgent missive. The last thing she wanted was any further interaction with Ash after last night's reckless abandon and today's humiliating reunion.

Didn't billionaires have teams of lackeys traipsing after them, doffing their caps and facilitating their masters' every whim? Why her?

But Ben would be in the air by now en route to New York. There was no escape. If she kept her head, kept her focus on the goal and not the infuriating, sexy-as-fuck Ash…her mission couldn't fail.

Get in. *Don't have sex with him.*

Acquire a signature. *Don't have sex with him.*

Get out. *Don't have sex with him.*
Simple.

Ash closed his eyes, braced his palms flat on the tile and let the steaming water pound down on his head. Perhaps it would rattle some fucking sense into his brain.

Stupid. Impulsive. Fantastic sex.

He curled one hand into a fist, knuckles bloodless.

He'd moved to London to claw back control of the wrong turn his life had taken, not to embroil himself in another personal shit storm of epic proportions. While he licked his wounds and disentangled his suddenly public personal life, he'd hoped to forge a new path away from Jacob Holdings. A fresh start. Something of his own, untainted by his father.

Sleeping with the intriguing and exotic stranger he'd met in the park had been beyond reckless. He should have vetted her beyond her flirtatious smiles, her sexy laugh and her astounding body. But he'd been charmed by her bubbly, ingenuous personality, so unlike the somewhat cynical sophisticates he normally bedded.

Cynical like him.

And she'd upped the intrigue factor with her hesitant confession of her relative inexperience.

Fuck.

Ash dumped a palmful of shampoo onto his head. But knowing exactly who she was only threw up more questions. If Essie lived in London, why the hell did she need a picture of one of its iconic landmarks? If she had a degree and a PhD, why was bar work so appealing? And what was the deal with her and Ben?

He scrubbed at his scalp, nails punishing. Now, not only did he have to work with her—fucking eyeball-scalding torture right there—but he also had to watch her prance her sexy ass around his club covered in those flirty little dresses she liked to wear, all the while keeping his libido under control and his hands to his damned self.

Screwed.

He rinsed his hair, welcoming the sting as the suds ran into his eyes.

Not that he'd known it at the time, but sleeping with Essie had broken one of his life's cardinal, cast-iron, unbreakable rules: Never screw a mate's sister—the golden bro code every decent male lived by.

And he was decent. He didn't use people. He didn't cheat. And he considered the consequences of his actions.

Usually.

Unlike his no-good, lying, asshole father.

His other rule—never more than one night—well, he hadn't broken that…yet. Although he'd been sorely tempted in his office earlier.

It was sure as shit going to test every single ounce of the rigid control he not only prided himself on but needed like oxygen in order to resist temptation. The minute she'd walked into his office behind Ben he'd wanted her again so badly he'd had to think of his whisker-chinned, sixth-grade music teacher Miss Lemmon to stave off his boner.

When he'd awoken at four that morning to find her gone, part of him had sagged back on the pillows with relief. He'd done his job. Shown her a good time—actually, a fucking fantastic time.

Yes, she'd understood the unspoken rules, sneaking out of his hotel room in the middle of the night. No number on the nightstand. No scribbled note demanding he call her. No hijacking his cell phone. But the sense of relief had done little to comfort him. A part of him, the part left restless by betrayal and humiliation, the part he'd hoped to leave behind in New York, had coiled like colic in his gut until he'd arisen before the dawn, taken a frigid shower and numbed his mind with several hours of legal work.

Despite walking away from Jacob Holdings, he still had unfinished deals for the family business, one in particular that, as shareholder, he had a personal interest in. No matter how much he might want to throw his father under the bus in retribution, he had his sisters' future inheritance to protect and his mother's share when her divorce from the old bastard was finalised. At least he could atone for causing the split by recommending a hotshot divorce attorney to get his mother a fair slice of the pie. But even drafting a complex and lengthy contract hadn't dragged his mind away from the fascinating Essie.

He sighed, succumbing to the inevitable. Every muscle clenched and his cock thickened. He gave it a couple of lazy tugs as the memory of Essie's whimpers and her cries echoed inside his head...

Ash slammed his eyes open and slapped the tile beside the showerhead. Here he was thinking about the other ways he'd like to fuck her, when there wasn't going to be a next time. There should never have been a first time.

He'd been done with women even before he'd set foot on English soil. Plus she was Ben's sister and now his club's temporary manager. An employee. And, more importantly, someone he couldn't trust.

Perhaps he could fire her? Employ a replacement manager before Ben returned from his trip and say it hadn't worked out with Essie. But Ben, quite rightly, wouldn't tolerate the slight. And if it came out that Ash had fucked his little sister and then fired her for humiliating him, their longstanding friendship wouldn't survive. And right now, Ash needed his friend—the only friend he could be certain hadn't known what his fiancée had really been up to all those years ago.

Her dumping him practically at the altar had left him struggling to trust the opposite sex, but his father's recent revelations and the public backlash had thrown Ash into a tailspin until he no longer knew which way was up and who he could rely upon not to snigger behind his back.

Of course, Ben didn't know the latest twist, the one that had prompted Ash's departure from New York. How the third wheel in his past relationship—the work colleague she'd claimed to have cheated with— had been nothing but a ruse. A decoy to stave off the marriage his ex had no longer wanted and conceal what had really been happening. Ash closed his eyes against his own reflection in the glass. Some things were so shameful they couldn't be shared, no matter how good the friend.

He completed his shower routine with a bitter taste in his mouth. A taste that morphed into the sweetest honey when Essie slipped back into his mind. With her blue eyes blazing and indignation thickening her accent and giving her extra height…he'd wanted to kiss her pinched-with-disapproval mouth and haul her spectacular ass out of his club at the same time.

She'd duped him. And no one duped him any more. He made sure of that in his professional sphere; his uncompromising reputation had become legendary.

And personally…? Fuck, there he was a mess. But he'd get there if it killed him. He'd claw back control, starting with his libido and the temptation threatening to derail him in the shape of Essie Newbold.

Now he had to spend the next two months both avoiding her and checking up on her so she had no opportunity to hoodwink him again. Not to mention hiding the fact he'd fucked her from his best friend, all the while fighting the urge to repeat the mistake.

Hi, Ben, how was New York? You know how I never date? Yeah, you understand why… Well, just FYI, I fucked your shiny new sister and I wouldn't mind having another crack at it, no strings. Hope you don't mind…

For a man who loved the law, loved truth and valued honesty and loyalty, he had certainly waded in some pretty murky waters recently. And it messed with his already reeling head.

He'd thought a satisfying night with the bubbly, curvaceous redhead would soothe his battered pride and redress the balance. But all it had done was land him deeper in the shit and reaffirm his stance on trusting no one.

Slamming out of the fogged-up cubicle, Ash threw a towel over his head and scrubbed at his hair. Looping that one around his damp shoulders, he quickly towelled his legs dry and then wrapped the second towel around his waist.

Just as he'd finished cleaning his teeth, he heard the noise and froze, every sense on high alert.

Someone was inside his apartment.

His SW1 penthouse apartment equipped with state-of-the-art security.

'Um, hello…?' A female voice.

Tossing the towel from around his neck, he strode from his en-suite bathroom, expecting perhaps to find the building manager or the cleaner he'd hired to ready the place for his arrival.

He came to a halt just inside his bedroom.

Essie stood in the doorway, her cheeks flushed as if she'd been running and her mouth hanging open as her stare took a slow, sensual meander over his naked torso. Her hot eyes settled on his groin.

He'd been hard most of the day, thinking about her and their night together. Hard in the shower, tempted to bang one out just to attain a measure of relief from the memory of her tight warmth gripping him. And now here she was. Wide eyes touching every inch of his bare skin, and the hard again parts of him behind the towel.

Her chest lifted and fell with shallow pants, which pushed her luscious, pert breasts in his direction. Having taken her time leisurely touring his body, she met his stare again.

He lifted one brow, lips twitching, tempted to fling off the towel so she could really go to town.

'You wanted something?' Had she come for a do-over? Fuck—that was refreshing.

It wasn't his usual style, but damn if he wasn't seriously considering bending the rules and bending her over. Just to clarify that it had been as ball-emptying as he remembered.

No. He didn't do second times. Clearly his libido was on New York time.

She stuttered back to life. 'I... I... Ben needs you to sign these forms for the bank. He couldn't get hold of you.' A pretty pink flush stained her chest above the neckline of her dress, which still bore this morning's coffee stain. It did nothing to diminish her allure. If anything, it heightened her attractiveness, a sign she was human, clumsy and lacked the vanity to rush home and change.

'I was in the gym and then the shower. How did you get in?' He took the folder from her and tossed it onto the bed. Perhaps he should offer her the use of his washer and dryer...get another glimpse of that phenomenal body.

Wishful thinking, asshole.

The phone in her hand buzzed, and she glanced at it, distracted.

He dropped his towel as if he were alone and strode to the dresser, selecting a fresh pair of black cotton boxers. If she chose to waltz into his home uninvited...

'For goodness' sake—do you have to?'

He shot her a look, the underwear he'd been about to don still dangling from his hand. Why should he be alone in this fierce, futile and, frankly, damned inconvenient attraction? Time to play with her a little.

'Hey, you saunter into my home, uninvited. If you don't want to find a guy naked, I suggest you call or knock first.'

He tugged the boxers on, noting with a slug of satisfaction the way her stare clung to his nakedness until the last second. Or perhaps she was gloating at his steely length, ready for action. But he was only human. She was a beautiful woman with a knockout body—but that didn't mean he'd act on his unconscious reaction to her. Or his conscious thoughts of splaying her over his bed and fucking her out of his system for good.

Her cheeks flamed.

Another buzz of the phone.

Someone was desperate to get hold of her.

'Got a hot date?'

She scowled a death stare at him, dropped the phone into her bag and then fisted her hands on her hips as if she couldn't quite believe his audacity.

Believe away, darling.

'None of your business.' She tossed her head with a haughty lift of her chin, the long swathe of russet hair gliding over her shoulders. How would that gorgeous hair look spread over her naked back as he took her from behind; the tips brushing her rosy nipples as he pinned her to the wall and sank to his knees in front of her; spread out over his stark white bed sheets as he pummelled her up the mattress?

'So first you accuse me of being a liar, and now you break into my home just to give me attitude?' He could live with the latter, but having his integrity questioned pricked at the crude stitches holding him together.

She glared but had the good grace to blush. 'Look. I…I'm sorry about calling you a liar. You didn't actually lie to me. I just… I was gobsmacked to see you again.'

'Apology accepted. And that made two of us.' Ash

moved to his walk-in closet, still visualising all the ways he'd like to make her come.

'But, I didn't break in,' she called after him. 'Ben told me where to find your spare key. And I *did* knock.'

'Ah, yes. Ben. A bit awkward, isn't it?' He selected a black T-shirt and poked his head around the door as he tugged it on, furious that his urge to touch her again was not only still present but seemed to intensify despite the stained dress, reminders of her name-calling and his own rigid rules. Well, if he had to suffer, he wanted answers. 'Tell me, what is a graduate with a PhD doing working behind a bar?' She was too smart for this job to be a career move, unless her degree was in hospitality management.

She bristled, her hip jutted to one side in a move that accentuated her curves and the shapely length of her bare legs. Legs he'd like to sink between… face first.

'I…I'm considering my career options. Ben was left in the lurch, and us working together is a good opportunity to get to know each other better.'

So she had a mission that involved spending time with Ben? Damned inconvenient for him and his raging inner battle, but equally intriguing, forcing her deeper into the crevices of his mind where she'd taken up residence since yesterday. He needed an eviction notice.

Another buzz from her bag. Why didn't she silence the damn thing?

'Why don't you answer that?'

She shook her head. 'It's just some…notifications.' She breathed a long sigh. 'Look, we're all grown-ups.'

She looked at him while she twisted a few strands of her hair the way she had yesterday. Perhaps, like him, her head was saying one thing while her body had ideas on a refresher.

But Ash didn't do regret over relationships any more—been there, done that. Look where he'd ended up after yesterday's lapse in judgment. And he was damned determined not to give in to the unfathomable desire currently dragging at him. A desire to have a second dip in the water.

'It was just a one-night thing. As I told you, unlike you, I'm no expert. But isn't it best to just…move on? Forget it ever happened?'

Was she convincing herself?

And she was right. His head had moved on pretty quickly—he'd trained himself well. But his libido, and his dick in particular, were as keen as mustard. It must be those damn flirty dresses that clung to her gorgeous tits like a second skin. Or her warm cinnamon scent infecting his bedroom. Or that pouty bottom lip her teeth kept tugging on…

'I'm sure it makes sense to you, too. After all, we have to work together.'

He emerged from the closet tugging up his jeans and buttoning the fly, trapping his still-eager dick behind a row of studs. If only he could trap his erotic musings as easily.

'Do we? Couldn't you resign? Tell Ben you've changed your mind?' Yes—remove temptation. She and Ben could get to know each other on their own time. His own sisters drove him crazy sometimes— how much time did they really need to spend together?

There was a small gasp as if he'd suggested abandoning kittens at the roadside. 'I'm not letting Ben down like that.'

'Surely he won't care.'

For a second she paled as if he'd struck a deep, throbbing nerve. 'Why would you say that? What has Ben said?'

Until today he'd never given much thought to Ben's news a year or so back that he had a half-sister in London. Their friendship had stretched over the years as careers took hold, their recent contact limited to a snatched beer after work or a trip to the gym. What was the nature of Ben's relationship with Essie? How close were they and why had she been out of the picture growing up?

One thing was certain: she didn't know Ben well enough to be confident in his reaction to her quitting. Interesting... He shrugged. 'I just mean I can replace you within the hour. No disruption to service.'

Fire shone from her stare. 'Oh, I just bet you could. Well, I'm not disposable and I'm not that easily substituted.' She stalked nearer, shunting his body temperature dangerously high with her teasing scent—summer, cinnamon and all woman. 'I'm not an inconvenience to be sidelined, quietly slinking away as if I don't exist.'

Whoa, where was all that coming from? He had clearly done more than touch a nerve—he'd sawed one in half and poured salt on the cut ends.

Her eyes danced over his crotch and then lifted. 'Couldn't you move back to New York?'

Not until the gossip-feeding frenzy had died down and his personal life was no longer entertainment news, but he wasn't sharing that shit. And why? So that she didn't have to feel embarrassed about over-sharing with her one-night stand? He parried with a step of his own. 'But then what would you stare at?'

'What do you mean?'

'You're practically drooling, sweetheart. I know I was a little wiped out last night, so if you want another crack at it…' He tilted his head towards the massive bed, which dominated the room like an elephant, every muscle tensed in anticipation of finally getting what he craved.

She closed the distance between them, eyes glazed and mouth open as if lust oozed from every pore.

'I'm perfectly capable of separating a meaningless fuck from the work that needs to be done at the club.' Her stare lingered on his mouth.

Was she waiting?

For the pithy reply banked up on his tongue, or another taste? His mind fogged as her proximity, her scent, her heat flooded his blood with the testosterone that had dogged him all day, just knowing she worked in the same building. Close enough to hear her throaty chuckle while she spoke to contractors and the soft humming that accompanied her fingers clacking on her keyboard.

'*My* club.' Time to remind Miss Compartmentalised who steered the ship. 'But are you capable of the work? Ben and I need someone honest, dependable, committed.' Ash ignored the flare that turned her irises to molten metal. He ignored the urgency of his own needs beating at his body until his muscles screamed with inertia. 'Tell me, who are you today?'

Her hands fisted on her hips, a move that tightened

the fabric across her full breasts outlining her erect nipples…begging for his tongue?

'What does that mean?'

'Yesterday a ditsy student tourist, today a competent professional in charge of *my* club? I don't take well to being deceived.' He battled for his legendary control, which he relied on as armour to protect himself. 'I don't trust you. So until I know my club is in safe hands, you and I will be working very closely together. Got that?'

Her stare narrowed but her eyes gleamed with something close to the incandescent flare burning through his veins. Perhaps that was the answer: to fuck this inexplicable chemistry out of their systems; to quench the fire. He'd said it wouldn't happen again, but that was before she'd stormed into his bedroom. Before all her talk about meaningless fucks and moving on. Before she'd drooled over his deliberate nudity and was still mentally stripping him with her hungry, slumberous stare.

Her mouth hung open while said stare burned the flesh from his features. 'I'd never do anything to damage Ben's business—you're just paranoid.' She dropped her bag and fisted her hands on her hips once more.

He inched closer, chest puffed. 'You've got that right. It works well for me these days.'

Her eyes blazed. 'I'm here to help my brother open *his* club. No matter how much you want me gone.' Her breath hitched. 'Unless I hear it from Ben that my services are no longer required, I'm staying, so you'd better get used to the idea.'

She jutted her chin forward, bringing her mouth

only centimetres from his, her breath fanning his face. She looked halfway to orgasm already—panting, flushed, her mouth saying one thing while her body strained in his direction.

Don't touch her.

Back away.

Too late…

In less than a heartbeat she'd pushed her hands into his still-damp hair and dragged his face down. But he'd been on the move himself. He scooped her around the waist and hauled her from the floor. Their mouths clashed and she gave a cry close to a victory wail as she parted her lips under the surge and slide of his ferocious kiss.

All reason fled. Their tongues touched, the thrust and parry of wildness a perfectly matched duel. Her body moulded to his as if they'd been forged side by side. Her passion seemed to enflame the lust that had been simmering in him since she'd swanned into his office this morning—his knees almost buckled. He wasn't alone.

Who was this woman he couldn't resist? Her wilful determination turned him on as much as it pissed him off and her demanding sexuality was…magnificent. His first impressions about her had been dead wrong. Essie fully embraced her sexuality—another fascinating aspect to her complex personality.

Like electricity and water, they sparked off each other. Her hands twisted his hair until he growled. Her greedy mouth sucked on his lips as if she wanted to consume him whole and her thighs clung to his waist as he hoisted her higher to press his steely length against her warm, wet centre, delivering the friction they both seemed to crave.

If he hadn't been staring her down, eye-to-eye, while they consumed each other, his eyes would have rolled back in his head. Her fantastic body aligned with his, her wet heat seeped through the denim covering his thigh as she ground herself there and her nipples poked through the two layers of clothing separating her chest from his.

A fresh surge of blood turned his dick to granite.

Yes.

One more time to banish this tigress masquerading as a pussycat from his system and restore his control over the explosive situation. He didn't need to trust her. He just had to fuck her. Just sex. Great sex. One last astounding time.

With one arm now curled around his neck like a vice, her free hand snaked between their bodies to rub him through his jeans before fumbling for the buttons of his fly. She writhed in his arms, all sexy little whimpers and catches of her breath. Fuck, she was a hellcat. Challenging, uninhibited, eager. He'd been doomed from the minute he'd opened his eyes to the sight of her yesterday in the sun-dappled park.

He spread his feet, cementing his balance so he could do a little exploring of his own. Cupping her ass in one hand, Ash delved beneath the hem of her dress with the other. His fingers skimmed her thigh, zeroing in on her to find the source of the warm patch on his jeans—her soaked panties. With their working mouths and challenging stares still locked, he slipped his fingers beyond the cotton and lace.

She was fiery hot and slick against his fingers, and

when he swiped forward and located her clit she broke free from the kiss with a moan. Her sultry glare—half *fuck you*, half *fuck me*—dared him. Spurred him on. Not that he required the encouragement.

In two strides, he'd deposited her ass on the edge of his dresser, which, like the rest of his home, was sleek, minimal and uncluttered. She spread her thighs, welcoming him into the cradle of space she created with a tug of his shirt.

While his fingers resumed the slip and slide against her, his other hand sought her pebbled nipple, strumming through the layers of fabric. But that wasn't enough for her. She released her grip on his shoulders long enough to unbutton the top few buttons of her dress and yank both it and her bra down, exposing one pale, creamy shoulder and a perfect, pink-tipped breast.

Fuck.

He groaned.

Perfection.

He dived to get his mouth on her. *Just one more taste.* Then he'd stop this madness.

But Essie was having none of that. One hand returned to his hair, her grip punishing and directive while the other drove him wild by rubbing his erection through his clothes. Her pert flesh filled his mouth and he sucked hard, drawing her in deeper and guided by her continued twisting and tugging on his hair and her repeated 'yes'es. Her hips shunted against his hand, as if she was as desperate for her release as he was.

Just one more time. Until he worked this baffling

urge from his off-kilter system. This time he'd walk away sated, equilibrium restored. Cured.

Pinning her to the furniture with his hips, he pushed two fingers inside her and feathered his thumb over her clit. His mouth returned to hers while his fingers strummed the damp nipple his mouth left behind.

True to the Essie of last night, she clawed his shoulders, her moans growing in frequency and volume.

'Tell me when you're close,' he mumbled against her lips, reluctant to break away from her breathy and frantic kisses.

She nodded, her eyes heavy and her hair a wild tumble around her flushed face. His clothing was practically cutting off his blood supply to his groin. But he couldn't move, couldn't have stopped now if he'd had a gun to his head.

He left her breast long enough to scoop one arm around her hips and shunt her ass to the edge of the dresser, changing the angle of her hips.

She cried out and tore her mouth from his. 'Yes, now… I'm…'

He dived on her exposed nipple once more, laving and lapping like a starving man as his fingers plundered her slickness and his thumb circled her swollen clit.

She detonated, her whole body taut as her orgasm jolted her forward. If he hadn't been there to block her fall the force of it would have tumbled her from the edge of the furniture. Ash kept up the sucking and circling until he'd wrung every spasm from her magnificent, trembling body. Until she pushed at his shoulders instead of clawing at them.

Her head fell forward, resting on his chest. 'Oh, wow…'

The scent of her hair made his eyes roll back. Thank fuck she couldn't see. He recited the most boring legal jargon he could think of to stop himself from burying his nose there and taking a deep, decadent inhalation. He'd fall asleep surrounded by her honeyed scent, just as he had last night…

Fuck.

His blood turned to liquid nitrogen.

What the hell was he doing?

He couldn't trust this woman.

He couldn't trust anyone.

His body turned rigid as reality dawned.

This had disaster written all over it. This business venture was his fresh start—a place no one knew him or his fucked-up family. A place of anonymity to regroup and wrestle back control. Why was he so fascinated in her? Why couldn't he stay away?

He stepped back, tugging his hand from Essie's underwear and avoiding her confused stare. He lowered her to the floor, steadying her by the elbows while she found her balance and righted her debauched clothing.

Too late for gentlemanly heroics now. Not that he claimed to be either. Not any more. That was a fool's game.

He sucked back a swallow that reminded him of all the reasons his head had been right about this illadvised encounter after all. He'd tasted betrayal—a different kind, but it sucked all the same. He was done with trusting the wrong person.

The humiliating scene at the Jacob Holdings offices flashed into his head. On discovering his father had been cheating on his mother, he'd lashed out at the man he'd worked alongside for ten years. He'd expected his old man to bristle, maybe tell him to mind his own business, but he hadn't expected the vile mouthful of home truths he'd received in return.

Fire snaked along his frozen blood vessels, reminding him of the subsequent damage he'd inflicted, especially on the mother he'd been trying to protect.

He turned away, adjusting his rapidly diminishing hard-on, which recoiled at both the bitter memories of his fight with Hal and the reality that he barely knew this woman he couldn't seem to leave alone.

'What? We're done?'

He turned back and offered a single, decisive nod. End it now. With his sanity and dignity intact, his fresh start still tenable and his principles only slightly grubby.

For the longest beat she stared, her expression neutral but her eyes stormy. Wordlessly she skirted him as if he were a shark and walked to his bed. She collected the file he'd tossed there earlier and returned to stand in front of him.

'So, counsellor—' she blatantly eyed the bulge in his jeans '—the defence rests?'

His fingers curled into fists to stop himself from kissing her sassy mouth once more. Pissed at him and flushed from her orgasm, she was even more breathtaking.

He ground his jaw clenched. 'I think it's best.' He'd never needed his attorney poker face more.

She barked a humourless snort. 'Don't worry. I may not be an expert at casual sex, but I am an expert at surviving rejection.'

What the fuck...?

She pressed the file to his chest, holding it there until his hand replaced hers.

'This needs to be scanned by six.' She slid one last look down his torso to his still-hard dick. 'Have a good evening.'

And she left.

CHAPTER FOUR

'EVERYTHING'S FINE,' Essie said to Ben. His partner
wanted to replace her as if she were…an inconvenience. She'd thrown herself at a man who'd had the
sense to resist. And she had no idea where Ben's head
stood and was too scared to ask. Sure, everything
was fine.

Essie hunched over the desk and rubbed at a non-
existent scratch. Perhaps that was why her joy at his
call was diluted. Fear that Ben, too, would agree
with Ash and fire her, then disappear from her life as
quickly as he'd appeared.

'Are you sure?' said Ben.

She pressed the phone to her face and hoped her
brother couldn't hear the blood pounding through her
head. She shouldn't be wallowing—she had work to
do. 'Of course. The decorators finished up today and
I'm meeting your head barman soon.' Ben trusted
her with his club, and she wouldn't allow her frenzied attraction to Ash to make waves or damage his
business venture.

No. She and Ash were done.

But the years of self-doubt had infected her fresh
start with Ben. Every childhood disappointment,

every time her father let her down and every cruel taunt from her overcritical ex rattled in her brain until nausea threatened.

Perhaps Ash was right. She should walk away.

No. She wanted a future as part of Ben's life. And their father had already robbed her of a past with her only sibling.

'How are things in New York?' Had he seen their father? Had Frank Newbold asked about her? She shouldn't care, but that little girl part of her, the part that had idolised him, had flown into his outstretched arms every time he'd come home, still craved his attention, even when she'd declared herself done with his toxic brand of parenthood.

'Someone's putting their hand in the cash register.'

Essie gasped. 'Oh, no, Ben. That's terrible.' A slab of guilt settled on her shoulders. Ben needed drama at The Yard as much as she needed another brush-off from Ash.

'I'll sort it out, don't worry. Did the bank get their signature in time?'

Essie's face heated with the reminder of what she'd done last night.

'Yes.' Despite all the reasons not to, despite Ash's obvious ability to resist, she yearned for the full-on repeat performance Ash had denied her yesterday.

He'd wanted her—the physical evidence, thick and hard behind his fly, had been irrefutable. She'd never have guessed a sexually charged man like Ash possessed so much command over his body. Or her so little.

The trust between her and Ash was non-existent. He seemed to think she was some sort of industrial spy out to ruin his investment and she couldn't be sure he wouldn't sack her at any moment, regardless of her relationship to Ben. But she wanted him anyway. Physically. Another new experience for her.

She'd trusted her ex with a blind faith that left her curled into a tight ball. She'd been so desperate to make just one relationship work that she'd ignored the warning signs—the criticisms, the bullying, the control. When he'd finally grown bored and left her on the grounds that she was too clingy, and she'd seen clearly for the first time how dysfunctional the relationship had been, she'd vowed never again to give someone that kind of power.

And she certainly wouldn't give it to Ash.

But, she'd known the minute he'd stepped from his en-suite bathroom, droplets of water dotting his sculpted torso with only the towel and his scowl as a barrier, she'd intended to make good on her plan to seduce him then walk away. A plan that had put the control of their rampant sexual attraction firmly in her hands.

But that chemistry between them had become a magnetised force field drawing her in, and her plan had backfired. She'd seduced him all right, but she'd bungled it. Failed to put a stop to the wild kissing and grinding that had scored her another orgasm, but scored Ash another point on his 'ability to resist her' scale.

'Are you and Ash getting to know each other?' Ben's voice pulled her back from thoughts of Ash's naked body, every inch of him hard and straining…

No.

Ash was getting to know how easily he could turn

her on to the point of spontaneous combustion. How eagerly she surrendered to their physical need that flared to life like a science experiment gone wrong. How her traitorous body succumbed to the pleasure he crafted so effortlessly.

The only positive outcome, aside from the fantastic sex, was that her blog post on one-night stands had been quoted on one of the UK's top online women's magazines and reposted over and over on social media. It seemed people loved *Illegally Hot*. The spike in followers and comments had, only this morning, spurred Essie into publishing another article featuring the panty-melting *Illegally Hot*, entitled *Dares; Disasters and Don't Go Theres*—those relationships we knew were bad for us, but we craved them anyway—drawing on last night's disappointing disaster. As if purging her thoughts, her fears, her doubts in cyberspace would cure her of her irresistible and seemingly one-sided attraction to Ash Jacob.

It was wrong, but she couldn't deny the buzz that the soar of popularity delivered. She'd always considered her blog as something of a hobby, but, with her PhD complete, perhaps the boost in credibility was just what she needed to take herself more seriously as a writer. She could even start running some pay-per-click ads… invite experts in the field to guest blog… She scribbled down some ideas while she zoned back to answering her brother's question. 'Not really.' Apart from Ash's bedroom skills and his considerable control, she knew zilch. A fact her analytical brain tolerated poorly.

'What's his deal? He seems a little…uptight.'

Plus he hated her, wanted to fire her and didn't trust her.

'Has he upset you?' The fact that Ben had protective instincts towards her left her gooey inside. But the only thing she needed protection from was her own reckless libido. The goo turned to brittle concrete.

'No, of course not.' Another lie. Because she *was* upset. Upset that she'd buckled to her searing attraction to the infuriating man, who displayed enough warning signs to send her running. And furious that she couldn't be certain, given half a chance, she wouldn't do it all over again.

'He…he said he doesn't trust people.' What was that about? Just her? Women in general? The entire world?

'He is a bit closed off…' A small sigh.

Closed off? A massive understatement. She'd need a pickaxe to excavate Ash's psyche.

No. Focus on the sex. Control that.

What was she thinking?

No more sex.

Her voice squeezed past strangled vocal cords. 'How are you two friends? You're such a lovely, warm person.' Ben and Ash had known each other a long time. Essie's stomach clenched. She'd gatecrashed a long-standing friendship with her ill-judged fling. But it was over now.

Ben chuckled and then went silent. 'He wasn't always so…uncompromising. It's not my story to tell, but let's just say he was badly hurt by an ex.'

Something they shared in common.

'It's left him with trust issues that make him a bit cynical.'

Cynical. Controlled to the point of snapping.

Of course a broken love affair would be to blame.

Essie knew both first-hand and professionally that only relationships had the emotional power to wreak such long-lasting havoc. The psychologist in her longed to probe Ash's secrets in light of this new clue, her resolve to ignore him stretched paper thin.

The least she could do, for Ben's sake, was try to give the exasperating man the benefit of the doubt professionally while giving him a wide berth personally. Ben deserved better than returning from his business trip to find his partner and his manager at each other's throats.

Perhaps, with a little subtle digging, she could help him deal with whatever held him back. Because if she knew anything, she knew Ash Jacob was on the run from something. Not a crime…more like a battered heart. She knew the signs—she'd spent years seeing them in the mirror. And she preferred to divert attention to other people's dysfunctional relationships than focus on her own.

The idea that Ash might be pining for a lost love left a bad taste in her mouth, one without an explanation. A change of subject. 'I'll have to speak to you some other time. Josh your star barman is due any minute.'

With her hollow assurances echoing in her head, and her mind racing with Ben's cryptic confession, she ended the call to her brother just as a text came in.

Josh had arrived.

Essie rushed to the rear entrance to welcome the twenty-one-year-old classics student. They headed to the bar and were halfway through introductions when Ash joined them without being invited.

Essie froze mid-sentence. Her body zinged from relaxed to nerve-tingling awareness.

Josh was handsome in that trendy, glasses-and-beard kind of way. But the mere presence of Ash in the space—his imposing height, intense, bright blue stare and commanding demeanour—shunted the room temperature to stifling. She couldn't even waft out the pheromones before they had chance to hijack her brain again and enslave her until she started clawing at his sublime suit.

Before she could question his presence, Ash stuck out his hand and introduced himself to Josh. 'I'm Ash Jacob, co-owner.' He flicked a curt nod at Essie and took a seat at the bar. 'Carry on.'

Carry on? Carry on? How was she supposed to do that when the mere sight of him decked out like the sort of lawyer she'd never be able to afford fried all her neuronal impulses not directly relayed to her lady parts and robbed her saliva-making capabilities?

And sitting in on Josh's orientation? He hadn't issued an idle threat or exaggerated last night. He didn't trust her. He intended to watch her every move in case she put a foot wrong and committed some sackable offence. She bristled. As if she'd *ever* do anything to jeopardise her brother's enterprise. Did he think she'd put her hand in the till or help herself to the vodka?

Jerk.

All her good intentions to make peace with him, to help him, fled. She'd prove to him that, not only was she one hundred per cent invested in this club, but she could employ similar levels of self-restraint to the ones he'd shown.

She was dreaming if she believed they could be

friends—the sexual-attraction barrier loomed in the way like an immovable boulder worthy of Stonehenge. But that didn't mean she had to act on her…urge. Again.

She led Josh behind the bar, seeking inspiration or at least a distraction from the persistent throb between her legs. How could Ash Jacob's brand of sex be so addictive? She'd only had one little taste…one and a half. He was orgasm nicotine and her poor brain's pleasure centres had taken a massive hit. No wonder she was reeling…

'Ben said you have lots of past experience so feel free to set up the bar area as works best for you.' The words squeaked past her constricted throat and she bent to slide a box of spirits out of the way.

Josh chatted away, filling the stilted silence with his relevant work experience and his ideas for making the bar space work.

She barely heard a word. Too aware of Ash scraping his keen eyes over her while his mouth formed a mildly amused smirk.

But, oh, what talent that mouth possessed. He should forget about law—his oral skills were seriously wasted in the boardroom. She'd never been so thoroughly kissed, nibbled, licked… Her nipples chafed against her bra and her legs grew restless, desperate to rub together to ease the ache at their juncture.

Sensing a pause in Josh's speech, Essie forced her mind away from Mr Jacob, orgasm whisperer.

'What about cocktails? Could you create a house cocktail, something unique, associated only with us?' She'd made that last bit up on the spur of the moment.

She seen it done at other clubs, and it matched the philosophy Ben had for The Yard.

Josh answered and Essie busied her hands with straightening a perfectly aligned row of shot glasses as a substitute for drooling over Ash, who'd narrowed his eyes and begun idly rubbing his lower lip with his thumb and forefinger while he listened and observed.

Forget drooling—she was half tempted to see Josh promptly on his way and ride Ash right where he sat. Or drop to her knees, release him from his sophisticated trousers and swallow him whole. Wipe that smug, self-satisfied grin off his face. Show him she could rile him up as easily, effectively and thoroughly as he did her.

No. They'd been there, done that. The sex was over. She'd humiliated herself enough.

Time to focus on her job and on Ben.

That was the relationship that required her energy. A rewarding sibling bond, family, longevity. Something she'd craved her whole life. After all, she'd put her beloved blog, her future career on partial hiatus just to work alongside her brother. And who knew how long he'd stay in London? If he moved back to New York, the opportunity to build family ties, to be a part of each other's daily lives, would be severely compromised.

Her stomach pinched as if she'd sucked one of the lemons sitting on the gleaming bar in a glass bowl. 'Well, I'll leave you to set up and familiarise yourself with everything.'

Josh smiled and started unpacking the box of spirits. Essie rounded the bar and Ash swivelled on his bar stool, the creak of leather drawing her attention to him spreading his thighs wider.

Man-spreading?

Staking his claim as the dominant male in the room?

When she looked up from his crotch, he held her gaze, one eyebrow raised in challenge as if he knew the flighty zigzagging of her earlier thoughts and their X-rated bent.

This was impossible. How was she expected to get anything done when he hovered nearby, watching her every move, tying her into sexually frustrated knots with just a quirk of his brow and some male posturing to which her qualifications and knowledge of body language should render her immune?

She turned a sickly sweet smile on Ash. 'Mr Jacob, do you have any questions for Josh?'

'No.' Ash rose to his feet. 'But I will speak with you in my office when you're ready.'

After Ash stalked through the staff door, Essie hovered in the bar area straightening chairs to gain a moment's reprieve from the hormonal maelstrom Ash induced.

With a deep breath she followed him, finding him behind his desk. She left the door open. Her, Ash, enclosed spaces…not happening.

'What the hell was that?' she snapped.

He shrugged, rising slowly from the chair and stalking to a halt mere inches in front of her face.

'What's the problem? I told you, until I'm certain my shiny new business is in safe hands, I'm all over you.'

Essie's eyes mentally rolled back with the fantasy

his words concocted. Him sweaty. Her writhing. More life-redefining orgasms.

Yes, please.

'I can't do my job with you…hovering. And surely you're too busy…preparing briefs or something?' Her unfortunate choice of words forced a rage of heat up her neck—he'd looked astounding yesterday, both in and out of his tight-fitting briefs as he'd strutted around his bedroom, a supreme specimen of rugged maleness. Every inch of him lean and ripped—all smooth golden skin with a dusky sprinkling of dark hair as near to black as the silky mop on his head. No inhibitions and no need for any.

And even though he'd only been partially aroused then, as he'd donned his underwear and jeans, the sight of him had still left her mouth pooling with saliva and her clit throbbing. *Astounding.*

What was wrong with her? She never obsessed over men, physically or emotionally. Well, not since her ex. Essie Newbold, psychologist, would-be relationship expert—at least on paper—was now far too well informed to fall victim to the games played in the name of those relationships. Ash could do all the male posturing he liked—she simply suffered from a bad case of lust. She could control those…urges. Writing about it helped.

'Actually, I have some instructions for you.' His grin widened, eyes turning feral.

She practically choked. 'You…what…?' Her knees wobbled while she imagined the kind of instructions she'd like to hear coming from his mouth.

Strip. Spread your thighs. Bend over…

Stop.

He lifted that one brow. Mocking. Testing. 'You do work here.'

'Yes, but—'

'Good. I want you to go home now and pack an overnight bag. Where do you live?'

Was he for real?

Where the hell was he sending her?

Had he decided to winkle her out from under his nose by stealth? Send her on some fool's errand and insinuate a replacement in her stead behind her back?

'I live in New Cross.' At his blank expression she added, 'South London. Where am I going?' Perhaps he'd decided to work her to death so she would quit. Did he expect her to pull an all-nighter? The Yard wasn't even open yet.

'You're coming with me to Paris. Do you have someone who can pack a bag for you? We leave at six.'

Paris?

With him.

No way.

'I…I have a flatmate. But I'm not going to Paris with you.' The words had barely escaped her mouth when the throb returned between her legs. Twice as ferocious.

Him.

Her.

Alone in the city of love.

Whoa there. Don't get carried away—this is real life, not some fluffy shit you made up for your blog. He's done with you physically and he doesn't trust you. Oh…and you've used his sexual prowess to validate your online relationship advice.

Her face flamed. Why *had* she done that?

He smiled, the feline kind of smile that told her he saw too much.

'Worried you won't be able to control yourself?' He closed in. His eyes dipped to her mouth.

Huh, right... The air trapped in Essie's lungs. He was so close, a cloud of heat rose from him, carrying the scent of whatever he'd used in the shower that morning to Essie's nose.

And then he leaned down so his breath tickled her ear and sent tiny muscular spasms skittering down her exposed neck to reawaken her nipples. 'Now who's flattering themselves?' He reared back, his expression hard, serious, uncompromising. All business.

Bastard.

'We have work to do. Didn't Ben mention it?'

She shook her head, her feeble body swaying as the adrenaline dissipated.

'There's a club we wanted to check out. The best in France. Perhaps the best in Europe.'

He slung his hands casually into his trouser pockets so the fabric stretched taut across his groin. Essie dragged her eyes away, desperate now to get away from him so she could regroup and fortify her defences with Ash-proof razor wire and hormone repellent spray.

'I didn't get where I am today by being second best. The Yard is going to be number one. So we're going to go see what the competition is up to.' He tapped the desk with two fingers and then levelled them at her.

'Call your roommate. My driver will collect your bag in—' he checked his watch '—thirty minutes.'

Essie's weak body veered from nuclear meltdown

to hypothermia. Her mind conjured excuses...*no pass-port...an ingrown toenail...an allergy to France.*

How would she survive a trip to Paris with Mr Rigid Control? There would be no way to escape the temptation of him for the hours of travelling time, trapped in a moving vehicle with only his astounding profile, catnip scent and magnetic sex appeal for distraction. Her poor ovaries would shrivel from exhaustion.

She lifted her chin. 'Will I be paid overtime?' She might as well make him suffer financially if he wouldn't be suffering from blue balls, although she doubted her meagre salary would hurt Mr Moneybags too much.

'Of course.'

'Separate hotel rooms?' She might be unable to refuse his reasonable, Ben-sanctioned request, but at least she would be able to escape the lure of lust when the work was over.

His mouth twitched.

'If you like, but surely that horse has bolted...' He shrugged.

Arsehole.

And why was he looking at her as if he remembered every detail of her naked? He'd turned away from her last night, put an end to the mad ride she'd have willingly enjoyed until the end. Perhaps despite his control he was still interested. That would certainly explain the way he looked at her. Her breasts throbbed and her clit tingled.

But where did that leave her and her tattered and grubby good intentions? Perhaps she should even the score; take back control of the physical attraction that showed no signs of abating, for either of them; remind him what he'd turned down. She narrowed her eyes. If she had to survive the extreme sexual frustration of being in his company she should definitely play him at his own game.

Her phone, set to send a notification every time someone commented on her blog, vibrated in her pocket, a timely reminder. *Aren't you already playing him? Writing about him?* Illegally Hot *is a real person.*

She swallowed and forced her thoughts back to ways of avoiding a repeat of yesterday's humiliating rejection. So he'd resisted once. So he wanted to pretend this insane chemistry would disappear. Time to up the ante. Bring out the big guns. Her mind scrabbled through the contents of her underwear drawer for the sexiest lingerie she owned—a treat to herself when she'd graduated with her first-class psychology degree. Some women loved shoes. Essie loved frilly knickers.

At least her roommate, Sarah, would be home cramming for exams today—she'd buy her flatmate something gorgeous from Paris to say thanks. A small smile tugged her mouth. Why should she suffer alone? The least she could do was take him down with her.

'Fine. And I insist on separate rooms.' She moved to the door, halting at his sexy drawl.

'Oh, and, Essie. Don't forget your passport.' With a wink that made a strangled gasp catch in her dry throat, he closed the door behind her.

The car probably cost more than her rented flat in South London—soft leather seats, sleek, shiny body-

work and chauffer driven. It even had a privacy screen.
Not that they'd need that. The minute Ash held open
the door for her and ushered her inside, he pulled out
his phone and began tapping away.

Essie normally enjoyed silence—you could learn
a lot about someone by people-watching. Their tells,
their habits, their unconscious body language. But
all she'd learned about Ash, apart from that the man
never looked anything less than seriously fuckable,
was that she wanted to know more.

Ben had told her Ash was from New York roy-
alty, his family dating back to a wave of nineteenth-
century immigrants. He'd worked for Jacob Holdings,
his family-owned real estate business, since leaving
college. He'd been to Harvard, and his net worth made
her light-headed. But why had he moved to London?
Who had broken his heart? And why couldn't he be
less attractive so she wasn't incapacitated by the urge
to jump him?

'Forgive me.' He looked up from his phone, his
deep voice interrupting her train of thought. 'The time
zones are messing with my schedule. I had some New
York deadlines to meet.' He pocketed the device and
gave her his full, panty-melting attention.

Essie shivered, hot then cold, sliding her own phone
into her pocket. She almost preferred being ignored.

The device buzzed immediately, halting whatever
Ash had been about to say.

'That goes off a lot. Do you have a bet on? Tracking
the stock market?' Playful glints sparked in his eyes,
but she couldn't enjoy the banter for the slosh of stomach acid burning inside her. Her fans loved *Illegally
Hot* and wanted more of him. She knew the feeling.

If only they could see him, edible in his crisp suit, his hair dishevelled and a scruffy smattering of facial hair reminding her how it felt to be kissed by that beautiful mouth.

'Something like that.' She shrugged, her cheeks hot. She should never have started the *Illegally Hot* posts. She changed the subject before she confessed.

'So, this club we're scouting—is there a dress code?' She only owned one little black dress, one she had asked Sarah to pack into her overnight bag. She'd seen plenty of photos of him with hot dates— gorgeous, sophisticated women: models, actresses, heiresses. Compared to the women he usually associated with, she'd definitely be the country mouse.

Except this wasn't a date. It didn't matter what she wore. She should have brought a bin bag, just so her libido stayed in check.

Ash turned and slid his gaze along the length of her body until she squirmed and heat flooded her panties. 'Whatever you wear will be fine.' A shrug. 'I know the owner.'

So it wasn't a date. That didn't mean she couldn't enjoy tormenting him while she suffered right alongside. Regardless of his impressive willpower, he looked at her as if she might as well be naked. His eyes wanted her even if the rest of him could resist.

'You can change on board. We'll be going straight to the club when we land.'

So they were still on the clock? Shame. Now she had him in a chatty mood, she'd like to unearth one or two juicy personal details to fill in the blanks. Like why he'd walked away from his New York life, his family business and what must be an extremely lucrative legal career. And why someone of his social standing, exceptional hotness and phenomenal bedroom skills was still single? No halitosis, in possession of a full head of luxuriant hair, and he wasn't a pervert.

'It's not my area of expertise, but Josh seems competent enough—would you agree?' He rubbed at his bottom lip, drawing her eyes there.

She'd probably agree to anything for the intense stare he settled on her and what it did to her pulse. How was she going to survive this trip when every nerve in her body vibrated, desperate to have him lose that control he wore like a second skin? Lose it with her.

'He does. It's not my area of expertise, either, although I can pull a pint.' Her cheeks warmed. She'd pulled him, too. In a park. She stuttered on, changing the veer of her thoughts. 'The DJ called to speak to Ben—know anything about techno house?'

Ash rubbed his jaw as if his scruff irritated him, and Essie's fingers twitched. That stubble had been amazing scraping across her sensitive nipple last night. How would it feel on her inner thighs?

Oh, no...don't go there.

Her experiences of oral sex were sadly unfulfilling. Her ex had claimed he didn't care for it, although he loved it when she returned the favour. She cringed at her younger self. Of course her ex had lacked skills in the foreplay and stamina departments, too—probably why she was struggling to resist the phenomenal Ash. She knew instinctively he would excel at oral sex— she'd kissed him after all, felt his mouth at her breasts... She discreetly blew at the wisps of hair clinging to her heated forehead. Another dangerous temptation to add to the growing list.

He smiled, the genuine, lopsided version that had landed her in this mess in the first place. 'No, not much. You?'

Essie shook her head. She loved to dance, but her clubbing days were few and far between. Long years of research-laden academic study had put paid to partying and wild nights out. And she hadn't been interested in the hook-up side of clubbing after she'd had her fingers burned with her ex.

'Perhaps we can leave that to Ben, on his return.' He leaned back in the seat and looked out of the window at the passing city, the route to London City Airport taking them parallel to the river. 'So, tell me about you and Ben. You didn't grow up together?' He turned a shrewd stare her way.

Great. So he wanted to make conversation and he'd chosen the one subject that made her skin raw and her scalp prickle. Her relationship with her brother was still so fragile, and brought all her insecurities to the surface like a rash.

Ben and Ash were friends. But Ash had barely heard of her... Was Ben ashamed of the connection with his illegitimate half-sister? Or perhaps she was so low down on his list of priorities... Been there, done that.

She shook her heavy head. 'We share a father, but I grew up here and, as you know, Ben in New York.'

It shouldn't matter that Ben hadn't discussed her with his oldest friend enough for Ash to remember her name. Yes, Ben had been the one to reach out after he'd discovered the truth about Frank Newbold's other life. But perhaps he now regretted the impulse. Did he consider her a cling-on? An inconvenience? Something else to be managed or swept under the carpet?

Could she really blame Ben for being ashamed to broadcast the existence of a sibling he knew little about, his father's sordid secret? The shame she'd felt growing up with Frank's constant absences and see-through excuses rose to the surface, boiling hot. Could she criticise Ben when her own father hadn't found her lovable enough for him to stick around?

She choked down familiar fears. 'What about you and Ben? He said you've been friends since grade school.'

Ash nodded, glancing away. 'He's a good friend.'

Well, that seemed to be the end of that.

'You don't give much away, do you?' The trust issues Ben talked about?

'Try me.' He lifted one brow, daring her.

So tempting. But she didn't want to scare him into brooding silence once more. Something easy. 'Do you have a sister?'

He nodded. 'I have two—twins. Younger. Both a pain in my ass.' He smiled, flashing the grooves around his mouth.

'What about girlfriends? Anyone pining for you back in New York?' Her throat grew hot and achy. Why had she asked that?

'No.' He shrugged. 'I don't do girlfriends.'

'Not ever?'

He shook his head, a slow measured action that gave his stare plenty of time to scrape over her heated face. 'Not for years.'

So the ex hadn't just hurt him, she'd ruined him. He

really was as closed off as she'd suspected. She took pity on the grey tinge to his handsome face. 'Human interpersonal relationships are…complex.' Hers included. All she knew about the opposite sex, beyond the theory she'd got from books and lectures, she'd learned from the behaviour of her selfish, largely absent father and her cruel, manipulative ex. She swallowed down the familiar lump threatening to make her feel two inches tall and changed the subject.

'Fun fact—did you know that having an older sibling can positively improve your mental health?'

He frowned as if she'd spoken in Russian.

She nodded, warming to her favourite subject. 'It… it's been scientifically proven. Ben and I have only connected recently, but…' She shrugged. She hoped it was true. Hoped what she found with Ben would positively impact both their lives for years to come.

His eyes narrowed slightly, as if he were seeing her for the first time. 'So Frank Newbold and your mother had an affair?' His lips formed a grim line, judgment hovering in his stare.

Essie squirmed as the acid in her throat burned its way through her internal organs. She bristled, lashing out instead of curling in on herself. 'Not exactly. Not every relationship is sordid—sometimes people are duped, lied to, manipulated.' The excuses kept on coming, as if she'd waited too long to purge. 'My mother didn't know about Ben and his mother until after I was born. Frank spun her the usual bullshit about having a rocky marriage and leaving his wife when the time was right…' Essie herself hadn't known until her fifteenth birthday. 'By then I was Daddy's little girl and Mum couldn't bear to break my heart with the truth that he'd probably never fully commit to us. I guess she always held out hope that one day we'd be a proper family.' Her throat burned so badly now she was surprised she could speak at all.

'So you didn't know about Ben?'

She sighed and shook her head. 'I was fifteen when I found out.' He stayed silent so she continued. 'My father was overseas, and I was angry that, yet again, he wouldn't be home for my birthday.' The burn invaded her eye sockets. Why tell him this? Speaking the words aloud wouldn't lessen the impact of the events. 'I stayed awake until the middle of the night, crept downstairs and called him at work. He wasn't at the office, but I was given another number I assumed was a hotel. A woman, Ben's mum as it turned out, answered the phone and I said I was his daughter. I'm not sure who was more shocked.'

A disbelieving frown. '*That's* how you discovered you had a brother?' Ash stopped just short of allowing his jaw to drop open.

She nodded, her face flaming. Not a pretty story, and one it seemed, despite his friendship with Ben, he'd never heard. She wasn't surprised. Why would Ben want to advertise such a sordid tale?

Ash's skin took on a green hue, his mouth now a fully blown grim line. Was he that appalled by her tawdry past? How dared he be so…judgmental?

The question stuck in her throat. She ripped it out, needing confirmation. 'Ben…never talked about me?'

He sighed. 'Not much. A mention here and there. But I…was busy…with work stuff at the time.' He grew pensive and turned to look out of the car window again. 'Perhaps if I'd known more about you, we might have avoided this…situation.' He spoke quietly, almost to himself. But the words stung just the same.

So now she was a situation? She wasn't the only one to blame for where they found themselves. 'So you usually screen all the women you sleep with, do you?' That must take up all his spare time, if the reputation Ben hinted at and the pictorial evidence was accurate.

He turned an inscrutable expression on her, but his eyes blazed. 'No. You didn't screen me, either, *your* first one-night stand. Perhaps we should both be a little more selective in future.'

She jutted her chin forward, humiliation making her irrational. 'What, next time you find an obliging stranger in the park?' She couldn't look at him, but she couldn't look away.

'Hey, you came on to me—all I did was make the mistake of sitting in a public place.' He leaned in, hard shards of metal in his stare.

What was wrong with him, making conversation one minute, lashing out the next?

What was wrong with her, digging for answers and then shooting the messenger?

'Well, all *I* did was make the mistake of sleeping with some sort of…Jekyll and Hyde character.' Could his signals be any more mixed? Just like the justifications and excuses currently spinning through her head and making her seasick.

They'd hissed the last few comments to each other, their faces drawing nearer and nearer as they made their respective points. Now, only a couple of centimetres separated them.

His warm breath caressed Essie's parted lips.

Her pants forced her breasts closer and closer to his chest with each breath.

His bold stare dipped to her mouth.

Her fingers curled into the leather upholstery.

She leaned in…

'Sir, we're here,' said the driver.

Essie flopped back, spent. This couldn't go on. They'd never survive sharing a workplace sexually sparking off each other like this, and the minute Ben came back from New York, he'd see straight through them and their barely contained animosity. Perhaps Ash would get his way—perhaps Ben would fire her.

Drastic circumstances called for drastic measures.

Damn, what was a girl to do?

CHAPTER FIVE

'YOU HAVE GOT to be kidding me…' Essie spun on him the minute they boarded the cute little Learjet he'd hired to take them to Paris. Her baby blues flashed and she popped out one hip as she glared in slack-jawed astonishment.

'What do you mean?' He was used to impressing women with his wealth. He'd never experienced what-ever snit had worked its way beneath her creamy skin.

She scanned the sumptuous interior, which was starkly white, from the plush carpeting to the soft leather seating.

'All this?' She spread her arms wide to encompass the luxury, her nose wrinkled as if he'd offered her a ride to Paris inside a dumpster. 'Ever heard of global warming? Carbon footprints? Scheduled flights? The Eurostar?'

Was she for real?

He swept past her, loosening his tie and shrugging off his jacket to drape it over one of the wide white leather seats that offended her so much.

'I'll plant a damn forest. Sit down.' Damn, she riled him up. Bubbly and playful one minute, vulnerable and hesitant the next and then hissing and wild when he overstepped some line he couldn't see. His cock stirred for the hundredth time that day. This torture had to end. One way or another.

After she'd left his apartment last night, his balls had been so blue he'd returned to his en-suite, switched the water to arctic and banged one out. Then he'd put out some feelers among his fellow legal professionals in the UK to see if anyone was looking to take on a new partner. As soon as Ben returned, he'd distance himself from the day-to-day running of The Yard. His commitment was always supposed to have been financial, with a spot of legal work thrown in pro bono.

When he'd walked into the bar this morning to see her smiling at Josh, he'd been so desperate to quench his constant need for her, his testosterone-addled mind had considered selling his stake in The Yard just to rid himself of her sunny smile and tinkling laugh, both of which he'd grown to crave as much as burying himself inside her again. What was it about her? And where could he get a shot to render himself immune?

But the more he discovered, unearthing the conundrum that was Essie Newbold as an archaeologist scraped away a layer of ancient dirt, the more he wanted to know. Who was this woman who intrigued him so much?

He had some answers—no wonder working for Ben, despite being overqualified, was so important to her. The need to connect with her brother shone from the vulnerable look in her eyes when she talked about him. And she wasn't secure in their relationship, a fact confirmed by the brittle tetchiness at Ash's clumsy comments.

What the hell had Frank Newbold done to her? Was that what she'd meant when she'd said she was an expert at rejection?

Well, they had an hour—plenty of time to fill in a few more blanks. He waited until she'd settled in the chair opposite his before he selected two glasses from the bar and an ice-cold bottle of white wine and then sat opposite. A small table separated them but it might as well have been a spider's web for all the protection it afforded. And he needed as many obstacles as he could get—the struggle to keep his hands off her grew more urgent every second he spent in her exasperating, but highly addictive, company.

He poured them both a glass while the two-man crew readied the plane for take-off. If he didn't occupy his hands and his mouth somehow, he was going to splay her open and drop to his knees on the plush carpet and taste something other than her sassy mouth.

Carbon footprints...

The car journey alone had been an exercise in extreme gratification avoidance—he deserved a damned medal. He'd never had to work so hard to keep his hands to himself and his dick in his pants. And the novelty had grown pretty thin. An hour's travel time to Paris... An hour of looking but not touching. Fuck, he was more of a mess now than when he'd left New York with his bags packed full of betrayal and indignation and paps nipping at his heels. But the conversation helped—he wanted to know what made her tick almost as much as he wanted to kiss her again and then lay her over this table at thirty thousand feet.

Fuck.

When Ben had suggested Essie accompany him to

Paris, he'd baulked at the idea. But Ben's proposal had made sense. After all, she was their temporary manager. This was the best way to iron out prospective teething problems before the doors opened. They'd only have one shot at making a first impression on the city.

Professionally, everything he touched became a success—The Yard would be no different. He wouldn't allow the failure that dominated his personal life to taint his work. And returning to Jacob Holdings with his tail between his legs after the public row between him and his father in their open-plan office area...not an option. The man was lucky Ash hadn't laid him out.

Ash took a slug of wine, wishing it were Scotch. He needed a distraction from the destructive thoughts and the dangerous urge to lose himself between Essie's magnificent thighs.

'What is your area of expertise?' He picked up the earlier conversational thread. He imagined her doctorate wouldn't be in bar work.

His question startled her—good. If he was to be off balance in her company... 'You said it's not bar work' He licked the wine from his lip and her eyes flared.

Yes.

Those pools of intelligence drew him in—she wanted him, too.

'I have a psychology degree and I've just completed a PhD.'

He frowned. Psychology? Well, that made sense. She was smart. She cared about people. And she could probably spot his bullshit a mile away. His collar tightened a fraction.

And then a fraction more. 'Why did you move from New York?' She jutted her chin in his direction.

Bingo.

He wasn't touching that one. Another millimetre tighter… New York was full of ghosts, full of reminders of his blindness and his failures and his guilt. And full of gossip on the state of his family and his past love life.

While she waited for his answer, Essie took a sip of wine. Her lips caressed the rim of the glass and she hummed her appreciation—blessedly distracting sound that shot straight to his aching balls.

At his prolonged silence she placed the glass on the table and narrowed her eyes. 'So it's okay to pry about my cheating father, my messed-up family, but you can't answer a simple question? Interesting.' She flicked her eyebrows up, her blue stare way too perceptive.

Fuck, the last thing he needed was her probing his head. He threw her a bone. 'Would it appease you to know I have a cheating father, too?' She stared, openmouthed. 'That my sister, Harley, grew up knowing our father had cheated on our mother with an old family friend but only recently confided in the rest of us?'

Ash had been defending Harley and his mother when he'd confronted Hal at the office that day. But all the arrogant Hal Jacob had heard was criticism—something the megalomaniac couldn't tolerate.

Essie's eyes widened as she waited for more. But sharing his sob story wouldn't change the outcome. She wasn't the only one with a crappy father figure.

Discovering his father had cheated on his mother and made Harley complicit in keeping the secret had turned his stomach. But it had been the blows to come that had nailed the coffin lid shut for good on his relationship with a man he'd worked for his whole adult life. A man who was supposed to love him.

Essie leaned forward, placing her hand flat on the table between them as if offering the support of her touch, something he wanted but didn't dare accept. 'Does your mother know? Is that why you don't trust people?'

Ash forced himself to take a slow swallow of wine. Her questions left him raw, reeling, the truth too shameful to speak aloud.

Half the truth. 'She knows.' Ash had been the one to tell her of Hal's final revelation, thrown at his son in a fit of extreme spite during that fateful argument— that Ash's fiancée's affair with one of his co-workers had been a ruse, one big cover-up, to hide the fact that the man she'd been screwing was him, his own father.

'It's okay.' She levelled sombre eyes on him, full of compassion. 'I understand. When someone betrays our trust, we just want to protect ourselves.'

Yes, Ash had battled betrayal. His fiancée had chosen the father over the son. Perhaps she'd hoped Hal would leave his wife. But his father's involvement had shown Ash's whole life to be one big lie. He swallowed the razor blades stuck in his throat.

'Are your parents still together?' Essie's gentle probing continued.

He should change the subject. She'd winkled out the truth as easily as if she'd stripped him naked. But he surprised himself by answering honestly, albeit a truncated version of the final shit storm that had had him walking away from his New York life.

'No.' He couldn't add his part. He hadn't thought the consequences through yet. The public row had been photographed by some Jacob Holdings employee, who'd passed the photos to the gossip rags. Ash had needed to ensure his mother wasn't the last to know.

He fought the urge to shrink down into the leather. His mother hadn't known about the second affair with Ash's fiancée.

He looked away. Intelligent, compassionate Essie saw too much. And the inside of his soul, the hot pool of guilt simmering there, wasn't pretty.

He grabbed a lifeline, any lifeline would do. 'Tell me about your PhD.'

Essie stared him down. She saw through his pathetic deflection technique—had probably learned about the tactic on day one of her psychology degree.

So his personal life had spiralled out of control. He focussed on the chemistry dogging his every interaction with this woman, present even in this quiet, albeit stilted conversation that dragged him too close to the edge of a cliff, but also offered deeper insights into the woman occupying all his thoughts and fantasies.

Was he seriously considering another tumble?

Another shot at distraction with the fascinating Essie?

She released a small sigh through those plump, rosy lips of hers, letting him off the hook. Lips he'd like to see wrapped around his... He discreetly adjusted himself under the table. The abrupt change of tack helped restore his equilibrium.

'I have a PhD in Human Relationships. Just finished it actually.'

Another choking sensation, as if his collar had now shrunk two sizes.

He gaped. Fucking perfect. The one woman who had threatened his one-night rule since he'd created it was some sort of...happily-ever-after guru. Totally understandable after her short-changed parenting from Frank. But Ash wasn't a happily-ever-after guy.

She didn't seem to notice the meltdown passing through his body.

She twirled the stem of her glass while she continued. 'My study looked at the social interactions in modern families in the Western model and compared them to those in other cultures—cultures with multi-generational family bonds, where people live in close proximity to extended family.'

Well, that sounded better—more science, less agony aunt. Ash released some air past his strangulated throat.

'So you're a...' he could barely utter the words '...relationship expert?' Next thing she'd be telling him she wrote one of those advice columns. What the actual fuck had he gotten himself into? And why was he more intrigued than ever? Even this revelation wasn't enough to dampen his need for her, a torture that surely rivalled anything on offer at the London Dungeon.

Instead of the glare he'd expected, she tossed her head back while she laughed a dirty laugh. His body reacted with futile predictability. He'd had first-hand knowledge of the silky soft taste of that neck—the way she moaned louder when he tongued that spot just below her ear.

Her hand clutched her chest. 'Oh...your face.' She grinned and took another sip of wine.

At least her mocking him had snapped all that confessional tension. Thank fuck.

'Don't worry. I'm not trying to trap you into marriage, counsellor.'

'What do you mean?' Was he *that* transparent? Could she see the sweat beading on his top lip? Hear his balls screaming while they ran for the hills? See how close he was to spiralling out of control?

'You have that deer-in-the-headlights look.' Her lip curled. 'Trust me—I know that look well. My father, Ben's father, perfected something similar every time I asked him if he'd make it to my school plays or my birthday parties. Every Christmas that look came out, as predictable as Christmas carols or the Queen's speech.'

She blinked and stared at her wine glass. Ash wished he'd just gone down on her instead of starting a conversation—at least he might have put a smile on her beautiful face.

'He had this look—a sideways glance, a shifty, non-committal murmur…and I knew my celebrations would be a single-parent affair. That I didn't matter to him enough.' Her glassy eyes took on a faraway look. If she cried, he'd be doomed.

But she sniffed and tilted her defiant chin up once more. 'Sorry…it's a bit early for wine.'

What the fuck…? So not only had Frank Newbold strung along two families, kept two women dangling, but he'd also done some serious damage to his daughter's self-esteem. Smart, emotionally intelligent Essie had been constantly let down, left waiting and wondering, probably questioning her worth. Ash sobered. 'I…I'm sorry.'

He'd met her father many times. He hadn't seemed like the piece of work she described, but then, he'd kept his mistress and his daughter a secret from everyone for more than fifteen years.

No wonder Ben hadn't said much on the topic—how did his friend feel about the revelations?

But what did Ash know about fathers? He was clearly an appalling judge of character where his own was concerned. He hadn't been able to see what was happening right under his nose, with the two people who should have loved him most.

So Essie was as messed up as him. Beautiful, intelligent, funny and caring—but probably none of those things in her own eyes.

With a slug of wine, she seemed to compose herself. 'Sorry. You probably got more than you bargained for with that question.'

True. But just meeting her had been a not unwelcome tornado, ripping through his already weatherbeaten soul. He wanted to pry further; to offer her words of consolation; to tell her she did matter. That she was all those things and much, much more. Tell her that he understood what it was like to have a shitty, selfish parent. But that would involve opening up his own pain for inspection.

Nope. Not an option.

His hand twitched, seconds from reaching for hers. But if he touched her now, he wouldn't stop until he'd slaked every need burning inside him.

Show some control, man.

She stood, all amusement leached from her pale face after her personal confession. She looked as sick as he felt.

'Look.' She braced her hands on the table so her delectable chest filled his vision, a distraction he indulged in for a dizzying split second.

'I understand you have…issues. Who doesn't? But, this—' she waved her hand between them, as if the constant crackle of sexual tension were a living breathing, visible thing '—isn't going away. I'm not letting my brother down because *you* can't separate sex from business.'

He sputtered, almost choking on his wine. Could she separate the two? A small smile tugged his mouth. It had been a very long time since anyone had surprised him as much as she had. Damn. Another magnificent point in her favour. And bringing talk back to the reason they couldn't stop looking at each other with lusty eyes—genius. Why hadn't he thought of that?

'So, I think we should find a way to work this from our systems.' Reaching for her wine, she took another slug. 'Now, please show me where I can change into something more appropriate for clubbing.'

Change…? No way.

He swept his eyes over her perfectly adequate, flesh-covering outfit. If she emerged in another of those flirty dresses that showcased her phenomenal body…

Doomed.

Again, her long legs featured in an X-rated fantasy— naked, draped over his shoulders, the heels of her shoes digging into his back… If he were to break his one-time rule to quench the insatiable fire, it would just be sex, until the flames dwindled.

With a resigned sigh, he directed her towards the

restroom at the rear of the plane. He couldn't argue with her logic, though. Where their intense, combustive attraction was concerned, they were all out of options.

'Jacob, good to see you, man.' His old friend Lucas slapped him on the back with a shoulder bump and slid his delighted smile over Ash's shoulder to take in Essie. Ash had been right to fear her change of outfit.

She'd emerged from the plane's bathroom wearing a wisp of black silk that hugged her breasts and hips like a second skin and completely bared her back. A pair of skyscraper heels completed the visual suffering. She'd even scooped her swathe of golden hair up into some sort of relaxed up-do so the gorgeous translucent skin of her neck, shoulders and back paraded for his greedy eyes.

She'd sat opposite him for the remainder of the flight engrossed in her ever-present phone while he'd indulged in his lurid imaginings.

Further conversation was off the table, not because he wasn't curious to know more about her past—which not only held her in its grip, but seemed to have guided her choice of career—but because he feared she'd turn the spotlight on him. Pick apart his freshly opened wound with her insightful, analytical psychologist's mind.

He'd tried to get some work done, but the words on his screen had blurred in and out of focus. His mind had reeled from her scent and every time she'd shifted in her seat and he'd caught a glimpse of another sliver of skin, he'd had to dig his short nails into the leather of the arm rests to stop himself from peeling her out of the dress that had become an implement of torture.

Lucas, already endowed with that effortless French charm, looked at Essie as if he possessed X-ray vision and could clearly see the delights the dress barely concealed. Well, fuck that. For as long as it took to extinguish this all-consuming need—one surely brought on by something in the English water—Ash would be the only one sampling anything Essie had to offer.

While he'd tied himself in knots, fucking around with trust and rules and control, the answer had been staring him in the face all this time. He was never more composed than when in the bedroom. She'd said she could separate sex from their professional relationship. Time to test the theory. A win-win situation.

Ash placed his hand in the small of her back, wincing when she turned a sharp glance his way, presumably with the shock. He didn't need to explain his actions—he was done fighting this forest fire of need—and she'd suggested he take the driving seat. Time to buckle up, Ms Newbold.

'Lucas, this is Essie Newbold, my manager. I've told her all about La Voute, so thanks for the tour.' Now he wished he'd simply brought her to the club anonymously, because all he wanted to do was get her away from Lucas and onto the packed dance floor so he could legitimately put his hands on her some more and draw her close enough to feel those nipples.

Lucas laughed, took Essie's hand and pressed it to his lips.

Smooth bastard.

He held out his arm and directed them to the bar. 'The best way to enjoy La Voute is to experience it.'

The barman had clearly been pre-warned, because, on seeing the boss, he brought over a tray of luminous shots that glowed in the neon lighting as if radioactive.

'The house speciality. Enjoy.' Lucas handed one to Essie and, without taking his eyes from her, swallowed the second. 'I've reserved you a VIP booth upstairs.' Lucas replaced his empty shot glass on the tray and nodded to the barman. 'Make yourselves at home, drink whatever you want and, if you have any questions, you know where to find me.' He shook Ash's hand, which rolled into a fist when he turned to Essie and kissed both of her cheeks.

Ash forced a smile, a move that almost cracked his jaw, the tension in his facial muscles was so pronounced. He downed the shot and jerked his chin at the barman to indicate another round, getting himself back under control. He never succumbed to such puerile emotions as jealousy. What was she doing to him? Perhaps the extreme self-denial had infected his common sense.

'This is fantastic.' Essie's eyes sparkled as she bobbed in time to the music. She'd stood on tiptoes to yell in his ear but she hadn't touched him.

Ash nodded, his eyes dancing over the unselfconscious sway of her body to the beat.

'You asked Josh to create a house cocktail. I liked that. What else do you want to do to The Yard?'

Her wary eyes warmed at his simple compliment. 'I love that graffiti art over there.' She pointed to a wall of exposed brick decorated with vibrant tagging. 'We could do that in the basement, get an artist in. Use neon paint so it glows in the UV light.'

He nodded and bent closer, although he'd heard her

just fine. His own lips were only millimetres from her ear so her delectable scent curled around him like an aphrodisiac cloud.

'He's right.' He flicked his head in the direction Lucas had disappeared. 'Clubs like this have the X-factor. We should immerse ourselves, while we're here.' He handed her the second shot and tossed back his own with a grin of challenge. 'Let's dance.'

She eyed him while she slowly pressed the rim of the shot glass to her plump bottom lip, holding it suspended there for what seemed like an age, taking his stare captive. At the last second, the tip of her pink tongue poked out and dipped into the blue opaque drink. And then she tossed it, slammed the glass bottom up on the bar and turned for the dance floor with a sassy sway of her hips.

He groaned, adding *seriously fucking sexy* to her growing list of attributes. Ash followed, walking with his hard-on torture. He took Essie's elbow to keep them together as they weaved through the crowds. The crush of bodies moving under the strobe lights hemmed them in on all sides, forcing them to dance in the bubble of close personal space that suited his intentions just fine.

Essie's eyes widened as he palmed her hips and tugged her close. So he'd made an abrupt about-face? Better to switch tactics and settle than go into negotiations with a weak case. And it seemed this captivating woman weakened his body, his mind and his resolve.

He kept his hands and his stare on her, sliding his grip from her swaying hips to her slim waist as they moved in unison to the thumping beat. Her hands reached for his forearms, fingertips just shy of gripping. She closed her eyes, tilted her head back and lost herself to the music, as completely and perfectly as she lost herself to her pleasure.

His hands snaked to the small of her back and he hauled her tight up against him, the small gasp she made and the excitement in the eyes she snapped open spurring him on. His erection pressed into her soft belly. She knew the effect she had on him, one he hadn't been able to conceal since day one.

She gripped his shoulders, her bottom lip trapped between her teeth as she swayed against him, all sensual movements and lust-drunk eyes. They danced for half a track, heated stares locked, bodies bumping and hands lingering like the most exquisite form of tactile torture.

Fuck this. Fuck the club. If he didn't get inside her soon, he'd need another cold shower. And he was done with pale imitation. He held the real thing here in his arms. If she'd been a property acquisition, he'd have already closed the deal.

Ash bent close, his lips caressing her delicate ear. The cascade of fine tremors down her neck slammed steel through his spine. But before he could utter one word of his argument, she turned her head so her lips grazed his.

Her stare lifted to his and then dipped back to his mouth.

His fingertips pressed into her waist. 'You suggested we work this out. We'll do it in my bed.'

She leaned back, eyebrows lifted.

'We will?'

He shrugged. 'Or yours, or the couch or wherever. As long as it involves me inside you.' He lifted a tendril of hair from her neck and wrapped it around his index finger.

'I thought you only did one night?'

He could no more explain his about-turn than he could walk away. It was an astounding turn of events for a man used to making verbal arguments and teasing out favourable deals for a living.

He gripped her bare shoulder, his fingers gliding over her shoulder blade.

'I'm making an exception. And there's something of an experience gap to rectify, so I'm told.' His thumb caressed the dip above her collarbone, setting off more tiny shivers.

She pursed her lips, as if giving the matter some serious thought. Fuck, if he'd had any issue with his ego he'd be snivelling at her pretty feet by now. But he hadn't become one of New York's top attorneys by misjudging the opposition's intentions. She wanted this as badly as he did. He hadn't changed his stance on relationships, but they could still have a good time.

'Tell me what I need to hear,' he whispered.

'Just sex.' She wavered, her lip trapped under her teeth for a moment.

He nodded, her confirmation music to his ears. 'I agree.' He pressed his thumb to her bottom lip, tugging it free from her bite. The only thought in his mind—how quickly he could replace her teeth with his—drowned out all else.

Essie stepped closer until the length of her body pressed to his, her nipples grazing his chest, the heat between her legs scorching his thigh.

He tilted her chin up, his eyes dancing with hers.

'I'm not the guy for you if it's a relationship you're after.' He couldn't reiterate that enough, especially considering her past and her profession. Now more than ever he wasn't relationship material.

She dipped her chin, capturing his thumb with her pouty lips and sucking on the pad. She tongued his digit and then released him with a pop.

'I'm not interested in a relationship. And if I were, you'd be the last man I'd consider.'

Ash bit back a groan and rubbed his erection into the soft mound of her belly.

'So we agree. You chalk up a few more…notches on your casual sex bedpost. We fuck this out of our systems. Then we walk away.'

She lifted onto her tiptoes and he bent lower to meet her halfway. Her lips feathered his neck as she whispered, 'We keep it fun—when the fun stops, we stop.'

She peeled back, challenge blazing in her mesmeric stare.

'I can do fun.' Only this time he'd take his time, savour every sexy inch of her, glut himself until he was spent and sated and his head straightened out.

A single nod. 'What about the tour of the club?'

'I've seen enough.' His fingers curled over her hips, the silky fabric of her dress bunching in his grip. The way his body coiled to the point of bursting, he could tear the damn dress in two.

He'd never brokered a more fulfilling merger and, as with the best deals, everyone would get what they wanted. He rolled his shoulders and followed her from the dance floor.

As if it had been painted in luminous orange paint across the ground, he was about to cross a line he'd long ago vowed out of bounds. But damn if he didn't want to throw on a pair of sneakers and sprint over, hell for leather.

CHAPTER SIX

Essie paused at the foot of the stairs leading to the VIP booths, dragging Ash to an abrupt halt. His brow dipped and he faced her, clasping both her hands between them.

'Second thoughts?' He cupped her cheek, pushing back wild wisps of hair from her hot face.

It's just sex. Fun.

She fought the wave of trembles that doused her from head to toe and shook her head, and then tilted it in the direction of the bouncer guarding the upper balcony.

'Lucas said we had a VIP booth.' She caught her lip between her teeth. Her breath stalled as she waited for Ash to get on the same page. Every inch of her craved him. Slickness coated her inner thighs, her core clenched in anticipation and her nipples chafed against her dress with every rapid breath she took. She'd never make it back to the hotel before flinging herself on him and demanding what he'd held out on for so long.

'I've never experienced sex in a public place… That could be…fun.' She tilted her head, her fluttering heart knocking against her ribs. They'd either consummate this new agreement in the back of the limo Ash had hired to drive them to and from the club tonight, or they'd do it here, in the privacy of the VIP area of this chic, sophisticated club. She held her breath. When had she become such a risk-taking exhibitionist? What was he doing to her, this sexy but closed-off man, who at first glance seemed to have it all?

Ash's eyes scorched her. 'You want me to fuck you here? Upstairs?'

She nibbled the inside of her cheek, her flush hopefully hidden by the alternating dim and flash of neon lights. He'd suggested she broaden her horizons, something that worked for her out-of-control libido. What better way to build on the success of her first one-night stand? Keep things playful and risqué. Embrace the heady sense of power she earned from their no-strings encounters. If she focussed on the sex, she wouldn't think about anything else. Her doubts, her past, her bad decisions.

She nodded, her belly twisting with delicious spasms.

Ash's stare bored into hers while he clearly mulled over her suggestion. This bold, uninhibited demand was so unlike her. But this was what he did to her, what he brought out in her. And what she hoped like hell he'd embrace. She'd been turned on all day, all week. It was his fault—time to atone.

Because right now she barely recognised the wanton woman he drew out. Hormones raged through her. She pressed her thighs together to ease the persistent thrum of her clit.

Ash scooped his arm around her shoulders, nodded briefly to the bouncer manning the foot of the stairs and escorted a tingling-from-head-to-toe Essie to the upper balcony.

Essie tottered alongside his determined strides, grateful he, too, saw the merits and timeliness of her risqué plan.

At the top of the stairs, he swooped on her, hauling her up with an arm around her waist and his hot and greedy mouth, demanding an uninhibited kiss. Essie clung, losing herself to the thrusting power of his tongue sliding over hers and his strong arms banded around her back, connecting them from shoulder to thigh. Her head spun. This was happening.

Ash released her. 'You sure about this?'

She nodded, too turned on for speech. And too enthralled for doubts.

He strode ahead, tugging her behind. Now they'd established the ground rules, he was all action. Thank goodness. She didn't want to have to resort to begging and pawing at him. So tacky.

The balcony overlooked the writhing mass of bodies on the dance floor below. To the left was a row of discreet curtained-off booths, each lined with low, banquette-style sofas and featuring an LED illuminated coffee table. Ash led the way to the last booth in the row, the one closest to what Essie guessed was a door leading to a fire escape.

Adrenaline slammed through her, shunting energy to every part of her body until her pulse thrummed right down to her fingertips. Her senses heightened, her skin buzzing under the glide of fabric, the music vibrating through the floor and into her bones and her vision eclipsed by the virile, determined man in front of her.

Ash tugged her by the hand and flicked the gossamer curtains closed behind them. If someone came close enough, they'd see through the filmy barrier. But the angle from the ground floor provided sufficient privacy to keep Essie invested in her reckless, spur-of-the-moment idea.

He kept hold of her hand, his body close, taut with energy.

'You're astounding, do you know that?' He scanned her features with heated eyes.

She shook her head, her throat hot. If he didn't touch her soon, or allow her to touch him, she'd disintegrate into a million pieces.

He flared his nostrils, sucking in a breath, and then said, 'Take your underwear off.' A husky command. He held up his hand, palm flat, waiting for her offering. If that was his lawyer voice…he probably sealed every deal he touched.

Essie's blood turned to melted wax. Ignoring the liquidity of her limbs, she tilted her head, eyebrows arched. Who knew she housed such a perverse streak? He couldn't get his way all the time, even when his demands benefited her.

'You're a long way from Kansas, counsellor.' But she obliged, because this daring tryst had been her idea. No time for coyness now, not when she was finally getting what she'd craved since the day after she'd met him, when she'd foolishly raised the stakes with her secret scribblings about *Illegally Hot*. Time to be all in, or get the hell out of Dodge.

She braced herself steady with one hand on Ash's forearm, while she shimmied her panties down her thighs and then stepped out of them, one foot at a time.

Holding his self-satisfied stare, she dropped her damp thong in the centre of his palm, with as seductive a smile as she could manage. Why deny the effect he had on her? That he'd agreed to this told her he was equally affected.

Whatever else they were, physically they worked.

Ash glanced at the lace and then grinned, tucking it inside the back pocket of his jeans. With one tug he brought their chests and thighs and mouths back together.

'You—' he cupped her face and slanted his mouth over hers, eyes open, bold stare pinning her immobile '—have been driving me out of my mind for days.' He took her hand and pressed it to the steely length of him, guiding her to stroke him through his jeans, his hand over hers.

'I could say the same about you.' He was rock hard. She squeezed her thighs together, seeking a modicum of relief.

'With the exception of this rather unorthodox and public time, we'll be taking this slow. I intend to get my fill of you. To taste every part of you, over and over until neither of us can walk.'

'Another new experience. I can't wait.' Essie clung to him, her eyes just shy of rolling back. 'I thought you'd never break.' She looped her arms around his neck and tugged his mouth down to hers once more as she pushed him backwards towards the low upholstered seats lining the booth.

Through kisses, she fumbled with the button fly on his jeans until she'd freed his thick erection behind. He hissed, his hand covering hers to still her frantic fingers.

'This time, it's your rodeo.' He cupped her breast through the fine silk of her halter dress, his thumb stroking the nipple to a hard peak. 'Next time, and the multiple times after that, will be my way. Understood?'

She nodded, ready to promise anything to get what she wanted—him, inside her, losing his phenomenal control.

Ash fished a condom from his pocket with a wry twist of his mouth.

'I was a Boy Scout.' He handed the foil square to Essie and sat back on the banquette, his arms stretched along the back and his stare flitting between her bare legs, her pebbled nipples and her face.

Essie's mouth filled with saliva. He was hers to play with. Sprawled out beneath her, hard, ready and willing.

Forcing herself to sidle slowly with a seductive sway of her hips, rather than bound onto his lap with embarrassing eagerness as was her natural inclination, she sauntered close until her thighs slotted between his, which were spread wide, the prod of his manhood rising above his open fly.

Essie placed the condom on the seat next to him and lifted her dress above her knees. When his gaze left hers to follow the path of the hem, she slowed the progress down, enjoying the way air gusted from his nose with every rise and fall of his broad, sculpted chest.

As payback for torturing her with his impressive stamina, she stopped just short of showing him everything, instinct telling her Ash was a man who always got what he wanted in the end. She might as well draw out the anticipation. Keep him on his toes. Drip-feed him, until he snapped and took what he wanted.

With her thighs bracketing his, she straddled his lap, rising up on her knees to force his head back on the cushion so she could kiss him the way she'd longed to since this morning.

She traced his lips with hers and then repeated her path with the tip of her tongue. She cupped his face and angled his head so she could deepen the kiss—a tangle and slide of tongues that left them both panting for air.

He groaned and his arms left the back of the sofa, one banding around her waist to hold her close and the other sliding up her thigh until his fingers delved between her spread legs.

He hissed. 'Fuck, you're soaking.' His fingers probed her entrance from behind while his mouth settled hot and demanding over one taut nipple.

'Yes. It's your fault.' A whimper caught in her throat as he sucked hard through the silky fabric and then scraped with his teeth.

She released her hold on his hair to untie the straps of her dress, which were knotted behind her neck. She wanted him skin to skin. To feel his sexy day-old stubble scrape her nerve endings alive.

He obliged. With an impatient tug, he followed her lead and pulled the top of her dress down until both her aching, heavy breasts spilled free.

He cupped one, his hot stare tracing her while his thumb tortured the nipple again and again with rough swipes. 'So pretty.' Then he swooped, his mouth covering the glowing bud with long sucks and flutters from his talented tongue.

Essie dropped her head back, too strung out to hold in the moan of delight his fingers inside her and his mouth laving her breast unleashed.

He pulled back. 'You're going to have to stay quiet. We don't want visitors.'

Stay quiet? Was he aware how good he made her feel? She didn't give a damn if the whole of Paris rocked up with popcorn and opera glasses. But she didn't want him to stop, so she bit down on her bottom lip and focussed on the silvery wallpaper behind his head to battle the strong sensations he was thrusting upon her willing, eager body.

Essie cradled his head as he leaned in for another taste, but this time fiery jolts of electricity slashed from her nipple to her core.

Enough.

She tugged at the hem of his T-shirt and collapsed forward so her face was buried in his divine-smelling neck. After two or three impatient tugs on his shirt hem, Ash released her flesh and between them they removed his shirt with hurried jerks.

Ash tossed it aside while Essie just stared at him up close.

Despite the time he spent behind a desk or in a boardroom, he somehow maintained the ripped physique now laid out for her. She spread her fingers wide as her hands glided over the smooth tanned skin of his torso and tangled in the thatch of dark hair covering his pecs.

His fingers clutched the fabric at her hips, releasing and then gripping again while she took her time exploring him. She kissed a path down his neck, the stubble scraping at her sensitive lips.

A strip of black hair ran from below his navel and disappeared into his boxers, which were tented with his ready erection. As if she had been jump-started, she flew into action. She grabbed the condom and tore into it. Ash, equally eager, shimmied his jeans and boxers lower down his hips, releasing his cock, which bobbed on his hard, grooved belly.

Essie licked her lips. She wanted to taste every inch of him. But the clock was ticking. And if she didn't get him inside her soon, she'd burst from sexual frustration.

He grinned. 'Later.' His voice was so low, he sounded like a stranger. In many ways, all the important ways, he was. But just like the first time, she wanted him anyway.

'Don't worry.' He grinned. 'I want to eat you, too.'

She'd been right about the oral skills—she couldn't wait. She rolled the condom over the hard length of him, her movements hindered by the inferno burning her up from inside and his constant fondling of her breasts and rolling of her nipples between his fingers and thumbs.

And then she rose up over him, gripping him between her legs and angling him back towards her entrance. Ash shuffled his hips under her and she braced one hand on his shoulder while between them they guided him inside.

She sank, stretched and filled to perfection so a cry escaped. Ash covered her mouth with one hand, a reminder of their public location. Although the expression on his face—his bunched jaw, his flared nostrils, his hooded eyes—told her he, too, struggled to contain the intense bite of pleasure.

This was what she'd craved since she'd walked into

his office that fateful morning. His surrender to this flammable chemistry that rendered her helpless. She wasn't alone—confirmation was etched into the harsh planes of his taut features.

With his hand still clamped over her mouth, Essie began to move, rocking back and forth on his lap. The angle rubbed her in the perfect spot and she picked up the pace, bouncing on his lap with renewed energy, delivering what they both craved.

Ash settled back and gripped her hips, allowing her to dictate the angle and depth of penetration. But he didn't lay idle for long. One hand cupped her breast, tweaking and pulling her nipple until lightning snaked across her belly. The other hand delved between their bodies until the pad of his thumb settled over her neglected clit, strumming and circling.

'Yes,' she half hissed, half whispered. No way could she stay completely silent, not when he lay sprawled beneath her looking sexier than any sight she'd ever seen. And not when he filled and stroked her with sublime perfection.

When he started thrusting up from below, each blow accompanied by a harsh grunt while his big hands held her hips firm to hit the same spot over and over again, she lost all strength in her upper body and collapsed forward. Her hands clasped his sweat-slicked chest and her hair formed partial curtains before her face.

'Damn, you're tight. You clutch me just right.'

She whimpered, his verbal encouragement, his deep thrusts and his thumb back on her clit working a unique brand of magic over her body.

She gasped, flinging her wild hair back over her shoulders, her neck arched.

'That's it, ride me.' He panted out, his gruff commands low but no less insistent. 'I'm going to make you come so hard.'

With one last swipe of her clit and three rapid-fire thrusts of his hips, she climaxed, her whole body tense as she fluttered and clenched around him. Her cries bounced off the walls, but they were both past caring.

He sat up, buried his face between her breasts and clutched her to him with breaking force as he convulsed and groaned out his own climax.

Essie swallowed past her dry throat, gripping his shoulders while the spasms petered out and her heart slowed.

The sheen of cooling sweat stuck their clammy chests together. Essie caught her breath at last. 'Well, that was fun.' She buried her nose in his hair, stifling a giggle.

He kissed her breastbone, between her breasts.

'Hell, yeah, it was.'

She cracked up, taking him along with her.

CHAPTER SEVEN

ASH WOKE TO the melodic sound of distant church bells.

He opened his eyes to find the hotel suite, which was situated in Paris's Eighth *arrondissement*, bathed in filtered sunlight and his body wrapped around a soft, warm, sleeping Essie. His morning wood nestled between the cheeks of her spectacular ass. He ground his hips, the bite of pleasure damping down the flare of panic that waking up spooning a woman had created.

He never spooned. He rarely spent the night with someone, usually leaving after the business end of the evening was over.

He held himself rigid until the wave passed, its grip on his chest lessening until he could once again breathe.

They'd agreed.

Just sex.

Fun sex.

Astounding sex.

And, seemingly to test him to the hilt, she wanted to experience new and adventurous sex. Would he even survive? She'd been incandescent last night. First agreeing to his renegotiated terms of engagement and then stating her own, which aligned with his so beautifully that he had discovered breaking his cardinal rule was easy. For the right woman. The right…inducement.

And then she'd blown him away by suggesting they fuck in the very upmarket club that they'd come to vet. Who knew studious, bubbly, relationship expert Essie concealed such a libidinous inner vixen?

Lucky him.

He'd gladly expose her to previously untried experiences—a tough job that he relished. This was the perfect solution. Keeping things fun and playful clearly delineated the boundaries, gave him back the control he needed like oxygen. And provided an out clause—because this would end. Sooner or later the fun would dry up. And they could walk away. No feelings hurt. A good time had by all.

He breathed deeply, preparing himself, just as he did in negotiations—take control, brainstorm all possible outcomes and, if all else fails, railroad the opposition. With that strategy in mind, Ash shelved the niggling seed of doubt and gingerly untangled his limbs from hers without waking her.

By the time they'd returned to the hotel in the early hours of this morning, they'd been beat. They'd shared a quick shower and collapsed into bed.

And now he wanted his breakfast.

Sinking beneath the sheet with slow stealth, he manoeuvred himself between her thighs. Essie slept like the dead, so she didn't wake until he'd opened her up and wedged his shoulders between her shapely legs.

She stirred, her head lifting from the pillow to level sleepy eyes on him. Eyes full of dawning realisation.

Fresh lust pounded through him, his dick burrowing into the mattress. 'Morning. Ever experienced wake-up oral?'

She shook her head, bleary eyes rounded.

'Do you mind?' His voice was gruff, from the sight of her rumpled and vulnerable, her hair a wild tangle around her face, and from the vision of her open and glistening before him.

Her eyes were tinged with growing excitement. She shook her head but continued to stare. Waiting.

Ash touched the tip of his tongue to his top lip, catching the flare of heat in her eyes and the way her breasts rose and fell with her shallow pants. Her scent enveloped him. He shifted her thighs until she was splayed to his satisfaction.

Perfect, pink and pouty. The strip of fiery hair neatly trimmed framed the most exquisite sight he'd ever seen. One certainly worth waiting for. Who needed the works of art housed at the Louvre, when they had a naked Essie in their bed?

'Are you going to watch?' A surge of blood flooded his groin and she dropped her head back onto the pillow with a hoarse groan.

'I don't think I'll be able to.'

He tutted. 'Your choice. But I will. I recommend the experience.'

She looked at him again, her cheeks flushed pink. 'I...I've never come this way before.'

Heat bloomed in his belly. Man, he loved a challenge. 'You will for me.' Leaning forward, he opened her lips with his thumbs and touched the tip of his tongue to her clit. She jerked. Her thighs slammed against his head and her hands flew to his hair to hold him in place. Not that he was leaving. Not until he'd gorged himself and left her begging him to stop. Until he'd ruined her and set the bar sky-high.

He'd warned her last night and he never made idle threats. They weren't leaving this hotel room until neither of them could walk.

Sucking the tiny bud between his lips, he flattened his tongue and laved at her, over and over. He watched her every reaction: the way she fisted his hair in her hands; the way, despite her proclamation, she lifted her head from the pillows every few seconds to stare at the action occurring between her thighs; and the way she urged him closer by lifting her legs over his shoulders and digging her heels into his back, demanding more.

She swelled in his mouth, her breaths now coming hard and fast.

'Yes…oh…yes. You're so good at that—' Her breath caught on a keen wail. He winced as she twisted his hair, drawing back for a second to part her and slide two fingers inside her tight, velvety heat.

'Having fun?' He scraped his teeth along one inner thigh, delighting in the trembles that snaked across her flat belly.

'Yes. Yes. Don't stop.'

'I have no intention of stopping. Best breakfast ever.' He dived back in, this time matching the rhythmic laves of his tongue over her swollen clit to the plunging of his fingers, which he angled forward to rub her walls.

When she released his head so he could pluck and roll her rosy nipples, her neck strained as she held her head up to watch his every move and he knew she was close. He gave her everything, sucking and humming and plunging until she cried out, her voice a broken, thready cry that spoke directly to his pulsing dick.

He drew out the torture while she continued to clench around his fingers and then she pushed him away and collapsed back on the mattress.

'Oh, wow.' She laughed. 'That was definitely fun.'

He clambered up the bed to lie beside her. 'Glad I could oblige.' He pushed the wisps of hair back from her flushed face. 'Your exes were no good at that?' Responsive, sensual Essie had been cheated.

She turned to face him, propped on one elbow. 'Ex. Singular. He didn't like it.' Her cheeks darkened and Ash wished he'd kept his mouth shut.

What a douche. Some men didn't know what they had in front of them. Her finger snaked through his chest hair in slow, pensive circles.

'Of course, he didn't like the way I dressed or laughed or the friends I kept, either.' Her brittle laugh failed to lighten the mood.

So on top of her shitty father figure, her only boyfriend had been a controlling, insecure bully? Ash swallowed, half tempted to further ruin their morning by demanding the asshole's address and investigating how well he liked Ash's fist in his face. 'Did he…lay a hand on you.'

She shook her head and looked away, her colour now a blaze across her cheeks.

'There are other ways, verbal and emotional, to diminish someone. I put up with it for longer than I'm proud of.'

His chest turned to a block of concrete. 'It's okay.' He trapped her hand under his, stilling her fingers.

'Sometimes it's hard to see what's right under our noses.' Insightful, analytical Essie, so in tune with others' needs, would hate that she'd tolerated a bad relationship for herself, just as he hated his own blindness and misguided trust.

'Fun fact,' he said, grinning when she levelled sceptical narrowed eyes on him. 'That guy wasn't worthy of the tip of this finger.' He lifted her pinkie to his mouth and pressed a kiss to the tip. 'Let alone the rest of you.'

Couldn't she see that? Didn't she understand any man would be fucking lucky to have her? He would have...once.

Essie broke the dark direction of his thoughts with an energetic kiss, tugging on his neck and then climbing on top of him and sitting astride his thighs. She sat back and looked down at him, her beautiful face soft with desire and doubt.

He gripped her waist, questions banked up in his tight throat.

'We have to go back to London today.' Her words gave him pause as if she'd added, 'Back to reality.'

And Ben would return from New York. Would that alter their new arrangement? 'I know. Still time for a few more experiences though...' He could feed the desire and banish the doubt. Just fun.

She smiled, her hand encircling him and pumping with lazy strokes and the perfect amount of pressure.

'Have you ever been to Paris before?' he asked. The urge to offer more than new sexual experiences lifted the hairs on his arms. He wished they could stay a week. Wished he could wow her, wine her and dine her, as she deserved. Wished he could show her everything the French capital had to offer by day and indulge in her by night. All in the name of fun, of course.

Her thumb grazed the sensitive spot beneath his crown. He cupped her pert breast, his thumb tracing the dark tip. She shook her head, her mouth parting on a gasp and his balls rose up.

'We don't have enough time to see everything, but I've planned some sightseeing, if you'd like a whistle-stop tour.' Anything to put that sparkle back in her eyes.

She glanced at the window and the view beyond. 'Well, I can see the Eiffel Tower from here.' Her thumb traced the head of his cock, spreading the bead of moisture her stroking had released. Then her eyes lit up. 'Can we get real croissants?' She bit her lip, which he'd come to learn was her vulnerability tell, and a damned sexy sight.

He nodded, warmth from his gut spreading to his chest at her simple request. No Learjets or Tiffany baubles for this woman.

'Great.' She stopped rubbing him and jumped from the bed.

He recoiled, every muscle in his body taut and pulsing with energy to drag her back and bury himself between those thighs.

'Time for a shower, then, because I'm starving.' Instead of heading to the en-suite, she twisted her hair while her stare lingered on his still-raring-to-go groin. 'I've never experienced breakfast in the shower...'

Within seconds he'd hustled her into the bathroom and turned on the spray. She laughed and dragged him inside the glass cubicle, which was big enough for two.

Her mouth met his, her smile stretched wide. 'I

wanted to do this last night. I'm sorry I was so tired.' And then she dropped to her knees on the tiles and gripped the base of his straining cock.

His eyes wanted to roll closed, so good was the sight of her on her knees. But he forced them open. He spread his thighs as the water pounded his back and cascaded over his shoulders. Essie smiled a sultry smile up at him, pressed her tongue to the base of his shaft and licked a path to the engorged tip. He braced one hand on the glass, terrified his jerking legs would give out before the fun was over.

Her warm mouth engulfed him, stretching her pink lips around his head. He grunted, an animal sound he was certain he'd never made before, and then he cupped her face, tangling his fingers in her wild, wet hair. An anchor.

She sucked hard and swirled the tip of her tongue over the sensitive crown, lingering on the spot that left him growling out her name and clamping his jaw so tight he worried for his enamel.

The minx had the audacity to smile around him, her mouth full, and then she bobbed her head, her eyes locked with his, full of challenge while she moaned and mumbled. He surrendered. He was always going to lose this fight. The sight of her on her knees with his cock in her mouth one he'd remember for ever. She worked him higher until every muscle screamed.

She was fantastic. Why had he battled so hard to fight this attraction? His balls tightened and boiled and fire flickered at the base of his spine.

'Essie…' The warning clear, no doubt by the look of twisted agony on his face.

Humming encouragement against him, she nodded

her head, giving her permission. The flames licked along his shaft, lightning striking the tip at the moment he erupted on her tongue with a harsh yell and a slap of his hand on the tile.

She swallowed him down, releasing him with a pop and satisfied grin. He hauled her to her feet and crushed her close while she gripped his ass cheeks in both hands.

He pulled back, smacking kisses on her swollen, grinning lips.

'Best.'

Kiss.

'Fun.'

Kiss.

'Ever.'

Essie pointed her phone at the majestic gothic spires of Notre Dame and snapped some pictures. The private pleasure cruise Ash had booked took them down the Seine from the Eiffel Tower to the Pont de Sully and back. A perfect way to see so many of the city's iconic landmarks and to fully appreciate Paris's endless stunning architecture.

After they'd dressed, they'd spilled out of the hotel and found a charming Parisian café where they'd sat on the pavement at a gingham-covered table for two and feasted on warm crumbly croissants that melted in the mouth. This new experiences game they were playing left her floating on air. She'd even forgone posting on her blog for that day and switched off her phone in reverence to her first orally delivered orgasm and her first visit to the French capital.

Ash approached with two flutes of what was probably real champagne—she was too scared to ask, because today had already had enough of a fairy-tale quality to leave her both swooning and restless.

Because she'd woken up in Paris next to a gorgeous man, any woman's dream, who lived a lifestyle she couldn't comprehend—one perhaps, had her parents been married, had she and Ben grown up together, she might have glimpsed. But that wasn't her reality.

Her reality had been the role of odd kid out—not quite like many other kids from single-parent families but not quite like the whole families, either. Her reality had been years of loneliness, confusion and pining for an absent father. Yes, he'd sent endless gifts and she'd never gone hungry, but her reality had been an illusion. Just as her and Ash cruising the Seine drinking champagne was an illusion.

'You look sad—Paris not what you expected?' He sat next to her.

She shook her head. 'It's beautiful.' Her lip took a severe nibbling while she tried to marshal her conflicted thoughts. 'Your parents' divorce... Was it while you were growing up?'

Ash sniffed as if the warm summer air offended him. 'They're in the process of it right now, actually. Turns out my mother could tolerate one affair, but not two. Why?'

She took the glass of champagne he offered and sipped. 'Just imagining what your childhood was like.'

He looked away. 'Pretty normal, I guess.' He shrugged and slid his arm along the back of the seat.

'Did you come here with your family?' She picked

at the scab, imagining fun-packed but rowdy Jacob holidays. All five of them together.

He nodded, eyes wary.

Essie's glazed-over stare found the view again. 'I only remember one holiday with Mum and my father. I was ten.' The memories rushed in like a tidal wave, stealing the last of her high. 'I'd begged and begged to accompany him on one of his business trips to New York, promised I'd be so good he wouldn't know I was there. He appeased me with a trip to Chester Zoo.' She picked at a sliver of peeling paint from the seat. 'I didn't mind—it was the best trip ever. He bought me a stuffed elephant, we got our faces painted and he taught me to play chess back at the hotel.'

Ash's hand slid to her back, his palm warm between her shoulder blades, the rhythmic sweep of his thumb strangely unbearable.

'So you didn't see much of Frank?'

She shook her head, her face hot. Why had she even confided such a deeply personal moment with the power to shrivel her insides? The memory of what she'd done to that beloved stuffed elephant five years later when she'd finally discovered her father's deception still brought heat to her face.

'When I discovered the truth, that he'd lied to me and to Mum and his real family...' She met Ash's stare, shame and defiance warring inside. 'I...I built a bonfire in the back garden. It didn't end well for the elephant.'

Ash pulled her close and pressed his mouth to the top of her head, the gesture more than that of fuck buddy. But she wasn't naive enough to see Ash's display of romantic, even comforting, touches as anything but good manners and an attempt to keep their insatiable chemistry on the fun track where it belonged.

She sipped the frigid wine, pushing dark, dangerous thoughts away, and focussed on the view to stop the dangerous slide towards obsessing. It wasn't just the fact that Ash was way out of her league. He possessed a quick wit and was sexy personified. He had a dry sense of humour and regularly called her out on her more outrageous bullshit. A very addictive combination for a girl sadly lacking in healthy, long-lasting relationships, either in her own life, or displayed by her parental role models. A girl who'd spent two years in a dysfunctional, emotionally abusive relationship because she was so desperate to be the opposite of her parents.

She'd promised Ash she didn't want more than sex.

But if she ever changed her mind, ever considered herself capable of maintaining the kind of trust and commitment she frequently wrote about from a theoretical point of view, Ash represented exactly the kind of man she'd want.

Pity it was never going to happen. Not because he couldn't be sweet and romantic as he'd just proved, as well as an astounding lover. But because he'd meant what he'd said.

The ex Ben mentioned had clearly hurt him badly enough that he'd sworn off anything beyond casual for good. Those closest had the most power to cause lifelong pain.

She shuddered. She'd certainly never been back to a zoo.

'Oh, look.' She latched onto a distraction and pointed at a couple on the walkway lining the riverbanks. A bride and groom, having their picture taken.

Ash followed the direction she indicated, and they stared for several stilted, silent seconds. Essie squirmed, covering the awkward moment with a blast of verbal diarrhoea to put him at ease.

'Ah, the city of love… Oh, fun fact. Did you know that falling in love has the same effect on your brain as snorting cocaine?' She wasn't fishing for a proposal, but she wasn't carved from stone like the gargoyles atop Notre Dame. Just because love hadn't worked out for her parents, for her, perhaps for Ash, didn't mean others couldn't find it.

Ash looked away from the beaming couple, his stare skittering anywhere but on Essie.

'Did you know the divorce rate in the Western world averages fifty per cent?' He curled his lip and sipped his wine.

She gaped. She wasn't wholly surprised—if more men were like her father and her ex…and his father… His cynicism was more than a hardened lawyer thing— it must be the woman…

The set of Ash's mouth told her now wasn't the right time to pry. Time to drag the conversation back to fun town. 'I didn't. But you're ruining the ambience, counsellor.'

He shrugged, a smile on his face, but his shoulders didn't drop to pre-shrug levels.

She rolled her eyes. 'Don't worry. I'm not hinting.' She nudged him with her elbow, trying to lighten the mood. 'From a scientific standpoint, I find it fascinating that something as nebulous as—' she made air quotes '—"love" is powerful enough to induce such a rush of euphoria on a neurological level.'

He stared for long silent seconds.

Essie brazened it out, but inside she wanted to roll into a ball and protect her soft parts.

'Do you really believe all that relationship babble?'

She bristled. Had he just ridiculed the basis of her entire research doctorate? The foundation of her precious and increasingly popular blog? The very doctrine she hoped to live the rest of her happy and contented life by, next time she was brave enough to dip a toe back into relationship waters? At least next time she met someone, she'd also have a sexual standard to measure them against, thanks to Ash.

For the first time in her life, she knew what all the fuss was about.

'I don't need to believe it. Just because we've never experienced it—it's science.'

'It's bullshit.' He flushed and then winced. 'It may be science, but science isn't for everyone. It isn't for me.'

Essie's heart rate accelerated. He was opening up. Had her earlier confessional mood infected him?

'Without changing my plea, I meant what I said last night—just fun—why the hefty dose of cynicism?' She glugged more champagne in case this conversation blew up in her face. The psychologist in her couldn't help but pry. And the woman who'd had fantastic sex with him was pretty interested, too.

She couldn't look too closely at why, preferring to believe her interest was a side effect of the spectacular orgasms, professional curiosity or her constant need to help her fellow man.

With his eyes shielded behind sunglasses, she had no non-verbal cues to help—Ash sat as still as a statue.

'I had a fiancée. Years ago. I thought myself in love, the kind you think exists, scientifically.'

Essie's throat tightened until she expected to hear choking sounds when she breathed. She clamped her lips shut, desperate for him to continue. To learn more about this closed-off man who had so much to offer and what had shaped him.

'Right up to the week before the wedding, when I discovered she was cheating on me.'

Essie stared, mouth agape.

Who would cheat on Ash?

A splash of icy champagne spilled on her dress, soaking through the fabric. She looked down, busying herself with wiping at the spill with the hem of her dress, to both gather her own scattered thoughts and give Ash some time to recover from his shocking confession.

But what did she say to a temporary lover on discovering he had indeed had his heart broken, something that had tainted all his future relationships? She knew what psychologist Essie would say. She even had an idea how relationship blogger Essie would handle it. But the woman who'd spent the night in his bed and was already struggling with the boundaries she'd agreed to Essie? She was all over the place.

'Have you…had anyone serious since then?'

He shook his head, confirming her theories. 'Casual works best for me.'

While part of her was happy that she and Ash were on the same page in their personal reasons for avoiding relationships at this stage in their lives, his confirmation came with an unpleasant hollowness in her stomach.

He'd really meant what he'd said.

'I'm sorry you were hurt. Your ex sounds a couple of sandwiches short of a picnic, if you ask me.' Humour seemed the safest option to claw back the light-hearted, Parisian vibe they'd had earlier. But it didn't banish the gnawing inside, or the restlessness of earlier. Or the urge to comfort Ash. But he'd hate that. She sat on her free hand.

Ash shrugged. 'I'm well over it. As I said, it was years ago.' He didn't appear over it. In fact, a greenish hue tinged his skin. 'I just think that whatever that emotion is—that drug-like high—it passes pretty quickly, and then what do you have?'

She had plenty of answers, but none she thought he'd want to hear. And perhaps he was right. What did she really know? Everything she'd learned about men came from her ex, a pathetic excuse for a man who'd needed to put her down to make himself feel like a man, and her waste-of-space father—a man who was only in her life thirty per cent of the time and never at the important moments. If she'd grown up with Ben, at least she'd have had a stable male role model, an older brother to fight her corner, vet her boyfriends and tell her she was worthy. But Frank had robbed her of that, too.

'Love didn't work out for you and the lazy, critical, controlling jerk-off...' He toyed with a strand of her hair, his stare searching.

'No.' As far as romantic relationships went, she'd proved her judgment was seriously lacking. She'd accepted meagre scraps, just like her mother. 'But that was my fault. People treat you the way you allow yourself to be treated, right?' Yes, she knew the theory down to the last detail, but putting it into practice for yourself... That was another matter.

Ash nodded in agreement, his stare fixed on the horizon.

'But, you're right. I haven't found it, yet. But I do know that as humans we're destined to strive for a meaningful connection, an interaction with other humans. We can't avoid it. It's evolutionary. A survival tactic.'

'Is that why your relationship with Ben is so important?'

Essie shrugged, feigning indifference while her insides shrivelled. 'You don't have to be a psychologist to see I have daddy issues. I grew up thinking I was an only child. I loved my father, idolised him as a little girl, but his betrayal ruined our relationship.' She shrugged, playing down the impact of her rolling stomach. 'I feel cheated—Ben's a great guy, as you know.'

Ash nodded.

And Ash? Another great guy who'd been hurt in the past, who she'd objectified on her blog in order to feel validated. Well, that ended today. No more *Illegally Hot*. And no more crazy ideas about Ash being anything more than a temporary fling.

Several beats passed.

'Hungry?' said Ash.

Essie nodded, despite her swirling stomach.

'Let's go to Montmartre for lunch. They have a street market today.'

And just like that they successfully hurdled the invisible barrier—with good, old-fashioned denial.

CHAPTER EIGHT

THE FOLLOWING SATURDAY night Ash emerged from The Yard's offices to find the bar awash with smart, glamorous opening-night customers. Cocktails and good times flowed. Essie and Josh had organised a happy hour to bring in office workers, and the online social media buzz she'd created had ensured it was standing room only. Their brand-new cocktail menu was inscribed in elegant script on the oversized contemporary chalkboard behind the bar. Every glass sparkled. The bar's state-of-the-art lighting created pockets of ambience, certain nooks and crannies of the chic space becoming intimate, dimly lit corners.

But instead of the satisfaction he'd anticipated, his body was strung taut, every muscle twitchy. Ash scanned the bar for Essie. He knew she wore the same slinky black dress she'd had on at La Voute a week ago, because just before they'd opened The Yard's door for the first time, she'd strode into his office with that slightly feral gleam in her eyes, locked the door behind her and perched her delectable derrière on his desk.

When she'd slowly bared her thighs, revealing that she'd removed her underwear, he'd been powerless to resist what had followed—him fucking her on his desk, a new experience she'd requested with a cheeky, 'For luck…?'

The restlessness dissipated as he recalled the past week of fantastic sex. They'd spent practically every spare minute screwing—starting with the flight back from Paris to London, where she'd ridden him in one of the wide leather seats at thirty-thousand feet, successfully earning herself a mile-high experience, and continuing at work, at his apartment and anywhere else they could get away with. The intense, couldn't-keep-their-hands-off-each-other phase was lasting well beyond the arbitrary time limit he'd set. Any day now, he expected the bubble to burst, the novelty to wear off, the fun to end and his life to return to normality.

But the desire was far from abating and Ash found himself in new territory.

Perhaps the out-of-body feelings rattling him were a symptom of having allowed the insatiable, enthusiastic Essie too much time in the driving seat? Time to wrestle back some of the control, dictate the…fun, suggest the next experience. His mind whirred with endless pornographic possibilities. Yes, that was just the right tactic to steer things back on track.

He spotted her at the far end of the bar and discreetly adjusted himself. She still carried the radiant glow her earlier orgasm had delivered to her translucent skin. She'd retamed her hair, twisting it into some messy topknot that left only a few wisps tickling her elegant neck. Just knowing that the halter dress she wore prevented her wearing a bra, and that her perfect tits were bare under the scrap of silk, flooded his groin with fresh heat. Heat that should have dissipated after their quick but thoroughly satisfying desk session. But no. It was as if the more he had, the more he knew about her, the more he wanted.

A very dangerous combination.

Ash set off towards the object of his disgruntlement, weaving his way through the throng. She chatted with Josh, who smiled at her and touched her arm. Essie laughed at something he said as she leaned close to speak over the general din of a hundred conversations and the vibratingly loud music.

Ash pressed his lips together and swallowed down the taste of acid. 'Fucking fantastic...'

A thump to his shoulder pitched him off balance.

'Go easy on her, man,' said Ben, who'd sneaked up behind him. Ben grinned at his friend and then looked at Essie, an indulgent smile playing on his mouth.

Ash slapped Ben's shoulder in greeting, his own shoulders cramping with the tension of lusting after Ben's sister. Add to that the very foreign stabbing pain under his ribs as he watched Josh and Essie together... He needed a lie-down and it was only eight thirty.

'She can't help helping people—it's who she is.' Ben stared at the couple chatting as if he was as enamoured as Ash, although likely in a different way.

He nodded as he flicked his gaze back to where she conversed with Josh. He could just imagine the kind of help the hipster barman wanted.

He'd developed quite an insight into Essie's magnificent, multifaceted personality. She was so different— different from him, a cynical, cut-throat lawyer with a reputation of being just like his ruthless old man; from most people he knew—out for themselves, inward-looking, selfish; and from any other woman of his experience, which was probably why he struggled to put a stop to their sex spree.

She was too good for him. Too good for her spineless ex and her careless father, too.

She laughed with Josh, her head tilting towards him in that way that made a person feel she was truly listening.

Fuck. He would hurt her when this ended. Yes, she'd said what he'd wanted to hear, but his instincts about her had been correct—Essie was a relationship kind of girl. She'd just lost her confidence at the hands of the worthless men in her life.

Ben loosened his tie. 'Josh is having boyfriend trouble,' he said. 'Essie can't resist a distress signal.'

Ash grinned, his head now so light it practically lifted off his shoulders.

Josh was gay.

As soon as he'd registered the relief pouring through him, it morphed into something else, something not unlike the itch of head-to-toe poison oak. What place did jealousy have in his orderly, controlled life? What place did any feelings have where Essie was concerned? She wasn't his—because that was the way he wanted it. Insisted on it. Made crystal clear from the outset. Why, then, did his insistence sound entirely self-directed?

'Hey, can you grab her? I have something I want to say to both of you.' Ben tilted his head to indicate the cordoned-off stairs leading to the basement dance club, which was quiet for now, but would soon be heaving with partygoers, if their ticket sales were any indication.

'Sure.'

Ash resumed his way across the bar to Essie, the idea of ending things tonight forming in his mind. Halfway there, she spotted him and he rebelled against the idea with a violent mind spew.

Whatever she'd been saying to Josh stalled on her lips, which hung a little open as she levelled her wide stare on an approaching Ash. Fire licked his balls. He'd come inside her not two hours ago. And already he wanted her again. She could do that to him with her open smile or her ready, but dirty, laugh. Even her irritating fun facts lent her an irresistible and refreshing air you couldn't help but adore.

He skirted around her and bent low from behind to speak in her ear—it was a club after all, the noise levels rendering that perfectly acceptable.

'Ben wants to see us downstairs.' A satisfying trill of shivers passed down her neck. Oh, yes, she battled the same hunger raging in him. Thank fuck he wasn't alone. Because that hunger was the only thing keeping him on an even keel.

Just sex—his rule.

Just fun—her rule.

He swallowed the panic and pressed his mouth to her ear. 'And I want to see you naked and splayed open for me,' he whispered. That would give her something to ruin those lacy thongs she wore, probably for his torment.

She tilted her hips and pressed her ass up against his groin, at the same time as leaning forward across the bar to tell Josh she'd talk to him later.

Not if he had anything to do with it—she'd be too busy coming around the cock she'd just flicked back

to life with her sassy stunt. She knew exactly what
she was doing, but payback would be fun.

He put his hand in the small of her back where the
dress dipped low and led her downstairs. Her skin
burned his palm. Her feminine scent buffeted his
senses. And if he slid his hand a couple of inches south
he could cup those rounded ass cheeks and ascertain if
she'd donned the panties again after the desk session…

At the last minute, he inwardly bit out a curse and
dropped his hand from her skin, seconds before they
entered the VIP booth where Ben waited.

He'd opened the good stuff—Cristal. Three tall
contemporary flutes sat on the table next to a small
gift-wrapped package. Ash bit the inside of his cheek.
He'd thought about giving Essie an opening-night gift,
but he'd talked himself out of it, too terrified by the
impulse and too worried it would blur the rigid lines
he'd demarcated.

Ben kissed his sister's cheek and poured the bub-
bles with a flourish. Ash struggled to share his friend's
enthusiasm. When they were all seated with a glass
in hand, Ben raised his for a toast.

'I just wanted to thank you both for all your hard
work these last two weeks, and for holding the fort
while I was away. We wouldn't be here, opening night,
without you two…so cheers. To The Yard.'

Ash and Essie joined the salutation, their eyes
meeting briefly. Ash saw in her expression what he
guessed was mirrored in his own—a flash of guilt.
Fuck.

What with the new and dangerous emotions en-
snaring him, and considering the potential mess when

this ended for him, for Essie, for his friendship with Ben…he should be a man. End it tonight, on a high.

We opened the club…what say you we call this quits and part as friends?

The mouthful of wine soured. He made a fist under the table.

'And, Essie…' Ben collected the gift and handed it to her '…I want you to have this. Thanks for stepping in when I needed you.' Ben stared, earnest, while Essie looked at him as if he'd just saved her, single-handed, from a burning building. And fuck if Ash didn't want to see her level that look in his direction, equilibrium be damned.

'As a kid, I always wanted a sibling.' Ben swallowed, visibly moved. 'I'm just glad it's you.'

She took the package, her lower lip trembling. As she fumbled with the bow and the paper, an unseen force made Ash reach discreetly beneath the table to touch her knee in silent support. This developing bond with her brother fed her soul, healing the cracks her father had created with his callous selfishness. Her old man and that douche of an ex had really done a number on her self-esteem. But Ash had underestimated the depth of her longing to be a part of Ben's life. To have more of a family. To belong. She deserved those things.

Ash had grown up surrounded by his family. Until recently he'd worked alongside them, every day. His sisters were still, and always would be, a massive part of his life. What must it have been like to never know when your parent was going to drop by? To wonder if this time, this birthday would be different? To feel unworthy of their time and attention, something that was a fundamental part of the parental role in Ash's opinion. He knew all about shitty fathers… But at least he'd grown up knowing he'd mattered to both parents.

He gripped her knee tighter. The next time he saw Frank Newbold…

Essie flashed him a brief, grateful smile and then she tore through the last of the paper and looked on in wonder. Ash forced his fingers to relax. She wasn't his business. They were just having fun.

It was a framed snap of Essie and Ben outside The Yard, their arms around each other and their grins, so alike, wide and beaming.

Essie's eyes filled and she threw her arms around her brother's neck.

Ash stilled, his breath trapped, a voyeur, an outsider on the growing sibling connection between these two. But he couldn't look away, or leave. A sick part of him forced himself to see what his selfish, indulgent actions put at risk. The siblings stood for a proper hug. Essie turned her face, which was pressed to Ben's chest.

Part of him had genuinely believed their chemistry would have petered out by now. That the insistent itch would have dissipated. But if anything, the need only intensified. Because now he knew Essie. He understood her quirky sense of humour. He could laugh at her strange English phrases and the way she'd translate them for his transatlantic education, and he reciprocated her enthusiastic desire for him, which seemed equally insatiable and only built in intensity with every day that passed.

Despite knowing the cost of deceit and betrayal— especially from a family member, one you should be able to trust with your life—the damage they wreaked. Despite knowing her past left her craving this relationship with Ben. Despite breaking his rules to have her only once, his resolve was steadfast. He couldn't, wouldn't offer her more than what they had right now. But was he ready to give her up?

He couldn't be what she needed. He owed it to her, to his friend, to let her go now, before the toll of his selfishness grew.

His blood stilled as if turned to concrete. Before he could make an excuse and leave on some pretext or other, he heard familiar voices. He turned around in time to see his sister, Harley, and the others arrive. *Perfect timing.* He'd forgotten they were coming to The Yard's opening night, he'd been so busy losing himself in Essie.

Harley flew at him with a squeal of excitement. He lifted her into a bear hug. She'd arrived from the States today with her fiancé, Jack, who split his time between Europe and New York.

Ash gripped his sister tighter than usual, earning him a searching stare when he released her to the ground. At least his sister hadn't blamed him for his part in their parents' split. She, too, had had her fingers burnt with Hal.

'You look amazing.' He kissed her cheeks, forcing his fingers to relax on her shoulders, and then shook hands with Jack and, behind them, Jack's friend Alex and his fiancée, Libby. Ash made introductions and the group settled around the table as a waiter brought more glasses and a second bottle of Cristal.

Essie, Libby and Harley quickly fell into animated and excitable conversation and the other men started a debate about some upcoming English soccer game Ash had no clue about. He sipped his drink, a sense of unease capturing him as he watched the interactions around the table, as if from a distance. He'd done enough emotional wrangling for one night. Damn, enough for a whole year. But the unwanted thoughts pushed their way into his head anyway.

Fraud.

Outsider.

Pretender.

He almost snorted champagne out of his nose. He'd long ago sworn off wanting what his sister and Jack's friend had. So why now did the hair at the back of his neck react to every look the couples shared, every touch, every unspoken communication? Because he knew he was short-changing Essie, like the men of her past.

He focussed on Essie, whose cheeks had pinked up nicely with the alcohol. She participated fully in the conversation with the other two women, who, Ash understood, had become close friends in recent months. But her gaze slid often to him, secret, non-verbal cues passing between them with every flick of her expressive eyes.

She was happy.

Ash's unease lessened. Perhaps he was overthinking this. She'd never hinted she wanted more than sex. Great, addictive sex. He should go with the flow tonight. Enjoy his and Ben's and Essie's success. Enjoy his sister's company and that of new friends.

The next time she looked up, he smiled back at Essie, his spirit lightening. During a brief lull in the chatter, Harley cleared her throat.

'So, we have something to ask you.' She glanced around the group, her eyes finishing on Jack.

Ash's shoulders tensed to the point of cramping as chills raced down his spine. Harley looked far too happy.

'We're getting married. Monday,' she said with a flourish and giggle.

The blow winded him. Married? They'd only just reconnected.

'What? Since when?' Ash reeled, his stomach tight.

Harley nodded, barely containing her joy. 'It's all arranged—we just planned it in the car on the way here.' She leaned over to kiss Jack while the others offered congratulations and indulgent grins.

Of course. Because that was how most people planned the most important commitment of their lives—spur of the moment. He hated to be the voice of doom, but they'd only been engaged a few months… And they had history.

More importantly, had she learned nothing from his experience? From their father's appalling behaviour, towards their mother, Harley herself and most recently towards Ash? All done in the name of so-called love.

Yes, he'd jumped in too soon, his engagement to Maggie impulsive, flushed with the enthusiasm of first love. And look where that had led. To heartbreak, and humiliation. To the ultimate betrayal. Its effects long-lasting, shaping him, controlling him, affecting his precious equilibrium even to this day. Affecting his ability to be open to someone new in his life.

He'd thought himself over it years ago, but now, years later, its effects still carried power. Because the lies outlasted all else. Discovering Hal had been the real partner in Maggie's betrayal and that he had concealed it from Ash, from everyone, long after the affair ended, had sealed the fate on both his working relationship with his father and his personal one. Ash's whole life as he'd known it had, in an instant, become untenable. His stomach rolled. He couldn't bear to look at his father, let alone work with the man.

'What about New York? Mum and Hannah?' No way would Harley marry without her twin sister present. And was Hal flying in for the ceremony? He couldn't be in the same room as him. Not yet. The betrayal was still too raw.

And what about divorce and infidelity and lies? He hadn't exaggerated when he'd informed Essie of the reality of divorce statistics. And he'd seen enough professionally—inevitable prenups, prolonged bitter wrangling over assets, the financial and emotional toll of a commitment that seemed like a good idea at the time but didn't last. Not to mention his personal prejudices…

'Mum and Hannah are flying in tomorrow. We don't want a big fuss, just a simple service. Alex said we can have the ceremony at his estate in Oxfordshire— this is what we want.' She clutched Jack's hand, some freaky silent communication passing between them. 'We'll celebrate with extended families separately.'

Ash could understand. There was no way their father and Jack's parents could attend the same event, not after they'd recently discovered the reason for the long rift between the former friends was another historic affair between Hal and Jack's mother. What a selfish bastard his father had turned out to be. He'd always known he was arrogant and uncompromising, but he hadn't realised he was such a shitty human being. Once a cheater, always a cheater.

Surely these were all perfect reasons for Harley and Jack to employ caution. To get to know each other better. To allow their relationship to stand the test of time before marriage. Why the hell did they have to marry at all? Why not just live together?

It warmed him that Harley, who'd struggled growing up because of her dyslexia, was happy. But could he stand to watch her go through the devastation a wrong choice now would bring? Jack seemed crazy about her, but you never really knew what lurked inside someone. Everyone had their ugliness.

As Harley turned to Ben and Essie, including them in the invitation to Oxfordshire, Ash battled his helplessness. It seemed, unless he could talk her out of this, he'd have a ringside seat. The least he could do was offer her some legal advice for when the shit splattered through the blades of the fan.

CHAPTER NINE

ASH TOYED WITH the ends of her hair, which still clung to his damp chest and the day's worth of stubble on his chin. Even at three a.m., after two rounds of opening-night celebratory sex, the oblivion of sleep evaded him.

Essie's head grew heavy. Had she succumbed to exhaustion? Should he slide out from under her and pound out the continued restlessness in the gym?

'Just tell me, Ash.' Her sleepy voice whispered over his skin, a soft caress that offered both release and a rising of his hackles. His body stilled but she stayed immobile and he was pinned beneath her sprawled, languid body.

'The problem shared, problem halved thing is true, you know.' She lifted her head and levelled warm, compassionate eyes on him. 'I won't judge you. I won't even comment. I'll just listen.' She settled her head back on his chest, but not before she brushed her lips over his skin with a small sigh.

Seconds stretched while he balanced on the edge, wishing he could be as brave and open as she was.

He could deny he had anything to confess.

He could huff and puff his way out of it.

He could even feign sleep.

But he wouldn't insult her intelligence.

With a sigh that lifted and then dropped her head, he drew his fingers back through her hair. The silky slide of the strands carried a hypnotic cadence he craved. Or perhaps it was just Essie.

'I think she's rushing into marriage.'

Coward.

True to her word, Essie remained quiet. Only her heartbeat, steady but fast enough, beating against his, indicated she was still awake.

'I've made no secret how I feel about it.'

She nodded, the slide of her skin and hair over his chest a soothing kind of torture, because it drew him out, a security blanket, lulling him to deeper confessions, ones at his very centre.

'You're probably thinking I have a right to feel the way I do. I told you about my fiancée, my parents splitting recently, my insider knowledge of the divorce courts from law school.'

He was making a meal of this. Was it better to say the words outright, to rip off the bandage with a vicious tear, that would bleed him out quicker, but shorten the sting? Or keep them in and protect himself.

'I discovered my father had cheated. More than the affair my mother knew about.' Essie stopped breathing and her pulse thrummed against his skin. 'I was the one who had to deliver that news. I didn't want her to hear it from someone who didn't care about her.'

Her head lifted, tugging her hair from between his fingers, her face wreathed in understanding.

'That must have been horrible for you.' She sat

up, crossing her legs and drawing the duvet into her lap to cover her nakedness. 'How did *you* find out?'

Ash nodded, the urge to flee the room and the shameful scrutiny strong. If he'd detected one hint of pity in her expression he'd already have hit the shower, but Essie's brow pinched in confusion.

'From the horse's mouth—my father told me. We'd…had a disagreement. He didn't like the way I'd dared to call him out on his bullshit so he lashed out, like he derived pleasure from inflicting the knowledge on me. The coward knew I'd tell her.'

He linked his hands behind his head as he shrugged it off.

'Some people are cowards. I understand your fears for Harley.'

'I just worry that she'll be hurt. As it is, she's marrying without her father present and our mother…' He sucked in a breath, and rose to sit on the side of the bed. 'She didn't know about that particular affair until I informed her.'

He swallowed bile. 'It turned out to be the last straw for her.' He stood and made his way to the door of the en-suite. 'So, you understand my trepidation about this…happy occasion?'

Essie's teeth worried at her lip, her eyes scraping him raw.

Tell her. Tell her everything.

He backed away. She had the sense to give him space.

He stepped under the steamy blast of the shower, welcoming the pound of the water as a replacement for the waves of self-directed emotion. He was a coward, too. Holding back, convincing himself he was happy. That he was justified in his mistrust.

And he still carried the full burden of guilt and self-loathing, not the half measure Essie had promised.

She joined him, as he'd known she would. She'd kept her promise, but offered silent comfort, just by her presence. Her touch, tentative at first, as if she was uncertain of her reception, grew bolder. She reached for the body wash and tipped a measure into her palm before sliding soap-slicked palms over his chest, abdomen and shoulders. When she moved behind him to soap his back, she pressed her mouth between his shoulder blades.

'I'm sorry that happened to you. Do you want me to go home?'

He turned to face her, scooping his arm around her waist and hauling her up so his mouth covered hers. 'No.'

Within seconds their lazy kisses grew torrid. Her slippery skin slid against his as she writhed and moaned in his arms, her hands clutching at him. Her fingers twisted in his wet hair and she angled his head and twisted her mouth away. 'I want you.'

He'd recovered sufficiently to be fully on board. Slamming off the water, he scooped Essie up and lifted her from the shower. In two strides, he'd deposited her on the bed, still sopping wet, and fell to his knees between her spread thighs.

His mouth covered her, a hint of soap and whole lot of delicious Essie. He worked her higher, her moans and gasps telling him when the time was right. With a curse, he tore his mouth from her and quickly covered himself with a condom.

When he pushed inside her, she gripped his face, her blue stare burning into him in unspoken unity.

They climaxed together, eyes locked, cries mingling and the blurred and broken lines of fun scattered all around them.

Getting out of London, especially for the romance of an impromptu wedding at one of the UK's most lavish private estates, complete with a boutique winery and hotel, carried a surreal quality akin to flying to Paris, just to go clubbing. Essie, giggly with excitement, relaxed back into the leather upholstery of Ash's Mercedes, and tried not to drool at the confident, manly way he handled the luxury car.

It was the same confident, manly way he handled everything, especially when commanding her pleasure with skilled, devastating proficiency.

Ash was quiet, a fact she wanted to attribute to him driving on unfamiliar roads, but she couldn't deceive herself after his late-night revelations. What should have been a joyous family occasion had huge potential to become a trigger. Hers wasn't the only dysfunctional family in the world.

Essie shifted in the seat, restless.

That Ash had opened up to her on Saturday night enclosed her in a warm cocoon. She longed to reassure him about today. That his own pain at being left by his fiancée would pass. That his mother surely didn't blame him for stepping up. That his sister had her own life to live with a man who wasn't Hal Jacob.

Perhaps he regretted opening up to her. Many men struggled to talk about their feelings. She'd bide her time. He had enough going on with his family drama.

She'd spent all of Sunday, after a late start, where she'd crawled home from Ash's apartment to catch up on mundane life things like laundry and bill-paying and checking on her flatmate. Of course, she also had to catch up on her latest blog post, entitled *Love is in the air—is it catching?* It was wedding season, after all. She glanced over at Ash, prickles of guilt dousing her high.

Her blog continued to attract new followers and the ads she'd incorporated on her website, featuring well-respected books on relationships, had high click-through rates. People couldn't get enough of *Illegally Hot*, if the comments were any indication. But she hadn't mentioned him in the last few posts. His pain was real—not entertainment fodder.

In the beginning, writing about her overwhelming attraction to Ash and his extreme bedroom skills had helped control the impact he'd had on her life. Helped her to rationalise that she was simply, for the first time, party to a healthy, equal-terms relationship based on spectacular sex. But now... She shuddered. Every social media mention, every new follower, every demand for more of *Illegally Hot* carried with it a hundred tiny barbs to her conscience.

Perhaps she should confess. Explain why she'd done such a reckless and thoughtless thing.

No. She'd never actually used any identifiers— he'd never know he was *Illegally Hot*. He'd never read the blog. And this wouldn't last for ever—Ash would move on and she would chalk up this experience and believe in herself and what she had to say.

Because she was no longer Essie the downtrodden, the ignored, the inconvenient. She was part of something wonderful, respectful and mutually satisfying. And with a man as incredible as Ash.

And her relationship with Ben was also looking up. Essie hugged the memory of his thoughtful present to her chest. She'd all but sobbed over him on Saturday night.

I always wanted a sibling... I'm just glad it's you.

That he would make such a heartfelt declaration went a long way to healing the past hurts and humiliations inflicted by their father. Ben respected her. He was starting to value her as a part of his life, as her inclusion in today's nuptials proved.

Ash exited the A40 to Oxford and headed into the green and gold countryside. The sun glinted off fields of barley, filling Essie with a momentary sense of the contentment she'd craved her whole adult life. She was spending time with her brother and his friends, welcomed into his social circle.

An equal.

Valued.

Important.

'What do you think of our English countryside?' So Ash wouldn't want to talk about Saturday night, or the wedding today, but they could still converse.

'Very pretty.'

'Don't you miss New York?' Of course she understood why working with his father at the family firm would be awkward, but why set up shop in London, why move away from your entire life?

He shrugged, non-committal. 'The Jacobs are never absent from the business pages or the gossip columns for long.' He concentrated on the road, his mouth a grim line. But Essie was more concerned about the growing constriction to her chest.

'My...confrontation with my father happened in the open-plan offices of Jacob Holdings. Someone snapped a photo. The next thing I know, the whole humiliating business is splashed online, as if our sordid, fucked-up family drama is entertainment.'

Her lungs seized. He'd left New York to get away from his personal life and that of his parents' divorce being played out like a soap opera on the internet?

He jerked his chin. 'It was my fault. I hurt my mother. I should have spoken to Hal in private. When he confessed his...affair, I acted hot, without thinking, and I caused her pain. Humiliation.'

'It wasn't your fault.' Her voice croaked past her scratchy throat.

He shook his head, nostrils flared. 'It's one thing to be betrayed by someone who's supposed to love you. It's another entirely to watch that devastation play out publicly, everyone judging, commenting, whispering.' His lip curled.

Essie's head spun. How could she tell him she'd used the amazing, no-strings sex between them as fodder for her blog? Poor, affection-starved, sex-starved Essie had cast aside her principles for a taste of success—the heady feeling of being taken seriously.

They'd travelled deep into the Oxfordshire countryside by now. Essie stared at the hedgerows without seeing the beauty, her mind churning in time with her stomach. Why had she been so impetuous? So irresponsible? Not only had she treated the man she'd come to know and to care for like a...like an object, she had no doubt Ash could slap her with a lawsuit that would blow her beloved blog and any future career as a clinical psychologist out of existence.

Should she tell him now about *Illegally Hot*?

He'd hate her. He'd call things off.

What if her poorly timed confession ruined the wedding? Harley deserved her big day. And his mother was flying in…

Hello, my name's Essie. I shagged your son and then used the experience to flavour my online career…

What if she lost Ben and Ash in one fell swoop? She'd only have herself to blame.

As the silent miles passed, Ash lost to his thoughts, Essie to hers, she made a vow. A reckoning of her own making was heading her way. All she had to do was choose the right moment to explain to this amazing man why she'd done what she'd done.

Piece of wedding cake.

CHAPTER TEN

HE DESERVED A damned medal. He'd spent the entire afternoon and evening with a fake smile plastered on his face, walked his sister down the aisle and kept his opinions to himself, when all he wanted to do was drag Harley aside and beg her to reconsider her rash decision. He couldn't deny the ceremony, under a rose-clad arbour, had been touching. And Harley looked so happy—even he'd had a lump in his throat, especially when he'd glanced sideways at a stunning Essie and seen her pretty eyes shining with emotion.

And he was man enough to accept that his feelings were about *him*. His issues. Nothing to do with Harley and Jack, who'd had the wedding they'd wanted today—intimate, full of laughter and in exquisite surroundings.

But he couldn't shake his demons.

His mother, too, looked beautiful, but her face was drawn and pale. She'd lost weight in the weeks since he'd left New York. It couldn't be easy for her being here alone at her daughter's wedding, her brave face fooling no one. And he'd left her behind to deal with the fallout of her rotten marriage. To deal with the public speculation. To deal with his shame.

Ash looked out across the gently sloping vineyards from the terrace where he'd detoured after a trip to bathroom. He sucked in air that felt too thin and willed his stray emotions back under control.

This whole fucking wedding thing had unsettled him anew. Not because he was still hung up on the ex not worth his consideration, but because Essie's gentle probing over the last few days and his cathartic confessions had thrown up comparisons, ones between him then and him now, and the evidence was growing increasingly hard to bury.

He'd struggled to answer Essie's questions about love, because the truth was he could hand on heart admit that he probably hadn't loved his fiancée. Not the way he should have. The way Essie described with her fun facts and scientific evidence. No wonder his ex had looked elsewhere.

And it wasn't the loss of that imagined love that had hurt so much. It wasn't even the lies, the deception. What hurt the most was that he'd handed over control of his happiness to those unworthy of it. He'd held himself back for so long after Maggie, believing the worst, something he never wanted to experience again.

All he'd done was live a half-life in between and then hurt others in his frustration with himself, his mother in particular.

Perhaps he was incapable of the kind of love Essie described. A chip off the old block. As ruthless, selfish and incapable of a meaningful, honest relationship as Hal Jacob. Genetics must count for something. But would he ever know if he refused to even consider the possibility?

Essie.

She was so open, so honest and so giving. Way too good for him with his issues and his rigid rules and his impenetrable guard.

Ash spun towards the festivities. He'd left her alone for too long. Not that he could claim her as his date, but, between him and Ben, they'd managed to keep both of their single sisters occupied on the dance floor all evening.

He re-entered the conservatory, his stare scanning for her. Her ready touch was the only thing to ease his restlessness. Her bright smile. And her dirty laugh. Even her fun facts.

The way she looked up at him. The way she embraced their chemistry with her cheeky sense of humour and her quirky logic. The way she commanded her femininity with grace and steely determination, and a massive heart.

He found her talking with Ben at the edge of the makeshift dance floor. The happy couple and Alex and Libby slow danced under the twinkle of a thousand lights.

Ben saw Ash approach and lifted his chin in greeting before kissing Essie's cheek and heading towards the hotel's main foyer.

Her porcelain skin glowed pale under the lights and her eyes peeled back his layers, leaving him raw and more conflicted than ever.

'Are you okay?' She stepped closer, her stare flicking to the dance floor before settling back on his.

Ash threw caution to the wind and curved his hand over her hip. He hated that he couldn't touch her when he wanted to. Hated that he'd left it to Harley to in-

troduce her to his mother as 'Ben's sister'. Hated that
the past he couldn't let go, his hang-ups, had placed
a filter across her pretty eyes.

'I'm fine. Are you having fun?'

She nodded. Her hand brushed his, fingers lingering for a second. 'You don't look fine.'

He couldn't fool her. 'I'm just worried about my
mother—she's lost a little weight. I feel responsible.'

Ash guided her to a chair and took the one opposite. Her small frown and worry-etched eyes slayed
him. He shouldn't have said anything. Should have
allowed her to enjoy the festivities while he attended
his pity party, solo.

He clasped both her hands in his while his mind
raced with all the ways he'd been an idiot.

'Have you talked it through with her? I'm sure she
doesn't hold you responsible.'

'She doesn't, but being the messenger of doom
sucks whichever way you look at it. I can never take
it back, or undo the pain.'

'But you were right. Better she heard it from you
than someone else.' She paled and looked away. 'I feel
guilty…about Ben.' Her teeth pulled at her lip. 'Don't
look at me like that.' She stared at her lap, where her
hands clenched.

He spoke softly, too uncertain of his own thoughts,
motivations and emotions. 'How am I looking at you?'
How did he feel about her revelation?

'Like you expect my brother to march you to the
nearest church with a shotgun aimed between your
shoulder blades.' She was too perceptive. Saw him
way too clearly.

'I—'

Had their secret-keeping days come to an end? A natural conclusion? Her limpid eyes lanced him, and he wanted to wrap her in his arms, to carry her out of here and kiss her until she looked at him as she'd done on Saturday night after their shower.

'Why don't we talk about it when we're back in London?' It was about time he manned up. Came clean with Ben. It was his responsibility. He hadn't been able to keep his hands off her, despite his damned pathetic rules. Perhaps if he ended things now, he could go to Ben in all honesty and say, 'It happened, but it's over.'

His guts twisted with eye-watering force.

The thought of going back to being friends with Essie, or even acquaintances, left him more impotent and off balance than when he'd sweated his way down the aisle this afternoon with his sister on his arm and a hundred different divorce scenarios in his head.

But Essie deserved a full relationship with her brother. He wouldn't stand in the way.

She looked over his shoulder to where Harley, Hannah and Jack were huddled around Hannah's phone laughing, probably at some atrocious selfie. 'You have a great family. Aside from my mum, Ben's all I have.'

Ash's chest grew tighter and tighter. Telling Ben about them would shift things between him and Essie far outside the realms of fun. But if he was honest he'd lost his precious control of this attraction days ago.

Fight for her.

Where the fuck had that come from?

She looked wearier than he'd ever seen her. He'd underestimated the toll this had all taken on her, or he'd seen it but ignored it because he was selfish and wanted her still. He cupped her cheek. 'Why don't you head upstairs? Take a bath? Things are pretty much over here. Just some mushy shit going on over there.' He jerked his head back in the direction of his sappy sisters, who were a bit tipsy and had sandwiched Jack between them on the dance floor for one last slow dance.

She nodded, her eyes glassy as she stared at their entwined fingers in her lap. And then she shook it off, her expression brightening as she watched the twin sandwich on display. 'Fun fact—did you know that simply holding hands with the person you love can alleviate pain and fear and reduce stress? It's the oxytocin the brain releases.'

He nodded, his throat so damned tight he had to loosen his collar. 'I'll tell the happy couple.'

She stood, glancing over at the dance floor. 'I think they know.' She smiled down at him, the saddest smile he'd ever seen, before she turned to leave.

He halted her retreat. 'Don't worry about Ben.'

She shook her head. 'Don't worry about your mum.'

She left him floundering at the centre of the monumental mess he'd made.

Ash tapped gently on the door to Essie's hotel room, his eyes scanning the corridor. He had no explanation for why he stood at her door at one a.m., for any of the wedding party who might spot him. He just knew a team of wild horses couldn't keep him away.

If this was to be their last night before he confronted Ben tomorrow, he just had to kiss her one last time. Hold her once more. See the rapture on her face as they shared one last intimacy. Somehow, between the fun facts and the fun sex, she'd worked her way under his skin. All of her—her beauty, her vulnerabilities, her thirst for new experiences.

The door flew open and there she stood, dressed in a baggy, oversized T-shirt that hung from one shoulder, her long, pale legs leading to the views of nirvana he knew were underneath. He had no right to touch her—he never had—but he wanted her anyway. With the same ferocity of need he'd experienced since the day they'd met.

How had he ever imagined himself immune to her? He was a fool and it was too late for a vaccine.

'Invite me in.' He tried to temper the gruffness from his voice, but he craved her so badly he could hardly draw breath. Perhaps it was the promise of one last time. But however he looked at it, he couldn't stay away. And he suspected it was simply Essie herself that drove his uncontrollable need. A need he'd have to quash soon.

Unless you keep her.

Fuck. She wasn't a possession. And she deserved way more than a commitment-phobic, cynical asshole like him. She deserved her happily-ever-after—the whole cake, not just the crumbs. Her scientific love. And he was the last man qualified to give her that.

But he could give her the only thing he'd ever given her.

A fun time. A new experience.

Why did it sound so empty? Hollow? Pathetic?

She held the door open and he stepped inside. As soon as she'd shut it behind him, she turned to face him. 'I need to talk to—'

Ash pressed his fingers over her soft lips. 'I know

what you need. What we both need.' He'd made his decision to talk to Ben. The mess he'd made of his personal life was old news and he'd be damned if he spent what little remaining time he had left with her trawling through his issues.

He might not be the man for her long term, but he could show her how rare and precious she was, and what she did to him and, hopefully, when they parted, she would feel her own worth and have nothing to regret.

She nodded, her breathtaking face lifted to his as he dragged her close with one arm banded around her waist and slanted his mouth over hers. Her soft lips parted under his with a sigh. As always, she embraced what they shared, never once pressing him for labels, or more than he could offer.

Did anyone deserve a woman as amazing as Essie?

Ash bunched the hem of her shirt in his fists and lifted it over her head, breaking from their kiss for the split second it took to dispense with the garment and slide his stare over her magnificent nakedness. He scooped his arms around her waist, hoisting her from her feet and stumbling backwards towards the bed so she sprawled over him, covering him from chest to thigh in a tumble of naked limbs and a cloud of Essie-scented hair.

Ash filled his lungs and his hands with her, memorising every nuance of this unique woman. With every passing beat, her kisses grew more desperate, the breathy moans in her throat more frantic and her fingers more insistent. And her ardour matched his.

Ash rolled them so she lay under him, her writhing body urging him on. She tugged at his shirt and he helped her, yanking it up from behind his head and tossing it aside.

Skin to warm skin.

Ash gripped one of her thighs, pushing her open to slot his hips in between. He captured one pink-tipped nipple, laving and lapping until she bucked in his arms and tugged at his hair, the wild, demanding side of her never far from the surface. His kisses followed the bumps of her ribs, the dip of her navel and the hollows beneath her hip bones.

He slid to the floor, tugging her ass to the edge of the bed until he was satisfied with her position. He spread her open, his gaze devouring every perfect pink inch of her.

Just one more taste.

He pressed a kiss to each thigh and then he leaned in to touch the tip of his tongue to her clit.

She sucked in a gasp, her hands fisting the bedspread. 'Ash...'

He pulled back, a rock the size of the Isle of Wight lodged in his chest. 'Say it again. Say my name.' Some base part of him needed to hear her call out for him, to know that he wasn't alone with his unrest. To know that she saw him and only him.

She nodded and he dived once more for the slick haven between her thighs. 'Ash...' She resumed her chant, his name over and over again, while he licked and flicked and suckled.

Every time she spoke his name, his fingers clung to her thighs with a fraction more force, as if he wanted to stamp his presence all over her from head to toe, leaving no doubt. He pushed the crazy idea aside, focussing on the catches in her throat as he forced her higher and higher.

She wasn't his.

'Yes…Ash…I'm close.' Her thighs juddered against his face and he ceased his efforts. He wanted to be inside her when she came, her muscles gripping him like a fist as she wailed his name for the last time.

She cried out, but when he tore into his fly, shoving his pants down with impatient jerks and pulling a condom from the pocket, she helped him, pushing at the denim and sliding her hands up and down the backs of his thighs.

Ash gripped the foil between his teeth and then covered himself. He shucked the jeans with a kick. Gripping her hips, he tilted her ass from the bed and plunged inside her with one thrust. Her body welcomed him, warm and tight and as close to perfect as he'd ever experienced.

He held himself still, allowing her to grow accustomed to him inside her and allowing him time to breathe around the block of concrete where his lungs should be. Ash held her stare while their chests heaved in unison, the patter of her heartbeat strong and rapid against his chest.

'Ash…' She sighed, her fingers dancing over his back, his shoulders and across his chest. He gipped one wandering hand, his fingers interlocking with hers while he pressed it to the mattress, and then followed suit with the other hand.

Her touching him with tender fingertips, while looking at him the way she was…it was too much. Too close to something he'd forsaken for good. Too raw a reminder that, one day, some other lucky bastard would be gifted this woman's love.

He rocked into her, his thrusts growing in speed and power as if he was chasing down his demons. Every time he slammed home a tiny gasp left her throat. It was a sound he'd remember his whole life. Her wide eyes clung to him as if begging. Only, he was the one who should be on his knees. Worshipping.

Her breasts jiggled, desperate for his tongue, but he'd reached the point of no return, reached his limit. He released one of her hands to scoop her thigh higher until it curved over his hip. Holding it there, he sank lower, the last inch into her tight heat.

'Yes…Ash…that's—' She never finished the sentence. Her orgasm struck, her head stretched back as she gasped a prolonged wail and clamped down on him so hard, he almost closed his eyes in ecstasy. But then he'd have missed her riding out her climax with her beautiful stare on him, her swollen mouth slack as her moans petered into pants.

His head swam as oxygen deprivation sucked him under.

'Ash.' She cupped his face, pressing her mouth to his.

He collapsed forward as fire raced along his spine and down the length of his cock. He buried his face in her neck as he ground his hips through the last of the spasms. He wasn't gentle. His facial hair would mark her, but he needed a minute to flounder in private from the purging flood of emotions he daredn't name. A minute to swallow the incredible high she'd often told him existed. He crushed her beneath him while he reeled, spent, panting and completely mindfucked.

Essie ran her fingers through his hair, her soft lips pressing kisses to his temples, his ear, the side of his neck. The see-sawing of his chest dwindled away until he struggled to suck even one molecule of air past his tight throat. His scalp prickled and the sheen of sweat on his skin turned icy cold.

He shifted, gently withdrew from her languid embrace and shuffled to the en-suite to dispose of the condom. He couldn't bring himself to look in the mirror while he washed his hands. He knew what he'd see. A stupid fuck who'd broken his number one rule in life and was now paying the ultimate price. The only thing he'd had to avoid and he'd gone and done it anyway.

His best friend's sister. A wonderful woman he couldn't have and didn't deserve. A woman professionally obsessed with relationships and romantic love—two things he sucked at and had spent years forsaking. A woman who deserved a man to love her one hundred and ten per cent. To be all in. To worship her and leave her in no doubt that she was his number one priority.

No way could fucked-up Ash be that man.

Keeping his gaze averted, he returned to the bedroom to find Essie wrapped in a white sheet, her face peaceful in sleep.

Indulging in one last, ill-advised move, he slipped into the bed beside her and fell asleep with her perfectly slotted into his arms.

CHAPTER ELEVEN

THE INSISTENT VIBRATION of a phone alert woke him. Ash opened his eyes to find the bed empty beside him and the sound of the shower from the en-suite bathroom. His body stirred fully awake at the idea of joining a wet Essie.

As he slid from the bed, Essie's phone vibrated again. He flipped it over and placed it on the nightstand, pausing when the screen lit up to reveal the string of notifications, which had sent the device into an early-morning frenzy.

You have fifty-three comments

What the…?

Ash's stomach pitched. Since his own brush with the gossip columns and the subsequent social media roasting around the story of one of New York's most influential families crumbling in the most sordid way, he'd deleted his own accounts.

Was Essie victim to a similar backlash? No, why would she be a target? Unless it was something to do with him…

Perhaps the gossip rags had caught wind of Harley's rushed, closed-door wedding. Perhaps they'd somehow acquired the limited guest list and sought a comment or a photo from Essie.

His scalp prickled even as he swiped his thumb over the screen.

It wasn't locked.

Every nerve in his body fired as he snooped—as soon as he'd verified that the messy, dirty Jacob drama hadn't spread to include Essie, he'd stop reading.

It took several beats for Ash to understand the content displayed on her phone. A blog.

Relationships and Other Science Experiments

So this was her little secret. Not quite an agony aunt. His mouth twitched at her sense of humour and her conversational writing style. He read on for a few lines, the latest post unsurprisingly one about the inexhaustible romance of weddings and the hidden tangle of complex relationships at play when extended families met, often for the first time in years.

One phrase, repeated in the comments at the bottom of the post, leapt from the screen and smacked him between the eyes. *Illegally Hot.*

Whatever it referred to, Essie's fans wanted more.

He shouldn't pry. No good ever came from snooping. But some unseen demon controlled his fingers, which scrolled the screen in search of earlier posts.

A familiar photo—the view of the London Eye taken from St James's Park. The photo he'd taken for her the day they'd met.

With each line he read, wave after wave of heat

flooded his body until his fists clenched and his jaw ached.

She'd written about their one-night stand. About their shock meeting the next day. About some arrogant asshole who'd rocked her world, but had the emotional intelligence of a rock.

He was paraphrasing, but one thing was glaringly obvious. *He* was *Illegally Hot*. And Essie had used him as tawdry inspiration fodder for her online musings. Exposing his hang-ups in a public forum…for humour…for entertainment… To humiliate him? To laugh behind his back?

No wonder the damned phone was never far from her hand. And every ping, every muted vibration represented someone new reading about or commenting on his sex life…

Ash tossed the phone on the nightstand, his stomach rigid as he sucked in a breath laced with razor blades. She'd put their relationship on the internet. For anyone to see? And kept it from him? All this time? While he'd agonised over the rights and wrongs of his attraction to her. All these weeks she'd made a fool of him…been laughing at him… Did everyone know? The Yard's staff? Ben?

His gut ached as if he'd taken a knee to the balls. He needed to get out of here.

Essie appeared in that moment, her open smile sliding from her face as she took in his posture. He stood, silently tugging on his boxers and his shirt—he was exposed enough.

'*Illegally Hot?* Did you come up with that all by yourself?'

Wrapped in a towel, her hair wet, she hovered,

breathtaking but paralysed, on the threshold. His vision tunnelled as he clamped his jaw shut and turned away from her to find his jeans.

She gasped, paling. 'Ash, I'm sorry, I—'

'You're fucking sorry? Is that all you have? Not quite your usual level of eloquence. Or is that reserved for your tacky sexploits?'

She moved towards him, a small anguished squeak leaving her throat. His outstretched hand stopped her dead in her tracks. If she touched him now, he might actually hurl, so tightly knotted were his intestines.

'Is everything entertainment to you? People's emotions? Their challenges? Their…pain.' What a fool he'd been. Again. He'd told her about his fiancée, his parents, his guilt over his mother… Would he read all about it online soon? Another science experiment?

How had he, only hours ago, imagined himself developing feelings for her? He didn't know her at all. Not this manipulative, deceptive version she'd hidden so successfully behind the bubbly, ingenuous, emotionally damaged exterior.

'I never meant to hurt you.'

Fuck, that sentiment sucked. 'So said every selfish person who ever acted in their own interest and only considered the consequences when they were found out.' Ash yanked on his jeans and scooped his own phone and the key to his room from the desk.

'Don't go. I can explain.'

'I don't give a fuck about your explanation. You used me. Not for one second did you consider my feelings before you published that crap—' he pointed at the nightstand and the offending device '—for anyone to read.'

'Ash…' She stepped closer, sucking the oxygen from the enclosed space until Ash's lungs recoiled. 'It was meant to be funny… I didn't name you.'

He snorted, expecting to see plumes of fire coming from his nostrils. 'Do you know why my family drama, my parents' split, was such salacious gossip, the kind you find funny?' He loomed over her, his chest working hard to oxygenate his blood before his head exploded. 'The juicy little details? The irresistible intrusion into our personal lives…all in the name of fair-game entertainment for the masses?'

Essie had the good grace to pale almost white and stay silent, a tiny shake of her head her only answer.

'The woman at the centre of the row between Hal and me, the final intolerable insult to my mother, the woman he confessed to fucking in front of my entire workplace, was *my* ex-fiancée.'

Her jaw dropped, and she swayed unsteadily on her feet, but it gave him no satisfaction.

Ash marched to the door, turning to cast one final look at the woman he'd almost trusted. Almost…

No.

'Forgive me if I have no intention of becoming a public laughing stock again.'

The door slammed behind him with a whoosh of air, blocking Essie's startled image from view.

Ash slapped his hand over the stop button on the treadmill in his apartment's fully equipped gym and wiped sweat from his eyes with a towel. He'd arrived home from Oxfordshire three hours ago, but he hadn't been able to quench the fire burning inside him any other way. Even now, after a solid hour of relentless pounding, when his noodle-like legs threatened to give out at any stage, the flames still licked at him— burning, taunting and mocking. Because he craved her still, when the taste of her betrayal should have turned his stomach for good.

Stupid fuck.

How could he have been so dumb? So taken in by her seeming ingenuousness and English-rose charm? When all the time she wielded a poisonous pen…or a noxious keyboard.

Of course he'd been right not to trust her. He'd been here before. Twice. Once with the lies his fiancée had told to keep her true affair with his father a secret, and once when Hal had finally tossed out the truth in a fit of malice for anyone at Jacob Holdings to hear.

Only this time, the pain slashed deeper, the wound gaping open. He'd thought she was different. He'd thought he'd learned his lesson and done everything in his power to protect himself.

Well, there was one more thing he could do. This time, he wasn't going down without a fight. He was done. Done with humiliation, done with being the last to know. Ash stumbled from the treadmill and eyed his phone where he'd switched it to silent. His fingers curled into his palm.

He wouldn't check.

How close he'd come to…feeling emotions that left him wanting to build barricades to protect himself! He needed fortifications more than ever, to protect himself from the feelings he'd realised last night were as foreign as the adopted country he'd chosen. Because whatever he'd felt for his ex, it paled in comparison to the unstoppable wave building in him now. He should never have let things go so far—caring for her hadn't been part of the plan.

A yell from his living room sucked him to his senses.

Ben stood framed in the doorway, his face slightly haggard with questions burning in his eyes. Ash had known this reckoning was coming, and yet he still recoiled. Telling your friend you'd slept with his sister was one thing. Telling him you'd allowed yourself to be duped, humiliated by not just one woman, but two…

Ash stalked to the kitchen with Ben trailing. He held out his arm, offering Ben a seat, and retrieved two bottles of beer from the fridge. 'What did she tell you?'

Is she okay?

No.

There'd be no asking about Essie, thinking about Essie and certainly no going to Essie.

'That it happened. That it was over.' Ben collapsed onto a bar stool, and accepted the beer Ash handed him. 'What did you do to her?'

Ash deserved the accusation in his friend's stare. He should never have slept with her after the first time. He had no defence. Never a good position for an attorney. But she wasn't blameless here. 'I met her the day before you left for New York. I didn't know who she was the first time.'

Fuck, that sounded all wrong.

Ben stared for long challenging seconds. 'I know Maggie hurt you and that you only do casual.' Ben gripped the bottle, his knuckles white. 'So why would you lead Essie on like that?'

Fuck, he didn't want to do this now, but there was no escape. 'We were just fooling around. She said she wanted the same thing. I should have told you.'

Ben paled even more, his lips thin and white. 'And now? You're done and she clearly wanted more because she's broken-hearted.' Ben speared his fingers through his hair. 'I offered her the job so I could get to know her, to make amends for the shit our father pulled. She's sweet and kind and fun. She's so desperate for approval…'

Ash nodded. It couldn't have been easy for Ben to find out he had a sister, either. A massive adjustment. 'I didn't know about your father, I'm sorry.'

Ben swallowed, his face twisted as he shook his head. 'Fuck… She's been treated so fucking shabbily by men, men who are supposed to care about her and love her and protect her, part of her believes she's unworthy of a decent relationship.' Ben took a swig of beer, wiping his mouth with the back of his hand. 'Please tell me you didn't take advantage of that.'

Had he? Had he unknowingly taken her fears and insecurities and used them for his own ends? He'd known Essie had a poor relationship with her and Ben's father, something Ash could relate to. Did she crave what she'd never had? Did she want it with him?

It didn't matter. It was too late. Over.

'If I did it was unintentional.' Ash ground his teeth together, willing truth into them—he'd told her his position from the start. But as he'd learned more about her, a part of him had known he would hurt her. He just hadn't guessed she'd hurt him in return.

Ben ignored his plea, as if lost to his own turmoil over his sister. 'He was never there for her. He kept me

and his wife a secret from her until she discovered his
lies by accident. Fuck. She deserves better than him.'

Acid flooded the back of Ash's throat. 'I agree. But
she's not blameless in this.' He should leave it alone.
Accept all the responsibility. But those fingers of mistrust still burrowed into his brain.

Ben stared. 'What does that mean?'

'Did you know about her blog?' The heat returned,
scalding, diminishing.

Ben frowned. 'Not until today, but what does that
have to do with anything?'

The words trapped in his throat, covered in barbed
wire. 'She's...been writing about us. About me.'

'So? She mentioned something... What's the big
deal?'

'Aside from the fact I don't enjoy reading about my
private life, my sex life on the internet...?'

Ben shrugged, eyes darting.

Ash took a seat at the kitchen bench, next to Ben.
'Did you...catch up on any gossip while you were in
New York?'

'What the...? You know that's not my style. What
does this have to do with Essie?'

Damn, the words stuck deep down in his gullet.
'Remember when...Maggie...called off the wedding?'

Ben nodded, one hand scraping over his haggard
face.

Ash gulped beer, the cool liquid soothing his
parched throat. 'Turned out the affair was a cover.
Some scapegoat schmuck. She was really fucking
Hal.'

Ben sputtered. 'Bullshit.'

Ash stared straight ahead. He couldn't witness whatever expression his friend wore for fear the humiliation would burrow into him so deep, he'd need a lobotomy to excise it. 'It's true. I didn't know it at the time, but Hal took great pleasure in informing me in front of a whole office of Jacob Holdings staff.'

Several beats passed. The occasional swallow of beer the only sound. 'Word spread. Before I knew it, the gossip rags were speculating on the demise of my parents' marriage, whether my playboy reputation would be damaged or enhanced and how destructive it would be to Jacob Holdings stock.' He faced his friend. 'That's why I came to London. I couldn't go back to work for Hal. I had paps chasing me down the street and, having created the mess, I had to rush to tell my mother before she heard of it at the gym or the grocery store.'

Ben shook his head, shock rendering him slack-jawed. 'I didn't know.'

Ash snorted. 'You and me both.'

'Does Essie know?'

Ash nodded.

They sat in silence. Then Ben said, 'She's sorry for what she did. Perhaps if you talked to her…'

Ash shook his head. He would. But not tonight.

'I think she's in love with you.'

No.

Ash couldn't deny they'd had chemistry from the start. And yes, she'd slipped under his guard, blind-sided him with her honest and refreshing outlook on the world, her ethereal beauty and her bubbly personality. But not love.

Ben glanced at his watch. 'I have to be at the club.'

Ash jutted his chin in silence. Where did these events leave him and Ben? Would he survive bumping into Essie down the track? She'd always be a part of Ben's life, quite rightly.

At the door, Ben turned. 'Ash. I'm sorry, man.'

Ash nodded. 'Me, too.'

And then he was alone again with only his restlessness for company.

Essie stacked the last chair into place and stretched out her aching back muscles. The basement club had been booked out for a private function that night—a fashion show and corporate party. The removal crew would arrive first thing to dismantle the temporary runway and extra seating.

The last place she'd wanted to be tonight was here with her happy face plastered on and the requisite nothing-is-too-much-trouble attitude, but she'd promised Ben she'd lock up the club, and in reality she'd rather have been here with the noise and the bodies than home alone with her self-recriminations.

Riding back to London earlier with Ben, she'd found hiding her desolation from her brother impossible. He'd coaxed the whole tale from her, his bunched jaw the only sign of any judgment. To his credit, he'd been supportive and understanding, something she didn't deserve for her role in hurting Ash, her own guilt a sharp blade slicing deep.

Flicking off the lights, she made her way upstairs, her tired feet encased in lead.

Her stomach clenched at the memory of Ash's face. She hated what she'd done to him. How much she'd devastated him through her thoughtlessness. She'd convinced herself he couldn't be identified, so he couldn't be hurt. But in light of his shocking confession about his father and his ex…

She'd betrayed his trust.

Humiliated him.

All because she'd been overwhelmed by their chemistry, in awe of the amazing sex and flushed with the heady power of holding her own in a relationship for the first time. And then later…

She only had herself to reprimand. If she'd been honest with him from the start, if she'd owned her feelings, said, 'This is who I am, take it or leave it,' instead of shoving them back inside for fear of his judgment or disapproval or indifference… He'd been honest with her from day one. He'd never once claimed to want anything beyond sex. She'd just misinterpreted his looks and his touches. She'd seen something, felt something that wasn't there. At least not for Ash.

She'd known the score going in and learned a long time ago that even when people said one thing, they usually did something else. Something that suited *them*.

But somewhere along the way, perhaps dazzled by the private jets and Paris and the glamorous clubs, she'd fooled herself into believing, just this once, she could have more. Have the real deal. An equal relationship where she was valued, cherished, respected. For once she'd ignored the loud and clear warning bells and imagined she could have someone for herself, someone who not just barely tolerated her, but actually wanted her in their life. Not an inconvenience, but as necessary as oxygen.

So the last time they'd been together in Oxfordshire had, at least for her, been way more intimate than all the previous occasions combined. She'd convinced herself they could be making love, not just banging each other. That didn't mean Ash had felt the same. She understood his anger, but could he run away so quickly if he shared one iota of her feelings?

Gnawing at her lip, she swung through the staff-only door. Yet again, she'd learned the hard way that relationships were fine in theory, the black-and-white science irrefutable, but disastrous in reality. She was an expert in one, but definitely a novice at the other. Nothing had changed. Only, this lesson carried a permanency that rolled her stomach and left her empty.

Bereft.

She slammed to a halt, her small gasp catching in her throat.

Ash stood in her office.

He wore running gear, his shirt dark with sweat as if he'd sprinted all the way with his backside on fire.

Perhaps sensing her behind him, he lifted his stare from a white envelope on her otherwise clear desk.

Essie's knees threatened to give way.

He was here.

To see her?

'Ash—'

'I came to deliver this. I…I assumed everyone had gone home.' He looked away and another part of Essie cracked and crumbled.

'I'm sorry. Please let me explain.' The words tumbled out in a rush.

Ash collected the envelope from the desk and Essie

spotted her name. He lanced her with a cold stare. 'Will your apology change the outcome? The facts?'

'No, but... Please...'

At his silence she ploughed on, certain he'd never forgive her, but desperate to have him understand. 'I didn't think I'd see you again after that first night. And then the next day you were my boss.' She lifted her gaze to his. 'I'd never had a one-night stand before. I...it made a good cautionary tale. Careful who you sleep with—it might turn out to be your boss.' Her voice trailed away with the ice of his stare.

She should have told him sooner. She'd been about to the night of the wedding. And then he'd looked at her as if he'd wanted more than sex and she'd succumbed, desperate to know if his feelings in any way matched hers.

'Yes, I can see that. Very entertaining.' He tapped the letter against his palm, his face an expressionless mask. His damp T-shirt clung to his ripped chest. If she hadn't needed every spare lick of saliva to lubricate her tight throat, she'd have drooled down her front.

'Ash, it wasn't like that. I never named you or wrote anything identifiable. And I didn't know about your... past—I would never hurt you like that. Only you know I was writing about us, well...just the incredible sex. I finally saw what all the fuss was about.'

Her excuses sounded all wrong. Her writing was exposition, scientific theory and a dash of poetic licence.

'I'm sure you didn't mean to be discovered. But lies grow. They twist and mutate and sprout claws. I could identify myself.' He thrust the envelope at her. 'I have a professional reputation. We fucked. That's it.'

Essie winced as if he'd slapped her.

'I don't want my sexual prowess to become a topic of public speculation. I'll be a laughing stock. I won't tolerate that again.'

'Ash. I understand you're angry with me.' She was furious with herself.

He pointed at the envelope trembling in her hand. 'Consider yourself severed. You can kiss your precious blog goodbye. Perhaps you'll be forced to sell out, practise what you preach, pedal your psychobabble for actual paying customers. You're about to find out the hard way, you can't hide behind theory for ever.'

'You…you're suing me? But—'

He stalked closer, pinning her with his steely glare.

Breathing became harder. His cold eyes flicked south to her mouth and then back again, the ice thawing. Or perhaps it was just her imagination. Just wishful thinking.

She pressed her back to the door, her palms flat to stop herself reaching for him. If he recoiled from her touch, backed away, she wouldn't survive.

This time her voice emerged a whisper. 'I'm sorry. Please let me explain.'

He was so close now his warm breath tickled her lips.

'My father was never there. Growing up, I would try to remember things I wanted to tell him, little things. I started writing them down until the next time he came home. And then later when I knew the truth, I used my blog to process my feelings. Writing about you was a lapse, a mistake—one I won't make again.'

If she took a deep breath, her nipples would brush

his chest. But she couldn't even draw in enough air to stop her head spinning.

He'd listened patiently but now he snarled. 'Well, some of us don't have that luxury—we have to deal, internalise, without publicly splurging every one of our feelings. Do you think you're the only person with a shitty father figure?'

'Of course not. I—'

'Oh, spare me your pity.' The pain in his eyes stole the last of her oxygen.

If she hadn't been leaning against the door, her legs would have given way. How could someone do that to their own son? She'd thought Frank was bad enough. No wonder Ash had fled from his life in search of a fresh start. And all she'd done was confirm his beliefs that he was right not to trust anyone.

'I understand that. But I was blindsided by our chemistry. I'd never experienced anything like it. For the first time in my life, I had some power in a relationship. It was heady, wonderful, but overwhelming. For the first time, I didn't feel worthless, and then when people liked what I wrote…I got professional validation, too. I messed up with the blog. I should have told you. I was trying to tell you the night of Harley's wedding.'

He placed one hand on the door above her shoulder and leaned close. At first she was certain he planned to kiss her, the heat in his eyes, the small catch of his breath, the way the tip of his tongue touched his top lip for a split second.

But then he must have changed his mind. He made eye contact and Essie shivered.

'I was right not to trust you.'

He wasn't listening. He'd shut down already. She'd done the damage and missed the opportunity to make it right.

He backed off as suddenly as if they'd been interrupted in an illicit, forbidden kiss. Essie's bones rattled from the icy chills of his frosty brush-off. That he could deliver such a blow without a flicker of emotion told her he'd be a formidable opponent in the courtroom. Something she hoped she'd never have to witness or experience, despite the legal document clutched in her hand.

'Ash, I humiliated you in a moment of stupid impulsiveness and I regret it.'

It was the now or never moment. Mustering every shred of her courage, she pressed herself back against the opened door to gain another sliver of space from his derision. 'But I kept the secret from you because I…I started to realise…I love you, and I didn't want anything to ruin that.'

Silence.

His cold stare remained unchanged.

Essie hovered for long, torturous, doubt-filled seconds. When he didn't move, didn't speak, she stumbled away, blindly barging through the exit and out into the night.

Much later, alone in a deserted Tube carriage, she looked down at the envelope still crumpled in her hand.

A bubble of hysterical laughter burst through her numbness.

How would she ever afford legal representation to fight him?

And why would she bother?

She loved him and she'd hurt him. It was time to face the consequences.

CHAPTER TWELVE

ESSIE'S TWENTY-FIFTH BIRTHDAY arrived with a predictability that left her gunning for a fight. At first, the card on the mat, addressed with an airmail sticker and recognisable handwriting, sent familiar chills down her bare arms and legs. But reading the dismissive, one-line greeting from her father fired her determination—today was the first day of the rest of her life.

A new Essie rose from the ashes. One who'd learned valuable lessons from the way she'd treated Ash. Yes, she'd hurt him and lost him—he'd already retreated behind the walls he'd constructed long ago, the defences she'd helped to refortify.

But Ash, and to some degree Ben, had taught her something. In loving Ash, she fully understood herself worthy of love in return. She wanted his love, even though she could survive without it. She had all the theory, and now the confidence in her ability to practise and live an authentic life. Not sit and wait for the scraps others tossed her way.

She took the annual cheque—her father's way of appeasing his own demons for his life choices and one she'd resolutely rejected since her fifteenth birthday—

and tore it in two. With the birthday ritual complete, she dropped both halves and the card into the bin, donned her sunglasses and left for the Tube station, her step lighter.

Half an hour later she waltzed into The Yard to find Ben and Ash drinking coffee together at the bar.

Her feet stalled for a brief second as Ash's eyes landed on her. She'd wronged him, hurt him in the worst way. He might not be able to love her in return, but she was done apologising for loving him.

'Good. You're both here. I need to speak to you.' Essie stood before them, clutching the straps of her backpack.

Two sets of wide, wary eyes followed her—one so like her own, her insides trembled—and what she'd come to say clogged in her throat. The other so blue, she imagined she could see inside Ash, to his deepest darkest fears. And maybe she could. Maybe she'd always been able to. But she couldn't see what she wanted to see.

She'd messed up, but she'd survive.

All humans shared the same basic longings—safety, love, acceptance. She deserved those things and so did Ash. But it was too late for him to find them with her. She'd ruined what tiny chance they'd had.

Essie turned her burning eyes away from Ash and focussed on her brother, her chin lifted. Slipping the backpack from her shoulder, she retrieved the letter she'd composed at six a.m. this morning after writing her latest blog post on the importance of self-love, self-acceptance and self-forgiveness, and handed it over to a puzzled Ben.

She cleared her throat. 'I'm handing in my notice.'

Ben took the envelope with a wince. Essie ploughed on—she needed to get all she wanted to say out, before emotion paralysed her vocal cords. Because she was done being needy. Done waiting for other people's approval. Done with scientific theory.

She would survive the practice and emerge improved, wiser, unstoppable.

Her bruised heart would heal eventually.

Essie cleared her throat. 'As we only had a verbal contract, I won't be working that notice, but you'll be fine without me.' Ash could wax lyrical on the ins and out of employment law as long as he liked. They wouldn't force her to stay. And Ben didn't really need her. His clubs were well-oiled machines. She suspected he'd offered her the job as some sort of olive branch, and she loved that he'd tried to make amends for their father.

'I know you only employed me because you somehow felt responsible for what Frank did. But there's no need. If you're short-staffed, I recommend promoting Josh to my position as manager, until you find someone permanent. He's way more qualified than I am anyway.'

She flicked her stare to Ash, her lungs on fire and pressure building behind her eyes so she was tempted to don the sunglasses. How long would it take him to replace her in his bed? Would he even bother? Perhaps he'd go back to his lonely one-night rule. She loved him enough to want more than that for him, even when, because of her foolish actions, it couldn't be her.

'Essie,' said Ben.

She held up her hand. She needed to say everything she'd come here to say. 'Going forward, I want us to have a real relationship. We have a chance to build a lasting bond, away from the usual influences of childhood sibling rivalry. I don't resent you for getting a phone before me or being allowed to stay up later and you never had to play dress-ups with me or read me dumb stories.'

He grinned, giving her the courage to continue.

'If you want to be a part of my life like I want to be a part of yours—' her breath caught, but she sucked in air through her nostrils, fighting the burn behind her eyes '—you'll meet me halfway.'

She shrugged, her whole body buzzing with renewed energy.

Ben nodded, his eyes sliding to Ash. 'Of course I want that.' He reached for her hand and squeezed her fingers. 'But what will you do without a job?'

She squeezed back. 'I have plenty to do. I want to put more time into promoting my blog to wider audiences, and I'm thinking of writing a book. It turns out I have something valuable to say about relationships. I'm a bit of an expert in the field, actually.' She winked at him. 'You know you're damned lucky I'm your sister, don't you?'

She swung her backpack onto her shoulder and offered a beaming Ben a small smile. She loved him. Always would. But her happiness was her responsibility—no more waiting around for someone else's acceptance or approval. No more settling.

And Ash...

Her eyes stung and she blinked away the burn.

Well, that was over. She'd hurt him, and he couldn't

love her back. But she'd meant what she'd said to him last night.

Her vocal cords constricted, almost choking off her newfound bravery.

As if sensing the private moment, Ben muttered something about making an important phone call and disappeared.

Part of Essie wanted to follow him. But it was time to own her mistakes and her feelings.

His expression was closed off, wary. The last shred of hope inside her withered and died. 'I know I messed up. I'm truly sorry I hurt you and I hope one day you can forgive me.'

Her voice broke, but she smiled through the scalding heat behind her eyes. 'But more importantly, and I'm saying this because I love you and I want you to be happy, I hope one day you'll want more with someone. You deserve more.'

He swallowed, his jaw bunched. Her hand itched to touch him, to feel the silk of his hair or the scrape of his scruff. She dug her nails into her palm and looked down, her own vision swimming. 'I allowed what my father did to hold me back but I'm done with that. Don't let yours hold you back, Ash.'

With a final, slightly wobbly smile, she turned her back on the man she loved and made her way out into the sun of a new day.

'What did she say?' Ben joined Ash at the window, where he'd moved to stare after a retreating Essie.

He shrugged, his lungs too big for his chest as he grinned at his friend. 'She's magnificent, isn't she?'

Every nerve, every muscle, every impulse in him

fired, urging him to chase after her. He'd missed her beautiful, ready smile, her effervescent personality and her dirty laughter over one of her own jokes. But he'd put paid to her trust with his bastard move last night. He had no intention of suing her. He'd been angry. He'd lashed out.

Asshole.

Now he had something his friend needed to hear. 'I love her.'

Ben swivelled to face him. 'Of course you do. Dick-head.' He thumped Ash's shoulder, making his point.

Ash sighed, a wistful smile tugging his mouth. He'd been blind long enough. 'I allowed my hang-ups to cloud my judgment. You don't need me to tell you she's the best thing that ever happened to me. To both of us.'

Ben nodded, still looking a little dazed by his sister's declarations. 'What are you going to do?'

Ash retraced his steps, his restless limbs unable to stand still for a minute longer, and tossed a note on the bar to cover the coffees. 'I'm going to do what I should have done at the wedding. I'm going to fight for her.'

Ben nodded. 'You'd better not hurt my sister again.'

Ash shook his head, his mouth pulled to a grim line. 'I will. I'm a fuck-up. But she'll put me right.' He grinned. 'Just like she did you.'

Ben nodded, another incredulous smile tugging his mouth.

Ash released a long sigh. 'Now, I'm going to say the same thing to you. You'd better always be there for my woman when she needs you. You're the man of her family—time to step up.'

Eyes rounded, Ben nodded. Then he grinned.

'Looks like we both have some ground to make up.'
He reached out his hand and Ash shook on it.
    'Good luck,' they said in unison.

CHAPTER THIRTEEN

ASH STEPPED INSIDE the relative gloom of the stuffy university hall, his throat so dry he'd never be able to say what he'd come here to say. He rolled his shoulders, scanning the mingling crowds for her golden hair. He'd come to present the most important closing argument of his life. No time for nerves or hesitancy.

This was what he did.

He won.

Every negotiation.

How he'd managed to fool himself he could live without her astounded him. For an intelligent man, used to getting his own way, how had he blocked his own path for so long?

He gripped the bag containing the rain boots tighter, the smell of new rubber reminding him of what was at stake. Had he waited too long? Woken up to himself too late?

He spotted her and his heart jerked out of rhythm.

A stunningly dressed Essie, as he'd never seen her before, stood not ten feet away. She wore a fitted green dress that outlined every one of her perfect curves, matching green skyscraper heels and a light smattering of make-up, which accentuated her rosy complexion and bright eyes. Her hair was loose, styled in soft waves that made his clenched fingers itch, and a formal graduation gown completed the look.

Damn, he wanted to mess her up. To peel from her the smart, professional outfit and tangle her hair while he kissed her senseless until she believed what he had to say. Believed it down to her bones. Because he meant it and he'd waited too long to tell her.

Ben caught his eye as he strode towards the siblings, his steps determined.

Essie turned at the last moment, the laughter at whatever Ben had said sliding from her exquisite face. A bubble of stilted anticipation enclosed them as the conversations around them muted into background noise.

'What's with the wellies?' said Essie, eyeing his bag. He deserved the cold shoulder after giving her that notice of legal action. But that wasn't Essie's style.

Ash pressed his lips together. Now wasn't the time for laughter. But of course she would say the thing he least expected. So full of surprises, so refreshing, so unique. His Essie.

Don't get ahead of yourself, asshole.

'If you mean these—' he held up the rain boots '—a graduation present. Congratulations, Dr Newbold.'

She eyed the spade sticking up next to the boots in silence, keeping his worthless ass on tenterhooks.

He should have come here today with champagne and flowers and a fucking brass band. But he'd got what he'd told her from day one he'd wanted—her out of his life, him out of hers.

What an idiot.

Her magnificent bravery and heartfelt declaration yesterday had been the final slap he'd needed to wake up. Ash himself acted as the only barrier standing in the way of contentment. He'd done the hard part, breaking free of his old life, free of the poisonous relationship with his father. The rest, loving Essie, was easy.

Now all he had to do was grab hold of this wonderful woman, pray she'd walk alongside him and never let go. If she'd have him.

That remained to be seen. But if forced to do this in front of this room full of gowned academics like some sappy idiot from a romantic comedy movie, he would.

Ben cleared his throat. 'I'll uh…go find your mum and get us some champagne.' With a look that said 'don't fuck this up', his friend offered them privacy.

Ash gestured Essie to accompany him to the less crowded foyer. She obliged and he followed the sway of her gorgeous ass that was unfortunately obliterated by her billowing gown.

In a deserted corner, she turned her big blue eyes on him.

'I bluffed about the lawsuit. I was angry. I'm sorry.'

The longer she looked at him, wary and hesitant, the more his intestines knotted. 'I fucked up, too.' He held her stare, willing her to hear the earnest regret in his voice. He stepped closer, taking an indulgent second to register how fantastic she smelled, how he wanted to wake up tomorrow with her scent in his hair, on his sheets, and every morning after that.

She pointed at the shovel. 'You bought me a shovel? Are we burying a corpse?'

This time he couldn't hold in the laughter. He was

messing this up. And she applied her usual quirky sense of humour to help him out.

His fingers twitched, desperate to reach out and cup her waist. To drag her closer. He eyed her full mouth, which was painted red. 'Someone once told me to consider my carbon footprint and I promised I'd plant a forest. Fun fact—did you know a flight from New York to London produces eighty-four tons of the greenhouse gas, carbon dioxide?'

She stared at him for so long, her features an unreadable mask, a countdown began in his head as if he waited for the gavel to fall.

'I know you're celebrating with your family, so I'll cut straight to my closing statement.' Not a flicker of her beautiful smile. Damn—his best lawyer humour… 'You were right. I allowed the poor way I'd dealt with my past to stand in the way of us, and I'd like you to consider taking me back.' Her lips parted a fraction.

'Now, before you send the jury out to consider, let me present my evidence.'

'Aren't you supposed to do that *before* you close?' She tilted her head.

Heat raced up his spine. She was magnificent. Keeping him on his toes, challenging him, calling him out on his bullshit. How had he been so blind for so long? How was he managing to keep his hands off her?

'Good point. The thing is, I've done a little research myself. I'm sure you know all about Sternberg's triangular theory of love?'

She shrugged, her colour heightening a fraction. 'I do.'

So far, so good.

'We definitely have the passion, or we did have, until I behaved like a douche and overreacted. We also have the intimacy down pat.' His hand cupped her waist, fingers flexing to draw her another milli- metre into his space. 'Two out of three isn't bad, as the song goes.'

She didn't step away, her eyes lifting to stare him down. 'The thing is, Ash, I'm no longer willing to settle for two thirds of what I deserve.'

His groin stirred at her proximity. At her demand- ing her absolute dues. Fuck, if this went his way, he'd hold on tight and never let her go.

'You don't have to, because I came here today to tell you I'm completing the triangle.'

She raised one eyebrow. 'Commitment?'

He nodded, an unfettered smile taking over his face. 'I'm all in. I want you. Every second I've spent with you has been the best fun. And, unless I fuck it up, which I plan not to, I know there's more fun in our future.' He dropped the bag and reached for both her hands, holding them between their bodies. 'I love you, Essie. Is it too late?'

She stared.

The gavel clattered to the block, the harsh clap of the hardwood echoing inside his skull.

He'd blown it.

But then she jumped into his arms, her hands tug- ging his neck and her body pressed to his as she kissed the shock from him with the enthusiasm he'd grown to expect. This woman was incapable of half measures, one of the things he loved most about her. Her hon- esty. Her emotional availability. Her complete lack of artifice. What you saw was what you got. And he wanted it all.

With his arms banded around her waist, he hauled her feet from the floor, groaning into her mouth as he swung her in a circle and then lowered her and broke free.

'I messed up your lipstick.' He wiped a smudge from her chin.

'I don't care.' She laughed, smearing the rest of the colour from his lips with her fingertips. 'That was quite a statement, counsellor.'

He shrugged. 'Some things are worth fighting for. You are worth fighting for.'

He swooped on her again, his tongue delving into her mouth and his hand slipping beneath her ceremonial gown to cup her waist and press her close. She pulled back with a small sigh, her eyes slumberous with lust.

'Wanna go to a stuffy degree ceremony lunch? I guarantee it *won't* be fun.'

He nodded, warmth spreading from his chest to the tips of his fingers, which held her a little tighter.

'As long as I can peel you out of this later, Dr Newbold.' He fingered the edge of the ceremonial gown. 'Or perhaps you could keep it on. That might be fun. Ever made love in a cap and gown?'

She laughed, shaking her head. 'Call me doctor again.' She writhed in his arms, waking up the parts of him inappropriate for the setting.

'Doctor.' He nuzzled her neck.

'Counsellor, I think you've just won your case.'

'No, I've won something better—you.'

They sealed the contract with a kiss.

* * *

Essie pushed the spade into the dirt and struck a rock. The field bordering a track of mature woodland on the Oxfordshire estate owned by Alex was marked out with rows of bagged tree saplings ready for planting. 'How many more do we have to plant before that delicious lunch you promised me?'

Ash laughed. 'Well, if you want to accompany me to New York for Christmas, you have to plant this whole forest.'

Essie pouted and attacked the rock in earnest. The quicker they planted the damn trees, the quicker she could get Ash naked. She glanced over at him dressed down in jeans and a T-shirt. As mouth-watering as ever. Who cared about greenhouse gases when Ash was around?

And he was hers. Her smile made her cheeks ache. She had two new men in her life. A fully committed brother and a proper boyfriend who was in love with her...

'Fun fact,' he said. 'Couples who play together, stay together.'

She picked up the inconveniently placed rock and tossed it to land at his feet.

He shot her a look that promised thrilling retribution.

She laughed, dropped her spade and went to him, wrapping her arms around his neck and tugging him down for a kiss. 'You totally made that up.'

He laughed. 'I did. But you're not the only one with a clever fact up her sleeve, Doctor.'

She sobered. 'Well, even if it is true, you'll be practising law again soon—not much time for playing or fun.'

He scooped her from the ground and she wrapped her legs around his waist, grateful she'd worn the cut-off shorts he could never resist as she felt the prod of his erection between her legs.

'There's always time for fun.' His lips brushed hers. 'But to be certain, ever experienced living with the man you love?'

She gasped and shook her head, which spun with his question as if he'd twirled her around in a circle.

'Good. Because I think we should move in together.'

Essie wriggled free, sliding down the length of his hard body. 'Seriously?'

He nodded, wicked light glinting in his eyes.

'But you live on the wrong side of London.'

He shook his head, holding her hips still and rubbing himself against her belly. 'I'm moving. New legal practice. New apartment. New girlfriend...'

She couldn't stop the grin that made her cheeks ache. He turned serious. 'Will you live with me— somewhere we choose together?' He cupped her cheek, his fingers tangling in her hair.

She nodded, flying into his arms once more. After a kiss that turned heated enough she scoped the nearby woods for a potential spot to take things further, he placed her feet on the ground and wiped what was probably a smudge of dirt from her cheek.

Taking her hand, he tugged her towards the car. 'Come on. Turns out I'm starving.' He winked, promising more than a delicious three-course lunch.

'But what about the trees? I want to see New York at Christmastime. I've never experienced ice skating in Central Park or the Rockefeller Christmas tree.'

'I'll hire someone to plant the damn things for us.'
He lengthened his stride, his steps more urgent now
he'd made up his mind.

'Are we driving back to London?' She didn't think
she'd be able to wait that long with the persistent buzz
between her legs.

Car sex...?

'No—I've booked a room at the hotel. We're going
to celebrate moving in together. I'm going to lick
champagne from every part of your body.'

'I'm not sure I'll survive that experience.'

'You will. It will be fun.'

She nodded. It totally would.

* * * * *

IF ONLY FOR TONIGHT

SHERELLE GREEN

To my sister, Kelsey, for your support and motivation. When I was crafting the character of Cydney Rayne, I was inspired by your adventurous spirit, mysterious demeanor, intelligence and beauty. You never pass up on an opportunity to enhance yourself culturally and challenge yourself mentally. I greatly admire your drive to live life to its fullest and your ability to always be on the go and not be stagnant in life. As little girls, we shared a bond that could not be broken, and as adults, I'm so elated that our bond has only gotten stronger. You walk with such confidence and embody so many wonderful qualities. I'm so proud to have you as a little sister and I appreciate all the literary inspiration! Without you, Cydney Rayne wouldn't exist. This one's for you, sis!

Prologue

Cydney Rayne enclosed her arms around her body as she inhaled the unique scent of the ocean. On the southeastern coastline of Anguilla, sounds from the sea creatures mingled with those constrained to land as midnight approached.

"So peaceful," Cydney whispered as she closed her eyes and listened to the sound of magnificent waves crashing against the rocky shore. Earlier that day, she'd soaked in the beauty of the bright sunset as it painted the sky a rusty reddish-orange. Now, as she opened her eyes, she admired the splashes of blue and gray that dusted the moon and the brilliant stars shining in the darkness.

Cydney walked over to one of the few light posts on the boardwalk and took off her leather sandals, letting the pinkish sand slide between her toes. Her vacation with her girlfriends from college was finally coming to an end, but she hadn't managed to track down the sexy guy she'd been running into all week. The ladies thought she'd made him up since they hadn't been around to spot him. But she knew she couldn't imagine the naughty conversations she'd had with the stranger or the sensations she felt in her body whenever he was around. She felt more intrigued by this man than any other man from her past. And she didn't even know his name.

She glanced around the deserted beach, wishing she'd brought her iPhone with her to keep track of the time. "Come on, mystery man...where are you?"

Her friends would kill her if they knew she'd sneaked out of the resort at night to track down a man she didn't know. But Cydney was known for being the daredevil of the group. The thrill of danger excited her, and even though her family disliked her adventurous ways sometimes, she couldn't help but be anyone but herself.

Deciding it probably wasn't the best idea to continue to walk around aimlessly in Anguilla, Cydney started to head back to the resort until she noticed she was near the beach house that she'd admired since her arrival. She knew she should keep walking since there weren't any lights surrounding the house, but she slowed down her pace, anyway. All the lights inside the house were off, and according to a local she had queried, the house wasn't occupied. But somehow she sensed someone was in the house, watching her from the front window.

She stood there for a few seconds before a porch light turned on and the front door opened. Out stepped a tall man who appeared to be shirtless. She could barely make out his face in the dim lighting. Her breath caught in her throat. The porch's lighting was just enough for her to tell that he was looking straight at her. She told herself to leave and hurry back to the resort, away from possible danger. But something kept her bare, toenail-polished feet planted in the sand as her blue summer dress danced in the night wind.

He stepped off the porch and began taking slow, purposeful steps toward her. A closer look at the man made her heart beat even faster. As he drew nearer, she told herself to be prepared for anything that the night had in store. After all, that was what she'd ventured to the beach for. She'd wanted to find her sexy mystery man, and there he was…in the flesh.

"So we meet again," he said in an alluring voice as he approached her.

"I guess so. You told me you'd be on the beach, but I didn't expect to find you in a deserted beach house."

The amused look on his face was undeniable.

"You didn't think I'd come, did you?"

"Not really," he said with a smile. "Beautiful women don't often go out into the night to meet a stranger they haven't even been formally introduced to."

What he said was definitely true considering she'd questioned her own motives several times while walking along the beach.

"Well, I guess I'm not most beautiful women then, am I?"

He walked closer to her and she confirmed her observation. He wasn't wearing a shirt, allowing her a nice view of his delectable six-pack.

"I guess not," he answered, studying her, as well. "My name is Brandon. It's nice to meet you," he continued. He offered a handshake as he removed one hand from the pockets of his khaki shorts.

Cydney wondered if she should give him her real name but decided against it. "Nice to meet you, Brandon. My name is Jessica."

She returned his handshake and felt an electric spark the minute their hands touched. She was totally caught off guard by the feeling and immediately dropped his hand. His eyes glinted with amusement.

"Very nice to meet you, too, Jessica. And might I add, I've enjoyed the conversations we've had this past week. Honestly, I can't say I've ever been this captivated by a woman before."

Cydney felt the same way but couldn't explain why she'd felt compelled to exchange naughty dialogues with the stranger. In fact, she'd been the one to start the conversations. She'd first seen him at a food market where he'd been buying coconut cake, a local dessert extremely well-known on the island. She'd waited until he was leaving, and being the daring person she was, she'd told him she'd love to lick the dessert off his body and then walked away, leaving him with a stunned look on his face.

He'd returned the favor the next day by walking into a local clothing store while she was shopping and saying he'd love for her to purchase the swimsuit she had in her hands just so that he could strip it off her later. He'd taken it one step further and explained everything he would do to her naked body.

Their back-and-forth naughty banter had continued every time they'd seen each other until finally he'd told her to meet him on the beach her last night in Anguilla. That night had finally come, and she didn't know if she was spontaneous or foolish for meeting with a man who had *just* learned her *name,* but probably remembered all the sexual positions she whispered in his ear for the past week.

"Brandon, I want you to know that I've never done

anything like this before," Cydney blurted out, although she wasn't sure why she cared since she didn't plan to ever see him again.

He grazed her cheek with the back of his hand. "I know. Believe it or not, I know what type of woman you are."

The gesture was sweet, but Cydney didn't believe him. What woman would believe a man in her position? She knew what he wanted, and it was fine with her because she wanted the same thing. She'd never had a one-night stand, but she didn't think she could stop herself now, even if she tried. The man was definitely in shape and had the build of a basketball player. His skin was the color of cinnamon and she'd never seen eyes like his. They weren't hazel or blue but more so a combination of the two. Sea-blue, she thought as she peered a little closer. He was hot....

"So what do you say, Jessica?" he said, breaking into her thoughts. "Will you come inside the beach house and spend the night with me?"

Cydney looked him up and down, her eyes lingering on his six-pack. *How can I say no to a man this fine?* She didn't live with regrets and after one more glance over his body, she knew she'd regret not taking him up on his offer.

"I accept," Cydney said, relishing in the desire reflected in his eyes. "But only on one condition."

"What's that?" Brandon said, his voice even sexier than before.

Cydney tilted her head to the side as she observed Brandon a little more closely. She was one day shy of twenty-seven and definitely not a stranger to the bedroom. But there were still certain things that she'd al-

ways wanted to try yet never entertained with other
men. If only for tonight, she wanted to live out one of
her fantasies. She glanced at the beach, and then back
at Brandon.

"I want to have sex in the ocean," Cydney finally
replied.

Brandon smiled at her and nodded his head in agreement. "That seems simple enough."

"But not just that," Cydney continued. "I want
us to continue our naughty conversations by talking
dirty while we explain every single thing we want to
do to each other...while having sex in the ocean. No
inhibitions...."

Cydney watched the fire build up in his eyes right
before he stepped closer to her. His hands gently grazed
her face again, only this time they didn't stop there. He
took one finger and dragged it in between her cleavage
before dropping his head to the side of her neck. There,
he placed soft kisses along her neckline, paying close
attention to the parts right above her breasts. Cydney
dropped her head back and enjoyed the way his lips felt
on her skin. She couldn't help the moans that escaped
her mouth with every seductive kiss he placed on her
upper body.

When he neared her mouth, she stopped him before
their lips could touch. Outlining his jawline with her
finger, she used her free hand to gently push him away
from her. She took that moment to provocatively lift
her dress over her head, revealing her spicy two-piece
bathing suit.

Her eyes were pinned to his lips as he licked them in
anticipation and slowly unzipped his pants before pushing them completely off. Cydney gasped at the sight that

was before her. Brandon hadn't worn anything underneath, displaying his enlarged sex. Her mouth watered as she took in the complete sight of his sexy nakedness. His arms and abs were so muscular that it made her want to lick every crevice of his body like it was a chocolate-ice-cream sundae.

He walked toward her, one mission clearly evident in his mind. Instead of getting nervous, Cydney flirtatiously smiled and met him halfway.

"I see you brought the swimsuit you were looking at in the store," Brandon said as he played with the string on the side of her bikini.

"I always keep my promises," Cydney replied, her voice catching as his eyes grew even deeper with desire.

"Come with me," he told her seductively while grabbing her hand and leading her to the ocean. Her inner voice warned her that a man this sexy could be dangerous for a woman's psyche. Men this fine were hard to forget and even harder to duplicate. But that inner voice was no longer present the minute their bodies hit the water. The only thought on Cydney's mind was making sure she remembered every moment she spent with her sexy island lover.

Chapter 1

Eight months later...

"Cydney Rayne."

She glanced up at the man who had whispered her name and prayed her eyes were deceiving her. They'd been formally introduced an hour before her sister Imani's wedding, and her body temperature still hadn't returned to normal. It had taken all her strength to stand up as maid of honor and not steal glances at the sexy man whose eyes had been glued to her the entire ceremony.

Imani and Daman Barker's backyard wedding reception was in full swing, and she didn't dare regard the man while being surrounded by her family and friends.

"Please follow me," she said quickly before leaving the reception and retreating to a nearby walk-in closet inside her grandfather's large house. As soon as she shut the closet door, she wondered why she hadn't found a less confined hiding spot.

As they stood there observing one another, she wondered who would be the first to speak. *Goodness, the man looked devastatingly sexy.* He looked even better than she remembered. His black suit looked tailor-made and now the foremost thought in her mind was how good he'd look out of it.

He licked his lips as his eyes practically burned a hole through her lavender maid-of-honor dress. He was obviously having the same thoughts she was. She wanted to kiss him badly, and seeing the fire in his eyes, she knew that he wanted to kiss her, too. But Cydney refused to start something with a man like him—the kind of man who oozed sex appeal and looked like he just walked off the cover of *GQ* magazine. She could lose her damn mind with a man like him, and losing her sanity over a man, no matter how good he looked, was *not* an option.

A month ago, when she'd gone to help her new brother-in-law move out of his Detroit condo, she had seen a picture of Daman with a man she couldn't quite make out. She could only see his profile in the picture, but she instantly knew that she had met the man previously. Refusing to believe her eyes, she put the photo out of her mind, hoping it was just a weird coincidence that he resembled *that* man she'd tried to forget about. Now, staring back into a pair of amused sea-blue eyes, she reminded herself that she never did believe in coincidences.

"So, Cydney Rayne, would you like me to call you Jessica, Cydney or do you prefer Cyd, the name everyone else has been calling you all day?"

She wished she could wipe that smirk off his handsome face. She wasn't the only one who'd made up a fake name. "Well, that depends. Do you want me to call you Shawn Miles or would you rather I call you Brandon?"

His eyes squinted together. "Although I loved the way you screamed my name that night in the ocean, I'd wished you were screaming Shawn rather than Brandon. Now that you know my real name, maybe we can make that happen."

Throwing her head back in an exaggerated laugh, she refused to let his arrogance get to her. "I'm sure your ears were playing tricks on you, but if that's the name your mother gave you, then Shawn it is. You can call me Cyd or Cydney, but if you think for one minute that we'll be sleeping together, think again."

He was still smiling and checking her out. She tried to keep a calm demeanor, but she was anything but relaxed. She couldn't even remember how Shawn knew Daman since she hadn't really listened to the introductions past learning his real name. The moment she'd seen his face before the wedding, she'd wanted to crawl into a deep, dark hole. However, Shawn had looked more amused than surprised. She'd barely returned his handshake when the enormity of the situation had hit her full force. Most people never saw their one-night stands again. Unfortunately for Cyd, her one-night stand came strolling through her grandfather's backyard for her sister's wedding. *Seriously?*

"How *do* you know Daman, anyway?"

He looked at her from head to toe one more time before responding. "I met Daman through Malik Madden, a mutual friend."

Cyd wondered if Shawn had known her true identity when they'd first met on the island.

"No, I didn't know we shared a mutual friend. Imani

and Daman hadn't started working on the gala they planned yet," Shawn said, interjecting her thoughts.

Cyd squinted her eyes together, soaking in his accurate assessment. "I didn't even ask you anything," she snapped. Even if he didn't know her then, she was sure he'd known about her before he got to the wedding because he hadn't appeared surprised when he saw her.

"You're right. I knew who you were before I got here today. After meeting with Daman and Malik one day, I used Google to search Imani when I heard she was marrying Daman. That's when I spotted a picture of you and your business partners."

Cyd rolled her eyes and shook her head when he read her thoughts once more. Clearly Shawn had done his research. Cyd, along with her sister Imani Rayne-Barker, cousin Lexus Turner and friend Mya Winters were proud founders of Elite Events, Incorporated in Chicago. The women were well-known for planning elaborate events that left lasting impressions with all who had the pleasure of attending.

"How do you know that's what I'm thinking? I could have been thinking anything." Cyd didn't like when people assumed they knew what was on her mind because usually they were wrong in their assumptions. But Shawn had correctly assessed her thoughts, and that didn't sit well with her.

Shawn pushed aside a coat that was partially blocking his view of Cyd. "That's true, but you weren't just thinking anything. And trust me, Cyd, I wanted to track you down the minute I found the information."

He was really starting to irritate her. He spoke to her as if they'd known each other forever instead of just being sex partners for one night. "Listen, you don't know me, Shawn Miles, or whatever your name is. So do us both a favor and stop acting like you do."

He leaned in closer, and she inhaled his enticing masculine scent. Being around him was a threat to her sanity, and her body was a ball of nerves. Her heart beat even faster as her eyes followed his hand that reached for her face. She couldn't help but lean into him a little more.

"I know you better than you think, Cydney Rayne or Jessica or *whatever your name is.* And I also noticed your hair. It's different than I remember. This color makes you look even sexier than you did the week we met."

His voice was so seductive that she squeezed her thighs tighter to try to ease the ache that was starting to develop. When she'd met Shawn, her hair had been light brown and styled in natural waves since she'd wanted a look suited for the island. Now her hair was jet-black and cut in soft layers that flowed around her shoulders. The dark color looked dramatic on her light butter-toffee complexion, and she'd definitely gotten a lot more attention since she'd dyed it.

Cyd slowly backed up into a corner of the closet, attempting to put some distance between them. Refusing to give her space, Shawn followed her into the corner and brushed a few fallen strands of hair out of her face with the back of his hand. The heat in the closet rose twenty degrees, and for the second time, she wished she hadn't chosen a closet as their hiding place. He leaned in, indicating that he was going to kiss her. She could feel it and even worse, she wanted it.

"What are you doing?" she asked, a little more breathless than she would have liked.

"If you have to ask, then I must be doing something wrong."

No, he was definitely doing everything right. But she was trying to stall the passionate explosion that she knew would come from his kiss. His six-foot-three-inch frame towered over her five-foot-nine-inch body. He'd successfully blocked her from any route of escape.

As his face grew closer to hers, she didn't have the willpower to stop him.

"I've been waiting to do this for eight months," he said as he dipped his head to hers. The moment their lips touched, she felt the burst of passion she'd been waiting for. Her tongue mated with his as she reacquainted herself with his savory taste. His hands went around her waist and straight to her backside as she wrapped her arms around his neck. When Shawn began to grind against her core, she lost all sense of reality. The fact that he had such a strong sexual hold on her was extremely unsettling.

When her back hit the closet wall, she lifted her right leg and was rewarded by his strong, masculine hand grasping her thigh to keep her in place. His hands were like fire as her body melted to his every caress. She was pretty sure she could come on the spot without him even trying. *That* was how badly she wanted Shawn.

"Cydney," Shawn said breathlessly in between kisses, "if we don't stop soon, I'm taking you right here, right now, no ifs, ands or buts about it. Like I said, I've waited eight months to do this, and after kissing you, all I want to do is fill myself with the sweet taste of you."

He pulled her even closer so she could feel his manhood press against the spot he wanted to bury himself inside. Cyd was so aroused, she could barely think.

She knew what she wanted, but she also knew that she shouldn't succumb to it. *Then again, when do I ever do what I should?* Being the bold person she was made the answer easy.

"Well, Shawn, if you think you can still handle me, by all means...*prove it.*"

She was thinking with the lower part of her body but this time she didn't care. She inched onto the tiptoes of her left foot and Shawn quickly lifted her so that both of her thighs were in his palms. A rush of anticipation shot through her body as she leaned against the wall while he pushed her dress high on her waist and tightened his grip even more.

Cyd assumed he'd just get down to business, but instead, Shawn leaned into her, licking from the base of her collarbone to the middle of her neck, leaving a trail of soft, wet kisses along the way. He methodically began grinding against her core while his hands gripped her butt, bringing her closer to the fit of him.

She wrapped her legs tighter around Shawn's waist as she gripped one of the closet poles to maintain her balance. When his lips found hers again, she was hungry and waiting. She could taste the remnants of wine on his lips, heightening her aroused state. She tried to think of any reason why she should stop Shawn from moving any further, but her mind was void of excuses. This man, her island lover with the cinnamon-colored skin and abs hard enough to bounce quarters off, was what all wet fantasies were made of. She couldn't deny herself the opportunity to make love to a man guaranteed to take her on a journey to ecstasy.

Cyd tore off his jacket and Shawn wasted no time tearing off his dress shirt and throwing it aside, as well.

His sexy arms flexed with each movement of their bodies and he never once let her feet touch the floor in his hastiness to remove his clothes.

Shawn reached in his back pocket and ripped open a condom packet. Cyd unzipped his pants and quickly put the condom in place, briefly massaging his member as she slid the condom over his shaft.

"I see you're prepared," Cyd murmured between kisses.

"Don't forget that I knew you would be here and I was hoping I'd get a chance to talk to you. I figured with you, I'd better be prepared for anything."

She wasn't sure if she liked the fact that he was prepared or offended that he thought there was a possibility they would have sex again.

"I guess if I think about the last time we were together, it makes sense that you were prepared."

Shawn stopped kissing her neck and gazed into her chestnut-brown eyes. She felt like she was under a microscope and her uneasiness increased when she couldn't make out his thoughts.

"I was hoping I'd be lucky enough to have another moment with you," Shawn said while rubbing his hands along her thighs. "I never forgot about the last time we were together, and I hung on to that hope that maybe you felt the same way about me and wanted to share another intimate moment. I didn't assume, but I damn sure hoped you did."

She melted at his reply. *Lord, help me.* The man had a way with words and she was being baited by his charm. Cyd always prided herself on knowing the difference between a man running game on her and a man genuinely expressing his feelings. Shawn was being genuine and the sincerity in his eyes was undeniable. But she couldn't get too wrapped up in the emotions she felt. This was only about sex. Instead of responding to his words, she adjusted herself and slowly guided his shaft into her core until he reached her hilt.

Shawn exhaled deeply and took over from there, gliding in and out of her wet center with ease. This was the moment she'd missed since their last encounter. This was the feeling she'd dreamed about, the sensations she knew only he could provide.

They'd been exchanging words since they'd stepped into the closet, but at this moment all words ceased. Shawn's eyes stared into Cyd's with an intensity she felt throughout her entire body. There was nothing sexier than a shirtless man sexing the hell out of a woman with his body and his eyes. All the coats and shirts hanging in the closet rocked back and forth to the movement of their hips.

Shawn never lost eye contact with her. There was never a man who wanted her this badly. The fact that he was so honest about his desire excited and scared her all at the same time. *Damn, what is it about this man?* Cyd had had good sex, but none of her past partners remotely compared to Shawn. Not even close.

Her orgasm was threatening to break free and Shawn increased his pace. She gripped his shoulders to maintain her balance as her body lifted more toward the ceiling with each powerful thrust into her core.

"Shawn," Cyd whispered. "We've been in this closet for a while and I know my family is wondering where I am. This time has to be a quickie."

She'd quickly realized her mistake in implying that they would have sex again in the future. The sly smile on his face proved that he'd caught her mishap and wouldn't let her forget about the implication.

"Who am I to disappoint," Shawn said, his eyes briefly lowering to admire the healthy amount of cleavage bursting through the top of her dress. There they were again, those slick words and that sexy look that had her insides twirling in a massive heap of desire.

"I want you to look me in the eyes as you come," Shawn whispered in her ear. Although she didn't want to, she obeyed his request and stared deeply into his sea-blue eyes. That was her undoing. The look in his eyes told her that even though this was a quickie, he was far from finished with her. In the time she'd shared with Shawn eight months ago, she'd realized he was a man who said what he meant and meant what he said. There was no doubt in her mind that they would have sex again, and she wouldn't even bother convincing herself otherwise.

"Cydney, it's time," Shawn said in a husky voice a little louder than before. Her faint moans were growing louder and on instinct, Shawn pinned her up on the wall even harder using only his thighs to hold her up while one hand gently covered her mouth. The movement brought him even deeper inside her and soon she mirrored his technique and covered his mouth to conceal his loud groans. Only using one hand for balance, Cyd bounced up and down as Shawn came completely out of her center only to bring her back down on him. He thrust harder twice more until they both released the passion they'd been holding inside. Cyd wanted to close her eyes as she became overcome with emotions she hadn't felt in months, but she kept her eyes open. She had no choice. Shawn was still staring at her, still

embedded deep in her core, warning her that this was
only the beginning. He had plans for her, or at least her
body. And with a man like him, she knew she had to
stand her ground or give in to temptation.

Chapter 2

Seductive moans swarmed around in Shawn's memory as he recalled every delicate feature of Cydney's curves. He should have been paying attention to the current topic of discussion at his weekly meeting, but he couldn't get his mind off her. For months, he'd dreamed about the unbelievable sex he'd had with his exotic lover, and this past weekend he'd sampled her sweetness again.

When he'd learned her identity a month ago, he'd wanted to contact her right away but he didn't think she'd respond well, since like him, she assumed they'd never see each other again.

I wonder what brought her to Anguilla eight months ago. He'd planned to ask her after they were formally introduced. But when he saw her, the only thing on his mind was getting her out of her dress. She'd looked even sexier than he remembered and he wasn't done with her yet. Far from it.

An undercover FBI assignment had led him to Chicago and he was definitely going to make the most of his time here after he solved the case. He'd need a good distraction after the upcoming months he faced, anyway. This case was one of the biggest of his career and for personal reasons, it was one of the most important.

"That's all for now, folks," said Chicago senior supervisory special agent Larry Wolfe as the meeting came to a close. "Shawn, can you follow me to my office?"

"Yes sir," Shawn said, putting his thoughts of Cydney on hold. When they arrived at the office, Shawn took a seat close to a window.

"Shawn, I wanted to talk to you about the assignment in a little more detail," Agent Wolfe said as he sat in a large desk chair opposite Shawn. "I'm sure I don't have to remind you how important this case is. The DEA and Chicago P.D. will be working closely with us. I know you've researched all the current employees for the Peter Vallant Company, but as acting chief information security officer, you need to be debriefed on all the new employees and volunteers for the company."

Agent Wolfe opened the top shelf of his file cabinet and pulled out a manila file folder. "I need you to go over everything in this file. As you know, Mr. Peter Vallant is the owner of the Peter Vallant Company, one of the top real estate firms in the nation. Mr. Vallant is throwing a series of customer appreciation events in Illinois and Indiana to thank all of the company's supporters and contributors who participated in their Rebuild Your Community program initiative. You'll be attending every event and Mr. Vallant is aware that you are undercover. He has agreed to assist you with any additional information you need while attending the events. I trust that your team is prepared."

"Yes, sir. My top four security guards are aware of

the situation and will provide extra sets of eyes during the tour for any suspicious activity. The rest of my security team will stay in Chicago and were told to be alert as they are with every security matter we handle." In addition to working with the FBI, Shawn had spent the past year building his own high-level security firm. He hadn't decided on a city to headquarter his company, but he had hired a top-notch security team of former members of the FBI, CIA, P.D. and U.S. military.

"Good. They leave on the appreciation tour later this week."

"I'll be ready," Shawn said as he stood from his seat.

"Oh, and, Shawn," Agent Wolfe called.

"Yes," Shawn said as he turned his head over his shoulder.

"Can you handle this?"

Shawn knew why he was asking and appreciated the concern. But there was no way he was giving up the opportunity to work on this case. He stood to lose too much and he knew that solving the case would bring him some closure. "Is there anything I can't handle?" he said sarcastically, demeaning the seriousness of the situation.

"Just making sure," Agent Wolfe said with a slight laugh.

Shawn then walked out of the office and into the busy hallway buzzing with agents and other personnel ready to start their Monday. Using his thumb to flip through the pages in the file, Shawn familiarized himself with a few new faces he hadn't originally researched as he shuffled around people walking past him.

When he was halfway through glancing at the

pages in the file, Shawn stopped short. "What are the odds," he said surprisingly as he studied the beautiful brown eyes of the woman who'd been sneaking into his thoughts way too frequently.

"Cydney Rayne, Elite Events, Incorporated. Lead planner for the appreciation series of events," Shawn said aloud as he read the headline on the page. "Damn." Yes, he was anxious to see her and continue what they'd started in the closet, but he didn't mix business with pleasure. When it came to his work, nothing and no one stood in his way, and he couldn't afford to compromise this case.

Shawn had a reputation as being one of the best undercover special agents in the bureau. A lot of agents were surprised to learn he ultimately wanted to leave the FBI and start his own company. But those who knew his story weren't surprised by his decision at all. For the past few years he'd tried to avoid coming back to Chicago, the second city he was assigned to when he joined the FBI. But a few months ago, he'd known he had to return and finish what he'd started. It was a miracle he even got on this case in the first place. Agent Wolfe was more than his supervisor. He was more like family. Shawn hadn't had the pleasure of knowing his biological parents and although he had great guardians, Agent Wolfe had been key in his development from boy to man. Agent Wolfe knew what Shawn stood to lose if he didn't solve the case, and since he cared about him, Agent Wolfe had appointed Shawn as the undercover agent despite the personal conflict. But Shawn wasn't too sure how Agent Wolfe would react if he knew about his relationship with Cydney.

"Miss Rayne, Miss Rayne. It seems I have a bigger

issue than I thought," Shawn said as he continued to stare intently at her picture. Since their relationship had been purely physical, he hadn't told her what he did for a living. He would have given her a fake job, anyway, but that would have further complicated the situation, so he was glad that he had kept his mouth shut. Cydney wouldn't like the fact that she would be working so closely with him, so she'd probably maintain her distance. At least that was what Shawn was hoping would be the case. He had a feeling that Cydney could be unpredictable at times and that could definitely pose a problem.

He looked from her eyes to her lips as he studied her picture one last time. For his sake, he hoped she would decide to keep her distance because if she didn't, he wasn't sure if he'd be able to resist her.

"Stay focused," he said to himself as he tried to reinforce his thoughts before leaving her page to finish scanning the rest of the documents in the file.

Cyd chanted Beyoncé's recent hit as she poured herself a cup of coffee and waited for her partners to arrive to the conference room. The song had been playing in her head all weekend and she was feeling good. Even better than good—she was feeling great. She wanted to ignore the fact that Shawn was the cause of her happiness, but she couldn't. The man had sexed her in a much needed way and she'd been on a high ever since.

After adding the perfect amount of cream and sugar to her coffee, she took a sip and savored the bitter yet sweet taste. She walked to a nearby window to enjoy the brilliant colors of the fall leaves, taking two more sips of the warm deliciousness. Each taste was better than the last.

"Hmm," she said aloud, not noticing that her partners had walked into the conference room. "Amazing."

"Okay," her sister Imani said, disrupting her enjoyable moment. "Who are you and what have you done with the real Cydney Rayne?"

"Very funny," Cyd replied. "I haven't been that bad."

Imani looked at Mya and Lex before turning her head back to Cyd. "You're joking, right? Do you even remember how you've been acting lately?"

"Well, let us remind you," Lex chimed in. "You've been tense over the past few months even though you've tried to hide it behind your usual sarcasm. To make matters worse, you missed the bridesmaids' group dance and the maid-of-honor toast on Imani's wedding day."

Whoops! Cyd had definitely forgotten about those last couple details. "Hey, I gave my maid-of-honor toast."

"Yeah, about thirty minutes late!" Mya replied. "And you disappeared for almost an hour. We couldn't find you anywhere."

"So true," Imani added. "Even though I refused to get upset on the most important day of my life, I honestly can't believe you pulled a stunt like that on my wedding day."

Cyd dropped her head backward and stared at the ceiling. She was slightly irritated that she was receiving the third degree, although part of her knew she deserved it. As she twisted her head to crack her neck, she immediately thought about Shawn placing soft kisses along her collarbone. She could still visualize every single moment of their sexual escapade in the closet.

"And you have the nerve to be smiling right now," Imani said, interrupting her thoughts. "Oh, man, you are so lucky that I leave for my honeymoon in a few days because I could strangle you! But I refuse to get arrested and miss my vacation with my new husband!"

"Sorry," Cyd said as she sat down at the conference table and thought about how her sister must feel. "If it's any consolation, I have a very good explanation."

All three women joined her at the table as they waited intently for her to finish.

"We're listening," Imani said impatiently when Cyd didn't jump right in with excuses. Cyd had planned on telling them about Shawn, but she was hoping they would be a little less tense if she waited until Monday. Times like this made working with her sister, cousin and friend really complicated. They were a large part of one another's lives and were also founders of a very successful business. Although she loved them dearly, sometimes she wished she could have a day or two to relax and take a step back from the family and business chaos. Luckily, a series of upcoming events would help her do just that.

Taking a deep breath, Cyd put on her big-girl pants and prepared to explain what happened.

"Do you guys remember meeting Shawn at the wedding?"

"Daman's friend?" Imani asked.

"Yes," Cyd replied as she watched each of her partner's eyes open wide with interest. "Well, something happened between us during the wedding."

"And what exactly might that be?" Mya inquired.

Cyd scrunched her nose as she thought about the right way to tell them. Slightly closing her eyes, she chose to be blunt about it. "We sneaked off to the grand walk-in closet in the foyer...and had sex." There, she'd said it.

As she fully opened her eyes, she laughed when she noticed all three women had their mouths hanging open.

Imani was the first to speak. "You mean to tell me that while I was wondering why on earth my sister and maid of honor had missed our group dance and the time for her speech, you were getting freaky in a closet?"

"Um...yes," Cyd said a little unknowingly, since she couldn't tell if her sister's high-pitched squeal and the fact that she was now standing was a good or bad thing.

Imani's face went from surprise to excitement in a matter of seconds. "Well, judging how fine Shawn is, I'd say you did well, little sis."

Cyd threw her head back and laughed. She should have known her sister would react that way.

"I shouldn't even have to ask based off that look you had a few minutes ago, but was the sex good?"

Cyd gripped her Starbucks mug a little tighter and took another sip of her coffee. "It was way better than good. Y'all saw how the man looked that day. I could barely control myself when we were introduced." No need to disclose the fact that it had actually been their second time meeting each other. She'd keep that bit of information to herself.

"He had to be good," Lex interjected. "I never remember you actually giving a man credit for being better than good in the bedroom."

"Or admit to not being able to control yourself," Imani added. "So I'm guessing he had a lot of qualities off your list?"

Instead of answering Imani's question, Cyd's mind

drifted back to the night she was with Shawn in Anguilla. She had spent a week with Imani, Lex and Mya
in Barbados before meeting her college girlfriends in
Anguilla. Lex and Mya had been on a quest to find sexy
islanders in Barbados and had succeeded. But nothing
could have prepared her for the likes of Shawn Miles
when she landed in Anguilla. As shallow as it sounded,
Cyd always knew the men she entertained weren't up to
her standard. The men who she believed were a great
match were often too nervous to approach her, further
proving her point that he wasn't "Mr. Right" in the first
place. So she settled for a bunch of "Mr. Right Nows,"
waiting for a man who would sweep her off her feet.

Imani cleared her throat, zapping Cyd back to reality. "No," Cyd slightly lied. "He doesn't have a lot of
qualities on my love list, but he does have almost every
quality off my lust list."

"Maybe you should create a 'you're full of it' list,"
Mya said with a laugh, her comment receiving snickers
from Imani and Lex, as well. Cyd knew they thought
her lists were stupid, but she didn't care. In her mind,
her lists were a necessity.

"Don't we have business to discuss?" Cyd said, directing her question to Imani since it was her turn to
lead the meeting. Imani gave her a look insinuating
that she wanted to say something else, but luckily she
dropped it.

"Okay, since Cyd will have her hands tied with the
series of appreciation events for the Peter Vallant Company, we will need to make sure we plan efficiently and
not overbook ourselves."

"Agreed," Mya said. "Let's make sure that we remind our assistants to constantly check our calendars."

"How much traveling is required?" Lex asked Cyd.

"Since the events are all in Illinois or Indiana, I will be living in and out of a hotel for the next month or so, but I don't mind. I'll find out more when I meet with Mr. Vallant in a couple days." Cyd loved to travel, and although small towns in the Midwest weren't exactly her idea of a good time, she'd enjoy herself nonetheless.

"Great. How about we go around the table and give an update on what we're working on," Imani suggested. "I'll go first."

Chapter 3

"Oh, my goodness, please let the weather stay this warm," Cyd said to the sky as she walked down the busy streets of Chicago's West Loop wearing her favorite designer sunglasses. The sunny October weather was unlike any she'd ever experienced in Chicago and she was enjoying every minute of it.

This afternoon she was meeting with Mr. Vallant to get the final details on the appreciation event tour for the Rebuild Your Community initiative. Elite Events, Incorporated was extremely honored to plan the events and Cyd was very proud of the agenda she'd created for each occasion on the tour.

She dodged through walkers, making sure she didn't roll over anyone's feet with her suitcase. "On your left," yelled a biker who was forced to use the sidewalks due to heavy traffic and street construction. Since the weather was so nice, Chicago construction was at its highest after the city decided to restructure several major streets in Chicago's West and South Loops. Cyd was glad she'd worn her most comfortable black high-waist skirt and heels. She'd completed her outfit with a teal blouse and complementing accessories.

Reaching her destination, she promptly signed the visitor logbook and waited in the tastefully decorated lobby for Mr. Vallant's assistant.

"Ms. Rayne?" said a woman with a questioning, raspy voice.

"Yes, I'm Cydney Rayne," Cyd replied as she shook hands with the woman. The woman didn't say anything at first, but observed her so intently, Cyd felt as if she were under a microscope.

"My name is Verona Neely and I'm Mr. Vallant's assistant," she said, her awkward demeanor growing perky in a matter of seconds. "Mr. Vallant invited a few other individuals to the meeting and he apologizes for not telling you about this change sooner. Please follow me to the conference room."

"Thank you, Ms. Neely."

When they arrived at the conference room with tall, floor-to-ceiling windows overlooking Lake Michigan, seven people were already seated at a large table. Cyd placed her belongings on a counter off to the side of the room.

"Ms. Rayne," said Mr. Vallant as he stood to shake her hand. "Allow me to introduce you to a few members of my executive team. We have Kim Lathers, chief marketing officer. Jim Pearson, senior vice president of business development. Jacob Early, chief financial officer. Brittany Higgins, senior vice president of client services. Tom Mendez, senior vice president of communications and Paul Jensen, general counsel. Everyone, this is Cydney Rayne from Elite Events, Incorporated."

Cyd made her way around the table as she shook

hands with each member before taking a seat in one of two vacancies. "Nice to meet you all."

"Throughout the next month members of the executive team will be present at a few of the appreciation events. I felt it best that we all attend this meeting to ensure that everyone understands the schedule. Team, I trust that you will make Ms. Rayne feel welcome during the tour."

Everyone nodded their heads in agreement and exchanged a few warm words. Adjusting herself in her seat, she tried to place the reason behind her suddenly quickened heartbeat. Her heart only beat this fast when she was nervous, but she usually never got nervous on the job. She momentarily stopped observing her behavior when she heard the conference door open. *No way.... No freaking way.* Now it all made sense. There was one new development in her life that seemed to be wreaking havoc on her nerves since the day she'd laid eyes on him.

"Ms. Rayne. This is the newest member of our team, Shawn Miles, chief information security officer," Mr. Vallant said, rising once again from his chair to make the introduction. "Shawn, please meet Cydney Rayne from Elite Events, Incorporated."

"Nice to meet you, Ms. Rayne," Shawn said with ease, once again giving himself away and proving that he wasn't surprised to see her at all. *Of course Shawn works for the Peter Vallant Company,* she thought sarcastically. What was it with this man! How did he manage to pop up in her life not once, not twice, but three times!

"Nice to meet you, too, Mr. Miles," Cyd replied, accepting his handshake and ignoring the electric surge that shot through her arm. He looked great in his navy blue suit, but she refused to give him a compliment. He never told her what he did for a living, but he'd admitted to researching her online. She guessed it was partially her fault for not researching him online, too. She'd much preferred to keep him a mystery, but had she just searched his name on the internet, she could have saved herself some embarrassment.

She was so sick and tired of Shawn getting the upper hand. Even if he was new to the company, he'd probably been told that she would be the lead planner for the appreciation tour. Cyd nervously glanced around the table before her eyes settled back on Shawn. She wished he'd wipe that smirk off his face. Better yet, she wished she could punch it off him. But Cyd had way more class than that.

"Let's all take a seat," Mr. Vallant said as he returned to his chair. As Cyd sat back down, she twisted in her seat so that her back was slightly to Shawn, directing her full attention to Mr. Vallant at the head of the table.

"I'll begin our discussion with the rotation schedule for the events. As lead event planner, Ms. Rayne will be attending every event. Here is the schedule for the rest of the events," Mr. Vallant said as he directed his attention at the material that had been placed in front of each attendee's seat.

Cyd didn't hear Mr. Vallant announce that as CISO, Shawn would also be present at every event, though a quick scan of the document made that fact evident, anyway. The hairs on the back of her neck stood on high awareness as Shawn leaned forward to pick up something he'd dropped on the floor. She sighed a little deeper than necessary as she gripped the mahogany table while uncrossing her legs just to cross them back again.

There it was again. The butterflies she couldn't stop from swarming in the pit of her stomach. Yet she managed to answer every question that was directed at her during the course of the meeting. Though she wasn't sure how she answered anything at all, given all her attention was secretly fixed on the man to the right.

She glanced at the clock on the wall and prayed that the already forty-minutes-long meeting would conclude in the next twenty minutes. She looked through a folder that Mr. Vallant had handed her a few minutes prior to see the list of hotels she would be staying at during the appreciation tour. Over the next month, there would be four stops. Cyd lived in downtown Chicago, but tonight she would be staying at the JW Marriott, host hotel for the Peter Vallant reception for the employees to thank them for all their hard work. On Friday, they left for their first stop, Springfield, Illinois.

At the sound of Shawn's voice, Cyd turned her head to listen to what he was saying, as did everyone at the table. She wanted to comprehend his words, but she couldn't. His lips looked too sexy today. He stuck his tongue in and out between sentences to moisten his lips, glancing at her after every lick. *I'll definitely be changing my panties after this meeting,* she thought. She was a visual person and right now the only thing she could visualize was seductively bouncing on top of him and riding him like the bull she'd ridden at her sister's bachelorette party.

"Is that okay with you, Ms. Rayne?" asked Mr. Vallant. *Crap, she'd missed the question.* "Yes, that's fine with me," she replied, hoping that her answer would suffice.

"Great. Ladies and gentlemen, that concludes our meeting. I'll see you all tonight at the reception."

Cyd quickly grabbed her belongings, politely smiling to the others as she tried to leave the room so she could seek refuge in the privacy of her hotel room, but Shawn had other plans.

"Are you ready?" Shawn asked, gently catching her arm before she dipped out into the hallway.

"For what?" she asked, trying not to notice his blatant appraisal of her outfit. He smelled of men's soap and aftershave that complemented his natural masculine scent. The fact that she could also detect that he was wearing a brand of Kenneth Cole's cologne to match the scent of aftershave both aggravated and aroused her at the same time. She'd never noticed those things about a man before, yet with Shawn she noticed every little detail. She nervously played with her hair, awaiting his response.

After one more look at her outfit, he finally decided to answer. "You agreed to let me take you on a tour of the building."

"No, I didn't."

"Yes, you did," he said, standing a little closer than before. "And you also agreed to let me escort you to your hotel to ensure that everything is well with your accommodations."

Cyd took a step back from him. "No. I. Didn't," she said a little slower than before. That was probably what Mr. Vallant meant when he'd asked her if she was okay with something. She just hadn't known what that something was until now.

"Look, Mr. Miles, I——" Cyd stopped talking when Shawn let out a hearty laugh.

"Mr. Miles? Seriously? After everything we've done, you want to be formal with me? Tell you what. How about you call me Mr. Miles when we're around everyone else. But when we're alone," he said, stepping back into her personal space, "I want you to call me Shawn just like I plan to call you Cydney."

Was that a request or an order? Cleary Shawn didn't know what type of woman she was. Cyd did *not* take orders from any man. "Listen, Mr. Miles. Had I known you worked for the Peter Vallant Company, I would have never…" Her words trailed off when he leaned in toward her ear.

"There is no way you wouldn't have been intimate with me, so save yourself the trouble and don't deny something you know was bound to happen, anyway."

Talk about cocky! He really thought he had her eating out of the palm of his hand. Although she was the first to admit that part was true, the fact that he wouldn't let her finish her statements was nerve racking.

"Tell you what," Cyd said, crossing her arms over her chest, not caring that his eyes followed her movement. "How about you be the good golden boy and tell Mr. Vallant that you showed me around the building and made sure my room was okay. In the meantime, I will head to my hotel *without you* and I'll make sure I have Mr. Vallant's assistant give me a tour some other time." With that she walked away, got on the elevator and hightailed it out of the Peter Vallant Company.

Only when she had paid the cab driver, checked into her hotel and settled into the confines of her luxury room did she absorb the situation. "For the next month or so I have to work with Shawn Miles," she said aloud.

A quick call to her sister in her cab ride to the hotel had eliminated the notion that Daman and her partners had known that Shawn worked for the Peter Vallant Company. Too bad Imani was laughing so hard that Cyd didn't have the chance to vent to her.

"Truly comical." She would be laughing at her situation, too, if she wasn't too busy freaking out. Cyd walked over to the floor-length mirror positioned on the wall to give herself a pep talk. "You can do this!" she chanted a couple times, taking deep breaths in between chants. "You're damn good at your job and you can definitely handle a man like Shawn Miles!"

But could she really? Could she handle a man who brought her to her knees with just one look? It may sound conceited but she didn't lust after men—men lusted after her! Yet somehow, Shawn had managed to make her crave his touch…and his touch only.

She cracked her neck as she placed her arms on each side of the mirror. "What I need to do is take control of the situation," she said, getting closer to her reflection.

"Why can't I enjoy Shawn while I'm on the tour? Participate in a little sweet seduction in between planning?" She was an adult after all, one who could enjoy sex with Shawn if she wanted to. Cyd always did as she pleased, but she was beginning to realize that there were some things she should have thought about before taking action. This definitely wasn't one of those times.

She sprinted to her suitcase and pulled out one of her grandmother's old diaries. When Faith "Gamine" Burrstone had passed away years ago, Cyd had been devastated. Her mother, Hope Burrstone-Rayne, could barely function after the loss. The entire family was shocked by Gamine's death, but luckily, Imani had stepped in and helped the family through the tragic time. While the death had affected Imani in ways she'd never admit, Cyd admired the strength that her sister had. The Burrstone clan was a loving, yet overwhelming, bunch at times. There were many reasons why Cyd was glad that her sister had found a man like Daman, the main reason being the fact that he helped Imani realize that she wasn't responsible for everyone's life.

Although they were sisters, she never did have the type of responsibility to the family that Imani did. But that didn't make things any less complicated for Cyd. Her role in the family was always a little more rebellious. She was the go-getter and adventure seeker. The one you ran to if you didn't need someone to bail you out of jail, but rather needed someone to sit in the jail cell beside you. Cyd had long ago decided to dance to the beat of her own drum rather than follow directions or fulfill obligations. As her mother affectionately told her, Cyd's antics oftentimes brought her parents to the brink of heart attacks. She had it all, brains and beauty. Class valedictorian, prom queen, and she was voted in high school most likely to run the world one day. She had a big heart and wasn't at all selfish, but she also didn't really care what people thought about her decisions. Men sometimes feared her confidence, falling into the friend category and staying there. And with each and every romantic downfall, she told each man the same thing: "I'm not the relationship type. I enjoy being single and free entirely too much to spend my days engrossed in a man. Trust me, you don't want to go there. But we can still be friends." To this day, her

friends and family didn't understand how she convinced
so many guys to actually agree to be friends with her.
"What can I say… I have a gift," she'd often respond.
But having that gift made the fact that she secretly
longed for a storybook romance so out of character.

Lying on the bed, she propped herself up on her elbows and began flipping through pages of the diary. Gamine had left her a few things in her will, but the most
important had been her diary collection. As soon as Cyd
had dived into the pages, she became engrossed in the
life of a woman she realized she hadn't really known.
She knew Gamine the mother and grandmother, Gamine the community activist, Gamine the best friend
to all who graced her presence. She even knew Gamine
the romantic since her relationship with her grandfather,
Edward Burrstone, had been one that everyone in the
family had admired. What she hadn't expected to find
in the diaries was a woman who understood her more
than she thought. A woman who used to be just like
Cyd when she was her age and a woman who'd dared
to dream big and live on the edge.

Cyd's fingers graced the page of her favorite entry,
written during a time in Gamine's life when she had
first discovered true love. Cyd was never much of a
reader, but she'd read Gamine's diaries so much that
every crème page was curled at the corners and tea
stains were evident on more than a few places.

"So romantic," she said aloud as she reread one of
her favorite lines. She wanted to find her Mr. Right,
which was the reasoning behind her creating her love-
versus-lust lists. Gamine's diaries had opened up a side
of Cyd that she'd often kept concealed…even from herself. Hidden in the pages of Gamine's deepest thoughts

were feelings Cyd longed to experience. An escape into a world that showed her, although she was one of a kind, many women shared her thoughts and feelings of finding the perfect man. It may not fit the persona that people were used to when they thought of the infamous Cydney Rayne. But it was how she felt, nonetheless.

She turned on her back and closed the diary, holding it close to her chest. Once again, the pages had given her the answer she desired. Shawn may have more "I don't" traits from her list than "I do," but a girl had a right to have fun. Who knew what things she could learn about herself through a man like that. Even though he'd caught her off guard and put her in her place a couple times, she liked that he was aggressive and not afraid to take her head-on.

Cyd got off the bed and put the diary back in her bag before heading to the shower. "Shawn Miles, wait till you meet the likes of Cydney Rayne." And she was certain he wouldn't know what hit him.

Chapter 4

At thirty-two, Shawn had finally met his match. He'd finally met a woman he couldn't get out of his mind, although part of him refused to admit it.

There were over three hundred employees and friends present at the Peter Vallant Company appreciation tour kick-off reception but Cydney Rayne was not yet amongst the crowd. Shawn tried to will his head away from the ballroom entrance as he checked for her in a pool of new attendees who entered. Still no Cydney. He barely registered all the women openly checking him out as he greeted employees he'd recently met.

Shawn usually had no problem bedding one woman after another, but after he'd met Cydney eight months ago, he hadn't felt compelled to have sex with any other woman. And he'd received plenty of offers. *Cydney.* He'd thought about calling her by her nickname, Cyd, but Cydney rolled off his tongue with such ease that he had to use her full first name. Plus, from the brief moments he'd gotten to observe her with her family at the wedding, he noticed that everyone affectionately called her Cyd and she played into the darling role. But when he was with her, he didn't see anything darling about her. She was a unique treasure. But his definition of treasure definitely meant in the bedroom. When he was around her all he saw was fiery passion, pure lust…all woman.

You should stay away from her, he reminded himself. He shouldn't even flirt with her. *But since when did it hurt to do a little flirting?* The voices in his head were not cooperating with one another and he could only assume it was a matter of time before the lower half of his body started siding with the less logical part of his brain. Shawn made his way across the room to Mr. Vallant, who was conversing with a few executives.

"Hello, Shawn," Mr. Vallant said as Shawn approached the group.

"Hello, ladies and gentlemen," he greeted. Curt nods from the men and polite smiles from the women were exchanged. Within two minutes he stopped a nearby waiter to ask for tequila on the rocks. He needed a shot of something to get through this night, anything to help him deal with uneventful conversations amongst an uptight executive team who had nothing better to do than kiss Mr. Vallant's butt. He didn't know why the men looked so tense. He didn't want any of the women in the group. There was only one woman on his mind. Only one woman he wanted to devour…whole, if he could. A woman with a sexy smile, succulent lips and a behind that fit so perfectly in the palms of his hands you'd think her butt was created just for him.

"You okay?" asked Paul Jensen.

Deciding to forget about Cydney, he focused his attention back to the group in front of him. "I'm fine. Just wondering what's the score of the football game."

"Bears are winning for now," responded Brittany Higgins, taking a sip of her drink while gaping at Shawn over her glass. When she fully lifted her head, her eyes told it all. He could sense that she'd wanted him from their initial meeting, and now had no qualms about making that fact obvious.

I really don't need this right now. After all, he was here to do a job, and if the FBI's suspicions were right, a man who worked for the Peter Vallant Company, more than likely an executive team member, played a significant role in the case. The team had been trying to demolish a huge drug operation for years and had recently tracked a van that was dropping off boxes of cocaine. The van traced back to the Peter Vallant Company and a lead informed them that someone who had higher ranking in the company was a key element in the operation. Peter Vallant, longtime friend of Shawn's boss, Agent Larry Wolfe, had agreed to help find the culprit, but Shawn knew he and his team had to pay attention to details. He needed to do more than just catch the person responsible. He needed to uncover the entire operation.

Shawn had always been great at socializing and after analyzing the group and providing a few key comments, the group was warming up to him.

"Here you are, sir," said the white-gloved waiter as he delivered his tequila on a silver platter.

"Thank you," Shawn said, taking the glass and sipping the strong drink. The cool liquor slid down his throat and the hairs on the back of his neck stood on alert. Shawn looked at the glass, surprised by the sudden kick he felt after only one sip. He quickly took another, this time feeling a kick in the lower part of his body. He shuffled his feet, his pants suddenly feeling too tight around his groin. *Maybe I shouldn't have had tequila after all.* He was seconds away from disposing of the drink when he heard the voice of seduction.

"Good evening," Cydney said as she sashayed her way to the group. He should have known she had entered the room. His body never reacted that way to a few sips of his favorite drink. *Why did she have to dress so sexy?* Her deep magenta dress clung to her curves while her jet-black hair was pinned back on one side and played over her shoulders. She didn't need much makeup but the slight makeup she had worn looked flawless on her smooth, buttery complexion and accentuated her natural beauty.

She found a place in the group standing right across from him with a glass of wine in her hand. *Why did she do that?* Why had she chosen to stand right across from him? He now had nothing better to do than imagine her sprawled across his bed, waiting to be enraptured by his body. Who told her to come down in a dress so tantalizing he swore he could see every crevice of her body?

But he wasn't the only one who'd noticed Cydney. The other men in the circle were on full alert, cracking imprudent jokes that caused her to giggle in delight. And Jim Pearson was the worst. Everything he told her made her slightly throw her head back in laughter and place her arm on his shoulder. But make no mistake, Shawn saw her glance at him every time she opened her sweet pink lips to let the cool wine enter her mouth. He watched her tongue slip in and out as if savoring the flavor before taking another sip, her long eyelashes fluttering with each taste. She was baiting him. He knew it. An unfortunately, the lower part of his body knew it, too.

Down boy, he inwardly cautioned to his piece, knowing he could spring out at any second if he continued to watch Cydney drink her wine. She wasn't going to make his undercover job easy, and now that he knew what he was dealing with, he would spend the night regrouping and reminding himself how important this case was. But right now, he needed to escape from the ballroom and away from temptation.

"Excuse me for a moment," he said to the group as he walked toward the exit and glanced over at Micah Madden, his lead security officer, to signal that he was leaving the premises.

Once Shawn was in the hallway, he unbuttoned his suit jacket and breathed in a sigh of relief. He quickly walked down the hall and found a conference room. He tried the handle and was relieved to find the door open. He kept the lights off and escaped to a nearby window overlooking the nicely lit city. Shawn loved nighttime and he appreciated the solace of the unoccupied room with the only sounds coming from nearby traffic and trains. Dropping his head and closing his eyes, he placed his hands on each side of the counter, taking a moment to calm his body. Cydney had him on edge. Wasn't it less than a week ago that he'd had her pinned to the wall of a walk-in closet?

"Reminiscing about great sex is not helping," Shawn said aloud to himself just as he heard the conference door creak open.

He stepped back from the window and placed his hand in the back of his pants, clutching a small pistol he always kept on him. As the intruder peeked their head through the crack, he quickly released his hold.

"Shawn, are you in here?" Cydney's sugary voice filled the empty room. She couldn't see him in the dark corner, but he could see her from the light in the hallway. For a few seconds, he thought about remaining quiet so she could leave, but decided to make his presence known.

"Yes, I'm here," he said, stepping back toward the window so the moonlight could shine on his face. As soon as Cydney entered the room and shut the door, Shawn knew he was in trouble. Even in the darkness he felt her get closer to him with each step she took. When she finally reached him, she stood there in observation, the moonlight caressing every part of her face.

"Why'd you leave?" she asked, her beauty catching him off guard even though he'd just seen her. Up close, he noticed all the little details about her that he hadn't noticed in the ballroom. Right then and there, Shawn knew hands down she was the most attractive woman he'd ever seen.

"Shawn? Why did you leave?" she asked again after several moments of silence. Shawn crossed his arms over his chest and raised his eyebrows at her question. There was no way she hadn't known why he left the ballroom.

"Really, Cydney," he finally replied. "By the way you were sipping that wine, you'd think you were purposely trying to seduce me."

She fringed a look of innocence as she shrugged her shoulders. "I don't know what you mean, Mr. Miles."

Unlike the terse way she'd said his name earlier that day, this time she said it in an alluring way that solidified his worries. *I should have kept silent,* he thought, referring to moments earlier when she'd asked if he was in the room. She took a step closer to him, her bold chestnut-brown eyes trapping his sea-blue ones in her sole captivity.

"Although I was surprised to see you in the meeting this morning, I must say that I do believe this is another sign," she said, playing with the collar of his suit jacket. Shawn kept his arms crossed for fear that if he uncrossed them, he'd have no choice but to kiss her senseless.

"I was surprised to see you, as well," he lied, hoping she believed him. She squinted her eyes together in disbelief before tilting her head to the side with a soft sigh. Then she looked up at him and smiled that smile he was becoming all too familiar with. "What is this a sign of?" Shawn asked, although he had a pretty good idea.

Cydney moistened her lips with her tongue before dragging his head closer to her mouth. He expected her to whisper something seductive or naughty in his ear. Instead, she gave his earlobe a quick lick before moving to his neck. He was pretty sure he had done this move on her a couple times already, but she was reversing the roles. Her sensual fragrance was mingling with her natural scent of arousal, further enticing his senses. The erotic aroma smelled like a combination of seductive slices of citrusy fruits and sweet wildflower honey. He couldn't help but uncross his arms and pull her closer to him. His hands ventured to her bottom and he palmed her cheeks as her mouth went to work on his neck. Her kisses were soft, light and wet. Her body was hot in his hands, proof that she was just as aroused as he was.

She stopped kissing his neck and gazed into his eyes. Her hands moved from their grip of his head and made their way to his chest, lingering on his dress shirt. "Another sign that our affair that should have been for one night only may not be so brief after all," she finally answered, lightly biting her bottom lip. She leaned closer to his face again, her breath fanning his lips. She didn't kiss him, though. Instead, she kept her face close to his and placed his right hand over her heart. The fast beats only stimulated him more and he was sure she could feel him jumping in his pants on full alert. But she didn't budge. And when she blinked, she did so slow and inviting.

"I'm going to head back to the party now," she said, gently pushing up from his chest while dropping her hands to her side. He didn't let her go right away as his left hand still palmed one of her back cheeks. Seconds later, Shawn let her escape his grasp. They stood there for one more moment, neither saying anything but letting their body language speak for itself. Then Cydney turned and exited the conference room door, briefly looking toward the dark corner Shawn was still standing in.

An hour later Shawn got to his hotel room and quickly discarded his tie and suit jacket. Pulling his dress shirt out of his pants, he plopped down on the bed and dragged his long fingers across his face. He suddenly felt sorry for any male who underestimated the determination of an irresistible woman. Cydney was a siren, a seductress with the grace of a cat, fortitude of a lion and craft of a fox. Blended together, those qualities equaled temptation at its finest. They were leaving for Springfield in a couple days, so Shawn had to focus on his duties and not stray from his goal. Fortunately, the case was so personal to him, he wasn't sure he even had a choice. Shawn knew all he had to do was remember that fateful day years ago and suddenly everything fell into perspective. It would take all of his willpower to treat Cydney like he treated the other Peter Vallant employees, but it was something he had to do. He would prevail in this case and finally close a chapter in his life whether his body agreed with him or not.

Chapter 5

"Ms. Rayne, here are the tablecloths you were looking for. And I also have the name tag you requested."

"Thank you, Verona," Cydney said to Mr. Vallant's
assistant as she took the tablecloths out of her hands
and clipped the name tag to her shirt. The first day of
the two-day golf tournament in Springfield, Illinois,
was going just as planned. The Springfield supporters
of the Rebuild Your Community initiative were really
impressed by the classiness of the event. Although Cyd
had been receiving plenty of praise from the Peter Vallant employees present, she owed a huge thanks to the
golf club and community volunteers who had helped
make the tournament possible.

Even with the hustle and bustle of supporters, volunteers and staff, Cyd couldn't help but notice Shawn's
every move. He was standing right outside one of the
large enclosed tents, so focused, intently observing the
entire tournament. Yes, he was the CISO, but something
about him seemed a lot more serious than he had been
when they first met in Anguilla. Maybe it was because
he was vacationing then, whereas now he was on duty.

Ever since the night of the reception, he'd avoided her like the plague. *Looks like playboy is playing hard to get.* But why now? Why the sudden desire to give her the cold shoulder? She had to admit that she did enjoy playing a good game every now and then, but could he really ignore her after the moments they'd shared?

One of the volunteers suddenly tapped her on her shoulder, interrupting her scrutiny of Shawn. In addition to the tournament, the golf club had been kind enough to let them use the land usually designated for weddings for their activity. Cyd hastily put out a few more fires and turned her attention back to Shawn. But he had vacated the spot he'd been standing at moments before.

"Hello, Ms. Rayne," greeted Jim Pearson just as Cyd was about to venture outside the tent.

"Hello, Mr. Pearson. How are you today?"

"I'm doing great. And please call me Jim."

"Okay, Jim it is. You can call me Cydney if you'd like."

"I'd like that very much," Jim said, the look of flirtation marked in his eyes. "Might I add that you've done an excellent job with the tournament."

Cyd could tell he was interested in her. He'd sought her out several times during the kick-off reception. She could admit that he was really attractive. His blond hair and blue eyes were enough to make any woman swoon, but he just didn't do it for her. He didn't give her the butterflies that Shawn gave her. But since Shawn was ignoring her and Jim wasn't, she had no problem entertaining Jim's flirtation.

"Why, thank you, Jim. This tournament is just the start of many events to come for the appreciation tour."

He was watching her lips as she spoke and Cyd wished she felt even a little stimulation from the look, but she felt nothing.

"Cydney, I was hoping that you could go out to dinner with me tonight. I heard about this great seafood restaurant in the area. Would you be interested?"

Her first thought was that he didn't say her full first name as sexily as Shawn did. Her second thought was that she was going to turn him down gently and let him know she wasn't interested. But before she could say any of that, Shawn walked back into the tent and leaned on the edge of a table a few feet away from them. He didn't look too happy with her, or maybe he wasn't happy with the situation. Regardless, his presence changed the direction Cyd was originally going with her conversation with Jim.

"That sounds great, Jim! How about we meet in the lobby of the hotel 'round 6:30 p.m.?"

Jim's eyes lit up with excitement. "Sounds like a plan," he said, gently reaching out to touch her cheek. Cyd didn't like the gesture and on reflex, she sidestepped away from his touch. Unfortunately, it seemed to amuse him more than turn him off. When she glanced over at Shawn, his jaw was tight as if he was clenching his teeth. He'd crossed his arms over his chest and was glaring at her with obvious disapproval. *Serves him right for ignoring me.*

Turning her attention back to Jim, she gave him a polite smile before she told him that she had to check with the caterer before she continued setting up a few tables for lunch. When she walked out of the tent, she breathed in the fresh air and smiled to herself. "Doesn't feel too good to be ignored now, does it, Mr. Miles?"

she whispered to herself. "Ahh," Cyd said with a gasp when she felt a hand tighten on her arm before she was pulled behind the main golf club building away from the crowd.

"That's what you think I'm doing?" Shawn said as soon as they were alone. "Ignoring you?"

"What's with the tight tree grip, Tarzan?" Cyd said sarcastically as she yanked her arm out of his hold. "Don't you know it isn't nice to sneak up on people when they aren't paying attention?"

Shawn crossed his arms over his chest again. Didn't the man know how sexy he looked when he did that?

"Don't you know it isn't nice to gossip about people behind their backs?"

"I wasn't gossiping about you behind your back," Cyd said, taking a step back from his imperial stance. "Gossiping would imply that I was talking about you to someone else. Quite the contrary, Shawn, I was talking to myself." How dare he pull her behind the building like she was a child being scolded? "What are you really upset about? The fact that you overheard something you weren't supposed to hear or the fact that I was flirting with Jim Pearson?"

His jaw twitched at the mention of Jim's name. Cyd definitely wasn't romantically interested in Jim, but Shawn didn't have to know that. After he'd ignored her for the past few days, a little payback wouldn't hurt.

Shawn shuffled from one foot to the other, his eyes burning a hole through her. "Why don't you stop this whole…thing that you're doing," Cyd said, flaring her arms around his stance, referring to the way he was trying to intimidate her. She mimicked his posture by crossing her arms over her chest, as well.

"Is there something else you wanted with me?" The gleam in his eyes proved that he'd caught her double meaning and he let out a slight laugh.

"Woman, you are unbelievable," he said aloud, giving her another laugh. "I want a lot of things from you." He took another step closer to her and uncrossed his arms, placing one hand in his pocket while the other tilted the bottom of her chin toward his face and stayed there. "I have a job to do, just like you do. You can flirt with whomever you want to, but when you're finished entertaining Mr. All-American Boy, I'm sure you'll be seeking me out."

Cocky, cocky, cocky... Why the hell did he have to make cocky look so damn sexy! Cyd uncrossed her arms, lightly smacked his hand away from her chin and placed her hands on her hips. Evidently, Shawn was used to playing this hot-and-cold game with women. But she hadn't forgotten all the things he'd said to her at the wedding. He could pretend like he was unfazed, but they both knew better.

"Who do you think you're kidding? Quit acting like you aren't jealous of Jim. I saw you staring at him like you were ready to come over and pounce him to the ground." She adjusted her blouse and bra, knowing he would look at her breasts bounce into place after the adjustment. Just as she hoped, he took the bait. "I'm going out with Jim tonight, and who knows, he may just be the type of man I've been looking for."

Shawn let out a hearty laugh. "I doubt it." She didn't miss the flash of jealousy cross his face. As he turned and walked back to the crowd of attendees, Cyd rounded the corner and admired his powerful walk as he retreated back to the standing position he'd had earlier.

He looked too good in his casual black slacks and blue polo. Cyd sighed to herself as she thought about her date with Jim. She'd pick fighting with Shawn over flirting with Jim any day.

When Cyd and Jim arrived at the restaurant, Cyd was already dying to get back to the hotel. She couldn't stand a man who only talked about himself and his accomplishments and didn't give anyone else an opportunity to get a word into the conversation. Within the first two minutes of their being in the cab, she was bored out of her mind. Then they arrived to the restaurant and had a ten-minute wait, which usually wouldn't have bothered her. But since she had to sit there and listen to Jim talk about the time he thought he wanted to be a restaurant owner, those ten minutes felt like an hour. Now she had ordered her favorite seafood dish and was at this beautiful restaurant forcing herself to be entertained and failing miserably. Not that Jim even noticed her boredom. He was too busy talking about his days growing up in Omaha, Nebraska.

"Are you enjoying your dinner?" Jim asked. Cyd looked down at her plate that was almost completely full. He was making her lose her appetite.

"Ah, yes. I'm enjoying my dinner," she lied as she took a sip of the red wine she'd ordered when they first arrived to their table.

"Great," Jim said as he flipped his head to get a piece of fallen blond hair out of his face. Even that move annoyed her because he flashed his pearly whites after every hair flip. When his cell phone rang and he excused himself, Cyd welcomed the alone time.

She was finally able to finish her meal in his absence. After the waiter cleared their plates and placed the check on the table, Cyd looked around since Jim still hadn't returned. She spotted him through the window, standing outside in what looked to be a heated conversation with someone on the phone. Although she'd known him for less than a week, she hadn't seen him get aggravated or angry, but he was definitely angry now. She stood and walked to the window to try to wave him inside so they could pay for the bill and leave. When he finally noticed her, he held up his hand in an extremely rude fashion and started pacing back and forth.

Cyd was growing more annoyed by the second so the quicker she paid the bill, the better. After she settled the check, she walked outside, a little apprehensive to approach Jim. She decided to walk slower when she neared him so he wouldn't hear her heels click on the surface.

"I understand," she heard him yell to the person on the other end of the phone. "I've done everything you asked. Now I need you to listen to what I'm saying. I have a bad feeling about this and I think we should hold off until after the appreciation tour."

Cyd tried her best to tie together the bits and pieces she heard him say, but it wasn't making any sense. His pacing had quickened and he was continuously brushing his fingers through his hair. When she took another step closer to him, her heel clicked to the ground louder than she intended. Instantly, Jim lifted his head to her as he placed his hand over his cell phone receiver.

"Do you need anything?" he asked abruptly as if they hadn't originally been out on a date.

"Um, no," Cyd replied uncertainly. "I was just letting you know we can head back to the hotel."

"Please take a cab without me," Jim said very briskly and straightforwardly as he turned his back to her and continued his conversation, lowering his voice this time.

The nerve of that a-hole, Cyd thought to herself as she got into a cab that was waiting in front of the restaurant. *That man clearly has issues.*

Chapter 6

"**S**hawn, we need to see you in room C3," stated the voice on the other end of his earpiece.

"On my way," Shawn replied into his two-way radio microphone connected to the collar of his polo. Last night he'd followed Cyd and Jim to the restaurant and had been up later than he'd planned. Shawn had been surveying Jim Pearson since he'd begun his under-cover work for the Peter Vallant Company, but besides a few fuming phone calls, he hadn't been able to catch anything else. Each time, Jim's call had been received from an untraceable number and the caller had hung up after a few seconds. But last night, Jim had stayed on the phone a little longer than expected. He was hoping Micah had been able to find something. Micah Mad-den, younger brother of his friend Malik Madden, had recently quit his job with Little Rock, Arkansas, P.D. after realizing the system was way more corrupt than he'd originally thought. Shawn had instantly told him about his goal to start his own company and Micah had jumped on the idea to help him.

When he reached C3, he swiped his key card to enter

the room. "What did you find out?" Shawn asked Micah
as he entered and shut the door. He grabbed a nearby
chair and plopped down at the desk that contained several laptops and various security devices.

"We traced that call to an abandoned warehouse
thirty miles from here, right by the lake. I sent four
members of the team to the location, but they didn't
find anything. Whoever was there was long gone by
the time we arrived."

"Do we know who the phone belongs to?"

"It's a disposable phone, but we're trying to run it
through a number of databases now. My guess is that
the phone was discarded into the lake."

"Did they find any prints?"

"No prints. This person was smart and did a good job
covering their tracks. Luckily, they couldn't hide their
tire tracks. Take a look at this," Micah said as he turned
the computer so that Shawn could get a better look.

Shawn got closer to the screen and analyzed the
tracks from the photo and video footage. They were
too small to be a truck or a car. "So our mystery man
rides a sports bike."

"Exactly," Micah said, snapping his fingers together.
"Now all we need to do is figure out the make and
model of the motorcycle. Could be a Ducati or a Kawasaki."

"Naw, the dirt lines from this baby are too smooth
and precise for a Ducati or Kawasaki," Shawn replied
as he pointed to the lines on the screen. "Looks like a
BMW. Probably the K1600 series, but I'm not sure."

"How do you know?"

"Take a look at the tire indentation," Shawn said, actually touching the screen this time. "From the way the

bike leans, it appears to have a narrower six-cylinder engine, like the BMW K1600 series. I did a lot of research when I was deciding on my motorcycle so I'm pretty familiar with sports bikes."

Shawn stood from his seat and leisurely placed both arms on the desk. "Have you found anything in the vans yet?"

"Not yet," Micah answered. "So far, Jim Pearson hasn't been anywhere near the vans since we started the investigation. No one from inside or outside the company has, with the exception of those who have clearance. And we've investigated all the drivers and employees who regularly use the vans, but they're all clean."

"Okay," Shawn replied as his forehead creased in thought. "Continue to monitor the vans. I need a few members of the team to head to Carbondale, Illinois, next week before the Peter Vallant Company arrives. The hotel has already been prepped so we have clearance to tap into their security cameras."

"I'll inform the men."

"Thanks. Did you hear anything from the private investigator?"

"They haven't found anything yet."

Shawn wasn't familiar with some of the newer members of the agency so he knew he needed to reach out to people he knew outside the agency if he was going to solve the case. "I need to make a few calls before the party tonight, including calling your brother," Shawn said as he stood to leave the room. "I also need you to head back to Chicago after we leave Carbondale to make sure we cover all of our bases." Micah nodded his head in understanding.

Jim Pearson was originally only appearing on two stops of the appreciation tour, but he had conveniently asked Mr. Vallant if he could attend all the events. After clearing it with Shawn and his team first, Mr. Vallant had obliged Jim's request.

As Shawn walked down the hallway toward his hotel room, he tried to shake the feeling in the pit of his stomach. Something just didn't sit right with him regarding the case. He knew as well as any law enforcement officer that sometimes the culprit was right in front of you, so Jim Pearson could definitely be their guy since he was the only executive team member who appeared to be into some shady side business. His demeanor during the investigation said as much. What he didn't know was whether Jim was the only Vallant employee who was involved in the drug case or if he was working with an accomplice outside of the company.

When Shawn reached his room, he went to the safe and took out all the paperwork he had on the case. Jim Pearson just didn't seem to have the mind-set of a criminal. He was guilty for sure, but was he the brains behind the transiting of the drugs?

As Shawn sat on the sofa and shuffled through stacks of paperwork, he thought back to that fateful day years ago when his life had changed. He'd been an FBI agent serving as a special deputy United States Marshal at the time. Not a day passed when he didn't wish he could rewind that entire day. So many more pertinent cases had surfaced since then, and FBI resources were needed elsewhere. But since that case was still open, Shawn was determined to do everything he could to find the person responsible. Although they'd captured Detroit's largest drug lord three years ago, the same marked drugs that were circulating through Detroit and Chicago back then were still circulating today. The DEA and P.D. in both cities were on the case, but Shawn needed to do more than solve the current drug situation. He needed answers that he'd been trying to get for the past three years.

He took out his Android and called his trusted friend and ex-FBI agent, private investigator Malik Madden. He answered on the first ring. "Hey, Malik, I need your help."

"Hey, man, what's up? Micah didn't mess up, did he?"

"Naw, man," Shawn said with a laugh. "You need to cool it on this big-brother kick. Micah's not that much younger than you." He heard Malik laugh. "I'm sending you a list of names that I need you to research as soon as you can. The FBI is coming up short and I think someone paid a lot of money to cover up their indiscretions."

"Say no more. Send me the list and give me at least a week, maybe two, to work with my connections." Malik was one of the FBI's finest and had been recruited while he was still attending Harvard University. But like Shawn, he'd always dreamed of operating his own business. After a little shy of ten years with the FBI, Malik had retired and opened his own private investigator firm.

"Thanks, man," Shawn said as he ended his call. "The FBI will do their research, and I'll do mine," Shawn said aloud before packing up his paperwork to begin getting ready for the party.

Once again, Shawn knew the exact moment that Cydney entered the banquet hall. He'd seen her hours prior directing the setup of the room and speaking with

the banquet hall staff. When Shawn had originally seen
Game Night: Come Represent Your Favorite Team! on
the agenda, he hadn't known what to expect. Looking around at the pool tables, dartboards, mini basketball hoops, Ping-Pong tables and other games staggered
around the large main room, he was greatly impressed.
Cydney had managed to turn a sporting event into a
classy production. There was even a section for hard-
core casino players that included roulette and poker
tables as well as several slot machines. Everyone had
on their favorite jerseys, team T-shirts or hoodies, but
no one looked as sexy as Cydney, who wore a clingy
Bulls jersey. Shawn took another swig of his beer as
he observed her outfit a little more closely. She'd tied
a knot in the back, successfully showing off her amazing body shape. Her dark blue jeans hugged her apple
behind in ways that made him jealous he wasn't denim
material. When she bent over to pick up something she'd
dropped on the floor, her shirt inched up, exposing the
soft, creamy skin around her midriff.

"Can't take your eyes off her, right?" said a male
voice standing behind Shawn. Shawn turned just as
Paul Jensen was approaching him.

"Excuse me?" Shawn asked, pretending he didn't
hear the question as he took another swig of his beer.
Paul laughed as he shook the ice in his drink to break
apart the cubes.

"Cydney Rayne? She looks damn good in that outfit, right?" Paul asked. "Although she looks great every
time I see her."

Before he could stop himself, Shawn cut his eyes
at Paul.

"Hey, man, I was just saying," Paul said, shrugging

his shoulders and laughing once again. *Keep your cool, Miles. She's not your woman.* Instead of responding he just smiled and initiated small talk about sports.

Ten minutes into their conversation, Brittany Higgins and Kim Lathers joined them.

"Hello, gentlemen," Brittany said, focusing all her attention on Shawn. While Kim led a conversation about the current status of the stock market, Brittany seductively sipped her wine, stealing glances at Shawn throughout the entire conversation. She was definitely an attractive woman and if Shawn wasn't so occupied with Cydney at the moment, he may have been inclined to return her flirtation.

"Shawn, what are your thoughts on the situation?" Brittany asked. Shawn didn't know if they were still talking about the stock market, or if they had moved on to another topic all together. He'd been too busy watching Cydney, who'd tried to watch their group discreetly ever since the women had joined them.

Shawn looked back at the group awaiting his response. "Ladies first," he said as he nodded his head toward Brittany, hoping she hadn't already answered.

"Oh, Shawn," Brittany said as she gently touched his arm. "You're too sweet." She tightly squeezed one of his muscles before she dropped her hand and answered the question, which luckily was still regarding the stock market.

As he pretended to listen to Brittany's response, he heard Micah's voice in his earpiece. "Jim Pearson has entered. East wing."

Shawn glanced discreetly at the east-wing entrance of the room in time to see Jim look around before his eyes landed fully on Cydney. Shawn wished the look he was giving her didn't aggravate him, but it did. Jim began making his way to her, but not before glancing over to where Shawn and the others stood. Jim's eyes zoned in on Paul and the two shared a look that didn't go unseen by Shawn. Both women had their backs turned to Jim, but there was no mistaking the contact between Jim and Paul.

Hmm. Interesting. Shawn was great at reading people, but he couldn't quite read the look on Paul's face. Was Paul involved in the transiting of drugs, as well? Was he the missing piece? Paul had never been on the FBI's radar, but then again, neither was Jim before Shawn began the investigation. A sideways glance at Micah proved that he was already taking note of both men's reactions to one another and had observed the exchange, as well.

Cyd straightened out the tablecloths draping the high tables as she tried to ignore the tinge of jealousy she felt. Watching Brittany Higgins flirt with Shawn was making her sick to her stomach. From where she was in the room, she couldn't tell if he was flirting back or not, but she was sure he was. What man wouldn't flirt with someone as attractive as Brittany? Cyd quickly glimpsed at the group again, just as Brittany laughed and flirtatiously leaned into Shawn.

Goodness, how tight is her jersey dress? Cyd thought. *Better yet, it looks like she just took a large jersey and tied it around her waist with a belt.* It didn't matter at that moment that she was just as guilty of wearing shirts as dresses just as tight, if not tighter herself. What did matter was that she hadn't foreseen

Brittany's interest in Shawn and chose to wear one of her scandalous dresses tonight.

"Cydney?" She turned around at the sound of her name and instantly wished she'd just ignored the person.

"Hello, Jim," she replied as she moved from straightening the tablecloths to fixing the centerpieces.

"I wanted to apologize for last night. I was extremely rude and I'm very embarrassed for the way the night went."

He's sorry? That's all he has to say after that hellish night? I'm sorry, too. Sorry for even going out with him in the first place.

"I understand," Cyd said politely. "I accept your apology." *Not!*

"Thank you," Jim replied. "I received an important phone call yesterday that needed my immediate attention. You know how it is when people want you to drop everything to help them...."

Cyd temporarily blocked him out as he went on another rampage about himself. Ever since Jim had arrived, Shawn had been looking her way a lot more.

"Am I right?" Jim asked, commanding her attention. She had no clue what he was talking about, but since it appeared she had Shawn's attention, she played into the doting-listener role.

"Yes, Jim," Cyd said with a slight giggle. "You are so right." She even playfully placed her hand on his shoulder, completely forgetting that she was supposed to despise him after the night from hell. She had to change their conversation to something even remotely interesting so she could keep playing her part.

"So why were you so angry on the phone yesterday?" Cyd asked, interrupting whatever he had previously been talking about.

"Just business," he said as he stuck his hands in his pockets. His jawline tightened and his eyes grew darker as if he were getting angry all over again. *Why the sudden change? He brought up yesterday first.*

"What kind of business?" Cyd asked. "Peter Vallant Company business?"

He shifted from the heels of his feet to the balls of his feet, his hands still in his pockets. He didn't answer right away so Cyd wasn't sure he'd heard the question. "What kind of bus—"

"Yeah, I heard you," he said gruffly, cutting her off. "I mean, yes, I heard you," Jim continued as he flipped his blond hair out of his face and flashed another all-teeth smile.

"Not Peter Vallant business, other business. I'm a man of many trades," he said, smiling once again. She wasn't sure if other women found his behavior attractive, but she definitely did not.

"Oh, really," Cyd said, ignoring his strange behavior. "Like what?"

He gave her a look that she couldn't quite read before answering, "Let's just say that my family is very wealthy and successful in the pharmaceutical business." By the way he responded, she assumed he thought she would be impressed. *Not likely,* she thought.

"That's nice," Cyd exclaimed. "Who owns the business?"

"Uh, my father does."

"Interesting. What's the name of the business?"

"Uh…it's Pearson Pharmaceuticals. I mean, Pearson and Company. I forgot they changed the name."

"Wow, interesting." *And by interesting I do mean the fact that you seem to be lying is what I find interesting.* "Why did they change the name?"

"You know, you sure do ask a lot of questions for someone who just met me."

Uh, DUH! That's typically what people do when they first meet.

"Just curious, I guess," she said instead. "I know people in that line of work. I was trying to figure out if we knew some of the same people."

"Babe, trust me. We don't know the same people," he said, as he stepped closer to her.

Cyd took it one step further and stepped even closer to him. "I'm not your babe," she said between her teeth as she tried to keep a smile on her face when all she really wanted to do was cringe.

"Not yet," he said, attempting to take another step toward her. Cyd stepped back before he got the chance. *Oh, man, he's so weird,* she thought as she observed his strange behavior.

"Okay, well, I have to get back to work," Cyd said as she turned to retreat to another part of the room. "I guess I'll see you around."

"Definitely," she heard him say after she had already turned her back to him. She went past the casino section of the room and out into a small hallway that led to the bathrooms. When she was alone, away from the crowd, she took out her iPhone and pulled up a Google web page to search Jim Pearson. Nothing popped up but the Peter Vallant Company website and articles associated with the company. Then she searched Jim Pearson, Omaha, Nebraska, after she remembered that was Jim's hometown. "Hmm, okay, that's strange," she said quietly to herself when nothing popped up in that Google search, either. She continued by typing in Pearson Pharmaceuticals in Omaha, Nebraska. Then she just typed in Pearson Pharmaceuticals. Followed by Pearson and Company. Zilch.

"So you're an ass and a liar," she quietly said aloud as she stuck her phone in the back pocket of her jeans. Since Shawn was ignoring her and she had two more cities of events before they returned to Chicago, she had to figure out what to do with her free time. The way she saw it, she only had one option. "Let's see who you and your family really are, Jim Pearson." Men lied to impress women all the time, but there was something about Jim Pearson that really got under her skin.

Chapter 7

Cyd dived into the hotel swimming pool and began doing laps. The day had been a long one, consisting of several family-oriented activities, relay races and many Halloween-themed events. Running after little children all day was exhausting and way beyond the duties of an event planner. She had so much built-up tension she could barely function.

It was day seven of her investigation on Jim Pearson and Cyd hadn't been able to track him down. *Why does he only bother me when I don't want to be bothered, yet when I'm trying to find him, he is nowhere to be found?* The Peter Vallant Company had arrived in Carbondale, Illinois, a couple days ago and Cyd hadn't seen Jim since they arrived, although he'd told her he would be here when they were still in Springfield.

Getting out of the pool, Cyd made her way to the whirlpool, anxious to relax after swimming several laps. She turned on the jets and submerged herself in the hot water, closing her eyes and soaking in the moment.

"Aah." She needed this. The water felt better than

she'd expected. She stretched out her legs and arched her back, preparing to take a quick nap in the water.

"May I join you?" she heard the deep voice say and prayed that she wasn't imagining him. Shawn hadn't been paying much attention to her since they'd started the tour so she knew it couldn't be him in the flesh, although she hoped it would be. She opened one eye first, expecting to see an empty space.

"Cydney…" He said her name breathlessly in a way she hadn't heard in weeks. She opened her other eye, taking in the complete sight of the man before her. She tried to speak, but she couldn't. His body had no business looking that magnificent. His swimming trunks were riding low on his hips. The indent of his pelvis bone was clearly visible. He'd grown a goatee that he hadn't originally had and goodness if that goatee didn't look sexy on him. His hair had grown out a little, too, so his fade was now a short crop of curls atop his head. She was taking too long to give him a response so he took it upon himself to get into the whirlpool with her. She felt like she was watching him in slow motion as he made the act of entering the water a truly provocative production.

When he was fully submerged in the water he looked up into the corner of the poolroom at the security camera before grabbing her waist and bringing her to the side of the pool not visible by the device. His back hit the opposite side of the whirlpool and she landed in between his legs, making a soft gasp when their bodies collided. He took one hand and tenderly brushed her wet hair out of her face.

"This is the other swimsuit you bought in Anguilla, right?" he asked as he played with the side of her purple bikini. It was getting harder for her to breathe under his unwavering stare. Although he looked sexier than ever, he also looked tired and a bit stressed.

So he sought me out instead of Brittany...interesting. Shawn and Brittany had been as thick as thieves lately and although Cyd tried not to be bothered by it, she was. But no matter how much Brittany flirted with Shawn and he flirted back, Cyd never saw him look at Brittany the way he looked at her. It was those moments that Cyd held on to.

"How did you know I bought this swimsuit in Anguilla?" she asked, finally finding her voice. Shawn gave her a killer smile before he answered.

"After I left the store that day, I watched you from the window to see if you would buy the other swimsuit I told you to purchase. I couldn't resist watching you."

Had any other man said those words to her, Cyd would have probably thought that it was creepy. But the fact that it was Shawn made her even wetter than the water they were immersed in. She leaned in a little closer and whispered into his mouth. "You watched me?" she asked.

"Yes," he said, his voice slightly cracking with desire.

"So you like watching me?" Cyd asked as she ran her fingers through his curls, breathing on his neck as she caressed his scalp.

"Yes," he said even deeper than before. His hands moved to cup her bottom, but she moved away from his grasp, careful to remember to stay out of the line of the camera. She leisurely untied the top of her bathing suit and placed the piece on the side of the whirlpool.

"What do you like watching me do?" she inquired

as she began to massage her breasts. The rise that she was getting from Shawn was motivating her to take her charade as far as he would let her. He hadn't answered her question, but it didn't matter. It was clear she had his undivided attention. She briefly turned to look at the poolroom entrance to make sure no one was entering.

"Don't worry. I locked the door," Shawn said, reading her thoughts.

"How did you get the key?"

"Don't worry about it," he said with a playful smile. She didn't really care how he got the key; she was just glad that the door was locked. She also didn't care that he had obviously planned to seduce her. Little did he know she had planned to seduce him first.

She continued her exploration of her breasts, massaging her nipples and throwing her head back in pleasure. The only way she could enjoy touching herself was if she imagined Shawn's hands caressing her instead of her own. So that was what she did. She imagined him caressing her…kissing her…licking her. Slowly, she rolled her tongue over her lips, softly moaning as she did. She brought her head back down and looked at Shawn. She hadn't seen when he'd removed his swimming trunks, but they were definitely discarded now and were lying by her swimsuit top. She stopped massaging her breasts and untied her bikini bottoms, throwing them by the rest of the wet clothes. Crossing one arm over her breasts, she took her free hand and allowed her fingers to glide up and down the side of her body, teasing him as he watched in anticipation and followed her hands to see where they would land. She reached out to flick a nipple at the same time she cupped her center, fully preparing to please herself and force him to watch. She didn't get very far because within seconds, Shawn had grabbed both of her arms, pulling her into his hold and onto his lap in the whirlpool.

"You are so naughty," he said right before his lips landed roughly on hers, his tongue enclosing over hers in his pursuit to make her pay for what she'd made him watch.

"I wasn't finished yet," she said in between his hungry kisses.

"You're finished," he stated in a fiery voice that confirmed he was done playing games. She'd successfully pushed him over the edge and didn't have any shame about it. He reached over to his trunks and pulled out a condom, his lips still plastered on hers. She lifted off his lap so that he could put on the condom and was in awe of how he continued to kiss all over her body and put on protection at the same time.

Seconds later, she climbed back on his lap and eased him inside her, clenching her vaginal muscles while he entered. The groan that escaped his mouth when he was completely embedded inside her was animallike. Gradually they began to move in a rhythm that was becoming all too familiar to them. Cyd rolled her head from side to side, overcome by the emotions shooting through her body as he cupped her butt cheeks and pumped inside her fervently. Thrust by thrust, he plunged inside, the tip of his manhood playing with the core of her essence every time he pulled out of her slender body.

"Cydney," he voiced on the brink of his orgasm.

"Me, too," she managed to say, her orgasm close to breaking free as a result of her body knowing his all too well. A few moments later, they both succumbed to their climaxes and experienced a feeling so powerful that the only thing they could do was hold on to each other tight and not let go.

What am I getting myself into? Shawn thought to himself for the umpteenth time as he walked down the hallway to the security room. He was in trouble. Big trouble. And it wasn't the kind of trouble he could talk his way out of. It was the kind of trouble that crept up on him quicker than he realized before he had time to truly react. Shawn wasn't even sure he could call it trouble. It was more like an obsession. He'd never been obsessed with anything in his life, not even solving the current case he was on that had ultimately changed his life. After years of thinking he was capable of solving any problem, he'd finally found a problem that he couldn't solve…and her name was Cydney Rayne.

Sex with a woman as gorgeous and intelligent as Cydney wouldn't normally be a problem for the average man. But Shawn wasn't an average man. His life wasn't an ordinary life and his past was far from normal. Therefore, Cydney Rayne was definitely a problem, and there was no doubt in Shawn's mind that he was, in fact, in big trouble. After their encounter in the poolroom yesterday, he'd successfully dodged Cydney any chance he got. She wasn't the type of woman to chase after a man, so one observation at his clear dismissal was enough motivation for her to ignore him, as well. But he hadn't missed the daggers she'd shot his way the night prior when he'd seen her in the hotel lobby. It didn't matter, though, because seeing her in another alluring dress had kept him up all night. She'd tiptoed into his mind, danced into his thoughts and hit him right where it hurt a man the most—his midsection.

"Shawn, Pearson has returned," Micah said as soon as Shawn entered the room. Shawn followed the direction of Micah's finger, which pointed to one of the mounted televisions streaming live security footage. The hotel had been extremely accommodating with his security team so they had been able to even place cameras outside of the hotel room Jim had been assigned to when he arrived.

"When did he get in?" Shawn asked, getting a little closer to the screen when Cydney's face came into view.

"Early this morning," Micah replied. "Nothing looked suspicious. Except…" His voice trailed off.

"Except what?" Shawn asked when Micah stopped talking midsentence. Micah shook his head and laughed, but still didn't continue.

"Except what?" Shawn asked again, growing slightly annoyed.

"I thought this was interesting," Micah finally answered as he reached for a remote and began rewinding the footage on the second television that was mounted on the wall. He slowed down the footage when he got to a part of the recording that showed Jim at Cydney's hotel room door before retreating to the elevator. Even in backward slow motion, Shawn was aggravated that Jim had been at her door.

"Just so you know, he followed her to her room. That's how he knew what floor she stayed on and her room number."

"What!" Shawn said a little more anxious than expected. He'd assumed she led him to her room.

"I figured you'd be pretty pissed when you found out."

Instead of responding to Micah, Shawn grabbed the

remote from him and began rewinding to the part when Jim started to follow Cydney to her room. Shawn balled his fists as he witnessed Jim intently observing her as she walked. It was either ball his fists or throw a punch at the television screen. He continued to watch as Cydney slid her key to open her door while Jim stood at the end of the hallway behind a large plant.

"That bastard," Shawn said aloud, not caring that he sounded like a jealous ex-boyfriend. Micah shook his head in pity. "Look, man, I don't know what's going on with you and Cydney Rayne, but I know that you need to get your head on straight. The FBI, DEA and P.D. are counting on you. Plus your company's on the line. You have a great team and she's a smart woman. Personally, I think she's just flirting with Jim to make you jealous."

Shawn cut his eyes at Micah. "Why do you think that?"

Micah laughed. "Um, I don't know. Could it be the fact that you have the hots for her? Or is it the fact that you can't seem to take your eyes off her anytime she's around? Or maybe it's the fact that you left me high and dry yesterday to sneak off and have sex with her in the poolroom?"

Shawn dropped his head back and dragged his hands over his face. "Crap. When did you know something was up?"

Micah looked at Shawn incredulously before he answered. "Are you serious, man? You know what, I'll pretend like you didn't just question my skills. You do a good job avoiding her so others may not know. But you don't pay me the big bucks to miss the obvious. After we solve this case, I think you'd better pick a location to headquarter our company and make me partner. You're reckless without me."

Micah slapped Shawn on the back as he finished reviewing the footage on the television. He laughed at his friend and soon-to-be partner because he was right. He was acting reckless, which was so out of character.

Before Shawn had even reached the poolroom yesterday, he'd known he was making a mistake. While he'd been reviewing the hotel's security cameras, he'd seen her enter the poolroom to take a swim. For a while, she'd walked around the edge of the pool in her cover-up and flip-flops as if she were contemplating between the pool and the whirlpool. When she'd decided on the pool, he watched her drop her cover-up, revealing a sexy bikini he'd recognized from their time in Anguilla. Within minutes, Shawn had given Micah an excuse about needing to relieve some stress and was out the door.

He'd questioned his motives up until the minute he opened the poolroom door and laid eyes on her in the whirlpool looking extremely sexy and appetizing.

"Shawn," Micah said, snapping a finger in front of his face. "Are you trying to figure out what Jim's doing with your woman or are you gonna sit there and day-dream about her?"

Shawn gave Micah a blank look before grabbing the remote from him to rewind the recent footage. "So Paul Jensen showed up, as well?" Shawn asked Micah when he saw Paul flash across the screen.

"Yes. It looks like most of the executive board has been sporadically arriving."

"Interesting…. So they aren't following the schedule that Mr. Vallant created," Shawn stated rhetorically as he got closer to the screen and watched the way Paul and Jim glanced at each other. "Did they arrive at the same time?"

"Yes. About ten minutes apart."

Shawn glanced over at Micah. "We need to make sure we keep our eyes on Paul Jensen, too." Something was definitely going on between the two men.

Chapter 8

"Come on," Cydney whispered to herself. "Match point. Time to take him down." She straightened out her black tennis skirt before throwing the ball in the air and taking a swing. She wasn't a huge fan of tennis, but she was determined to show Jim Pearson her skills, anyway. When he'd asked her out for a game of tennis yesterday, she'd instantly declined his invitation despite the indoor tennis court being on the grounds of their hotel. Shawn's dismissal had really gotten to her. But upon remembering her investigation on Jim, she'd recanted her response and eagerly accepted his invitation. With the exception of a few chance meetings at the bar, they hadn't gone out on another date. Despite declining his previous invitations, she'd followed him on several occasions and had concluded that Jim was indeed keeping a secret.

"Yah," she yelled as she swatted the tennis ball. "Yah," she bellowed again, returning the ball and hitting it harder than before. Beads of sweat dripped from her forehead and her socks were slowly creeping deeper into her black-and-white shoes. She was, however, extremely competitive so she ignored her discomfort, determined to win the game.

"Yah!" She returned his ball with such force, Jim couldn't react fast enough, resulting in match point. Her win!

"Yay," she shouted as she placed her tennis racket under one arm while doing a fist pump in the air with the other arm. "Oh, yeah…oh, yeah," she said as she did a little happy dance, oblivious to the observant glances from neighboring tennis players. She stopped cheering when she noticed Jim's fixated stare.

"Okay, that was fun! Do you want to have lunch now?" Cydney asked. "I'll buy," she continued in a cute voice, swaying back and forth with a look of childlike innocence.

"Sure. Why not," Jim responded as he twirled his tennis racket in his hand in obvious frustration. For a brief second, he looked as if he wanted to throw the tennis racket into the wall, but that look left as quickly as it had come.

"Come on," she said as she made her way to him and linked her free arm through his. He reluctantly followed her down the hallway to a breakfast-and-lunch café. They were quickly seated and placed their order right away.

"So why weren't you on the tour for the past few days?" Cyd watched as he raised one eyebrow, undoubtedly taken off guard by her question.

"I had business to attend to," Jim responded drily as he played with his silverware on the table. He looked as if he didn't want anything to do with her at the moment, so Cyd was forced to try another tactic. She leaned over the table and gently placed her hand over his, twirling her fingers in a circular motion.

"I missed you a little when you were gone," she said, trying not to squirm as she voiced the words. She gave him a half smile, gently moistening her lips with her tongue. She had to remind herself not to go too far since Jim's personality had proved to be unpredictable.

He matched her movement and leaned into the table, as well. "How much did you miss me?" he asked as he made a smacking noise with his mouth as his tongue brushed over his teeth. He probably thought he sounded sexy, but the sound was both annoying and unattractive.

Cyd removed her hand from his, pushed her chair back from the table and crossed one leg over the other. "Oh, I missed you a lot," she continued with a laugh. "I realized that we never had a complete conversation. One of us always has to leave or work gets in the way."

"Really?" Jim said, clasping his hands together on the table. "You enjoy talking to me?"

Cyd contemplated her next words carefully. "I think there is a lot I don't know about you, Jim Pearson," she said as she let her voice drop a little lower. "And I definitely think there's more to you than what meets the eye."

His eyes lit up as if she'd said exactly what he'd been thinking. "That's so true," Jim stated, bringing his chair closer to the table. "All my life people haven't given me enough credit. I have a range of talents, but I hardly ever get credit for what I do!" His voice was rising as he talked.

Now we're getting somewhere.

"I understand completely," Cyd replied. "No one understands how talented you really are, Jim. Especially when it comes to handling business."

"Exactly," Jim exclaimed as he pointed at her as if she'd just pronounced a problem he'd been dealing with his entire life. "People underestimate me all the time. Especially when it comes to business. They need to realize that I'm an asset to this line of work and the sooner they realize that, the better it will be."

Cyd wondered what type of business he was referring to, considering he was the senior vice president of business development and had a large role in the company. She would understand more if he were the low man on the totem pole, but senior VP? It didn't make sense to her. *He must be talking about another type of business. Hmm...his family's business?*

"I agree. The sooner they realize, the better. Don't they understand that you could take over the business if you wanted to? Don't they realize your potential?"

Jim threw his hands up in the air. "That's what I've been trying to tell them for years. They just don't get it." Cyd observed his demeanor as his eyes squinted together in contemplation. "They really don't get it. After everything I've done and accomplished, disregarding the consequences, they still don't get it. Especially the one person who should."

"Exactly," Cyd added. "You're worth more than that."

"Damn straight," he said. "Especially when they are the reason I'm even in this line of work."

Her gut was telling her that the line of work he was referring to was definitely illegal. Cyd wanted to ask him who that person was, but she didn't want him to clam up if she pried too much. So instead she just sat quietly at the table and watched the range of emotions cross his face. Anger. Frustration. Revenge. And surprisingly, guilt.

She knew he was an intelligent man, but right now, he wasn't acting like a senior VP of a top real estate firm. He continued to talk, staggering his words as he spoke, nothing really making much sense. He would say some words in a higher tone, then he would lower his voice. Cyd had never met anyone who made her feel this uncomfortable. He wasn't directing any of his explicit words to her, but his behavior was unsettling nonetheless. She felt like she should stop their conversation, but instead she let him talk, unsure of what she would even say to him if she were able to get in a word. Luckily, their food arrived, causing him to stop his vocal rampage.

Jim looked down at his food, then back up at Cyd, coming out of his troubling trance. "This looks great," he said, his disturbing behavior suddenly stalled. Instead, his face instantly calmed and his frown was replaced with an award-winning smile.

What the hell? What was it with this guy? Cyd briefly contemplated distancing herself from Jim. But Shawn was still ignoring her so she didn't feel like she had much of a choice. She hated being bored, and at least focusing on Jim gave her a distraction. There was no doubt in her mind that Jim was a little dangerous, but he was an employee for the Peter Vallant Company so she didn't think he was a danger to her. As they began eating, once again, Jim began talking about himself.

"Tell me a little about yourself," Jim said, halfway through their meal. *Was he seriously asking about her?* He hadn't shown any interest in her personal life since they met.

"There's not much to tell," she replied, trying to keep the conversation impersonal. "As you know, I'm a co-owner of Elite Events, Incorporated and business is definitely booming."

"That's great," Jim said, taking a bite of his food. "What is your family like?" *Wow, he's two for two,* Cyd thought as she forked her salad.

"We're just a typical family," Cyd replied, minimizing the successes and accomplishments of her family. The Burrstone family was known for their many accomplishments in business ownership, community advocacy and entertainment. Usually, Cyd boasted about her family because she was so proud of everyone, but in this case, she appreciated the fact that she could withhold information because she had her father's last name—a name that had clout, but wasn't as well-known as her mother's family name of Burrstone. Besides, Jim didn't strike her as the type to research her on the internet. She turned the conversation back to him. "My family probably isn't as interesting as your family. I know people in the pharmaceutical business, but your family actually owns their business. What is your family like?"

The smile dropped from his face the instant she mentioned his family. He stopped eating his food and cracked his knuckles. "We aren't close. They've never accepted me and my decisions."

"I'm sorry," Cyd replied sympathetically. "Maybe they will come around someday."

"I doubt it, but it doesn't matter." Jim cracked his neck and resumed eating before he continued. "I have another family, so I don't need them or their judgment."

Cyd took a sip of her water. "That's good. What are they like?"

He didn't clam up as he had moments prior. But his current expression wasn't a pleasant one, either. He looked down at his plate. "They take me for granted, but they are a better family than my family ever was to me. I'd do anything for them."

"So when you were talking about your family earlier, you were referring to your other family? Why would you do anything for them if they don't appreciate you? That's not fair."

His face rose from his plate, void of expression. *Looks like I went too far.* He went from looking at her like a confidant to looking at her as if she were a threat to his "other" family.

"I'm done with lunch," Jim finally said as he waved over the waiter to get the check. Cyd looked down at her half-finished salad, forcing her eyes to stay down, avoiding Jim. He was still staring at her and even though there were other patrons in the café, the look in his eyes was a little intimidating. Cyd realized she was intimidated because he was void of emotion. She was pretty sure she had irritated him by asking so many questions and he was finally realizing how much he'd told her.

When they left the café, Cyd excused herself by saying she had to change before tonight's festivities began. They were headed to Indianapolis in the morning, so it was their last night in Carbondale.

"I'll see you later," Jim said, stopping her in her tracks. She turned back toward him and noticed his relaxed smile. The smile was even eerier than his being angry with her. Cyd gave a quick head nod and hurried away from him.

As she walked farther down the hallway, she couldn't

help but turn around to see if he was watching her. Surely enough, his eyes were glued in her direction.

Cyd opened a large manila envelope and poured the contents on the bed in her hotel room. She glanced at the array of pictures and notes she'd accumulated since she'd started investigating Jim. She found out a lot of valuable information at her tennis date with Jim earlier that day. She also realized that she needed to leave this situation alone.

Growing up, Cyd was always a bit of a detective. She loved the idea of solving the case of a missing sock or having a Q&A with her cousins on who ate the cookies from the cookie jar. She even entertained the idea of being a detective or investigator while she was in college, but she quickly realized that planning events was definitely her passion. When she was younger, her spy antics hadn't put her in any danger. Now she wasn't so sure. Although she didn't think Jim was really dangerous, she knew it wasn't smart to continue to investigate him. She honestly had no idea why she'd thought it would be a great idea in the first place. *Because you needed to occupy your time and get attention from someone else since Shawn was ignoring you.* The voice inside her head was right. Even though she disliked Jim to some extent, she did like the attention he was giving her.

Shawn. His named crawled into her mind for the first time all day. Shawn was the chief information security officer, so it only made sense for her to tell him about the suspicions she had about Jim.

"But how would I explain why I started following him in the first place?" she asked aloud. How was she supposed to explain to him that since he was ignoring her, she was bored and liked the attention she was receiving from Jim? She wouldn't dare give him the satisfaction of knowing how badly his dismissal affected her.

"But what other choice do I have?" She glanced at the pictures and notes again. Jim talked on the phone four times a day at precisely the same time every day. Twice, she'd noticed that the call came up unknown, which wouldn't seem like an issue except for the fact that he always seemed to leave her abruptly and answer like he knew the person. Her conversation with Jim today was icing on the cake.

Cyd began placing the pictures and notes back into the large envelope. "You have to tell him," she said to herself as she put on her gym shoes and texted Shawn to meet her in the lobby. She left her hotel room and headed to the elevator. As soon as the elevator door opened, out stepped Jim, running right into her.

"Oh, sorry," Jim said as he gripped her arms to help her maintain her balance.

"That's okay," Cyd said, slowly easing herself out of his grip. "Why were you walking so fast, anyway?"

"I guess I was just anxious to see you," he said, although Cyd didn't believe him. She straightened out her T-shirt and yoga pants, making sure she tightly gripped the envelope, holding it close to her chest.

"I have to meet with the hotel staff before I finish getting dressed," she said, thinking quickly. She tried to move around him to get on the elevator, but he stepped in front of her. "Do you have to leave right now?" Jim asked as he bent down to tie his shoelace while stationed in between the elevator and floor. "I was hoping we could have a little wine before the events later today."

Only then did Cyd notice the wine bottle and glasses in a tote bag on the floor of the elevator.

"Sorry," Cyd exclaimed as she finally made it around him and into the elevator. "I have a lot to do tonight and before we get to Indianapolis. Can I take a rain check?"

Jim stood there for a few seconds and Cyd prayed he wouldn't give her a hard time. "That's fine," he finally said as he stepped back into the elevator with her and pressed his floor number.

"Great," Cyd exclaimed in relief. After Jim got off on his floor and the elevator let her off on the ground level, she spotted Shawn waiting in a corner of the lobby. His head immediately turned as she approached him.

"Hello, Shawn." He had on a pair of worn jeans and T-shirt. On any other man, the outfit would look casual, but on Shawn, it looked rugged and sexy.

"Hello, Cydney," he responded in his raspy voice. "What did you want to talk to me about?"

Cyd glanced around and pointed in the opposite corner of the lobby that had a couple chairs and a table. "Do you mind if we sit over there?"

"Sure, why not," Shawn said as he followed the direction of her hand. When they arrived at the chairs, taking seats right across from each other, Cyd opened the manila folder, but didn't remove any contents. "I wanted to talk to you about an employee who I believe may be up to something."

Shawn's eyes squinted together as he placed his forearms on his knees and clasped his hands together. "I'm listening," he said, giving her the green light to continue.

Cyd explained the entire story, leaving out the part about her wanting attention from Jim due to Shawn's decision to ignore her. The corner they were stationed at was very private, so Shawn was able to unobtrusively skim through the pictures and notes without looking suspicious.

"So you've been following him?" Shawn asked, although the question had to be rhetorical since she'd already told him that. "Why did you think that was a good idea? Do you know how much danger you put yourself in?"

Cyd was taken aback by the way he was speaking to her. She felt much younger than her twenty-seven years. "Seriously, I'm an adult, so I'd appreciate it if you talked to me as such."

Shawn threw his head back in a sarcastic laugh before leaning over to talk lower. "For an adult, you certainly weren't thinking like one when you created a plan to investigate Jim Pearson." He leaned even closer to her. "Cydney, I will look into this. But I need you to stand down and drop this investigation. You're liable to get hurt."

She wished his concern warmed her heart. Instead, she was irritated and a little embarrassed that he thought her investigation was so childish. She'd wanted to tell him because she'd known it was the right thing to do. What she hadn't planned on happening was her feeling stupid for even coming to him in the first place. When she'd first met him in Anguilla, she'd felt a passion unlike any she'd ever experienced. When she'd seen him again at her sister's wedding, she'd felt desire at the highest peak. Ever since she saw him in the conference room, he'd made her feel minuscule and unimportant, with the exception of their time in the whirlpool.

"I understand," Cyd exclaimed, her voice rising

slightly. "I was only trying to…" Her voice trailed off as she noticed the look of irritation in his eyes.

"I know what you were trying to do," Shawn said in impatience. "I can't believe you'd be so irresponsible and put yourself in danger. I'll handle it from here."

His heartless words were like daggers to her pride and self-esteem, making it impossible for her to hold in her feelings.

"Well," Cyd said as she stood to retreat back to her hotel room. "Thank you, Shawn." She counted to three to try to get her emotions under control. "I hadn't known what rejection and humiliation felt like until I met you. But somehow you've made me feel both in a matter of weeks."

"Cydney," he said, standing and reaching for her.

"Don't touch me," she all but yelled as she moved away from his hands. She then brought her voice back down to a normal level. "I gave you control when I let you use my body in ways I'd never allowed any man." She got the courage to look him straight in the eye before she brought her lips to his ear. "Rest assured, Shawn Miles, I will *never* make that mistake again."

Chapter 9

"You're an idiot," Shawn said aloud to himself as he walked around the outside premises of the host hotel for the Indianapolis Customer Appreciation Cultural Fair. Yesterday, Shawn and Cydney had been placed on the same bus on their commute from Carbondale, Illinois, to Indianapolis, Indiana. He'd tried to talk to her several times and apologize, but each and every time he was rejected.

You deserve it after talking to her the way that you did, he thought to himself. Even worse, he should have been happy that she was just following Jim and wasn't actually attracted to him. He'd been following them both and had been unsure if Cyd was using Jim or if she actually enjoyed Jim's company. Shawn hadn't known what had come over him that day. He'd had a feeling that she was going to talk to him about Jim, but instead of being understanding, he'd reprimanded her as if she was a child.

Early this morning, he'd called Micah and told him there had been a change of plans and he needed him to reroute and meet him in Indianapolis. Micah was due to arrive soon and Shawn needed to debrief him on his recent findings. It was actually more like Cydney's recent findings. She'd gotten close enough to Jim to have some intimate conversations with him and the information she'd found out had given Shawn an idea.

"Man, what are you doing out here?" Micah asked as he approached Shawn. "I know it's still fall, but it's a little chilly."

"I guess I don't feel anything," Shawn said as he led Micah through a gathering of trees near a creek. He handed Micah a flash drive. "I scanned and uploaded all the files I received from Cydney. I need you to go through them while I prepare the team for the cultural fair that's starting in a couple hours."

"No problem." Micah placed the flash drive in his pocket.

"Great. I need to call Malik and see if he has an update."

"I talked to him on my drive over here. He wants to verify some of his findings, but he expects to give us an update tonight or tomorrow."

"That's perfect. After reviewing everything that Cydney found out, I think that Jim may be hiding more than we thought. For starters, there's no way Jim Pearson is in this alone."

"I thought the same thing weeks ago," Micah added. "He didn't go under the FBI's radar without any help from the inside."

Shawn was about to respond to Micah's statement when he noticed they were being watched from the window. "Did Malik tell you anything about Paul Jensen?" Shawn asked.

"Malik said he's clear. There's nothing in his background that would indicate otherwise."

"Well, he's definitely watching us right now from the window. Something about him doesn't sit well with me."

"Me, neither," Micah added, knowing he couldn't turn around to take a look. "Let's wait and see what Malik has found before we count him out."

"Definitely," Shawn agreed as he watched Paul leave the window. "Let's get to work," he continued as he began making his way back inside the hotel.

As soon as they entered through a side door near the lobby, Shawn wished he had stayed outside for a few more minutes.

"Shawn, there you are," Brittany said, briskly walking toward him.

"I'll go play catch up and review the files," Micah whispered in Shawn's ear before patting him on his shoulder and turning to leave.

"Hello, Brittany," he said when she grew nearer.

"Hey, yourself," she replied when she reached him. She looked attractive in her snug-fitting skirt and blouse, but she didn't make his body feel any bit the way it felt when he was around Cydney.

"So what time are you heading to the conference room for the festivities?" she asked as she played with the collar of his shirt. His eyes trailed from her manicured hand to her heavily made-up face. Despite her being attractive, he never did go for the prima-donna type. *I really don't need this right now.*

"Probably in a couple hours," he stated, making sure he looked her in the eye even though she'd perked out her chest, hoping he'd sneak a peek. "But I'll be on duty."

She closed the small gap between them and puckered her lips in a pout. "Not if I have anything to say about it." He had enough on his plate tonight and entertaining Brittany wasn't on his agenda at all. He noticed someone in his peripheral vision and slightly turned his head to get a better look, hoping it wasn't who he thought it was.

When his eyes landed on Cydney, she quickly turned her back to them but she wasn't quick enough. He'd seen the look of hurt on her face. Brittany noticed his attention was projected elsewhere and turned toward the direction of his gaze.

"I swear that woman spends too much time looking at you. Hasn't she gotten the hint already? You ignore her every chance you get." Brittany placed her hands on both sides of his collar and pulled him closer to her. "You'd think she'd save herself the embarrassment." She voiced the last statement a little louder than the others. Without turning around, Cydney walked out of the lobby, clearly having overheard some of the conversation.

Shawn grabbed both of Brittany's wrists and pulled her hands away from him. "I don't know what you're talking about, but I suggest you keep your mouth out of things you know nothing about."

"Ooh, so now you're done with me and you're all over Little Miss Perfect, huh?" Brittany flipped her weave over her shoulder. "It's cool, though. Just wait until you see my dress tonight. You won't even be thinking about her. You'll only see me."

Was she delusional? How did I even get myself wrapped up in a love triangle? Shawn knew whatever he said would only make the situation worse, so he excused himself and went to the security room, glad to find Micah in there reviewing the documents he'd received from Cydney.

"That woman is crazy," Shawn said as soon as he closed the door and took a seat next to Micah.

"I can tell that much from the little episode that just happened in the lobby," Micah said with a laugh as he pointed to the television screen with the camera aimed at the exact spot Shawn and Brittany had been standing. "Man, you've got these women all over you."

"I guess so," Shawn responded. "Why me and not you, I have absolutely no idea."

"Me, neither," Micah said with another chuckle. "I'm younger and more attractive."

"You may be younger, but you wish you looked as good as I do," Shawn laughed. "Okay, on to more important matters," he said, quickly changing the subject. "I spoke with Agent Wolfe and Mr. Vallant to update them on our progress. Mr. Vallant will actually arrive in thirty minutes. How much did you cross-reference between our footage and Cydney's?"

"Enough to know we need to regroup and call all the men together before tonight's cultural fair. My gut is telling me we need to be on alert tonight."

Shawn had the same feeling in the pit of his stomach. "My sentiments exactly."

The cultural fair cocktail hour had begun thirty minutes ago and so far, everything was running smoothly. The Peter Vallant Company had several rebuilding initiatives in the Middle East and Africa, most of the contributors and investors coming from Indianapolis and Chicago. Mr. Vallant had arrived and uttered his appreciation for all of their hard work so far and the attendees really seemed to be enjoying the worldly theme in dedication to the different countries they'd helped.

Cyd looked down at her iPhone when she heard it ding, indicating that she had a text message. The cultural event in Indianapolis and the formal ball in Chicago were the two large events she had planned that required her to have contact information for the entire executive staff in case someone who was scheduled to give a speech couldn't attend. Unfortunately, that meant that she had to give them her contact information as well, which included Jim Pearson. Though up until now, he hadn't texted her.

In case you are looking for me, I had to step out for a minute. I'll be back in time for my speech to the attendees.

"Of course he had to step out," Cyd said aloud to herself. She just texted him a simple "okay" and got back to working the event. She wasn't going to concern herself with Jim anymore. It was too stressful and there was no doubt that Shawn would be watching her every move now. He'd been watching her from the minute she arrived in the hallway connecting all the conference rooms, his eyes glossing over her attire, fixating on the curve of her hips that graciously filled the beautiful black-and-teal African-themed dress she'd chosen to wear.

After seeing Shawn with Brittany, Cyd had given herself a pep talk before she'd left her hotel room. She was worth more than a man who only wanted her on his time and treated her as if she was a child instead of a grown woman. She'd expected them to have a respectful conversation, but all she'd gotten was an unpleasant lecture. *Maybe I needed him to act that way so that I could work him out of my system?* She realized when she'd decided to seduce him that he wasn't her Mr. Right, so in all honesty, she shouldn't even be angry at his behavior toward her.

But he seems so different than that man I met in Anguilla. She couldn't get over the fact that he seemed so infatuated with her one minute, yet the next, he could flirt with another woman right in her face.

"Ms. Rayne, everyone is gathering in conference room A for the kick-off speech for tonight's events."

"Thank you, Verona," Cyd replied. When she arrived at the conference room, Jim was nowhere in sight. Mr. Vallant was giving the kick-off speech, which meant Jim was the next executive member to speak.

"Kim," Cyd said as she approached the CMO. "Can you say a few words before Jim?"

"Sure thing."

"Thanks so much," Cyd responded as she made her way through the crowd to find Jim. Shawn's right-hand man was standing near Mr. Vallant. She briefly looked around for Shawn so she could tell him she was going to search for Jim, but decided against it when she noticed Brittany twirling in front of him in a dress so tight, Cyd could see the imprint of her thong.

"Forget this," Cyd said to herself as she also dismissed the idea of telling another member of Shawn's team. She made her way to the elevator and pressed the floor number that she'd seen Jim press when they were in the elevator together. She didn't even know what room he was in, but she hoped she would run into him in the hallway, unless he'd left the building.

She stepped off the elevator and looked down both ways of the hallway. After she didn't see anyone, she briefly placed her ear to each door she passed, hoping that he would be on a phone call so she could hear his voice. When she neared a room at the end of the hall, she placed her ear on the door and it pushed open. She looked at the cracked door and contemplated her next move.

"Jim, are you in here?" she asked as she clicked on the light and pushed the door open a little more. No answer. She stepped into the entryway. "Jim?" she called again, in case he was in the bathroom. Still nothing. The room looked spotless...even cleaner than it would be after housekeeping. Cyd dragged a nearby potted plant to the door to keep it propped open before she walked completely into the room. It was the same size as her suite, only everything was on the opposite side. She checked in the bathroom and closet with no sign of Jim. As she got closer to the coffee table, she turned on a lamp to see if there was any sign that this was Jim's room. She noticed a thermos with the initials J.P. etched on the side sitting on the table. Jim usually carried the thermos to all the hotel breakfast buffets every morning and filled it with coffee, so she was confident this was indeed his room.

Right next to the thermos was a small heap of documents. The contents spread out on the table stopped her in her tracks. She picked up a few pictures and notes that were paper clipped together. Removing the paper clip, she shuffled through the documents.

"Oh, no," she said when she noticed they were the

pictures and notes that she had taken of Jim. Racking her brain, she remembered when she'd bumped into Jim on the elevator. At the time, she hadn't thought she'd dropped anything. Then she remembered that he had stepped out of the elevator when he hadn't needed to and stepped back in before it closed. *Had he pushed the pictures into hiding when I ran into him?* She suddenly dropped the pictures on the table when she noticed a picture of herself clipped to a file folder. The picture was taken the day she'd arrived at the Peter Vallant Company.

Her fingers were trembling as she flipped open the folder and spotted several more pictures of herself and a timeline of her daily schedule since the start of the appreciation tour in Springfield, Illinois. When she left for her morning jog and the time she had lunch every day. But then she noticed more pictures in the back of the file that included her life before the appreciation tour. Jim had pictures of her leaving a clothing store and walking out of Union Station in Chicago. Cyd brought one hand to her mouth to cover her gasp as she noticed more personal pictures of her walking down the street to work and others of her leaving her condo. And another when she entered her condo's parking garage to get to her car. She looked at her outfits she wore in the pictures and realized they were all taken after her first meeting at the Peter Vallant Company months prior.

"Oh…my…God," she said, dropping all the contents in her hand as they landed on the table and partially on the floor. *How could I not notice I was being followed,* she thought. She became instantly overwhelmed by the information she'd just uncovered, and Shawn's cautionary words that she had put herself in danger popped into her mind.

She lifted her head as her heartbeat quickened. He was there…with her in the room. He had to be. It felt like a setup and she was pretty sure she'd fallen right into his trap. She lifted her head and noticed a shoe sticking out from under the curtain in her peripheral vision.

The best thing you can do is pretend you didn't see his shoe and make a run for it, she thought to herself as she tried to slow down her heartbeat. Within seconds, she leaped over the table and ran toward the door. One more leap over a plant and her right arm and leg were already out the door. But he was quick on her tail and caught her left arm and placed his leg in front of her left one.

"It's about time you found out my secret," Jim said to her as he pulled her into his chest and kicked the plant that was propping the door open out of the way.

Cyd screamed, but Jim placed his hand over her mouth as his arms pressed into her abdomen. She chose not to say anything else for fear that her mouth over the past few weeks had already gotten her in enough trouble. He brushed her hair out of her face and pulled a handful to his nose.

"I always loved how your hair smelled," he said to her as he pulled her unwillingly to the balcony. He opened the door and dropped two rope ladders over the railing. "It's time for us to take a little trip," he said before he told her to remove her heels and climb down the ladder.

"In case you think about pulling any funny business, this should help diminish those ideas." Cyd felt the cold handgun pressed against her side and she nodded in understanding. *Oh, no…. What have I gotten myself into?*

Chapter 10

Something isn't right, Shawn thought as he dodged around Brittany, who had been flaunting her outfit in front of him since she'd arrived. He glanced at Kim Lathers as she was concluding her speech before he opened the agenda and noticed that Jim Pearson had actually been supposed to speak before her. He could barely hear himself think over the flirtatious words Brittany was throwing his way.

"Brittany, my apologies, but I'm definitely *not* interested. Why don't you find another man to intrigue," Shawn said as he gently pushed her away from him. She muffled an expletive under her breath before flipping her hair over her shoulder and sauntering away from him.

"Any visual on Cydney Rayne or Jim Pearson?" Shawn said silently into the two-way radio microphone. The voices on the other end of his earpiece all voiced no. Micah got offstage and headed over toward Shawn. "Paul Jensen is toward the front of the audience, but no sign of Jim."

"Or Cydney," Shawn said, moving across the crowd.

He gave his men orders to be on alert while he and Micah left the room.

"I'll check Jim's room and you check the security cameras," Shawn said to Micah.

"Right away," Micah replied before running down the hall to the security room. Shawn took the stairs in hopes that he would find Jim or Cydney in the stairwell. No such luck. When he reached Jim's floor, he pulled out his pistol before opening the door to the floor.

The level was quiet and as Shawn made his way to Jim's door, he hoped that his suspicions weren't true. When he reached the door, he opened his wallet and took out a credit card. He entered his room key card into the slot, knowing it wouldn't unlock the door, but needing it to at least prompt the process of recognizing if the key was correct so he could slide his credit card into the side of the door at the same time. After three tries, it worked and the door popped open. Shawn did a quick, yet thorough, scan of the suite and concluded that neither Jim nor Cydney were in the room.

"Shawn," Micah called into his earpiece. "The cameras show Cydney entering the room that had been left open and not exiting. It's hard to say, but I think she tried to get out because five minutes later, there appears to be an arm that reached out of the door before the door closed."

"Crap," Shawn voiced into his two-way mike as Micah confirmed his suspicions in the same moment that he noticed pictures of Cydney spread out across a coffee table. Shawn saw the window curtains sway as a soft breeze floated into the room.

"Micah, he's got her and apparently he's been following her since before the tour," Shawn said as he ran to the balcony, immediately noticing rope ladders hanging over the edge. "Check the outside security cameras. Men, one of you is to stay alert in conference room A while the other two check the lobby and inside the hotel."

Shawn placed both arms over the balcony and scanned the grounds below, trying to find anything in the darkness. He noticed a couple walking in the distance and knew from the way the woman walked that it was Cydney and Jim. Since she wasn't screaming, Jim had to have a gun.

"Men, they're outside in the south wing." Without giving it a second thought, Shawn leaped over the balcony and began climbing down one of the ladders.

"The speeches have concluded in conference room A," voiced one of his men. "But I noticed a few extra men that hadn't been present the entire night."

Shawn's hands tensed on the rope as he listened to one of his men request that the other two stay alert in the hallway. Now that the kick-off meeting had concluded, it was harder to keep eyes on everyone. Shawn waited until he was on ground level before speaking into his microphone again. "I need someone here to assist me in the south wing. Pearson is in sight."

"I'll be right there," replied one of his men.

If Shawn knew anything, he knew that he didn't have time to wait for help to arrive. There was no way he was letting anything happen to Cydney. Shawn reached them in record time and hid behind a bush to see why Jim had stopped walking. Then he noticed the parked van covered by tree branches. It looked just like the Peter Vallant Company brown vans but a glance at the number on the side of the van proved that it wasn't one of the originals. *He duplicated the van,* Shawn thought as a few other pieces of the case began melding together. There was no telling how many had been duplicated.

Shawn got a little closer to them when he saw Jim place his gun on the top of the van and dig in his pocket to answer his phone. From Shawn's angle, he saw Cydney glance around the area as if contemplating what her next move would be. *She probably knew the call was coming,* Shawn thought as he remembered the personal investigation Cydney had conducted. Jim yelled into the phone, distracted by the caller and in obvious disagreement with the plan the caller must have stated. Jim's distraction gave Shawn his opening to rescue Cydney.

He quietly approached Jim and Cydney, only pressing his pistol to Jim's back when he heard him end his phone call.

"I suggest you don't make any sudden movements," Shawn said as he used his other hand to knock Jim's gun off to the other side of the van. "Now release your hold on Cydney."

Jim did as he was told, and as soon as he did so, Shawn pushed Jim against the car before turning him around and securing his arm under Jim's neck.

"Shawny boy, you're way out of your league with this," Jim said in a strained voice when his eyes landed on Shawn.

"We'll see about that," Shawn said as he pushed his arm farther into Jim's neck and took out his handcuffs.

"You're right," Jim said with a vindictive laugh. "We will see. We'll see how macho you are when they get a hold of your stuck-up princess over there," Jim yelled as Shawn pushed his head farther into the van, after the handcuffs were secure. "You'd better watch your back,

Ms. Rayne," he added with a malicious laugh. Shawn roughly took him off the van and prepared to walk him toward the hotel, but Jim lunged toward Cydney as if to scare her more than he already had.

Thinking out of anger and pure irritation, Shawn bashed Jim's head against the door of the van and knocked him unconscious. He picked up his lifeless body and turned him on his back. Shawn looked up at Cydney, barely able to see her in the darkness.

"Cydney," Shawn called aloud. "I know you're angry and scared, but I need you to help me." She got closer to him and only then did he notice the unshed tears in her eyes. She looked down at Jim before squatting to help Shawn. Together, they pulled Jim's body a few feet as one of Shawn's men appeared.

"Micah, what's your location?" Shawn said into his mike after one of his men assisted in locking Jim away in a secure location just outside of the hotel.

"The west wing. Shawn, you need to see this."

Without waiting another second, Shawn gripped Cydney tighter and told his security officer to watch Jim. When he arrived outside the west wing, Shawn spotted Micah crouched down near a group of bushes. Micah turned at the sound of fallen leaves crunching under their feet.

"Take a look at this," Micah said, pointing in the distance as he handed Shawn his binoculars. "See any familiar faces?"

Shawn took the binoculars from Micah to observe the situation. About two hundred yards away stood a group of men barely visible by the lights in the parking lot. "Who are they?" Shawn asked Micah as he continued to view the men.

Micah glanced over at Cydney and then back at Shawn. "Check them out one by one," he suggested discreetly.

Shawn pushed a couple bush branches out of his way to clear his line of vision as he took a look at each of the men individually. "No, come on," Shawn said as realization hit him as to who the men were. In the parking lot in what appeared to be a business deal stood a couple of the Midwest's most influential businessmen, including men he'd seen on several occasions in the Detroit and Chicago P.D. offices.

"This is worse than I thought," Shawn said, for Micah's ears only. He peeked over at Cydney, who was now sitting on the grass with her head on her knees, no doubt still trying to comprehend what had *almost* happened to her. As if she'd heard him, she lifted her head and looked directly at Shawn, her big mahogany eyes full of questions that Shawn wasn't sure he could answer right now.

"Even worse," Micah said quietly to Shawn so that Cydney couldn't hear. "The hotel manager sensed something was wrong and called Indianapolis P.D. before I could stop her. She thought she was helping. Don't you find it odd that these men would feel comfortable enough to do business right in the open when you can hear the sirens in the distance headed this way?" Micah asked quietly so that Cydney couldn't hear.

"I guess there's no reason to leave when you have partners on the inside," Shawn said, passing the binoculars back to Micah and removing his phone to send Agent Wolfe a text message with a code they used in case one of them needed to discuss an urgent matter.

As he was typing the message, he noticed he was receiving a call from Agent Wolfe.

"Miles," Shawn said as he answered the phone, purposely leaving out the word *agent* before he stated his name.

"Agent Miles, this is Agent Wolfe. Something has just come to my attention that may affect your case."

"I was just about to message you about another matter," Shawn said, firmly knowing Agent Wolfe would understand exactly what type of message he was referring to.

"I definitely need to hear what is going on there, but unfortunately I was going to call you, anyway, once I received notification from our inside drug source in Detroit. It appears that a few new pictures are circulating of people who are assumed to be a new threat to their operation. I'll give you fair warning that your picture surfaced as one of them and so did one of Paul Jensen."

"What? That's impossible," Shawn said lowly into the phone as he took a few steps away from Cydney and Micah. "With me being CISO for the Peter Vallant Company, I understand why I'm a threat, but Jensen is one of our secondary suspects." It wasn't his first time being targeted and probably wouldn't be his last.

"Jensen should still be watched closely," Agent Wolfe replied. "We need to keep all our options open in case this is a setup. In the meantime, I need you to be extremely alert. We take threats against an FBI agent very seriously, although I'm sure I don't need to remind you of that. However, my source did confirm that they don't know you're FBI, so we still have that working in our favor. Jensen will need to be watched 24/7 and you will need to put one other person under immediate surveillance."

"Right away, sir," Shawn said in reply to Agent Wolfe's request. "Who is he?"

"It's not a he," Agent Wolfe said with a little more concern this time. "It's Cydney Rayne. She's the third person being targeted."

Shawn's back stiffened at the sound of her name as he pinched the middle of his forehead in an attempt to stop the headache that was rising. He hadn't had this particular feeling of apprehension in three years, and suddenly past situations flooded the forefront of his mind as thoughts of something terrible happening to Cydney swarmed in his head.

"Miles, are you there?" Agent Wolfe asked. Just to be sure that he'd heard the correct name, he asked Agent Wolfe to repeat the third person being targeted once more. Hearing Cydney's name again did nothing to ease his worry. Shawn confirmed that both Paul and Cydney would have around-the-clock watch and then he updated Agent Wolfe on the current course of events. Shawn agreed to set up a conference call with Agent Wolfe, Mr. Vallant and himself in a few hours so they could update Mr. Vallant on the case and decide if they needed to postpone the rest of the appreciation events. "Keep me in the loop," Agent Wolfe said. "I have a feeling since someone has connections with the Indianapolis P.D., they won't make a big deal about the possible kidnapping. They wouldn't want to bring too much attention to themselves, but they will be looking for Jim soon, so I may have to send reinforcements."

Shawn agreed with Agent Wolfe's assessment and as he was hanging up the call, Indianapolis P.D. began to arrive at the hotel. Shawn walked over to Micah and told him they needed to get the P.D. in and out as quickly as possible. They wanted to follow protocol so that no one suspected Shawn was FBI, but they needed to maintain a low profile, as well. And Shawn needed Cydney to be on board in order to successfully do that. He walked over to Cydney, who was still sitting on the grass, and squatted down beside her.

"Cydney, I know you're scared, but you're in my care now, so you're safe." He lifted her hands in between his in an attempt to bring her comfort. Her eyes that had been staring out into the distance turned to meet his gaze. They were still watery, but she seemed to be more at ease.

"I need you to trust me," Shawn continued as he helped her rise from the grass to stand up. "In a short while, the P.D. will probably need to talk to you about what happened." He began rubbing his hands up and down her arms. "I need you to tell them that you had stepped out to get some fresh air and were grabbed. But someone heard you scream and came to your rescue."

Cydney squinted her eyes in confusion as she observed his face. "Why do I have to lie?"

Shawn chose his next words carefully. "I need you to fabricate the story, not lie."

"It's the same thing," Cydney retorted in frustration.

"Cydney," Shawn said a little softer this time. "As CISO, I need to do my job, and there is something going on here that we haven't figured out yet. My team and I want to make sure that everyone is safe."

"Isn't that why we have the police? How would you and your team do a better job than the actual police?"

"Because my team is aware of more than the police

at this time. Something isn't adding up and to be on the safe side, we need to talk to some of our connections in Chicago before information is spilled into the hands of the Indianapolis P.D."

Shawn could tell she wasn't buying his story, but he didn't need her to believe him. He just needed her to follow directions.

"Cydney, please trust me on this one. You know from the short investigation you did on Jim Pearson that something is going on way beyond the everyday crime. Don't you want to get to the bottom of this?"

He knew he had her on his side when her face softened in understanding. "Okay," she said with an easy sigh. "I trust you."

"Thank you," he said then he gave Micah a positive head nod and encompassed Cydney in a hug.

Chapter 11

Shawn sent Micah to the secure location where they were holding Jim before requesting that one of his other security guards keep watch of the situation. *Hmm... P.D. only sent two cars,* Shawn noticed in suspicion and surprise. He darted behind the side of the hotel when a couple of the businessmen he'd been watching went to the police to inquire about what was going on, stating they were contributors of the Peter Vallant Company. Although they really could be contributors, Shawn didn't believe that the cultural fair was their main reason for being in Indianapolis. In case they had connections on the inside and had seen a photo of him being passed around, Shawn couldn't risk being seen.

Once he had a secluded hiding place on the side of the building where he could still hear everyone speaking, Shawn looked over at Cydney, who was talking with a police officer. It was evident that she was still shaken up, but she was handling the situation like a pro. He overheard her sticking with the fabricated story of needing fresh air and being taken by a masked man before screaming and being rescued by someone who she didn't know.

Shawn's attention was taken away from Cydney when he noticed one of the police officers a few feet away from her. The way he was watching her made Shawn uneasy.

"Take a look at the officer on your left," Shawn said into his mike to his security guard that wasn't standing too far from Cydney. His guard turned his head slowly as if surveying his surroundings before motioning with a subtle nod that something was definitely suspicious.

The police officer looked at one of the businessmen and nodded his head in Cydney's direction. The gesture was so quick that one might not have noticed the elusive way the officer acknowledged the businessman. But Shawn was trained to notice the slightest of movements and his quick eyes followed the way the men observed one another before they both settled their eyes on Cydney.

Moments later, she had wrapped up her conversation with the police officer and had turned to walk back into the hotel. "Stay with her at all times," Shawn said to his guard as he continued to observe the men outside. Once Cydney was inside the hotel, the officer who had jotted down the details of her story walked over to the other officer and was joined by one of the businessmen. They looked from the hotel entrance and back to each other, no doubt trying to develop a plan of action.

"Shawn, Cydney is refusing to follow me and insists she be allowed to go to her hotel room to change. I'll stand guard outside," Shawn heard in his earpiece.

"Absolutely not," Shawn stated into his mike. "She

needs to be taken to our office. She's too accessible in her hotel room."

Just then, the officers got back into their police cars, and two of the businessmen walked back into the lobby. *Man, I know that guy,* Shawn thought as he observed one of the businessmen. He'd seen him on a billboard or something, but he couldn't quite place his name.

"They're coming in," he said on his mike to his security guard. "Don't take the elevator to Cydney's room, take the stairs to our location. Do you copy?"

"Shawn," Micah's voice said into his earpiece. "The light isn't flashing that indicates his mike and earpiece are on. You need to go check it out. Last place I had him was outside Cydney's room." Seconds later, Micah's voice filled the mike again. "I have a visual. Our security guard is fighting another man on the floor. The other guy is taking Cydney to the stairwell. The rest of us are on our way for backup. "

Reacting as quickly as possible, Shawn entered the hotel through a side door and entered the stairwell, taking two steps at a time. When he was almost near her floor, the stairwell door above him flew open and he could hear Cydney's distressed voice.

Shawn was two floors down from them so he quietly opened the door to the floor he was on, preparing to catch the culprit off guard. Once Cydney and the man passed the door Shawn was stationed behind, he swiftly opened the door and entered the stairwell, knocking the man on the back of his neck with the bottom of his pistol. The man tumbled to the ground and almost took Cydney with him, but Shawn was quick to rescue her. Grabbing her hand and jumping over the unconscious man on the floor, Shawn didn't waste any time getting

Cydney out of harm's way. "I have her, but the guy is unconscious on the third floor," Shawn said when they exited the stairwell and ran right into a crowd of people. The event was coming to a close and attendees were beginning to leave the cultural fair.

"We caught the other guy, too," Micah's voice said through the earpiece. "We're on our way to get the guy you knocked out now." Shawn sidestepped through the mass of people as he tried to make his way to their secure office. Cydney wasn't fighting him, making the trek through the crowd a whole lot easier.

Suddenly, the hairs on the back of his neck stood on alert. Shawn stopped walking for a few seconds as he did a 360-degree turn around the crowd, making sure he kept Cydney safely tucked on his side. There were several men sprinkled in the crowd who no doubt had him and Cydney as their main course of interest.

"Cydney, we have to go for a little ride," Shawn said into her ear as he tugged her arm and ventured toward a side exit.

"Shawn, I'm scared," Cydney exclaimed behind him as they ran through the door. As suspected, a glance over his shoulder proved a few of the men were hot on their trail.

"I know, but we have to get out of here," Shawn said as he made his way to one of the vehicles he'd requested in case of an emergency. Shawn and Cydney darted through a parade of trees, leaving the hotel grounds with darkness working in their favor. The car was hidden in a parking lot behind several houses in a nearby neighborhood. Once they were inside the car, Shawn called Micah on his phone since his earpiece and mike were now out of range.

"Micah, we had to leave the hotel. There were several more men in the hotel lobby. I'll make some calls, but you and the men need to be alert. We can't trust the Indianapolis P.D. so I need you to make some calls to Chicago P.D."

"You got it," Micah replied. "We also found Paul Jensen in one of the utility closets near the conference rooms. He'd been beaten up pretty badly, but he'll be okay."

"Thanks. I'll make a call so he can be put under immediate witness protection." Shawn hung up, then hit number one on his speed dial, ignoring the curious look Cydney shot his way before he turned his head back to the window. The number he called went straight to voice mail so he was forced to leave a message.

"Agent Wolfe, this is Agent Miles," he said as he heard Cydney gasp before she placed her hand over her mouth and turned her head toward him. "We have a situation and we need backup immediately. I have Cydney Rayne, and the other victim needs to be placed under witness protection. My team is aware of the situation." He dared to look at her and instantly regretted it. Her eyes squinted together and her breathing grew more rapid. She was fuming. He could tell that she felt betrayed. He saw it in her looks and body language, but he didn't have time to dwell on the situation. He had to figure out where to take her until the FBI was able to get more answers. He didn't trust anyone right now and he refused to let anything happen to her. He knew seizing Cydney and escaping to a secure location out of the reach from any P.D. or drug-related gangs was against protocol, but reason had flown out the window the moment he'd noticed she'd been taken earlier that night. "Call me back ASAP."

After Shawn hung up the call, Cydney wasted no time asking the obvious question. "Agent Miles…as in an FBI agent?"

He looked from the road to Cydney, surprised that after tonight's events, she still looked as sexy as ever. He had enough experience to know that victims of any type of traumatic experience sometimes lashed out at those around them if they felt betrayed in any way. In this case, he didn't expect any different from Cydney.

"Yes, I'm an FBI agent," Shawn finally stated, watching Cydney as she put her head in her hands. When she lifted her head back up, her eyes were full of disbelief and astonishment.

An FBI agent? How in the world had she missed the fact that he was an FBI agent? "So," Cyd said with a slight drawl of her tongue. "What are you doing at the Peter Vallant Company?"

"Well, I run my own security firm," Shawn stated as he stared out into the dark road. "But I'm also working undercover for the FBI to try to solve a case that has taken three years to resolve."

"How long have you been with the FBI?" she asked quickly.

"Ten years," Shawn answered just as fast.

"How old are you?" she asked, a little surprised at herself for not asking him that earlier.

"Thirty-two."

"And you run your own business and work for the FBI?"

"Yes, my business is in the beginning stages."

"Then you must have a lot of resources to track people."

"I have resources and connections in the government or otherwise."

"You know a lot about me?"

"I know enough."

Hmm. "Do you mean you know me because you ran a background check or do you mean you know me sexually?"

"I take it that that is a rhetorical question, right?"

"No."

"Then the answer is both. I ran a background check and—" he said as he turned to look her straight in the eyes "—I definitely got to know you sexually."

Cyd's breath caught in her chest. *Don't salivate over him, girl. Get it together!*

"When will I be able to go home?"

"Hopefully in a week."

"A week! Where are you taking me?"

"Under witness protection…with me." *Aw, heck, naw!* She couldn't handle that. Asking him questions was not only taking her mind off what had *almost* happened to her, but it was also solidifying the fact that Shawn was a man she shouldn't be involved with. Not only was he missing attributes on her list, but he also had a dangerous job with severe consequences.

"What if I demand to go home?"

He gave her a sidelong glance. "I highly doubt you'd choose to be put in danger."

Only then did Cyd realize she'd been sitting as straight as an arrow in the passenger seat, afraid to relax until she understood what was going on. Their back and forth Q&A was exhausting, yet it was helping, and she tried to convince herself not to get upset at the man who'd recently saved her life not once, but twice. But she couldn't help how she felt, no matter how hard she tried. The fact that he hadn't told her his true occupation hurt, although deep down she understood why he couldn't. But the real kicker was the idea of her being forced to stay with him for a few days in who knows where. *That* really boiled her blood.

Cyd finally relaxed in her seat as the enormity of the possible circumstances that could have occurred enveloped her consciousness with brute force. She loved to live on the edge of danger, but she'd always gotten her thrills by leaping out of airplanes or diving into deep coves. Almost being kidnapped—twice—was *not* her idea of living dangerously. That was just plain dangerous. *Did I get myself into this trouble when I began my investigation of Jim Pearson?*

"Don't think it's your fault, Cydney." Shawn interjected her thoughts. "He'd targeted you long before you targeted him, but you're safe now."

"You know," Cyd said as she placed her right hand on the dashboard and leaned into him, "you really need to stop this whole mind-reading thing. It's beginning to creep me out." She gave a derisive look to match her sarcastic tone.

Instead of responding to her comment, Shawn gave her a penetrating stare that momentarily labored her breathing. Even with all the commotion that had happened earlier, his masculine scent encircled her nostrils and induced her desire. When he turned back to the road, Cyd took the opportunity to admire his profile. She noticed the worry lines in his brow, evidence that he was concerned about her. His right hand tightly gripped the steering wheel, flexing as he passed by cars as he switched lanes. Cyd's head dropped to the right as she studied his firm jawline. She had so many more questions she wanted to ask, but if she was honest with herself, she'd realize that she was afraid to learn all the answers, at least for tonight. She also realized that she didn't really know much about the real Shawn Miles, the man behind the devastatingly good looks and charming personality. Of all times to be mesmerized by a man, now was definitely not the best time. She thought he was mysterious before, but the man she observed now was far more mysterious than she'd imagined.

"Where are you taking me?" she asked as she leaned back to an upright forward position in her seat. He didn't answer right away and when he did, he kept his eyes glued on the road.

"I'm taking you someplace away from the public until I get a handle on what's going on."

Away from the public? "Like in the woods or something?" Cyd asked with a slight rise in her voice.

Shawn laughed at her question. "Or something," was his only answer. Only then did he glance over at her again. "Why don't you take a nap and I will wake you when we get there?"

"What about my family? They'll want to know what's going on."

"I'll call your brother-in-law Daman and he can inform your family. I want to check on a few things before you contact them directly."

"What about the rest of the events for the Peter Vallant Company?"

Shawn sighed before he responded. "Cydney, a lot has happened to you today and I need you to trust me.

I promise we will talk more once we get settled in our location."

   She took one last glance at him before she rotated to look out of the window. She felt safe with Shawn, and that was really important, but she wasn't sure she liked the idea of being placed under witness protection…with him as her protector. It wasn't because she thought he couldn't protect her from the people after her. He'd already proved he could. The reason she didn't like the idea was because he was now her sole protector, and not being intimate with him was going to be an impossible task. Her mystery lover had reentered her life only to save her from evils she hadn't known were lurking. And now, headed to an unknown location, Shawn had managed to land right where she hadn't known she craved him most—her heart.

Chapter 12

"We're here," Cydney heard Shawn say as she opened her eyes and stretched her back. She'd slept for much longer than she'd anticipated, but at least she felt more relaxed than she had earlier. She yawned as she looked over at Shawn, who was exiting the car. A quick glance at her surroundings made her breath catch in her throat. It was breaking dawn outside and the autumn trees were blowing in the wind. The brilliant colors of nature and soft hum of a nearby lake was breathtaking and Cyd could have appreciated the ambiance even more if they had been standing outside a hotel rather than a cabin. A camper was one thing Cydney Rayne was not. It was not that she detested camping; she just didn't enjoy the idea of roughing it in the wilderness. There was something about the dark of the night and uncertainty of what animals prowled around that had always been her reasoning for declining any invitation to go camping. *But you've definitely never camped with a man like Shawn Miles,* the voice inside her head reminded her.

"Um, where are we?" she asked Shawn as she joined him outside the car. Instead of responding to her, he smiled and made his way to the front porch of the cabin. Cyd followed Shawn through the dirt, her bare feet growing even filthier than before. She wanted to curse Jim for numerous reasons, one, probably the silliest reason, was that he'd made her discard her shoes before they climbed down the ladder at the hotel. Shawn took the stairs two at a time and Cyd was quick on his heels, swatting at a few flies on her way to the front door.

Opening the cabin door, Shawn stepped back to let her enter. "Welcome to my cabin in Gatlinburg, Tennessee."

"Tennessee!" she exclaimed as she walked through the door, not believing that they had crossed several state lines in the middle of the night. Cyd had stopped in Tennessee briefly years ago on her way to visit some relatives, but she hadn't been able to visit much of the area. "You own this cabin?"

"Yes, I do," Shawn said as he closed the door and began opening the blinds. "This is by far one of my most favorite homes."

"One of your favorite homes?" she asked him questionably.

"Yes, I own several homes including that beach home in Anguilla. But this cabin is one of the most rural, yet relaxing, places I own."

Who is this guy? CISO turned FBI agent turned multihome owner. Seriously? "Well, your cabin is very nice."

"Thanks," he replied as he continued to open the blinds. "There are two levels, four bedrooms and two bathrooms, a fully equipped kitchen and a Jacuzzi on the back patio that I will make sure is ready for you in case you need to relax."

She followed Shawn as he took her on a tour of the cabin. Cyd admired the rustic interior with fur rugs, solid wooden chairs, enormous ten-person dining table and large-mantel fireplace. The cabin was truly gorgeous, decorated with warm colors and a comfortable setting that felt very homey. Cyd instantly felt at ease even though they were still in the middle of the wilderness. It helped that there were also large flat-screen televisions in most of the bedrooms and living room.

"When will I be able to go shopping for clothes?" Cyd asked when she realized she hadn't been able to grab anything out of her hotel room.

"My team will ship all your belongings back to Chicago. In the meantime, I called my neighbors and had them stock the shelves and the closet in your room. You'll find clothes, socks, shoes and undergarments in there."

"Is that safe? To tell your neighbors I'm here?" Cyd asked, knowing they were supposed to be in hiding.

"Definitely," Shawn replied. "I trust this couple with my life."

Just as Shawn was finishing his statement, they arrived to the room on the second floor where she would be staying. Cyd was suddenly overcome with an uneasy feeling that she couldn't shake. She didn't like the idea of other people packing up her private belongings, including her undergarments and grandmother's diaries that she treasured. The only thing she'd managed to grab before she was snatched from her room was her purse that contained a little makeup, one of the diaries and other odds and ends that she knew wouldn't do her any good now. She didn't even have her iPhone since she'd dropped it during the attack.

"I'll let you get settled," Shawn said after he'd shown her where everything was in her room. Once Shawn left, Cyd opened a couple drawers and observed the different sizes and styles that had been gathered for her. Next, she went to the closet and ran her fingers over the dresses and jeans that were hanging there. Unlike the spicy pine smell of the cabin, her room smelled of fresh lavender. Usually the smell of lavender was very calming to Cyd, but today it was a reminder that she was far from home and away from the comfort of her loved ones. She'd been through a whirlwind the past twenty-four hours and she hadn't thought she needed much comfort…until now.

Cyd plopped on the bed and dropped her head into her hands, overwhelmed by the new emotions that overtook her. She felt like her nerves had been playing a game of Ping-Pong ever since the first attack, and even though she was safe now, she still felt on edge. *Please don't cry, please don't cry,* she chanted over and over to herself. She was a strong woman who could overcome anything and she refused to let Jim and whoever else was after her get the best of her. But even as she chanted the words, she could feel the tears in the back of her eyes demanding to be released. Her adolescent ways of playing detective were long gone. Not in her wildest dreams did she imagine that one day she'd be involved in an actual case and have to be placed under witness protection.

Deciding she couldn't be in her room any longer, she made her way downstairs to the only bedroom on the lower level, the one that Shawn said he would be occupying. Instead of the bedroom, she found him on the back porch checking on the Jacuzzi. He stopped suddenly and Cyd assumed he'd noticed she was watching him through the glass door. He didn't look up at her; instead, he looked at his wet shirt as he discarded it and continued cleaning the Jacuzzi. Her eyes had a mind of their own as they took in the complete view of his naked chest. It had to be forty degrees outside, but Shawn didn't seem fazed by the weather. "Hot-blooded male," she said to herself as she continued to watch him.

After he'd checked and cleaned the Jacuzzi, he swept the fallen leaves off the porch. Watching him clean the porch with the beautiful mountains in the distance was a picturesque scene Cyd wished she could keep with her forever. *There should seriously be a rule against a man looking that handsome.* His rugged look gave him the appearance of a mountain man, further proving that she hadn't really known the man behind the city swagger and captivating wordplay. Her center grew wetter the more she stood and watched him in his element. *Oh, no, please don't chop the wood,* she thought as she watched him pick up an ax and walk over toward the tree stumps on the ground near the porch. She could barely keep her legs closed now, so watching him chop wood without a shirt would no doubt soak her panties even more. As suspected, he went about chopping several pieces of wood, her pink essence throbbing with each chop of the ax. *Lord, have mercy.* Why did he make everything look so damn sexy!

When he looked as if he was coming back into the cabin, Cyd made a beeline dash to his room to wait for him. She didn't know why she didn't just wait for him in the living room where she'd been watching him outside. All she knew is that her first thought was to catch him in his room.

This is insane, she thought to herself when she quietly sat on his bed in the most erotic pose she could think of at the moment. She had almost convinced herself to leave his room and meet him in the living room when his six-foot-three frame engulfed the bedroom doorway.

"Where are you going?" he asked her in a husky voice as he leaned one forearm against the entryway. This man had the ability to make her feel like a nervous schoolgirl, adding another emotion to her already growing list of her current feelings since the incident.

"Um, I figured I would go take a shower," Cyd lied as she fully rose from the bed and tried to make it past him.

"I saw you watching me," he said as his arm enfolded her waist and gently tugged her to his damp cinnamon chest, halting her quest to get out of the bedroom. Cyd took several breaths before she got up enough nerve to look him fully in the eyes. And when she did, all the apprehension she felt was replaced by fiery need and potent attraction. His sea-blue eyes ventured to her lips only to return with a clear agenda. "You're sexy as hell," he said to her as his eyes darted from her lips to her dress.

"I can't look sexy after everything I've been through," Cyd replied shyly. She couldn't think straight when he looked at her with such inhibition. It was rare that she'd gotten to actually see him look at her quite like that. His lips curled up in the sexiest half smile she'd seen on him yet.

"I disagree," he said, right before he leaned in a little closer to her mouth. Once he was mere centimeters away, Cyd noticed the slight look of concern in his face.

"Are you okay?" he asked in the sweetest voice. Instead of responding, she nodded her head to indicate that she was.

"Are you sure?" he asked her again, not convinced.

"At first I wasn't," Cyd admitted. "That's why I sought you out."

"And now?" Shawn said as he placed his hand gently on the back of her neck while the other remained around her waist.

"Now I'm more than okay," Cyd replied, leaving his hypnotic eyes and landing her gaze on his juicy lips. Shawn then pulled her head closer to his, their mouths fusing together in a perfect union. A moan escaped Cyd's mouth when Shawn's tongue slid through her lips evidently on a mission to bring her to her knees in desire. *Mission accomplished,* she thought as she felt herself being lifted in the air and placed gently on the bed. He slid between her legs with grace and style as his hands pushed her dress to her waist. His lips never left hers as his tongue dipped in and out of her mouth, allowing more moans to escape. He left her mouth and began placing hard kisses on her neck. His lethal tongue was no doubt leaving imprints on every part of her body that he touched. When his mouth found hers again, his kisses grew slower. Shawn stopped kissing her and lifted himself onto his hands as he gazed down at her face. When he didn't say anything but continued to look at her, she noticed that the mask that was usually blocking his true desires was left uncovered for her to observe. She felt like there were still many secrets left untold, but what gave her hope was the fact that his look proved he wanted her to know some of those secrets.

She lifted one hand to his cheek as she searched for more reasoning and answers. The passion still lingered in the depths of his eyes, but vulnerability and intense desire were also present in his look. Apparently, deciding he'd shown her enough, he rose from the bed and helped her get up, as well.

"How about we both take showers and then we'll make something to eat?" Shawn asked.

Cyd smoothed out her dress as she tried to organize her thoughts. "Sounds like a plan," she said and gave him one quick peck on the lips before escaping upstairs to her room to shower. Once she was on the other side of the door, she lay on the bed and looked up into the ceiling. *Cydney Rayne, you've really done it this time.* Although Shawn had said none of this was her fault, she suspected he was trying to ease her worry. She'd always been told that her antics would get her into trouble one day, and finally she understood just how much trouble, reflecting again on the situation she could have avoided. Now she was stuck in Gatlinburg, Tennessee, supposedly in witness protection, and all she could think about was sexing the hell out of Agent Shawn Miles. *Way to have your priorities straight, Cyd,* she said to herself sarcastically as she got up to take a much-needed shower. *Maybe all I need is some me time.* She actually hadn't relaxed in weeks and although she wasn't much of a reader, she'd noticed the bookshelf was full of great novels. "Yup, a good book should do the trick." And if it didn't, it would at least prolong the inevitable.

Chapter 13

"Come on," Shawn said to himself as he adjusted his pants for the third time this morning. He'd had a hard-on ever since he'd kissed Cydney yesterday and it still hadn't gone down. She'd politely excused herself from lunch and dinner, leaving him horny and irritated. He left her food on the outside of the door and each time, he returned to find an empty tray.

Shawn figured she was avoiding him, for what reason, he had no idea.

"Cydney, are you ready?" he yelled up the stairs. His neighbors had invited them over for brunch and Shawn was going to use the time after brunch to pick up some necessities and call Agent Wolfe. He knew his neighbors would keep Cydney busy while he handled his business and went into town to get some supplies.

Mama Jessie and Papa Willie were more than his neighbors, they were his godparents and the couple who had raised him. Mama Jessie was best friends with his mom, and Shawn would forever be grateful for the love and support he'd gotten from them.

"Here I am," she said as she made her way down the

stairs. She had on a pair of blue-jean capris and a navy blue blouse that would look modest on most women, but on Cydney, it looked sensual. "I may be a little cold, but it was hard to find pants that fit the way I needed them to," she continued to say.

"You look great," he said when she reached the bottom of the stairs, his eyes glued to the part of her legs that were showing beneath the capris.

"You look nice, too," she said with a slight gleam in her eyes.

"Finally I'm getting you out that room."

Cyd raised an eyebrow at his statement. "It's only been a few hours," she said, crossing her arms over her chest. "Besides, I'm reading a great book." Book or no book, she was definitely avoiding him. But if she wasn't ready to admit it, he wasn't going to force her. Sooner or later, she'd have no choice but to come to terms with her feelings for him.

Slow down, Miles, he warned himself. The last thing they both needed was to get too deeply involved before the case was solved. Feelings clouded judgment and Shawn was already in too deep with Cydney.

"I called Daman last night," Shawn said as he and Cydney made their way to the front door. "My neighbors live a couple miles away, so you can call your sister when we get to the car. She's expecting your call."

"Thank goodness," Cydney said as she jumped up and down with glee. "I need to talk to her so badly."

As crazy as it seemed, Shawn felt a tinge of jealousy that he wasn't the reason behind her happiness. They got into the car and Cydney wasted no time hurrying Shawn to hand over his cell phone. Imani answered on the third ring.

"This is Imani Rayne-Barker."

"Sis, it's me, Cyd."

"Oh, my God, Cyd, are you okay? Daman told me he spoke with Shawn. I've been worried sick."

"I'm fine. It's been an insane couple days, but I'm finally safe...thanks to Shawn," Cyd said as she momentarily glanced at him.

"Honestly, I would have probably gotten the girls and driven to Indianapolis myself had it not been for Shawn."

"I know," Cydney said with a sigh. "I can't believe the mess I've gotten myself into."

"Daman wouldn't tell me details, but I highly doubt any of this is your fault," Imani replied. When Shawn had told Daman some of the story, he'd left it up to him as to what he told his wife.

"Thanks, sis. Did you tell Mom and Dad I'm okay?"

"Yes, I told them that you'd fallen for Shawn and the two of you took an impromptu trip out of the country and you left your phone." Shawn choked back a laugh when all the color drained from Cydney's face. He was trying not to eavesdrop on their conversation, but it was hard considering his phone was connected to the car's speaker.

"What!? Imani, why would you tell them that?"

"So they wouldn't worry, why else! They met Shawn at the wedding and Shawn gave Daman permission to tell them he's in the FBI. They agreed to keep it secret and Mom was thrilled that you'd finally met a man." That time, Shawn couldn't hold back and let out a hearty laugh.

"But Shawn and I aren't a couple! What happens when I have to tell Mom and Dad the truth?"

"Well, little sis, my gut is telling me that you and Shawn are way past friends. Are you telling me y'all haven't had sex again since my wedding?"

"Imani, he can hear you! You're on speakerphone."

Imani laughed on the other end of the call. "Duh, I know that. Why do you think I brought it up?"

"Okay," Cyd said, clearly even more embarrassed than before. "On that note, I think I'll hang up now."

"Don't hang up on my account," Shawn interjected. "Hey, Imani," he said, greeting Cydney's sister.

"Hi, Shawn," Imani eagerly replied. "Thanks for taking care of my sister."

"It's been my absolute *pleasure*," he said, purposely insinuating that he was doing more than just protecting her. He was rewarded by a hard punch on the shoulder by Cydney.

"Cyd," Imani said. "Before I go, Lex, Mya and I have a message for you."

"Oh, really," Cyd said as she looked over at Shawn again with a look of innocence.

She wouldn't be looking at me like that if she knew how badly it made me want her, he thought.

"And what might that be?" Cyd continued.

"Daman mentioned that you'd be somewhere for a week, so if you can go grocery shopping, make sure you buy a few cans of pineapples to stock in the cabinet. Fresh pineapples are better, but I'm not sure where you are and what you have access to."

"Why would I need a bunch of pineapples?" Cyd asked in confusion. Shawn knew exactly what Imani was talking about. Pineapples were his favorite fruit and he'd read more than a few articles about its benefits.

"Pineapples are known to make the female juices

taste better," Shawn responded to her question. "The more you eat, the better you taste." He was well aware of the double meaning in his statement and his eyes landed on hers as she looked at him with awe.

"Seriously," Cyd replied in a soft, yet disbelieving, voice. "How do you know that?"

"I happen to love pineapples," Shawn answered matter-of-factly. He purposely licked his lips as he overly enunciated the last words of his next statement. "I even heard that using the fruit while making love makes for a very delicious kind of sex." His eyes darted between the road and Cydney, mesmerized by the desire building in her eyes.

"Okay," Imani said, interrupting the silence and sexual tension in the car. "Now I feel like I'm violating a special moment between you two, so I'll let you both go. Cyd, I love you! Shawn, make sure you let my sister call and check in!"

"I love you, too," Cydney said, her eyes still glued to Shawn.

"Will do," Shawn replied before disconnecting the call and turning toward Cydney again. The road demanded that he focus, so he had no choice but to retreat from her gaze. He picked up his water bottle to take a sip, grateful that he'd chosen to bring the cool liquid with him on the short trip to his neighbors' home. His body needed a dose of coolness to bring back down his suddenly hot temperature.

"I wonder what I taste like…." Cydney stated in a come-hither kind of voice that caused him to almost spit out the water in his mouth. "Guess I need to invest in some pineapples."

Once again, his eyes darted between her and the

road, the road losing the concentration battle. "From what I remember, you already taste sweet," he said, barely finding his voice after her surprise statement.

"But your tongue hasn't really dived into me yet," Cydney replied as she smacked her lips to get her point across. *Why the heck was she saying this stuff now and not when they were back at the cabin?*

"Cydney," he said in a ragged voice when he reached his neighbors' house and parked the car in their dirt driveway. "You decide to flirt now...after you ignored me most of yesterday?"

Instead of answering his question, she tilted her head to the side and gave him her million-dollar smile. He was sure that smile had brought many men to their knees in surrender, so he might as well just give up now and add his name to her list of captives.

"If this is payback for me being hot and cold with you during the appreciation tour, then I apologize. I was just trying to do my job."

She didn't say anything and her smile turned to an expression of temptation, slowly drawing him in. She deliberately stuck out her tongue and then bit her bottom lip as she placed her hand lightly on his thigh. *Don't do that.* He needed her *not* to touch him right now. They had a brunch to attend and being *excited* at brunch with neighbors he hadn't seen in a few months was a *very* bad idea. Luckily, she removed her hand after a couple strokes up and down his thigh.

Shawn had an acute ability to read between the lines, but he wasn't seeing any lines between him and Cydney.... Only an open field to play a passionate game of touch football. She had to know what she was doing to him, but she made the act of seduction look effortless.

She blew out a deep, long sigh before he heard the word *pineapples* slip through her lips. She leaned in closer to his ear and flicked the lobe with her tongue before opening the passenger door and hopping out of the car. By the time Shawn had gotten out of the car, Cydney was already on his neighbors' front porch, waiting for him to join her.

Her sister should have never mentioned pineapples. Now she had ammo to use against him, and there was no doubt in his mind that she would use this knowledge to her advantage. Hell, she'd already started using the information against him. When he got out of the car, he looked toward the sky and held out his hands in surrender.

By the time he arrived at the stairs, Willie and Jessie Johnson had already answered the door. "Shawn," Mama Jessie yelled as she ran up to him to give him a hug. "Hey MJ," Shawn said as he returned her embrace. When he was a child, unlike most three-year-olds, Shawn knew that Willie and Jessie Johnson weren't his parents. Even at a young age he'd had a keen sense of awareness. So instead of calling them Mom and Dad, Shawn referred to them as Mama Jessie and Papa Willie. "Cydney Rayne, this is Mama Jessie and Papa Willie, or MJ and PW as I affectionately call them."

"Nice to meet you both," she said as she gave each of them a hug.

"Oh, she's a beauty," Mama Jessie said as she took Cydney's hands and led her into their house.

Papa Willie slapped him on his back as they followed the women into the house. "You did good."

"Thanks, PW," Shawn replied. "But we're just friends." Cydney overheard his reply and tucked some fallen hair behind her ear before turning to give him a quick smile. *She looked sexy.*

"Shawn," Papa Willie said when they'd fully entered the home. Only then did Shawn notice he was still fixated on Cydney.

"Yes," Shawn said at Papa Willie's successful attempt to get his attention. Papa Willie looked from Shawn to Cydney once more before giving Shawn a slight nod of disbelief.

"Whatever you say, son," Papa Willie said before closing the door and leading Shawn to the dining room.

After brunch and a quick run to a nearby hardware store, Shawn returned to the Johnsons' home and went straight to the den to call Agent Wolfe, who wasted no time informing him that Jim hadn't budged and wasn't talking.

"The FBI has ways of making criminals talk, and Jim doesn't strike me as the type who can withstand any rough handling."

"My sentiments exactly," Agent Wolfe agreed. "As far as the other men, we're trying not to bring the media into this. One of the men who was trying to kidnap Ms. Rayne was Bob Noland, CEO of one of the largest fast-food chains in Illinois."

"I knew he looked familiar," Shawn interjected.

"Our assumption is that they hadn't expected to get their hands dirty and tried to take matters into their own hands when they noticed Cydney had escaped," Agent Wolfe continued. "He called his lawyer and some people in the media are beginning to get suspicious since we postponed the rest of the Peter Vallant Company appreciation tour, so we may only be able to keep this under wraps for a few more days. One thing's for sure—you need to keep Ms. Rayne safe until we find out more. Is your cabin stocked with supplies just in case?"

Agent Wolfe wasn't talking about normal supplies, but rather equipment that would help them in case they were attacked or felt threatened. The FBI had trained him well so he was ready for any situation. "Yes, I'm prepared."

"Good, I'll keep you updated. Oh, and, Shawn," Agent Wolfe continued, "other agents were questioning why you didn't bring Ms. Rayne to an FBI secure location so she could be placed in witness protection. I vouched for you, but you'd better not disappoint me."

"I assure you, sir, she will be safe here."

Agent Wolfe was the only one in the agency who knew where they were and Shawn wanted to keep it that way.

"I'm confident that you will, but I'm not stupid. You're an excellent agent and you're always on high alert. Don't let your relationship with this woman cloud your judgment."

Shawn knew that Agent Wolfe would eventually bring up the obvious. Though he hadn't really known he was going to take Cydney to the cabin until she'd fallen asleep and he felt himself turn the car in the opposite direction.

Shawn ended his call with Agent Wolfe and walked into the living room just as Mama Jessie was taking out old photo albums that contained photos of Shawn and the rest of his family. Shawn knew Cydney would have questions for him once she noticed he was in the photo albums a lot.

"Did you use to spend every summer here?" Cydney asked as she studied each page.

"Yes, something like that," Shawn replied as he adjusted himself on the sofa. Cydney flipped through a few more pages, glancing at him in between pages.

Shawn ignored the look that Papa Willie and Mama Jessie gave him as Cyd went through pictures of him with their two sons. They could obviously tell he hadn't told her his situation based on the way she was reviewing the pictures. But he didn't see any reason to tell her just yet. *I'll just tell her when we get back to the cabin,* he thought as he started a conversation with Papa Willie to get the attention off him.

"Aw, this baby is so adorable," Cydney gleefully exclaimed. "Who is the little cutie? Is this Shawn?"

Shawn, who had been engrossed in a conversation with Papa Willie, suddenly whipped his head toward the photo album. He walked over to the album to get a closer look at the picture. *That is me....* He hadn't seen a baby picture of himself in years and he honestly didn't know how he felt about seeing the picture.

"Is that you?" Cydney asked again when no one responded.

Instead of answering her, Shawn looked from Papa Willie to Mama Jessie. "How long have you guys had this picture?"

Mama Jessie got up and began stroking his back. "Willie took this picture a year after you were born, so we've had it ever since then."

Mama Jessie walked over to her husband and leaned into him as they watched Shawn's reaction to the picture. Shawn picked up the album and ran his fingers over the picture, feeling so disconnected to the people in it. He might as well be staring at strangers...himself included.

Cydney rose from her seat and placed her hand over his arm. "I'm sorry if I said anything wrong."

Shawn looked up from the picture and over at Cydney. "It's me and my parents," he whispered, surprised and angry that he'd almost forgotten how they looked. Cydney's eyes studied his face in confusion and concern. She had no idea how monumental this moment was for him, yet she was still trying to find a way to comfort him. In that moment, his breathing quickened for two reasons. One, he hadn't seen pictures of his family in over fifteen years and two, he'd never felt comfort from anyone the way he was receiving relief from Cydney.

"They died when I was three," Shawn said, a little above a whisper this time. He left out the part about how they died and luckily Cydney didn't ask him any questions. "They were both only children so I didn't have any living relatives. Papa Willie and Mama Jessie raised me like their own son and although they were great godparents and guardians, I was a very angry teenager. I got into more fights than anyone else in my school and in a rampage one day, I ran to the woods with a suitcase of family pictures and burned everything." Shawn waited for Cydney to stare at him in disbelief or shock, but she didn't. Instead, she just listened and continued rubbing his arm.

"Papa Willie eventually found me, but it was too late—I'd burned everything that was left of them. It took a day or so, but I eventually realized what I'd done." Shawn looked back down at the picture of him and his parents again. "I'd decided that from that point on I would stop thinking 'why me' and reacting out of anger and instead I would focus on being a better person…a better man. When I turned twenty-one, I bought my first property…the cabin we are staying at."

Shawn looked at Papa Willie and Mama Jessie before turning back to Cydney. "They both really helped me mold myself into a better man."

Mama Jessie dabbed a few tears. "His mom and I were best friends, and I love Shawn like one of my own," Mama Jessie said to Cyd. "And your parents would be so proud of you," she said as she looked at Shawn.

"I agree, they would. You turned out to be a remarkable man," Papa Willie said with a smile as he held his wife.

Years ago, Shawn had chosen to join the FBI to make the world a better place and to better himself in the process. He was far from perfect, and some people from his past never failed to remind him that he used to be a bad boy without a care about anything or anyone. But that was the old Shawn. The new Shawn had spent the better part of his life striving to be the best he could be. He wasn't sure if he'd ever be the type of man that left a legacy, but he planned to succeed at everything in life. *Succeed…or die trying.*

Chapter 14

As Cyd watched Shawn stare intensely at the picture, her heart ached for him. *He never told me about his parents.* She wished she'd known before she asked who was in the picture. Although he wasn't moving away from her touch, she felt his body tense under her hand.

"I'll be back," he said suddenly as he placed the album on the coffee table and began making his way to the front door.

"Shawn," Mama Jessie said as she took the picture of Shawn and his parents out of the photo album and walked over to where he was standing. "We want you to have this." She handed him the picture, but he didn't reach out for it.

"Take it," Mama Jessie said, placing the picture in his hand. Shawn gripped the photo and enveloped Mama Jessie in his arms. Cyd gave Shawn a smile when he looked at her over Mama Jessie's shoulders. When they detached, Shawn left out the front door, obviously craving fresh air. Cyd walked over to the living room window to see if he was going anywhere. She assumed he would go for a walk or get into the car and take a ride.

Instead, he paced back and forth on the dirt driveway, looking at the ground and kicking small rocks that were barely visible. *Goodness, that must be a terrible feeling,* Cyd thought to herself. She didn't even want to think about losing her parents. *I wonder how they died?* She was afraid to ask him when he had told her that they'd passed away, but she was so curious.

"He really likes you, you know," Mama Jessie said, interrupting her thoughts.

"Honey, stop," Papa Willie said playfully to his wife. Cyd turned around when she heard movement behind her. Mama Jessie came to stand beside her at the window.

"You like him, too," Mama Jessie said a little lower so her husband couldn't hear. Cydney didn't say anything. She really had no idea how to respond to Mama Jessie's comment.

"So, Cydney, let me ask you something," Mama Jessie stated. "How does Shawn seem to you right now? Outside kicking dirt and looking overwhelmed by his past. He's grown a lot since his rebellious teenage days, but—"

"I used to be rebellious, too, so that doesn't bother me," Cydney interrupted, although she hadn't meant to.

"What I'm saying is that right now, he doesn't look like the successful and confident man he has grown to be. Going down memory lane is reverting him back to those teenage years and provoking those feelings he used to have when he believed it was him against the world."

"Part of him still feels that way," Papa Willie added, proving he could still hear them talking. "Sorry, honey, you never could whisper."

Mama Jessie gave her husband a forgiving smile before turning her attention back to Cyd. "So what do you think he needs right now?"

Cyd tilted her head to the side and observed Shawn a little more closely. Every now and then, he would look back to the house as if he was waiting for something… or someone. He looked so defeated and all Cyd wanted to do was make him feel better, like he was king of the world—her world.

She shook her head slightly to clear her mind before answering. "He looks like he needs comfort or something to get his mind off the past that is clearly haunting him right now."

"Bingo! Told you she was a smart girl," Mama Jessie said with a laugh as she turned to her husband, then back to Cyd. "So why are you still in here with us?"

Cyd looked at Mama Jessie to respond but couldn't think of anything to say. *Is she suggesting what I think she's suggesting?*

"Go ahead," Mama Jessie said while she led Cyd toward the front door, with Papa Willie right behind them. "He needs comforting, and you want to comfort him, so you're wasting time being in here with us."

When Mama Jessie opened the door, she called Shawn to the door and gave them both hugs goodbye. Cyd expected Shawn to ask why they were leaving, but he didn't say anything. He actually looked relieved, although he hadn't said anything since she'd stepped out of the house. When he started up the car, they waved goodbye and began their short journey to the cabin. During the entire two miles, Shawn didn't say anything to her. She couldn't even tell how he was feeling. *Was he mentally exhausted? Angry? Sad?*

When they reached the cabin, Shawn got out of the car, promptly took some bags out of the trunk and went over to open the passenger door for Cyd. It was dark outside now, but she noticed him study their surroundings outside before he opened the cabin door. She waited until the door was fully closed, the alarm was turned off and a couple lamps were turned on before she said anything to him.

"Shawn, are you okay?"

"I'm fine," he said as he kicked off his gym shoes and dropped the bags on the floor near the door. "Just hungry as hell."

"Okay, no problem. I can fix you something to eat," she responded, kicking off her shoes, as well. "We haven't had dinner yet. What do you want to eat?"

He walked to stand in front of the couch, but the light from the lamp didn't quite reach his face so Cyd walked over to where he was standing. The minute she reached him, he pulled her to the couch, landing her on the side of him. When the light hit his eyes, she didn't see anything reflected in them but untamed animalistic lust, and the sight made her breath catch in her throat.

"I'm not hungry for food, Cydney," he said as he gently grazed her cheek with the back of his hand. "I'm hungry for you." With that, he adjusted her perfectly on her back, his hands already unzipping her capris and sliding them down her legs.

Now would be the time to stop him, she thought to herself when her capris slipped completely off, followed by her shirt. When his hands reached the top of her panties, he gazed up at her. At first, she thought he was waiting for confirmation so that he could continue. A closer look proved he wasn't waiting for confirmation at all. From the times they'd made love, she'd realized that he liked to look into her eyes when they connected in such an intimately indescribable way. He was doing that now. Intently watching her before they connected. Before he ravished her body. She opened her mouth. To say what, she wasn't sure. It didn't matter what she'd planned on saying because the only sounds that escaped her mouth were echoes of her surrendering to the sweetest seduction.

Shawn grabbed a remote off the side table and pressed it toward the stereo. Instantly, one of Robin Thicke's latest hits began playing through the speakers. Shawn snapped her panties off within seconds and entered two fingers deep inside her core. Cyd moaned even louder as her body began moving to the rhythmic pump of his fingers. Without warning, Shawn replaced his fingers with his mouth as he slightly lifted her off the couch so that he could grip her butt in his hands and secure her to his mouth.

"Oh, my," were the only words that escaped her lips as his tongue lapped her like a melting ice cream cone. She was supposed to be making him feel better, yet he was definitely exciting her in ways he hadn't before. When his tongue circled her nub and gently sucked her essence to the beat of the music, Cyd was sure she'd squirt her juices all over if he continued.

"I'm...close...to...climaxing," she warned him, her words scarce and scattered. Instead of stopping the erotic pleasure, his strokes grew deeper and stronger. When his tongue left her nub and dived into her center, she could hear the wet noises ringing off the walls.

She climaxed—hard. She was overflowing with desire and barely comprehended that Shawn hadn't stopped after her climax. She placed her hands on his head to push him away since the feeling was too powerful and never had she come twice back-to-back. Her hands denied her request and instead of pushing him away, they held his head in place as her hips lifted to meet each plunge of his tongue into her center.

Without warning, Shawn got off the couch and kneeled down while flipping Cyd to sit upright. He threw both her legs over his shoulders and pulled her closer to his mouth. *Oh, my goodness, what is he doing to me?* The stimulating foreplay she was having with Shawn definitely beat the basic canoodling she'd experienced with past lovers. When she felt herself on the brink of another orgasm, she didn't even bother to warn him. He knew what he was doing to her and Cyd wasn't sure her body could handle a stronger onslaught of his mouth.

"Oh...my," she screamed as her body combusted into a billion pieces of passionate pleasure.

"Hmm...your taste reminds me of delicious diced pineapples laced with brown sugar," Shawn said as he lifted his head and wiped the remnants of her juices from around his mouth.

Shawn quickly went to the discarded bags at the door, opened a box of condoms and took one out. He took off his jeans and shirt and put the condom in place before making his way back to Cyd to remove her bra, the only clothing she was still wearing. Only when Shawn had effortlessly lifted her off the couch did Cyd notice a large bearskin rug sprawled out in front of the fireplace. He placed her there, gently, before he positioned himself on top of her. Although his mouth had gone to work on her center moments earlier, he eased into her nice and easy so that she could familiarize herself with the length of him again.

Shawn looked into her eyes when he began moving in and out of her with purpose and skill. What she saw embedded in the depths of them nearly took her breath away. It may seem crazy, but Cyd swore Shawn looked at her as if he never wanted to let her go. As if she were a prize that he wanted to keep forever. Cyd knew there was no way that was true, considering they'd known they weren't meant to last forever, ever since the first time they'd made love on the beach of Anguilla. But if only for tonight, she planned on pretending that he really wanted to keep her forever. She entertained the blissful idea that he could actually be her Mr. Right. That he could be that one man who she'd realize she couldn't live without.

Stroke for stroke, Shawn managed to go deeper than before, implanting himself in parts of her inner body she hadn't known existed. The curve of his manhood poked and played with her G-spot, threatening to give her another release more powerful than the past two. She wrapped her legs around his waist and lifted her hips to the movement of his.

"Cydney," he grunted with a loud and powerful rasp as they both indulged in the sinful pleasure. Shawn pumped even faster and his head dropped back toward the ceiling. Cyd couldn't understand his incoherent speech, but his sporadic actions proved he was close to his breaking point.

Cyd wanted to wait until he released himself so they could climax together. A few minutes later, he surrendered to his desire and came inside her with a force much stronger than Cyd had expected. She freed her third climax along with his, savoring the satisfying feeling that overtook her body. When the feeling subsided, Shawn lay down beside her.

"That was amazing," Shawn said as he stretched out his body.

"I agree," Cyd said, rising just enough to prop herself on the palm of her hand. She was well aware that she was still completely naked and giving him a great view of her body by leaning up, but she didn't mind. She wanted him to see her—all of her. And after everything they'd done, it seemed silly to cover herself.

The room grew quiet, each of them apparently wrapped up in their own thoughts. "Do you want me to make you something to eat now?" Cyd asked as she thought about how that question had gotten her in trouble the last time she asked.

"Sure," Shawn said as his hand began rubbing up and down her arm. "We need to eat something to keep up our strength."

"I agree," Cyd said with a slight laugh as her eyes ventured the entire length of him spread out on the bearskin rug. *He even makes breathing look sexy,* Cyd thought as she continued her admiration. *How crazy is that! Since when do I find a man sexy after sex?* She could admit to herself that she was more of a love-'em-and-leave-'em type of woman, never wanting to cuddle after sex and most times not even finding the man that tempting afterward. Her friends often teased her by saying she was more of the man in a relationship and usually, she agreed with them...until now. Shawn made her feel *all* woman, which begged the question, was there ever any man in her past who she even felt remotely connected to like Shawn? The answer was simple—never. *Gracious, the man looked sexy loung-ing on the rug.* If she didn't get a grip, she'd be the per-son initiating another round of lovemaking.

Instead, she leaned over and gave him a soft kiss on the lips. Shawn pulled her on top of him, his hands grip-ping both back cheeks as the kiss deepened. Her hands made their way to his hair, enjoying the soft silkiness.

"We should probably make dinner," Cyd said, break-ing the kiss. Shawn gave her two more sweet pecks be-fore he nodded his head in agreement.

Cyd stood first and helped Shawn to his feet. She was heading to the kitchen, but stopped when she felt Shawn's hand on her arm.

"Thank you," he said, pulling her into his embrace. "I needed that." She didn't need him to explain what he meant. She knew he'd needed her once she saw him pacing outside Willie and Jessie Johnson's home. To be honest, she was glad that he'd needed her. It made her feel like she was more to him than just a bed partner, and *that* was a feeling she was definitely holding on to for as long as she could.

Chapter 15

While Shawn was in his office checking emails, he could hear the click-clacking of dishes in the kitchen. Last night, Cydney had whipped up steak and mashed potatoes that were so delicious Shawn's mouth was still watering. Tonight, Cydney had insisted on washing the dishes since he'd cooked his famous lasagna for dinner. He hadn't originally planned to cook the lasagna, but when he noticed he had all the ingredients, he wanted to cook something special for Cydney after a full twenty-four hours of intense lovemaking. Never had he wanted to cook anything special for a woman before. Most women didn't even know he could cook. Mama Jessie had made sure that Shawn had all the makings to be a great husband and provider, but Shawn had never chosen to share his attributes with a woman...until he met Cydney. Since meeting her, his life felt more purposeful and all he wanted to do was make her happy. But he knew his time with her was short-lived.

Shawn had made a promise to himself years ago that he would never bring a woman into his world. He'd seen a lot of stuff in his line of work and because of some tough cases that he'd cracked, he had more than a few people who wanted to see him dead. One could argue that a lot of those men were now behind bars, but the fact still remained that criminals often had people on the outside who continued to do their dirty work while they were locked up. News about the arrests that Shawn had successfully helped make years ago was dying down, but he was still on a quest to solve the last piece of the puzzle.

He reopened an email from Malik that had been sent to him and Micah. Everyone they'd originally investigated seemed to be clear. He received the same message from the FBI. *Damn, what am I missing?* Leaning back in his office chair, he closed his eyes and crossed his hands in his lap as he did every time he was gathering all the facts in his head. *Lead Detroit drug dealer locked up three years ago? Check. Peter Vallant van used to transport drugs? Confirmed. Jim Pearson is the mole in the Peter Vallant Company? Yes. Leading businessmen involved in dirty crime. Affirmative.* His phone rang, interrupting his thoughts.

"Agent Miles," Shawn said as he got up to close the office door.

"Shawn, it's Malik. I found some more information."

"Shoot."

"It turns out that Paul Jensen is a cousin of TJ Desmond." Shawn fell back into his desk chair at the mention of TJ's name.

"Are you sure?"

"Absolutely. It took me a while to find out the information. Looks like Paul went to great lengths to conceal his identity, no doubt trying to get revenge on someone. My guess is that Jim Pearson was his target or he thought he could lead him to his target."

"That explains a lot," Shawn responded as he thought back to Paul's behavior during the appreciation tour. "Did you find out anything else?"

"Not yet, but if I do I'll give you a call."

"Thanks, Malik," Shawn said before he hung up the phone and made a call to Agent Wolfe. Agent Wolfe was happy to get the information and put in a request to question Paul Jensen right away.

Shawn thought back to Agent Wolfe's words during their last conversation. Was Agent Wolfe right? Was being around Cydney making him lose his focus? Truthfully, no one would have known about Paul since it was clear he'd paid someone off to cover his true identity. And Shawn had indeed known that something was up with him, he just hadn't placed exactly what it was. But still, Agent Wolfe's words haunted him and made him second-guess his ability to be successful at his job and fall for a woman at the same time. *Fall for a woman....* Oh, yeah, he was definitely falling hard. *What am I going to do about my feelings for her?*

His head jerked when he heard a knock on the door. "Come in," he said as he waited for Cydney to enter. She peeked her head in the door first before coming completely into the office. She was wearing a black jumper that she'd put on after a recent lovemaking session. *Is there anything this woman wears that doesn't make her look sexy?* Even in clothes that Mama Jessie had stocked for her, Cydney still looked beautiful and stylish.

"I'm finished washing the dishes and started a movie. Do you want to watch the movie with me?"

A movie with Cydney sounded great, but Shawn

had way too much on his mind to focus on a movie. "I think I'll pass," he said as he tried to give her his best genuine smile.

"Okay," she said, although she didn't leave the office. She tilted her head to the side and squinted her eyes like she always did when she was observing his behavior.

"What's wrong?" she asked, crossing her arms over her chest.

"Nothing," Shawn lied as he closed out of his email.

Cydney squinted her eyes once more. "I don't believe you," she said as she made her way to him, pushing a few papers on the desk out of her way before she sat down. Shawn leaned back in his chair and looked up at her. She looked good sitting on his desk, and immediately his mind started thinking about all the naughty things they could do in his office.

"Get your mind out of the gutter, Miles," Cydney said with a giggle. "Tell me what's wrong. I already know that something is going on, but I don't know any details. Considering I'm here with you under witness protection, I think I deserve to know what's going on."

Shawn ran his fingers down the front of his face as he contemplated what he should do. He knew he shouldn't tell her everything, but something inside him wanted to open up to her. He kept so many secrets bottled inside and only a few select individuals actually knew the real Shawn Miles. Most people only knew the persona that he portrayed to the outside world. But Cydney wasn't just anyone. She was a woman who had sneaked her way into his heart before he knew what hit him. He wasn't ready to completely come to terms with his feelings for her because he suspected that she felt the same way. Shawn had accepted years ago that he would never, ever fall for someone to inevitably put them in the lines of danger. But no matter what the future held for them, he wanted to tell her the truth.

"Do you remember when I told you that my parents died when I was three?"

"Yes, of course."

"Well, they didn't exactly die when I was three," Shawn said, taking a deep breath. "They were murdered in our Detroit home."

Cydney's hands rushed to her mouth to cover her loud gasp. "Oh, Shawn…"

"I know, it took PW and MJ years to tell me the story," Shawn said, secretly encouraging himself to continue. "My father owned a cleaners that was located right under our apartment. He never turned away customers and was a community activist in our neighborhood. A lot of people looked up to him and at the time, my father believed he could turn any criminal into a man of God. One day, a young cat by the name of Leon Roberts walked into my dad's cleaners, walked straight to the front of the line and demanded my dad take him before his other customers because he had spilled something on his favorite shirt. My dad, being the fair man he was, told him that he had to wait in line like everyone else, despite the fact that the people standing in line had allowed Leon to cut them rather than be subject to problems later. But my dad wasn't having that. Leon took his clothes and left, but not before he yelled a bunch of expletives and threatened my dad that he'd be back."

Cydney sat still on the desk, her hands now removed from her mouth and placed on the sides of the desk. Shawn adjusted himself to sit more upright in his chair before continuing.

"After that day, my dad found out that Leon Roberts was assumed to be the up-and-coming drug dealer, having recruited young men and women from all over the state of Michigan. My dad was furious and began rallying others in the community to take a stand and fight for their community. From what PW and MJ were told from people in the neighborhood back then, Leon and his growing team quickly looked at my dad as a threat. He couldn't even walk down the street without someone following him or yelling at him by claiming that he wasn't really a black man and shouldn't even be in their neighborhood."

"Why would they say that?" Cydney asked.

"Because my dad was a Creole from Louisiana with lighter skin and blue eyes and my mom was a Detroit native who used to date Leon's uncle before she met my dad and realized she deserved better."

"Oh, my goodness," Cydney said as she moved closer to Shawn. "Was Leon's uncle in the drug business?"

"Until the day he died of lung cancer," Shawn replied. "Leon's father died young so his uncle, who wasn't that much older than him at the time, was more like a brother to him and no doubt had told Leon all about the situation with him and my parents."

Shawn stopped talking as he gathered together his next thoughts, realizing just how long it had been since he told this story. "By the time I was born, my dad was still fighting for a greater cause, but after five years of fighting, my parents decided to leave Detroit after my third birthday and make a permanent home in Tennessee."

Shawn looked at Cydney's eyes that were already

filling with tears. "Maybe I should stop this story. It's pretty depressing."

"I can handle it," Cydney said as she scooted closer to him. Shawn wasn't sure he wanted to continue, but Cydney was intently waiting to hear the rest, so he kept talking.

"Word circulated in the neighborhood that they were leaving, and the night before they were scheduled to move to Tennessee, my dad's cleaners was robbed. He went down to stop the culprit and was shot and died instantly. And the robbers didn't stop there. They went upstairs to find my mom and me. We were hiding in the closet. By the time police arrived, both of my parents had been killed and for whatever reason, they'd decided to let me live. Everyone knew Leon was behind their deaths, but back then, so many people were getting killed, the police had their hands tied. No one could touch Leon and his team."

Shawn noticed Cydney shiver a little as the tears that had formed in her eyes began to fall. He stood up in front of her and began gently wiping the tears from her face.

"That's so terrible," Cydney said as she pulled Shawn into a hug. "I'm so, so sorry."

Shawn accepted her comfort and leaned his chin on the top of her head as he continued to hug her. "What happened to Leon Roberts?" Cydney asked as she looked up into his eyes.

"That's a better story," Shawn said with a slight smile. "After I got my act together, I realized that I excelled in all the qualities needed to be a successful FBI agent. One of the main reasons I joined the FBI was to help fight for families who went through what my family went through. I met my boss, Agent Wolfe, when I was in college and was quickly recruited to the FBI shortly after. I had a lot of small cases in the beginning, but then I got put on the case to bring down Leon Roberts. After years of wanting to put that man behind bars, I helped the FBI convict him, and he's currently serving life imprisonment without parole."

"That's great to hear," Cydney said with a smile.

"It is," Shawn responded. "Only we weren't able to eliminate the entire drug operation. We had a key witness who was a teenager named TJ, who for whatever reason had become one of Leon's favorite rookies. When he got caught stealing, the FBI made a promise to reduce his jail time if he helped them bring down Leon. The boy agreed and I was placed on his case to protect him. But Agent Wolfe noticed I was getting too close to the boy and took me off the case."

Cydney started rubbing her hands up and down Shawn's back when he didn't continue right away. "I saw something in him," Shawn finally stated. "I had flashes of myself when I was a teenager and instantly I wanted to help the boy. I made a promise to keep him safe and one rule that FBI agents are always supposed to follow is to *never* make promises. The day TJ was to appear in court, he was shot on his way to the courthouse and permanently paralyzed."

"Oh, no, Shawn," Cydney said again as she continued to rub his back. "I know you were devastated."

"I was," Shawn said. "The case was pushed back and we were still able to convict Leon without TJ's testimony. But TJ and his family never forgave me for not being there. I haven't seen him since that day at the hospital when he was told he would never be able to walk again."

"But it wasn't your fault. You were taken off the case."

"Yeah, but I still should have protected him."

"Shawn," Cydney said, taking his face in her hands. "You aren't Superman. You can't save everyone. You couldn't have predicted something would happen to TJ on his way to the courtroom just like your dad couldn't predict that his refusal to serve Leon before the other customers would result in years of watching his back."

Shawn looked into her eyes that were still misty with tears. "You're an amazing man with compassion and loyalty for others. What you've overcome in your life is truly admirable. Don't you know how great you are?"

My compassion? Didn't she know that her compassion was the only thing that had given him the courage to tell her the entire story? Thinking back on the past times he'd told the story, he remembered leaving out key points that he didn't leave out with Cydney. Surprisingly, telling her the entire truth gave him a very serene feeling, which completely contradicted the way he should be feeling after sharing such a devastating story.

She's got you, Miles, the voice inside him said. *She's stolen your heart and you've given her a piece of yourself that will forever be hers.*

Chapter 16

The bulge in his pants began to rise the longer he looked into her eyes. He'd already released so much pent-up emotion, yet all he wanted to do was release himself even more…preferably deep inside of her.

"Wrap your legs around my waist," he told her. She quickly obeyed and when she was secure, he lifted her from the desk and took her into his bedroom.

"Do you realize that we haven't actually had sex in the bedroom yet?" he asked her as he placed her on the bed.

"Then what are you waiting for, Agent Miles?" Cydney replied as her breasts popped free when she pushed her jumper as far down as she could while he was on top of her. He took care of the rest, discarding their clothes in the corner of the room.

"I want to get on top," she said as she scooted from underneath him. He obliged her request and lay on his back.

"You are one sexy man, Agent Miles," Cydney said in a seductive voice as she crawled in between his legs.

He waited for her to make her way up his body, but when she reached his midsection, she lingered there.

"Have I told you how badly I've been dying to taste you?"

Say what? Did she just say what I think she said? Shawn swallowed a big gulp of air. "Taste me?" he repeated to clarify if he'd heard her correctly.

"Yes," she said as she placed her hand completely around his shaft. "Taste you." She licked her lips to emphasize her point and was rewarded by his member jumping at the sound of her voice and the movement of her hand. Cydney lowered her mouth onto him, taking in his complete length, which was *not* an easy task. Some women couldn't even handle him sexually because he was larger than they expected, yet Cydney had managed to completely surround him in her mouth.

"Ooh wee," were the words that escaped his mouth as she began to move up and down. "How are you—" His speech was momentarily staggered when she began to move her mouth faster, moaning every time he reached the hilt of the back of her throat.

"I did throat massages earlier today," she stated in between licks. "I wanted to make sure I could take *all* of you."

"You did not just say that," Shawn said at the idea that sucking him into submission was something she had preordained and even practiced for.

"Oh, yes, I did," Cydney said, moving her hands up and down as she played with his tip. "You should probably buy more bananas."

"Never, and I mean never, have I met a woman like you," he said breathlessly as he gripped the sheets when she began fondling him, as well. *Dang, she says what-*

ever is on her mind. Shawn was so engrossed in the foreplay that he knew he was on the brink of a hard and long orgasm. But he didn't want to release himself that way. He wanted to feel her wrapped around him. Tight. Wet. But Cydney wasn't having that.

"Cydney, I want to come inside you," he exclaimed as he leaned up on his elbows and tried to switch positions. She looked up at him, her mouth still attached to him as she licked his shaft up and down, her eyes never leaving his.

Cheeks clenched. Jaw set. Hands in motion. Shawn had to accept the inevitable—Cydney Rayne wasn't letting him go anywhere! In all his thirty-two years he'd never come during oral sex. After living a life where nothing had been in his control, Shawn decided long ago if it were in his power to control, then he would definitely do things on his own terms. But clearly Cydney Rayne didn't know that about him. Or she knew that he liked to be in control but didn't care.

"Oh, shoot," he said aloud, dropping his head back to the bed when he felt a tingling sensation start at his feet and make its way up his legs. Cydney must have sensed it, too, because she quickened her licks, suckling him in between the strokes of her tongue. Within seconds of his statement, he released himself into her mouth as his body jerked at the intensity of his climax.

When his spasms had subsided, Cydney crawled up to him and curled herself into the nape of his neck. "That was amazing," she said as she wrapped her arms around him.

"Amazing for you?" he exclaimed. "Hell, that was incredible, remarkable and any other word you can say to imply that something was out of this world."

She laughed at his statement and tenderly kissed him on his cheek before her eyes fluttered closed. He followed suit and closed his eyes as he pulled her even closer to him. *Way to go, Miles. Way to fall for the one person you should be protecting.* He'd probably fallen for her way before he'd known she would need his protection, but that was the crux of the problem. Shawn popped open one eye to gaze down at the now-sleeping Cydney. She was everything he'd always wanted and had convinced himself he couldn't have. Now that he'd found her—the one woman he couldn't live without— there was absolutely no way he was giving her up.

Cyd was the first to wake the next morning. The rays of sunlight shining through the blinds on the window landed right on Shawn's body, accentuating the entire length of his naked masculinity. With one hand, she ran her fingers over his abs, admiring how magnificent they looked when he flexed them during their lovemaking sessions.

They had both woken in the middle of the night when Shawn's phone had rung. After his call, he'd explained the rest of the case to Cyd and told her how the Peter Vallant Company, Jim Pearson, Paul Jensen and now Bob Noland, CEO of a chain of fast-food restaurants, played a part in everything. Toward the end of the story, she'd asked him if she was in a lot of danger and he'd told her no, but not before she'd seen his hesitation. He seemed to be keeping something from her, and if she had to guess, she'd assume that someone in the drug business hadn't liked her snooping and was still after her.

Her eyes left his abs and went to his face. She was

honored that he felt close enough to her to discuss his past and in some ways, his present, as well. He'd gone through more pain in his thirty-two years than many people went through in a lifetime. Yet he'd chosen to take his pain and use it as a platform to mold himself into a better man.

Cyd eased herself out of bed, careful not to wake Shawn. Once she was out of the bedroom, she tiptoed up the stairs to her bedroom and went into her purse to find the only diary she had with her. She plopped onto the bed and positioned herself on her elbows as she skimmed the back pages, trying to find the list Gamine had written about the signs of knowing you're in love. Once she found the passage, she read each and every number on the list carefully with a newfound understanding of the meaning behind each number. She paid particular attention to the last and final number on the list. "Number twenty. He may not be perfect…but he is perfect for me," she read out loud. It was a simple line that contained a whole lot of meaning.

Closing the diary, Cyd lay on her back and stared up at the ceiling. Based on the way they'd met, Cyd would have never guessed that she would fall for Shawn Miles. She'd never thought he had any of the qualities she desired in a man to *love,* only a man to *lust.* But in actuality, he had more qualities of a man you love and lust instead of one over the other.

"Oh, goodness, I've fallen in love with him," she said to herself as she placed her hands over her face. She'd fallen for a man that she'd never seen coming and had given him a piece of her heart that she feared she'd never get back. Not that she wanted to get anything that she'd given to him back. She wanted him to keep every piece of her that he had for as long as he wanted, and *that* was a huge thing for her to admit. The fear came from the fact that she didn't think she could ever find a man more perfect for her than Shawn if they didn't end up together.

She analyzed everything that had happened since that fateful day they met in Anguilla. Shawn hadn't actually expressed any interest in building a relationship with her, which gave her an uneasy feeling in the pit of her stomach. *What do I do if he doesn't want a relationship with me?* She could tell by the way he looked at her that he had feelings for her, but she didn't dare ask him if he wanted a relationship. Although she now knew why he'd blown her off those times before, she couldn't shake the feeling of rejection that was his doing. She was hoping that he would make the first move and indicate what he wanted from her and what he was feeling. The more she thought about Shawn, the more she realized he was the type of man who probably didn't attach titles to his relationships. *But that's exactly what this feels like....*

"When did you leave the bedroom?" Shawn asked as he filled her doorway. She hadn't even heard anyone moving in the house.

"Sorry," Cyd said, sitting upright in the bed. "I didn't want to wake you."

Shawn made his way over to the bed and leaned down to give her a kiss. The sweet kiss quickly turned into a full-on make-out session that was obviously heading to something else.

"I have to take a shower," Cyd said when Shawn's kisses had moved from her lips to her neck. He stopped kissing her and flashed a wicked smile.

"Shall we shower together?" he asked, already standing and leading them both to her bathroom.

"You're insatiable," Cyd said with a laugh as she let him lead her to the bathroom.

"What can I say, baby," he said, joining her in laughter. "My loving is limitless." He pulled her into another kiss at the same time he masterfully turned on the shower. Cyd knew what he meant by the description of his sex drive, but she was hung up on the "my loving" part of his statement. *I wish you really did love me,* she thought to herself, finally, completely admitting that she was craving Shawn in every way possible.

Shawn got in the shower first, allowing Cyd a few moments to watch the water hit his body from a short distance away. When she entered the shower, Cyd squeezed some shower gel into the loofah and began rubbing the lathered suds all over Shawn's body.

"I must really like you," Shawn said with a laugh.

"Why do you say that?" Cyd asked as she continued to clean his body.

"Because I'm letting you wash my body with this girly soap."

Cyd looked at the bottle before she resumed washing him. "It's vanilla, a gender-neutral scent."

"No, it's not," Shawn said with another laugh. "Women say that so poor suckers like me won't complain when a gorgeous woman rubs the scent all over their body."

"So you think I'm gorgeous, huh?" Cyd said as she wiped his chest in a circular rotation.

"You're all right," Shawn answered.

"Not funny," Cyd exclaimed as she softly punched him in his arm.

"I'm just joking," he said as he took the loofah, squeezed on more shower gel and began rubbing it over her body.

Cyd relished in the seductive way he massaged the soap into her body. "You're absolutely gorgeous," Shawn said between strokes.

"Thank you," Cyd said placing her hand on the wall of the shower.

"Open your legs for me," Shawn requested. She did as he asked, her desire building stronger every second.

Shawn took the loofah and rubbed it between her legs, paying close attention to her throbbing bud of nerves. Her labored breathing made him increase his hand motion and push her even closer to her breaking point.

Oh, wow, she thought as she forced her eyes to hold Shawn's gaze. She'd never known how much pleasurable friction one could get from a loofah and hot water. Or maybe Shawn was just that great at understanding the inner workings of the female body.

"I'm just that good," he said, reading her thoughts once again. Cyd didn't even question it anymore and accepted the fact that this man was just connected to her and knew her better than most people she'd known for twenty-seven years. Right before she was about to come, Shawn suddenly stopped and connected their bodies with one quick thrust. Cyd looked down at their connected bodies and noticed the end of the condom peeking out between them.

"When did you put that on?"

"Like I said, I'm just that good," Shawn replied with a wink. "Lift up your left leg."

Once her leg was lifted, he grabbed her thigh to keep

her in place as he thrust in and out of her body. The combination of water hitting her clit while he rhythmically danced in her core was nearly her undoing. She watched him drop his head back and let the water hit his face. She had no idea how he was able to breathe, but watching him sex her with the water running down her body was way more erotic than she'd ever imagined.

Since arriving at the cabin, their sex and foreplay had been lengthy and satisfying. This time was definitely going to be just as satisfying, but she doubted it would be long. She'd give them two more minutes before they were ready to release the tension that was building up in their bodies.

"Oh, man, Cydney, I'm about to come," Shawn yelled, signifying that her prediction of two minutes was way too long.

"Me, too," she declared as she leaned into his thrusts by moving her waist in a circular motion while he continued to pump in and out. Her movement pushed Shawn over the edge, causing him to howl at the ceiling after his release.

Once they floated down from cloud nine, they quickly rinsed their bodies and got out of the shower. Shawn seductively dried her off before drying himself. Shawn then carried her to the bedroom, lightly placing her on the bed. He was just leaning down to kiss her when his phone rang.

"Hold that thought," he said before hopping off the bed and running down the stairs. *That was amazing,* Cyd thought in regards to her first time making love in the shower. Shawn was an expert lover, and a quick stretch of her body proved that she'd worked muscles she hadn't used in a long time. And those muscles had definitely never been worked the way Shawn worked them.

After several minutes, Cyd went downstairs to see why he hadn't returned yet. She found him in his bedroom, still on the phone. He gave her a quick smile when she walked into the room and sat on his bed.

"Yes, I will. See you soon," he said as he hung up the phone.

"Who was that?" she asked, noting that he didn't seem as happy as he'd been moments prior to the phone call.

"That was Agent Wolfe," Shawn said as he placed his phone back on his nightstand. "I guess the honeymoon is over. I need to bring you back to Chicago. We'll leave this afternoon."

Cyd noticed that he was searching her face. *Did he think I'd be excited by the news? Heck, no!* She still had no idea where their relationship stood and going back to Chicago meant going back to reality.

"So they caught everyone involved?" she asked.

"The FBI and P.D. are confident that they've caught everyone involved and the DEA is setting a plan into place to bring down the entire operation. Paul Jensen sang like a canary when he was questioned and admitted that he had been after Jim Pearson ever since he'd gained employment at the Peter Vallant Company. Paul figured Jim was key in his quest to get revenge for TJ. He also admitted to knowing who I was the week I began working for the company. Like his family, he also blamed me for allowing harm to come to TJ, but he believed there had to be a reason I was at the company three years after the case. I guess he was conflicted when we met because we got along so well and he wanted me to do whatever I needed to do to find justice. I don't think he's a bad guy, but he'll probably do some time for premeditating revenge, even though he never actually got the chance to harm anyone."

"That's sad," Cyd said, sympathizing with Paul. Shawn had a look of apprehension on his face and Cyd could feel his tension. "Are you confident they caught everyone?"

He looked at the floor before looking back at her, as if he were trying to gather his thoughts. "No," he said as he sat on the bed next to her. "But of course, I've been told that I'm paranoid at times. Until I feel comfortable with this situation, I'm not letting you out of my sight."

She saw the worry in his eyes, and although it warmed her heart, she wasn't sure if his worry was misplaced. "Shawn, if the FBI and P.D. are satisfied, maybe you're overreacting and—"

"I'm not," Shawn said, cutting her off. "Make me a deal."

"Okay," she said since she felt like she really didn't have a choice.

"Promise me that you will let my men watch you 24/7 until I get to the bottom of this."

24/7.... Was he crazy? "Shawn, I don't think that's necessary."

"Promise me," he said in a stricter voice. She studied his face for any sign that he would drop the around-the-clock security idea and concluded that she was wasting her time.

"Okay," she said with a sigh. "I promise."

Chapter 17

"Shawn, is this really necessary?" Cyd asked him for the third time that day. Since returning to Chicago last week, Shawn had been accompanying Cyd everywhere. News had broken out about Jim Pearson, Paul Jensen, Bob Noland and a few others the day after they'd returned to Chicago. The FBI was credited for being a key part in demolishing the huge drug operation, and the identity of the woman who'd almost been kidnapped remained a mystery to the public. Agent Wolfe informed Shawn that he should be elated that the entire operation was destroyed and a case that had been open for the past three years was finally closed. The damage that was done in the cities of Detroit and Chicago was far from over after it was uncovered just how many individuals were involved with Leon Roberts. At least convicting Jim Pearson and Bob Noland was a huge plus and had exposed many layers of the drug operation.

Nonetheless, Shawn couldn't quite pinpoint why he still felt the need to follow Cydney. She thought he was crazy, and from the looks he'd been receiving from Micah, he believed he was crazy, too. At least Micah's

brother Malik obliged his request and opened his search
to other employees at the Peter Vallant Company. He
couldn't shake the feeling that he hadn't found out if
Jim had another inside source.

"Shawn, are you listening to me?" Cydney asked
when they reached the front door of her parents' house.

"I'm sorry, what did you say?"

She gave him a look of irritation and placed one
hand on her hip. "I said that Sunday brunch is very
important for my family. My mom and partners will
probably throw questions at you left and right about
our relationship. Make sure your answers are concise
and to the point, especially with my mother. You don't
want to stumble over your words and give her ammo
to use against us. Understood?"

"Of course," Shawn said as Cydney rang the door-
bell. "But you make it seem like we're going to battle.
It's just brunch, right?"

Cydney gave him a look of frustration. "No, it's not
just brunch. If you say the wrong thing, my mother will
have planned our wedding and named our kids before
the day is over."

"Yeah, right," Shawn said with a laugh. "She can't
be that bad."

Cyd smacked her lips and shook her head. "I love
her dearly, but don't say I didn't warn you." The minute Cydney finished her statement, the door opened
and Hope Rayne, Cydney's mother, wrapped her in a
big hug.

"Mom, I'm okay, really."

"I know, but I still needed to hug you."

"Mom, you came to see me the day after I got back
to Chicago."

"And I haven't seen you since then," Hope replied as she moved to let them in the door.

"Hello, Mrs. Rayne," Shawn said as he leaned in to hug her.

"How are you, Shawn?" she asked with a smile before leaning in to give him a hug.

"Crazy busy since every day I have to convince your daughter to let me protect her."

"She may be stubborn, but I don't want you to let her out of your sight."

"I won't, ma'am," Shawn said, returning her hug and greeting Mr. Rayne, who had walked over to shake his hand. Shawn hadn't seen her parents since Daman and Imani's wedding, but he felt as comfortable around them as he felt with Mama Jessie and Papa Willie.

Shawn followed Mr. and Mrs. Rayne into the living room where Cydney was giving hugs to her partners.

"Hey, man," Daman said as he slapped hands with Shawn.

"Hey, man, how are you?"

"Good, now that my sister-in-law is safe. Imani was freaking out when I told her what happened."

"I figured," Shawn said, stealing another glance in Cydney's direction. "It was a scary moment for me, too."

"Yeah, I can imagine," Daman stated. "Having the woman you love almost kidnapped not once, but twice. That's scary for any man."

"Exactly," Shawn replied, only hearing part of Daman's comment.

"Oh, so you do love her?" Daman asked.

"Wait, what?" Shawn replied while shaking his head. "Did you ask if I love her?"

Daman shook his head and laughed. "Man, you're usually more alert than this. Does Cyd know?"

Shawn looked from Daman to Cydney, then back to Daman again. The way he saw it, he had two options—either deny the truth or admit he had feelings for her. Neither option suited him at the moment.

"Don't worry, I won't say anything," Daman said, slapping him on the back. "If it's any consolation, I think she feels the same way."

"Really?" he asked, although he hadn't meant to sound so eager.

"Yeah, really," Daman replied, laughing once more. "I know how you feel. My love for Imani sneaked up the same way. One minute, you think you're just having sex with an incredible woman and enjoying her company. And the next, you realize that no woman you ever meet after her will compare or make you feel complete. Next thing ya know, you're down on one knee proposing."

"Naw, man," Shawn said, waving his hands in front of him. "Cydney will definitely expect more than a knee proposal. She'd want the works. You know, something to tame that spontaneous side she has."

Daman gave Shawn a look of confusion. "You do realize that you basically just admitted to the fact that you're ready to propose to her, right?"

Shawn glanced back over at Cydney and shook his head. "Damn," he said with a chuckle. "When the hell did that happen?"

"Oh, sweetie," Mrs. Rayne said as she touched his shoulder with her hand. "Love just has a way of sneaking up on you."

Shawn turned his head at the sound of Mrs. Rayne's

voice before he turned to Daman, who was sipping his untouched soda and masking a laugh.

"Um...Mrs. Rayne, I... Um..."

"Don't worry, sweetie," she said, giving him another squeeze and winking at Daman. "I won't tell her anything. It's best if she hears how you feel about her directly from you. But if you need my advice on when and where to propose, Daman can give you my cell number."

"Sweetie, how about we set the table for brunch?" David Rayne, Cydney's father, asked with a smile on his face as he led his wife away from Shawn and Daman.

"You've done it now, son," Mr. Rayne said for Shawn's ears only. "Welcome to the family."

A few seconds later Shawn was still standing there with a stunned look on his face while Daman laughed harder than he had since their arrival. Even the women looked over to see what was going on. Cydney gave Shawn a look of confusion and waved her hand toward the direction of her mom, who was walking out of the room with her dad with an extra pep in her step. Shawn didn't know what to tell her so he rose up his hands in defeat and mouthed *sorry*. Cyd's eyes got bigger as she mouthed *I warned you* before turning back to talk with the women.

Mrs. Rayne popped her head into the living room and asked Shawn to help her set the table. When he didn't answer quickly enough she flashed a smile and asked him again. As he made his way to Mrs. Rayne, he heard Daman's voice behind him.

"Enjoy the talk with your future mother-in-law," Daman said with a chuckle.

Shawn was about to comment, but Mrs. Rayne stuck her head back in the living room before he could. "I heard that, Daman," she said as she pointed her fingers to her eyes before pointing at his eyes. "I'm recruiting you to help me clean up after brunch so you can explain how long you plan on making me wait before you give me some grandkids."

"Aha," Shawn said as he laughed and pointed at Daman before going into the dining room to help Mrs. Rayne.

"Shawn is sexy," said Lex.

"I agree," stated Mya. The women had escaped to the upstairs den so that they could talk and gossip without any interruptions.

"Ladies," Cyd said, getting the attention of Lex, Mya and Imani. "I think I've really fallen hard for this man."

"Oh, sis, we already know that," Imani said as she waved her hand in the air. "The two of you have barely stopped looking at one another the entire day. And Mom and Dad are on cloud nine."

"Yeah, I can tell they like him," Cyd responded.

"Like him?" Imani said in a surprised voice. "Have you forgotten how many crazy antics you usually get yourself into? All the times you've unexpectedly left the country without warning just because you felt like it? Shawn's an FBI agent and Mom and Dad love the fact that he seems to keep you more grounded."

"I didn't need to be more grounded," Cyd retaliated.

"Oh, yes, you did," Lex interjected. "Need we remind you about the mess you recently got yourself into? Following a man who turned out to be a dangerous criminal?"

Whoops! They have me there. "Okay, but that's over now."

"Because your knight in shining armor saved you," Mya responded.

"Twice," Lex added.

"Geesh," Cyd said as she slunk down into the sofa chair a little. "You almost get kidnapped twice and no one lets you forget it."

All three women just gave her blank stares. "I'm kidding, guys," Cyd said with a laugh before sitting upright in her chair again. "Tough room."

"You scared the crap out of us," Imani said. "But we don't just like Shawn because he saved you. We also like Shawn because as complicated as you are sometimes, he understands you and lets you be yourself."

Cydney looked down at her hands before looking back at the women. "I know," Cyd replied. "He understands me more than I understand myself sometimes. And I understand him, too, and connect with him way past an intimate level."

"So what about your list?" Lex asked. "I think I remember you stating a few of the attributes that you needed for Mr. Right, and if I remember the Mr. Wrong list, Shawn's career definitely puts him at the top of that list."

"Yeah, you're right," Cyd said with a sigh. "But while we were cooped up in the cabin I started to realize that although he may not be perfect, he's definitely perfect for me," she continued, quoting Gamine's diary.

"And that's all that really matters, sis," Imani said as she gently squeezed Cyd's hand.

"So," Lex said as she curled her feet Indian-style on the couch. "You have to tell us about this cabin hideout with Shawn. We've been dying to know what it's like to be in witness protection with a man like that."

"Oh, this is definitely something I can tell you all about," Cyd said with a laugh, as the women got comfortable so they could listen to all the juicy details.

Just as she was about to start the story, Shawn popped his head in the den.

"Sorry to interrupt, ladies, but, Cydney, can I talk to you for a minute?"

"Um, sure," she said, looking from her partners to Shawn. Each woman had a look of interest in her eyes, wondering why he needed her at that particular moment.

Shawn waited until she was in the hallway to talk to her. "I just had a three-way call with Agent Wolfe and Peter Vallant. Due to all the bad media that the Peter Vallant Company has been associated with, Mr. Vallant still wants to have a final formal ball here in Chicago to wrap up the appreciation tour. He decided to pass out awards to the top contributors as well, so he'll need both events combined. And he still wants you to lead the planning, although he said he would understand if you don't feel up to it."

Cyd let out a big sigh, not prepared for what Shawn had just said. "Well, I guess since all the other events were canceled, it's not fair that Mr. Vallant's company has to suffer because of the recent course of events. What do you think?"

He lightly touched her cheek before he spoke. "I think that it's your decision, but know that me and my security team will definitely be there during the entire ball. I don't want you to think you're alone in this."

"We're all here," Imani said as she stepped out into the hallway with Lex and Mya right on her heels.

"We will be at the ball, too, sweetie," her dad said, standing next to her mom and Daman at the end of the stairs. Cyd followed Shawn's eyes as he looked around at her family members with slight disbelief.

"We don't keep many secrets in this family," Mrs. Rayne said in response to his confused look.

"I'm beginning to see that," he said, smiling at Mrs. Rayne before he turned his attention back to Cyd.

"One of us could also oversee this event," Imani added.

"No, that's okay," she said, looking at her sister before her eyes landed back on Shawn. "With your security team and all my family and friends around me, I should be fine at the event and it will be easy to plan, depending on how much time I have. When did Mr. Vallant want to reschedule the final event?"

"He was interviewed by the *Chicago Tribune* yesterday and told them that he would be having a formal right after Thanksgiving."

"Okay, that gives me about a week and a half," Cyd said as she clamped her hands together. She didn't know why, but she couldn't shake the uneasy feeling she had in the pit of her stomach. "Then I guess I have a lot of work to do before then."

"We'll put some of our projects on hold and help with this event," Imani said as she went to her sister and gave her a quick hug.

"Don't worry," Shawn said as he gave her a hug right after Imani. "I'll be right by your side every step of the way. Just breathe," he continued while holding her close to his heart as her suddenly quickened breaths started to subside.

Cyd noticed her mom lean into her dad as they watched the scene unfold between her and Shawn. She buried her face in his chest before looking up at him and giving him a peck on the lips that quickly turned more intimate. After that kiss, her family would definitely be more suspicious of her relationship with Shawn, although in that moment, she didn't care. She'd needed his kiss more than ever.

"Okay, ladies," Cyd said, clapping her hands together and trying to liven up the mood. "Shall we continue our conversation?" She looked toward her partners, who excitedly nodded their heads.

Her parents and Daman made their way back downstairs and eventually, Shawn followed suit. When she was at the doorway of the den and he'd descended a few stairs, he looked up at her and gave her a half smile. She returned his half smile and softly bit her bottom lip. Even from a distance, she could see the desire build in his eyes before he turned and walked down the rest of the stairs.

As she sat with the ladies and began telling them her story, she thought about her reaction to planning the formal awards ceremony for the Peter Vallant Company. She'd definitely underestimated how much the situation had affected her, but she had a great event to plan and she wasn't letting anything stand in the way of planning a successful one. Besides, there happened to be a lot of people in her corner who were willing to keep her safe. And with Agent Shawn Miles by her side, and in her heart, she felt safer than she'd felt in her entire life.

Chapter 18

After almost two weeks of restless nights and extensive planning, Cyd and the staff of Elite Events, Incorporated had worked day and night to bring the Peter Vallant Company Formal Awards Ceremony to life. She was exhausted, but she'd wanted everything to be as close to perfect as it could be, given the bad press that the Peter Vallant Company had received because of Jim Pearson. But luckily the company also had extremely loyal clients and contributors who RSVP'd despite it all.

Cyd gave herself a once-over in the hotel room mirror, pleased with her choice to wear an elegant black floor-length gown and stylish black stilettos with only earrings for accessories. Her hair was pulled to the side with soft curls flowing over her right shoulder and pinned with a delicate Swarovski crystal clip. She took out her blueberry lipstick to retouch her original application when she heard the hotel door open.

"You look absolutely stunning," Shawn said as he entered the room and walked straight toward her, pulling her into his embrace.

"And you look extremely sexy, Agent Miles," she

said as she gave him a quick peck on the lips, careful not to mess up her second application. Shawn had gotten a fresh haircut and trimmed his goatee, giving him a very clean-shaven look. It was hard not to want to sex the man senseless when he wore a classic black tuxedo and fashionable dress shoes, enhancing his natural sex appeal.

Shawn stepped back to admire the entire length of her outfit, his sea-blue eyes piercing through her and igniting the fire between her center. "I'm a lucky man," he said as he pulled her back to him and planted a hard kiss on her lips. Within seconds, she forgot all about the fact that she was trying not to mess up her lipstick.

They'd been spending every waking minute together since they'd left Tennessee and although they hadn't had a conversation about officially being in a relationship, it was a proved fact between their friends and family that they were definitely an item. It wasn't in either of their characters to have an official conversation confirming their relationship since with them, words had never been necessary.

On occasion, they introduced one another as boyfriend and girlfriend, but Shawn hadn't said the three magic words that Cyd longed to hear. Quite frankly, she worried that given his past, he was afraid to express his love to her for fear that something would happen to her. She honestly couldn't blame him since that fact had unfortunately been proved true with his parents and TJ.

"Was everything okay while I was gone?" Shawn asked, although he'd only been away from the room for thirty minutes.

"Let's see," Cyd said as she curled her arms around his neck. "You have two guards at my door and every five minutes they knock to see if I'm okay. Don't you think you're going a little overboard with this 24/7 watch idea?"

"Absolutely not," Shawn said as he placed sweet kisses along her collarbone. "There's no such thing as too much protection."

Cyd put her hands on her hips and gave him a look of disbelief. "Seriously!"

He didn't say anything, but he crossed his arms over his chest and observed her stance. *Crap, he always likes it when I stand this way.*

"I need you to focus," Cyd said as she took a few steps back from him. "Forget I asked the question. Let's just head to the formal."

"Um…no," he said firmly. "You know how I get when you put your hands on your hips like that." When her back hit the wall, she had nowhere else to go.

Just like that, she felt the sexual tension in the room rise to a higher level. She gazed into his eyes and realized he was at the point of no return. Shawn took another step closer to her and continued his original mission by placing wet kisses on her neck before his lips and tongue ventured to the top of her breasts.

"Shawn, we have to get to the ballroom for the formal," she said again, more breathlessly than before. Her words only made him kiss her quicker and in more places. His hands bunched her gown in his fists before they walked up her thighs, one hand pushing her panties aside and landing on her essence. Her thigh lifted on its own accord, landing in the palm of his hand at the same time that he stuck one of his fingers from his free hand precisely in her core. There, he moved his finger in and out until she was wet to his satisfaction.

Then he added another finger, playing with her clit at the same time.

"Shawn…" She moaned when she felt herself shiver at the sign that a strong orgasm was right around the corner. She gripped his neck tighter as he took his finger completely out before dipping back into her dripping-wet core. After a few more tweaks of his fingers, she released a forceful orgasm, crying into the ceiling as she did. Only then did she release her grip on his neck.

Shawn grabbed a piece of cloth out his pocket and dabbed her center clean. "Hmm, maybe I should take a quick shower," she said when she noticed remnants of her juices on his hands.

"You don't need one," Shawn said as he licked his fingers clean. "Most of your juices are on my hand. Besides," he continued. "I plan on finishing what I started after the formal and after I'm finished with you, you'll definitely need a shower."

"Point taken," Cyd said as she sashayed to the bathroom to freshen up. After ten minutes of washing up and refreshing her makeup, they were finally ready to head to the formal. As they walked into the ballroom, Cyd admired the great work her and her team had done. The simple, yet classy, decorations definitely made a statement and Mr. Vallant had expressed his utmost gratitude for everything she and her team had accomplished on such short notice.

A lot of the attendees were still arriving, but her parents and partners had arrived early.

"Cydney, I'd like to officially introduce you to my partner, Micah Madden," Shawn said as Micah extended his hand. Of course, Cyd already knew who he was, but she'd never been introduced to him properly.

"I'm going to survey the premises," Shawn said as he kissed her cheek. "I'll be back as soon as I can."

"Okay," Cyd said as she resumed conversing with her family. Ten minutes into the conversation, she excused herself to check with the caterer. She'd only taken a few steps before she noticed Micah hot on her tail. She ignored him at first and continued toward the kitchen. After her conversation with the caterer, she walked over to Mr. Vallant and the executive team to make sure they knew their speaking order for the awards portion of the night.

"Did you need something?" she asked, although she had a pretty good idea why he was still following her. Micah just looked at her and offered a quick smile before his face turned stoic again.

"Seriously," she said, crossing her arms over her chest. "Even during tonight's event, Shawn wants someone watching me at all times. I thought I only needed to be watched before and after the formal ceremony?"

"I'm just following orders," Micah said, as if that answered everything.

"Sure you are," Cyd said as she let out a frustrated breath. "Look, I still have to talk with a couple contributors who are presenting their success stories to the crowd in an hour. Can you do me a favor and actually say something when I approach them?"

"What do you want me to say?" Micah asked.

"I don't know," Cyd said as she wailed her arms. "I know you're usually more lively than this, so how about you actually introduce yourself this time?"

"I can do that," Micah said right before she met the next group.

"Hi, I'm Micah," Micah said awkwardly as she approached everyone. *Could he sound more monotone?* Cyd thought as she shot him a look of irritation. She figured Shawn must have told him to act professional because she'd definitely seen Micah more relaxed. After she finished speaking with the group, she tracked down her sister, Imani, and brother-in-law, Daman.

"Daman, do you know Micah?"

"Uh, yes," Daman said as if he could tell she was fishing for something.

"Great! I need you to tell him to back off." Cyd watched Daman and Micah share a head nod before he answered her with a solid, "No!" Imani began laughing until Cyd shot her a death stare that made her stop laughing instantly.

Cyd glanced over at Micah, who was now wearing a smug look on his face. *This is going to be a long night,* she thought as she grabbed a glass of wine from one of the passing waiters.

"Malik, this is Shawn. Have you found anything yet?" Shawn asked from inside a secure room down the hallway from the main hotel ballroom.

"Not yet," Malik said on the other line. "I haven't seen any red flags, but I'm still making it through the second list you gave me. So far everyone's been clean."

"Dang, okay," Shawn said as he shook his head. Waiting for Malik to find something when there may be nothing left to find was truly an agonizing process. "Man, call me if anything changes."

"I always do."

Shawn hung up the phone and reminded a few of his security men to make sure they kept their eyes open. The FBI and P.D. were no longer involved in the case since they'd already resolved what they needed to solve or conclude in the resolution of the case. Truth be told, he didn't think that either government team even cared about Cydney's safety since so many people involved were already behind bars.

Shawn made his way down the hallway to the main ballroom. "Hey, Micah," he said, tapping him on his shoulder. "We're switching positions."

Cydney turned at the sound of his voice and lifted one eyebrow. "If it isn't Prince Charming here to relieve his loyal follower," she said in a sarcastic voice. Evidently, she didn't think she needed protection during the formal ceremony. Micah mouthed *good luck* before leaving the ballroom.

From the way she was glaring at him, he was going to need a whole lot of luck. She was an independent woman in every sense of the word, so he knew this was hard for her. "Well, rest assured that the way I plan on protecting you will be a helluva lot better than Micah," he whispered, briefly kissing her behind her ear.

"Is that a promise?" she asked, softening the hard defense exterior she'd apparently built upon learning she wouldn't go anywhere at the formal without an escort. "I missed you," she said as she played with the collar of his shirt. Shawn was in the middle of his response when he noticed her looking past his shoulders at something that had gotten her attention.

He glanced over his shoulder and spotted Brittany Higgins walking into the event way past fashionably late.

"Don't worry about her," he said when he turned back to Cydney. "By now she's probably heard that we're dating."

"Is that all we're doing?" Cydney asked him questionably.

"No, that's not all we're doing," Shawn answered, realizing that the sight of Brittany had made her uneasy. "You're the only woman for me, Cydney." He gently grabbed the bottom of her chin. "I can't imagine being with anyone else." Although he'd realized he loved and wanted to spend the rest of his life with her before they'd left the cabin, he didn't feel like now was the best time to tell her.

"Do you mean that?" she asked as she searched his eyes for confirmation.

"Absolutely," he said as he leaned down to give her a kiss, not caring that there were many onlookers and people from the media there to witness the moment. By the time they stopped kissing, he'd had his Cydney back. *His.* He loved the sound of that.

Mr. Vallant walked over after the kiss. "You know," he said, slapping Shawn on the back. "I have a rule against people dating in my company. But I guess since you both are contract employees with tonight being your last day, I'll make an exception." The three of them shared a laugh.

"That was some kiss," Kim Lathers said to Shawn and Cydney after Mr. Vallant left.

"Oh, man, that was hot," said Verona, joining them, as well. "And, Cydney," Verona said as she opened her purse and moved around a few things before pulling out a black bracelet. "Before I forget, I found this in the bathroom. Isn't this yours?"

"Yes, it is, thank you," Cydney exclaimed before studying the piece and sliding it back on her wrist.

Shawn watched Cydney search the room, apparently searching for someone.

"I never did understand women and purses," Shawn said to try to distract Cydney as he watched Verona struggle to stuff a few contents back into her clutch. Shawn knew who Cydney was searching for because he was trying to find the same person.

"Men don't need to understand," Cydney said as both women joined her in laughter. Once Cydney was engaged in a conversation with the women, Shawn finally spotted Brittany and detected that she wasn't too happy with their open display of affection. She was at the bar with a drink in her hand, glaring at them from across the room.

"Did you see the look on Brittany's face after y'all kissed?" Kim asked Cydney.

"Not really," Cydney responded.

"Goodness," Kim exclaimed. "She practically burned a hole straight through you guys," she said to Shawn and Cydney as Verona nodded her head in agreement. *Maybe I really shouldn't have flirted back at her,* Shawn thought, although he couldn't change the past now. But he definitely knew he had to keep his eye on Brittany. She originally hadn't been on his radar, but now that he thought about it, no one was ruled out.

"She makes me feel uncomfortable," Cydney exclaimed after Kim and Verona left.

"Ignore her," Shawn said as he led her to another corner of the room. He didn't need Cydney concerning herself with Brittany, but as always, something definitely didn't feel right to him. There was something in the air…something that was making him uncomfortable, too. He didn't want to worry Cydney, but he felt like he was missing a very important detail of the puzzle. Although everyone thought he was paranoid, his gut had never steered him wrong. *Time's running out, Miles,* he thought. With the event coming to a close, it was going to be even harder to figure out if there was anyone else after Cydney, but he knew he wouldn't stop until his gut established that she was safe.

Chapter 19

"Thank you so much for everything," Mr. Vallant said with appreciation as he extended his hand. The lines of stress that had frequented his forehead lately had not been present the entire night.

"You're very welcome," Cyd responded sincerely, returning his handshake. Mr. Vallant and a few of the last attendees walked out of the ballroom and expressed their gratitude for a great night. The final event of the appreciation tour had been a huge success and the awards ceremony to honor top contributors had been a great addition to the formal. With the exception of Brittany Higgins, who'd stormed out of the ballroom shortly after her and Shawn's public kiss, everything had gone smoothly.

"Do you need help with anything?" Imani asked.

"I'm fine, sis," Cyd replied as she gave her a hug. "I just need to make sure the hotel sales manager doesn't need anything else from me."

"Okay, we'll be at the house," Imani said as she motioned for her partners and Daman to follow her. Her parents had retired early and the rest of them were going to Imani and Daman's estate for drinks to celebrate another successful event.

Cyd wrapped up the final details with the sales manager while the hotel staff continued to clean the ballroom.

"Are you ready to head out?" Shawn asked, with Micah close behind.

"Yes, I'm ready," she said, holding her clutch and taking one last glance at the ballroom to make sure they didn't leave anything behind.

Cyd was so relieved that the appreciation tour was officially over. It had been way more intense than she'd originally prepared for, but planning such a huge series of events was definitely great for her company.

When they reached the lobby, the wine and water she'd been drinking all night was finally catching up to her. She was so busy she'd been holding her bladder the entire night and that definitely wasn't healthy. "Shawn, I have to go to the bathroom before we leave."

"Um, okay. I'll go with you?"

Cyd stopped short. "You mean you'll wait here in the lobby while I go to the bathroom, right?"

"No, I mean I will wait in the bathroom with you. I just won't go in the stall." *Goodness, is he for real?*

"Come on, Shawn. I've been real accommodating all night," she said.

"Aha, yeah, right," Micah chimed in with a laugh.

"Zip it," she said to Micah, laughing along with him. "I promise to be quick and besides, how will you explain your presence to the women who go in and out of the bathroom?" She waved her hands around the lobby at all the women present to validate her point.

Shawn gave her an uneasy look before doing a 360

around the crowded lobby. Most of the attendees who'd left the formal had settled at the bar. "Okay, I won't go in the bathroom, but I'm definitely waiting right outside the door."

"Deal," Cyd agreed as she headed to the bathroom to release her bladder.

"Hello," she said to a woman who was exiting the bathroom.

"Hi," the woman replied before leaving. There was one stall that was occupied, a couple that were a little unclean and another that would have to do. After Cyd washed her hands, she took out her lipstick to reapply a fresh coat just as the other occupied stall opened.

"Hey," Cyd said to the familiar face that walked out of the stall.

"Hey yourself, princess," said the other female in an icy voice right before Cyd felt the solid poke of something hard on her side. "If you try to scream or say anything, I'll shoot you quicker than you can voice one word."

Cyd looked at her through the mirror, her heart beating so fast that she was sure she would have a panic attack at any moment. *Is she serious?*

"Aw, does that look mean you're confused as to why I'd want to hurt you?" the woman said as she yanked Cyd's head backward by grabbing a fistful of hair. Cyd almost yelped at the sharp pain that shot through her neck at the forceful snatch, but she thought about the woman's threatening words. "I'm here to finish the job that my partners clearly couldn't finish. And mark my words, princess," she said as she pushed the hard object even more into Cyd's side. "I won't mess up like they did."

Cyd stared into her eyes to see if she could see any signs of empathy, but saw nothing in her eyes but amusement. She was enjoying this. *Oh, I knew I got a weird vibe from this woman!* The woman yanked her hair a little more before pointing to the window.

Shawn, where are you? Cyd thought as she was forced to stand on the sink and climb through one bathroom window while the woman climbed out of the other at the same time. *Should I just scream and call her bluff?* It seemed like a good idea, but Cyd was certain that she would be shot if she didn't follow directions.

"Walk," the woman said in a mighty voice as she waved her hand toward the alley. At one point, Cyd thought about tackling the woman to the ground, since she was taller than she was by at least a few inches. But the woman had her by at least forty pounds. *Come on, Shawn, where are you?* She had no idea how to get herself out this situation and before she had a chance to formulate any more thoughts, she was knocked out cold.

"Nobody move!" a woman yelled at the top of her lungs as she hopped on a table in the lobby wearing a wedding veil, white party dress and no heels. "If you do, I'm liable to hurt anyone who crosses my path." People in the lobby and bar gasped in surprise at the crazy woman on top of the table. A quick observation of her hands proved she didn't have a weapon. Suddenly, she did a little happy dance while singing "Happy Birthday."

"Hahahaha, just kidding," the woman said as she tried to get off the table and was instantly surrounded by girls wearing T-shirts with the word *bridesmaid* written on it. *Man, I hate that stuff,* Shawn thought as he reflected on a previous time where he'd been on high alert just to find out that the sneaky-looking women were actually participating in bachelorette party antics.

Shawn looked at Micah and nodded for him to check out the scene, anyway. *Cydney,* he thought when he realized she hadn't come out of the bathroom. He knocked before peeking his head in.

"Cydney," he called, but received no answer. He walked completely into the bathroom and instantly noticed the open windows.

"Crap," he said as he hopped on the sink and peered out the window down both ways of the alley. Nothing. Not a single person. Before running out of the bathroom, he pushed open each door just to make sure she wasn't in there and didn't find anyone. But he did find a scarf.

"Micah," Shawn yelled as he ran up to his partner who was now surrounded by the bride and bridesmaids.

"Shawn, what's wrong?" Micah asked in concern.

"Someone got to her," Shawn whispered in his ear. "We have to move ASAP!"

"Oh, crap," Micah said as he quickly discarded his tie and handed it to one of the women.

"Why are you giving her that?"

"The bride has a list of things she has to accomplish before midnight and her time is almost up."

Shawn shook his head and made his way toward the hotel desk to inform security. As Shawn and Micah ran out the front entrance, Shawn heard someone from the bridal group state that she was so glad she'd gotten the list from a strange woman. Something clicked.

"Who did you get this list from?" Shawn asked the group as he backtracked a couple feet.

"Some lady," one of the bridesmaids said. Shawn took the lipstick-written list from the bride's hand and noticed that the list had specific times and places to do everything, including getting a piece of clothing from the first man who helped her off the table.

"How long ago did you get this?"

"I got it, actually," said another bridesmaid who was standing off to the side. "I'm the maid of honor and I just got it when I went in the bathroom. I was hanging up the phone with my sister and expressing how I needed to spice up the bachelorette party. This woman jotted something down for me real quick and I showed the ladies the list." Shawn studied the bridesmaid's face and remembered her walking out of the bathroom just as Cydney had entered.

"Do you remember how she looked?" he asked the bridesmaid.

"Not really," the bridesmaid said, obviously a little taken off guard by all the questions. "She was wearing that scarf you have in your hand and all her body parts were covered."

Shawn wanted to ask them more questions but everyone in the group had obviously been drinking so he was lucky he'd been told anything at all.

"Let's head to the alley," Shawn yelled to Micah. "Call the team and tell them to talk with the security guards at the hotel. They don't have cameras inside the bathroom, but I noticed a camera that was pointed in the direction of the bathroom, so we should be able to see who went in and never came out."

As Micah made the call to the team, Shawn called Malik.

"They took her again," Shawn said into the phone

as he and Micah arrived at the empty alley. "And since they captured her in the women's bathroom, a witness confirmed there was another woman in there with Cydney. Anything on the other employees?"

"I'm only through searching everyone with a last name that begins with *L*. As far as the woman in the company who interacted with Cydney, Brittany Higgins is clean. So is Kim Lathers."

"Damn," Shawn said as he massaged his forehead. "What am I missing?"

"You're too personally involved," Micah said as he entered the conversation. "Take a step back and think."

Shawn did as Micah suggested and passed his phone over to Micah, who began talking with Malik. He walked over to the side wall of the building and began thinking.

Okay, it's definitely a woman. More than likely, a Peter Vallant employee who interacted with her. Suddenly, his mind went to his time earlier with Cydney when they were in the hotel room. "Bad timing," he said quietly to himself as he thought about his hands roaming up and down her body, landing on her butt and caressing her breasts.

Focus, Miles, he said quietly to himself, but his mind was still remembering the intimate moment between them in the hotel room. He leaned his head back on the wall and closed his eyes. He let his mind wander back to their time in the hotel room, since his gut had never steered him wrong. In his memory, he was on the outside observing the scene as their foreplay unfolded before him. He witnessed Cydney as she lifted her leg and he saw himself grab her leg to keep her steady. He watched himself stick his finger inside her as she dropped her head back in satisfaction. He could hear the moans escape her mouth as the passion overtook her body. He witnessed her release her orgasm in an explosion of desire before coming back down to earth, and he could see himself arch his back to plunge even deeper as her juices flowed over his hand.

As his eyes remained closed he watched Cydney give him a seductive smile as she unlatched her arms from around his neck. And that was when he saw it. That was when he noticed the one detail he'd wished he'd recognized hours sooner. There, as clear as ever, he noticed that both of her wrists were bare...clear of all accessories.

"How did I miss that?" Shawn said aloud and he ran back over to Micah and grabbed the phone out his hand. "Malik, I know who it is, I know who took Cydney."

"Who?" Malik asked on the line at the same time Micah asked in person.

"Verona Neely," Shawn said to them both. "Malik, I need you to find everything you can on Verona Neely immediately!"

"Right away," Malik said, hanging up the phone.

"How do you know?" Micah asked in confusion as to how Shawn had just come up with Verona as the person of interest seemingly out of the blue. Shawn placed his hand on his forehead again. He'd just thought of another detail.

"Earlier today, Verona gave Cydney a bracelet that she claimed Cydney left in the bathroom. But I finally remember from earlier that Cydney wasn't wearing a bracelet tonight. Matter of fact, Cydney was looking at the bracelet funny, but she was too distracted by Brittany Higgins to question anything. We both were. And now I remember seeing something that was black and leather sticking out of Verona's purse when she took out the bracelet. I'd bet any amount of money that those gloves are biker gloves."

"You think she's the owner of those motorcycle tracks we found back in Springfield?" Micah asked, finally catching on.

"Definitely," Shawn said as he took out his phone to call Agent Wolfe. Although Malik was on the case, he needed to call the FBI in case Cydney's disappearance was related to anything else currently going on in the city.

"I understand, sir," Shawn said in response to Agent Wolfe's orders to stand down until he could send the team out there. "But with all due respect, tonight I'm not an FBI agent." He glanced over at Micah, who was listening intently. "Tonight I'm just a man trying to save the woman he loves."

Chapter 20

Shawn paced the entire length of the security room as he awaited a call from Malik and the return of Micah and another agent who'd gone to Verona's apartment. He'd called Daman, who had brought Cydney's parents and sister back to the hotel after they'd heard the news. Agent Wolfe was also present in the room and Shawn's security team, along with two FBI agents and friends, were discreetly patrolling inside and outside the hotel for clues. Although Agent Wolfe often went by the book, he'd dropped protocol when Shawn had expressed his love for Cydney.

Cydney had been missing for two hours and Shawn couldn't believe he had let someone get to her again. *I knew I should have followed her into the bathroom,* he thought for the hundredth time since the incident.

Shawn stopped pacing and sat in the chair to try to calm his nerves. No such luck. Mrs. Rayne gave him a look of sympathy, but he saw the pain in her eyes from holding back remaining tears and frustration from unanswered questions. Shawn had spent the first hour she'd gone missing walking up and down the streets and alley trying to find any clues that would help them figure out where she was. He'd even thoroughly checked an abandoned building several times before he was forced to stop to explain the situation to Cydney's family when they'd arrived.

Shawn nodded his head toward Daman to indicate that they should continue the search when his phone rang.

"Hey, Malik, you're on speaker. What did you find out?"

"For starters, Verona Neely's real name is Victoria Noland, the daughter of Bob Noland, that fast-food-chain CEO who tried to kidnap Cydney in the first place."

"I never read anything about him having a daughter in the papers or online."

"You wouldn't," Malik added. "Looks like Victoria, or Verona, was kept out of the public's eye since Bob's family forbade him to have an illegitimate daughter with Verona's mother, an African-American woman. But I guess…like father, like daughter."

"Yeah, that makes sense," Shawn said, understanding a few more pieces of the puzzle.

"And guess who she's dating? Jim Pearson, of all people. His record is still pretty clean, so he probably got suckered into doing what the father-daughter duo wanted him to do when he joined the Peter Vallant Company."

"What about Mr. Vallant?" Shawn asked, glancing over at Agent Wolfe, who appeared to be holding his breath as he awaited news on his dear friend.

"No, he's clean," Malik confirmed.

"I'll call and inform the FBI on the other news,"

Agent Wolfe said as he went to the corner of the room to inform the FBI of the new developments in Jim Pearson's and Bob Noland's cases.

"That's all I was able to find in a couple hours, but I'm still researching and reaching out to a lot of contacts to piece together other red flags I've found. Once I learned that Verona Neely was really Victoria Noland, I uncovered a lot more. Looks like Bob somehow convinced her to put a lot of things in her name. I also called Micah since I knew he was at Verona's home and I needed him to check out something for me." Malik continued on the phone. Shawn was just about to request that Malik elaborate on what info he was researching about the Nolands when the door opened.

"I think I found what you're looking for, Malik," Micah said as he and the other agent entered the room.

"What did you find?" Shawn asked.

"Way more than we suspected," Micah replied as he opened his bag. "Besides the fact that Verona, or should I say Victoria, definitely led a double life, it looks like dear daddy leads a secret life, as well."

Micah opened his bag and took out a large file. "All the information in my bag was locked in a safe, but I cracked the code." He tossed the largest file toward Shawn.

"Lead Assassins Combat? What company is this?"

"Well, LAC, as it's stated on numerous files, is owned by Bob Noland, but most of the filed paperwork is in Victoria Noland's name."

Shawn flipped through the papers and looked questionably at Micah when he didn't respond right away.

"Malik, your suspicions were correct," Micah said to his brother on his phone. Malik let out an expletive.

"What?" Shawn asked Micah.

"Well, LAC is apparently a company you go to when you want to hire a hit man. Bob Noland's been in the business for almost thirty years and five months ago, his daughter joined him, although he'd been falsifying documents in her name for the past decade."

Shawn closed the file as the hair on the back of his neck stood on edge. *No way,* he thought as Malik handed him another file. Shawn skimmed through the file and page after page was filled with detailed accounts of the people who had contracted the LAC and their targets, starting with the most recent. His fingers began moving in slow motion as he got toward the end of the file. When he reached the last page, there were only five names listed as targets for that year. Even worse, that entire page listed Leon Roberts as the person who hired LAC. *Really! A drug dealer who hired a professional hit man?* Shawn's anger skyrocketed the more he studied the page.

"Why did they take Cydney?" Shawn all but yelled to Micah, who walked over to him and placed his hand on his shoulder.

"Why?" Shawn repeated as he closed the file and slammed it on a nearby table.

"What's going on?" Mr. Rayne asked in aggravation since most of the individuals in the room were in the dark about the situation.

"Sir, ma'am," Shawn said as he looked over to Cydney's parents. "According to the file, my parents were killed by someone at LAC twenty-nine years ago who was hired by Leon Roberts, a drug dealer I helped lock up three years ago. Since recently I helped bring down the entire operation, including the fall of Bob Noland, my guess is that his daughter wanted revenge and since she couldn't get to me...she decided to take Cydney."

Cydney's family gasped in shock and devastation at the news Shawn had disclosed.

"Shawn, that's not a proved fact," Malik said on the phone.

"I know," Shawn responded quickly although he felt partially to blame. Deep down, he knew he shouldn't blame himself. He'd always known that Leon was behind his parents' deaths and he was actually happy that he finally knew the truth. But he had no time to wallow in self-pity, although he did allow himself a quick second to relish in the relief that his parents' deaths were solved. He guessed that a deeper look into LAC would probably prove that TJ was a target, as well.

"Malik, can you pull up a list of all the properties Bob Noland owns?"

"Already done," Malik said over the phone. "I'm sending it to both your and Micah's phones now."

"Great," Shawn said as he opened the message on his Android. "Micah, take two security-team members and check the last two locations on the list. Agent Wolfe, you take an agent and check the middle one. And Daman," Shawn said as he made his way to the other side of the room, "we will take the first two."

"I'll stay here with my wife and daughter," Mr. Rayne said. "Oh, and Shawn," he continued as he walked over and gripped him on his shoulder. "I need you to bring my baby girl home safely."

"Sir," Shawn answered, momentarily glancing at Agent Wolfe. "You have my word that I will bring her back safely. I promise." He hugged Mrs. Rayne and whispered the same words into her ear, hoping they provided her with a little comfort.

Shawn looked at Agent Wolfe again as he nodded his head in approval. He knew he was breaking all kinds of protocols, but at the moment, all rules ceased to exist in his mind. There was no way he was losing another person in his life—absolutely no way.

Cyd lifted her head and opened her eyes, unaware of how long she'd been unconscious. The few sporadic lamps offered some visibility but no one appeared to be in the room with her. *Is this a warehouse?* she wondered, since the space she was in looked a little empty and almost like a large garage. She had no idea where she was or how Verona had managed to get her there, and the loud heavy-metal music that bounced off the walls sounded worse than nails on a chalkboard. The back of her head was still pounding in the spot that Verona had hit her, but she refused to close her eyes again. She had to be alert, and there was no doubt in her mind that Shawn was on his way to save her. She was confident of that.

Cyd tried to crack her back as she adjusted herself in the hard chair. She couldn't tell how her hands were tied, but she knew they were confined by plastic. She twisted her arm to try to squeeze her hands free.

"I wouldn't do that if I were you," Verona said as she walked out from a dark corner.

"Why are you doing this?" Cyd said, trying not to act as startled as she felt.

"Isn't it obvious?" Verona asked with a laugh. "You stuck your nose in where it didn't belong, just like your little boyfriend did a few years ago."

"What are you talking about?" Cyd asked, although now she was pretty sure Verona and Jim were working together.

"My dad told me to leave you alone, and so did Jim at one point. But honestly, I wanted to see if I could kidnap you and get away with it."

Cyd watched Verona as she began circling her. *Jim? Her dad? What is she talking about?*

"Bob Noland is my dad, by the way," Verona said. "And Jim and I have been dating for years, so all that time he was with you, he was doing it for me."

Cyd wanted to tell her that she could have that sorry excuse for a man, but she didn't want to say anything reckless. However, she couldn't help but ask a few questions.

"Verona, why did you have Jim pretend to be interested in me?"

"Ugh," she responded as she stomped around the room. "My name isn't Verona…it's Vic, short for Victoria."

"Okay," Cyd said in a calming voice. *Remember, Cyd, you can't argue with crazy,* she reminded herself, already concluding that Verona, or Vic, had lost her freaking mind.

"To answer your question, princess, I just wanted him to learn more about you. I love my baby, but he isn't the sharpest tool in the shed. Although going to jail for my plan was the smartest thing he's done since I met him."

Out of nowhere, Vic started dancing in circles and chanting that her dad would be so proud that she'd successfully kidnapped her first person.

"I can't believe he failed to kidnap you but I didn't!

I was pissed when Jim told me that others in our organization were targeting you, as well." Vic stopped twirling and crossed her arms in a pout. "You were my kidnapping, not theirs." Instead of continuing to dance, she slowly walked closer to Cyd.

What the heck is she doing? Cyd thought when Vic was mere inches from her face.

"I want to make sure I remember every detail about you in this exact moment," she said as she deeply inhaled and exhaled before stating that she even wanted to remember Cyd's scent. Cyd kept a solemn face, but inside, her nerves were jumping through hoops.

"I like the combination of lavender and vanilla," Cyd said with a discomforting laugh as she tried to get think of a way to get inside Vic's head. Vic let out a brief chuckle before her face grew serious and she took another breath. *Goodness, she looks creepy when she does that!*

"So," Vic said as she leaned over right in front of Cyd and flicked a hand through her hair. "I don't have anyone else to talk to, so what's the first thing you want to talk about before I start torturing you?"

Torture? Is this chick for real? Cyd thought as she glared up at her with mass confusion. *Oh, heck, no. I refuse to be killed by this crazy woman.* Between the sniffing, exhaling and the dancing, the situation was growing more irritating by the minute. Cyd wasn't demeaning the dangerousness of the situation, but she also thought if she had to die at an early age it would be in a situation a whole lot more exciting than a kidnapping by a crazy woman.

"Come on," Vic said in a whiny voice. "What do you want to talk about? I know," she stated as she snapped her fingers. "Let's talk about why I wanted to kidnap you in detail. Well, for starters, you always dressed way too nice."

Oh, come on!

"And *all* the men in the company liked you. That's really bruising to a girl's ego, you know?"

"And third, you're really slender so you were the easiest of the women to target and kidnap. Jim tried flirting with Brittany Higgins and Kim Lathers to get me my first kidnapping, but they wouldn't flirt back," Vic said as she crossed her arms over her chest and poked out her lips in a pout.

Lord, help me, Cyd thought as she listened to Vic rattle off insane reasons for wanting to kidnap her. *Okay, maybe I'll just close my eyes until she finishes.*

"And fourth, I…" Vic's voice trailed off and Cyd popped her eyes open again.

"You what?" Shawn said as he pressed the pistol into her side.

Oh, my goodness, thank you, thank you, she thought as she looked up toward the ceiling.

"Daman, untie Cydney," Shawn ordered as he handcuffed Vic.

"Brother-in-law, I'm so happy to see you," Cyd said as she stood up slowly and finally cracked her back.

"Me, too," he said as he gave her a big hug. "Let me call the police and then I'll call your sister and parents."

"Did you secure the premises?" Cyd asked, not knowing if there were more criminals in the warehouse.

Shawn gave her his best "what do you think" look before he started toward a door in the distance.

"Shawn, don't you know who I am?" Vic yelled as they made their way outside. Cyd looked around, surprised to see that they were near a few office buildings and a forest preserve. She could hear the police sirens getting closer with each step they took.

"I'm a Noland," Vic said as she attempted to kick her way out of his grip. "I wasn't going to hurt her. I only wanted to pretend to complete my first kidnap. This gave me such a bigger adrenaline rush than I got when I helped the druggies use the mock Peter Vallant vans to transport cocaine. With kidnapping, it's all about me."

Shawn shook his head in skepticism, not believing that she was a bigger mole in the Peter Vallant Company than Jim. "Just so you know," he said to Cyd. "We didn't find any weapons in the warehouse…only a BB gun and boxes of drugs that I'm sure will link back to the case."

Cyd's head whipped around to Vic. "A BB gun? Seriously? You kidnapped me with a freaking BB gun?"

Vic didn't say anything and just continued to laugh hysterically. She was still laughing when the police arrived to take her off to jail.

A BB gun? Cyd thought again, still surprised that she'd actually let someone kidnap her who didn't even have a real gun. She leaned against a stationary police car as she watched another police car take Vic into custody.

"Are you still thinking about that BB gun?" Shawn asked as he leaned on the car next to her.

"Of course I am," Cyd said as she waved her hands in the air. "I can't believe I let her kidnap me with a fake gun."

"Better a fake one than a real one," Shawn said in a serious tone. When he gazed back at her, she noticed the worry lines in his face.

"You know that my kidnapping wasn't your fault, don't you?"

After a couple seconds, he gave her a soft smile before he laughed. "After hearing the crazy explanation Vic gave you, yeah."

"Good," she said with a slight smile.

Her hair caught in the chilly wind and slashed across her face. Shawn tucked the tousled hair behind her ear. "You know, I was worried sick about you," he said as he pulled her a little closer to him.

"I know," she responded. "But I knew you would come for me."

"You were that confident?" Shawn asked as he searched her eyes for confirmation.

"Yes," she said, choosing her next words extremely carefully. "I figured if you loved me any fraction as much as I love you, there was no way you'd stop searching until I was found."

Shawn gave her a deep smile and softly pecked her lips before speaking. "I'm so glad to hear you say that because I happen to love you very, *very* much." He tightened his arms around her waist and stationed her right between the fit of his legs.

"Why, Agent Miles, I do believe you just professed your unyielding love for me. I could have sworn I was just another notch on your list of women."

"Not another notch," he said as his face grew serious. "You're the only notch, the only woman I want to spend the rest of my life with."

Cyd bit her lip and tried to hold back her huge smile. "Even if I tend to get myself into trouble sometimes?"

Shawn looked around at all the parked police cars, and listened to the sirens in the distance from a fire truck and ambulance that were still headed their way. "Yeah," he said with a laugh. "Because I can't imagine you getting into more trouble than this."

Cyd laughed along with him before bringing him closer to place a passionate kiss on his lips. "I love you," she said again, just because she liked the sound of those three words.

"I love you, too," he said as he placed a couple kisses along her neckline. Even the smallest peck on her neck brought her desire to a heightened level.

"Did you ever think one night in Anguilla would turn into love?" she asked out of curiosity.

"I didn't know it would turn into love, but I knew one night with you would never be enough. I thought about you every day after Anguilla."

Cyd touched her hand to his cheek and looked into his eyes. "I did, too—my mystery lover with the sea-blue eyes. But nothing could have prepared me for the real Shawn Miles, the man behind the mysterious mask." She let both hands settle on his chest. "The more I learned about you, the deeper I fell in love. You're it, Shawn…. You're my perfect man."

Cyd watched a slight mist fill his eyes before he pulled her in for a tight hug. He didn't say anything for a couple minutes and Cyd cradled his head to her shoulder, giving him a moment to soak in her words.

When he lifted his head and brought his face mere inches from hers, her heartbeat quickened as she studied his eyes. She didn't see any more secrets reflected in his gaze. Gone were the last of the barriers he'd set in place, and before her stood a man who not only deserved her love, but accepted it.

"So tell me something, Ms. Rayne. What does a man

have to do to get you to agree to be the future Mrs. Miles?" Shawn asked.

Cyd looked around at all the chaos that surrounded them and gave him a questioning look.

"What?" Shawn asked her in concern. "What's wrong?"

"Well," she said as she curled her arms around his neck. "Is this an official proposal?"

"Goodness, woman," he said with a laugh as he shook his head. "I warned Daman this would happen."

"Huh? Warned Daman about what?"

"You are something else," he said in his best Kevin Hart imitation as he shook his head in disbelief. "If you must know, this is not the way I plan to officially propose to you. But it is my way of getting an idea on what a man needs to do for a proper proposal that meets Cydney Rayne's standards."

She giggled and swayed back and forth in his arms. "For starters, I think you should seriously consider proposing where it all started!"

"I actually wanted to hear your ideas, but not the place. Now you'll know I'm proposing the next time we travel to Anguilla."

"Not if we go to Anguilla every couple months," she said with an innocent look on her face.

Shawn laughed as he placed a sweet kiss on her lips. "How did I get so lucky?"

She looked into his hypnotizing eyes and gave him a sneaky smile before responding. "I was just asking myself the same thing," she said. "How did you get so lucky?"

* * * * *

d at the body before she resumed washing

STEPPING OUT OF
THE SHADOWS

ROBYN DONALD

CHAPTER ONE

HEART thudding more noisily than the small plane's faltering engine, Rafe Peveril dragged his gaze away from the rain-lashed windows, no longer able to see the darkening grasslands of Mariposa beneath them. A few seconds ago, just after the engine had first spluttered, he'd noticed a hut down there.

If they made it out of this alive, that hut might be their only hope of surviving the night.

Another violent gust of wind shook the plane. The engine coughed a couple of times, then failed. In the eerie silence the pilot muttered a jumble of prayers and curses in his native Spanish as he fought to keep the plane steady.

If they were lucky—*damned* lucky—they might land more or less intact...

When the engines sputtered back into life the woman beside Rafe looked up, white face dominated by great green eyes, black-lashed and tip-tilted and filled with fear.

Thank God she wasn't screaming. He reached for her hand, gave it a quick hard squeeze, then released it to push her head down.

"Brace position," he shouted, his voice far too loud in the sudden silence as the engines stopped again. The woman huddled low and Rafe set his teeth and steeled himself for the crash.

A shuddering jolt, a whirlwind of noise...

And Rafe woke.

Jerking upright, he let out a sharp breath, grey eyes sweeping a familiar room. The adrenalin surging through him mutated into relief. Instead of regaining consciousness in a South American hospital bed he was at home in his own room in New Zealand.

What the *hell*...?

It had to be at least a couple of years since he'd re-lived the crash. He searched for a trigger that could have summoned the dream but his memory—usually sharply accurate—failed him.

Again.

Six years should have accustomed him to the blank space in his head after the crash, yet although he'd given up on futile attempts to remember, he still resented those forty-eight vanished hours.

The bedside clock informed him that sunrise was too close to try for any more sleep—not that he'd manage it now. He needed space and fresh air.

Outside on the terrace he inhaled deeply, relishing the mingled scent of salt and flowers and newly mown grass, and the quiet hush of the waves. His heart rate slowed and the memories receded into the past where they belonged. Light from a fading moon surrounded the house with mysterious shadows, enhanced by the bright disc of Venus hanging above a bar of pure gold along the horizon where the sea met the sky.

The Mariposan pilot had died on impact, but miraculously both he and the wife of his estancia manager had survived with minor injures—the blow to the head for him, and apparently nothing more serious than a few bruises for her.

With some difficulty he conjured a picture of the woman—a drab nonentity, hardly more than a girl. Although he'd spent the night before the crash at the estancia, she'd kept very much in the background while he and her husband talked business. All he could recall were those amazingly green eyes in her otherwise forgettable face. Apart from them, she had been a plain woman.

With a plain name—Mary Brown.

He couldn't recall seeing her smile—not that that was surprising. A week or so before he'd arrived at the estancia she'd received news of her mother's sudden stroke and resultant paralysis. As soon as Rafe heard about it he'd offered to take her back with him to Mariposa's capital and organise a flight to New Zealand.

Rafe frowned. What the hell was her husband's name?

He recalled it with an odd sense of relief. David Brown—another plain name, and the reason for Rafe's trip to Mariposa. He'd broken his flight home from London to see for himself if he agreed with the Mariposan agent's warnings that David Brown was not a good fit for the situation.

Certainly Brown's response to his offer to escort his wife back to New Zealand had been surprising.

"That won't be necessary," David Brown had told him brusquely. "She's been ill—she doesn't need the extra stress of looking after a cripple."

However, by the next morning the man had changed his mind, presumably at his wife's insistence, and that evening she'd accompanied Rafe on the first stage of the trip.

An hour after take-off they'd been caught by a wind of startling ferocity, and with it came rain so cold the woman beside him had been shivering within minutes. And the plane's engines had cut out for the first time.

If it hadn't been for the skill of the doomed pilot they'd probably all have died.

Of course! There was the stimulus—the trigger that had hurled his dreaming mind back six years.

Rafe inhaled sharply, recalling the email that had arrived just before he'd gone to bed last night. Sent from his office in London, for the first time in recorded history his efficient personal assistant had slipped up. No message, just a forwarded photograph of a dark young man wearing a look of conscious pride and a mortarboard, a graduation shot. Amused by his PA's omission, Rafe had sent back one question mark.

Last night he hadn't made the connection, but the kid looked very much like the pilot.

He swung around and headed for his office, switched on the computer, waited impatiently for it to boot up and smiled ironically when he saw another email.

His PA had written, *Sorry about the stuff-up. I've just had a letter from the widow of the pilot in Mariposa. Apparently you promised their oldest boy an interview with the organisation there when he graduated from university. Photo of good-looking kid in mortarboard attached. OK to organise?*

So that explained the dream. Rafe's subconscious had made the connection for him in a very forthright fashion. He'd felt a certain obligation to the family of the dead pilot and made it his business to help them.

He replied with a succinct agreement to London, then headed back to his bedroom to dress.

After a gruelling trip to several African countries, it

was great to be home, and apart from good sex and the exhilaration of business there was little he liked better than a ride along the beach on his big bay gelding in a Northland summer dawn.

Perhaps it might give him some inspiration for the gift he needed to buy that day, a birthday present for his foster-sister. His mouth curved. Gina had forthright views on appropriate gifts for a modern young woman.

"You might be a plutocrat," she'd told him the day before, "but don't you dare get your secretary to buy me something flashy and glittering. I don't do glitter."

He'd pointed out that his middle-aged PA would have been insulted to hear herself described as a secretary, and added that any presents he bought were his own choice, no one else's.

Gina grinned and gave him a sisterly punch in the arm. "Oh, yeah? So why did you get me to check the kiss-off present you gave your last girlfriend?"

"It was her birthday gift," he contradicted. "And if I remember correctly, you insisted on seeing it."

She arched an eyebrow. "Of course I did. So it was just a coincidence you broke off the affair a week later?"

"It was a mutual decision," Rafe told her, the touch of frost in his tone a warning.

His private life was his own. Because he had no desire to cause grief he chose his lovers for sophistication as well as their appeal to his mind and his senses. Eventually he intended to marry.

One day.

"Well, I suppose the diamonds salvaged a bit of pride for her," Gina had observed cynically, hugging him before getting into her car for the trip back to Auckland. She'd turned on the engine, then said casually through the open window, "If you're looking for something a bit different, the gift shop in Tewaka has a new owner. It's got some really good stuff in it now."

Recognising a hint when he heard one, several hours later Rafe headed for the small seaside town twenty kilometres from the homestead.

Inside the gift shop he looked around. Gina was right—the place had been fitted out with taste and style. His appreciative gaze took in demure yet sexy lingerie displayed with discretion, frivolous sandals perfect for any four-year-old girl who yearned to be a princess, some very good New Zealand art glass. As well as clothes there were ornaments and jewellery, even some books. And art, ranging in style from brightly coloured coastal scenes to moody, dramatic oils.

"Can I help you?"

Rafe swivelled around, met the shop assistant's eyes and felt the ground shift beneath his feet. Boldly green and cat-tilted, set between lashes thick enough to tangle any heart, they sent him spinning back to his dream.

"Mary?" he asked without thinking.

But of course she wasn't Mary Brown.

This woman was far from plain and an involuntary glance showed no ring on those long fingers. Although her eyes were an identical green, they were bright and challenging, not dully unaware.

Her lashes drooped and he sensed her subtle—but very definite—withdrawal.

"I'm sorry—have we met before?" she asked in an assured, crisp voice completely unlike Mary Brown's hesitant tone. She added with a smile, "But my name isn't Mary. It's Marisa—Marisa Somerville."

Indeed, the assured, beautifully groomed Ms Somerville was a bird of paradise compared to drab Mrs Brown. Apart from the coincidences of eye colour and shape, and first names beginning with the same letter, this woman bore no resemblance to the woman he'd seen in Mariposa.

Rafe held out his hand. "Sorry, but for a moment I thought you were someone else. I'm Rafe Peveril."

Although her lashes flickered, her handshake was as confident as her voice. "How do you do, Mr Peveril."

"Most people here call me Rafe," he told her.

She didn't pretend not to know who he was. Had there been a glimmer of some other emotion in the sultry green depths of her eyes, almost immediately hidden by those dark lashes?

If so, he could hear no sign of it in her voice when she went on, "Would you rather look around by yourself, or can I help you in any way?"

She hadn't granted him permission to use her first name. Intrigued, and wryly amused at his reaction to her unspoken refusal, Rafe said, "My sister is having a birthday soon, and from the way she spoke of your shop I gathered she'd seen something here she liked. Do you know Gina Smythe?"

"Everyone in Tewaka knows Gina." Smiling, she turned towards one of the side walls. "And, yes, I can tell you what she liked."

"Gina isn't noted for subtlety," he said drily, appreciating the gentle feminine sway of slender hips, the graceful smoothness of her gait. His body stirred in a swift, sensually charged response that was purely masculine.

She stopped in front of an abstract oil. "This is the one."

Rafe dragged his mind back to his reason for being there. Odd that Gina, so practical and matter-of-fact, couldn't resist art that appealed directly to the darker, more stormy emotions.

"Who's the artist?" he asked after a silent moment.

The woman beside him gave a soft laugh. "I am," she admitted.

The hot tug of lust in Rafe's gut intensified, startling him. Was she as passionate as the painting before him? Perhaps he'd find out some day...

"I'll take it," he said briskly. "Can you gift-wrap it for me? I'll call back in half an hour."

"Yes, of course."

"Thanks."

Out of the shop, away from temptation, he reminded himself curtly that he'd long ago got over the adolescent desire to bed every desirable woman he met. Yet primitive hunger still quickened his blood.

Soon he'd invite Marisa Somerville to dinner.

If she was unattached, which seemed unlikely in spite of her ringless fingers. Women who looked like her—especially ones who exuded that subtle sexuality—usually had a man in the not-very-distant background.

Probably, he thought cynically, stopping to speak to a middle-aged woman he'd known from childhood, he'd responded to her so swiftly because it was several months since he'd made love.

From behind the flimsy barrier of the sales counter Marisa watched him, her pulse still hammering so loudly in her ears she hardly heard the rising shriek of the siren at the local fire-brigade headquarters.

She resisted the impulse to go and wash Rafe Peveril's grip from her skin. A handshake was meant to be impersonal, an unthreatening gesture...

Yet when he'd taken her outstretched hand in his strong, tempered fingers an erotic shiver had sizzled through every cell. Rafe Peveril's touch had been unbearably stimulating, as dangerous as a siren's song.

If a simple, unemotional handshake could do that, what would happen if he kissed her—?

Whoa! Outraged, she ordered her wayward mind to shut down that train of thought.

For two months she'd been bracing herself for this—ever since she'd been appalled to discover Rafe Peveril lived not far from Tewaka. Yet when she'd looked up to see him pace into the shop, more than six foot of intimidating authority and leashed male force, she'd had to stop herself from bolting out the back door.

Of all the rotten coincidences... It hadn't occurred to her to check the names of the local bigwigs before signing the contract that locked her into a year's lease of the shop.

She should have followed her first impulse after her father's death and crossed the Tasman Sea to take refuge in Australia.

At least her luck had held—Rafe hadn't recognised her. It was difficult to read the brilliant mind behind his arrogantly autocratic features, but she'd be prepared to bet that after a jolt of what might have been recognition he'd completely accepted her new persona and identity.

She swallowed hard as the fire engine raced past, siren screaming. Please God it was just a grass fire, not a motor accident, or someone's house.

Her gaze fell to the picture she'd just sold. Forcing herself to breathe carefully and steadily, she took it off the wall and carried it across to the counter.

Gina Smythe was the sort of woman Marisa aspired to be—self-assured, decisive, charming. But of course

Rafe Peveril's sister would have been born with the same effortless, almost ruthless self-confidence that made him so intimidating.

Whereas it had taken her years—and much effort—to manufacture the façade she now hid behind. Only she knew that deep inside her lurked the naive, foolish kid filled with simple-minded hope and fairytale fantasies who'd married David Brown and gone with him to Mariposa, expecting an exotic tropical paradise and the romance of a lifetime.

Her mouth curved in a cynical, unamused line as she expertly cut a length of gift-wrapping paper.

How wrong she'd been.

However, that was behind her now. And as she couldn't get out of her lease agreement, she'd just have to make sure everyone—especially Rafe Peveril—saw her as the woman who owned the best gift shop in Northland.

She had to make a success of this venture and squirrel away every cent she could. Once the year was up she'd leave Tewaka for somewhere safer—a place where her past didn't intrude and she could live without fear, a place where she could at last settle.

The sort of place she thought she'd found in Tewaka…

Half an hour later she was keeping a wary eye on the entrance while dealing with a diffident middle-aged woman who couldn't make up her mind. Every suggestion was met with a vague comment that implied rejection.

Once, Marisa thought compassionately, she'd been like that. Perhaps this woman too was stuck in a situation with no escape. Curbing her tension, she walked her around the shop, discussing the recipient of the proposed gift, a fourteen-year-old girl who seemed to terrify her grandmother.

A movement from the door made her suck in an involuntary breath as Rafe Peveril strode in, his size and air of cool authority reducing the shop and its contents to insignificance.

Black-haired, tanned and arrogantly handsome, his broad-shouldered, narrow-hipped body moving in a lithe predator's gait on long, heavily muscled legs, he was a man who commanded instant attention.

Naked, he was even more magnificent...

Appalled by the swift memory from a past she'd tried very hard to forget, she murmured, "If you don't mind, I'll give Mr Peveril his parcel."

"Oh, yes—do." The customer looked across the shop, turning faintly pink when she received a smile that sizzled with male charisma.

Deliberately relaxing her taut muscles, Marisa set off towards him. He knew the effect that smile had on women.

It set female hearts throbbing—as hers was right now.

Not, however, solely with appreciation.

In Mariposa his height had struck her first. Only when he'd been close had she noticed that his eyes were grey, so dark they were the colour of iron.

But in Mariposa his gaze had been coolly aloof.

Now he made no attempt to hide his appreciation. Heat licked through her, warring with a primitive sense of approaching danger. She forced a smile, hoping he'd take the mechanical curve of her lips for genuine pleasure.

"Hello, Mr Peveril, here's your parcel," she said, lowering her lashes as she placed it carefully on the counter.

"Thank you." After a quick look he asked, "Do you give lessons in parcel wrapping and decoration?"

Startled, she looked up, parrying his direct, keen survey with a mildly enquiring lift of her brows. "I hadn't thought of it."

A long finger tapped the parcel. "This is beautifully done. With Christmas not too far away you'd probably have plenty of takers."

Easy chitchat was not his style. He'd been pleasant enough in Mariposa, but very much the boss—

Don't think of Mariposa.

It was stupid to feel that somehow her wayward thoughts might show in her face and trigger a vagrant memory in him.

Stupid and oddly scary. It took a lot of will to look him in the eye and say in a steady voice, "Thank you. I might put a notice in the window and see what happens."

As though he'd read her mind, he said in an idle tone at variance with his cool, keen scrutiny, "I have this odd feeling we've met before, but I'm certain I'd remember if we had."

Oh, God! Calling on every ounce of self-preservation, she said brightly, "So would I, Mr Peveril—"

"Rafe."

She swallowed. Her countrymen were famously casual, so it was stupid to feel that using his first name forged some sort of link. "Rafe," she repeated, adding with another meaningless smile, "I'd have remembered too, I'm sure." Oh, hell, did that sound like an attempt at flirtation? Hastily she added, "I do hope your sister enjoys the painting."

"I'm sure she will. Thank you." He nodded, picked up the parcel and left.

Almost giddy with relief, Marisa had to take a couple of deep breaths before she returned to her customer. It took another ten minutes before the woman finally made up her mind, and while Marisa was wrapping the gift, she leaned forwards and confided in a low voice, "Gina Smythe's not really Rafe's sister, you know."

"No, I didn't know." Marisa disliked gossip, so she tried to make her tone brisk and dismissive even though curiosity assailed her.

"Poor girl, she was in a foster home not far from here—one she didn't like—so she ran away when she was about six and hid in a cave on Manuwai."

At Marisa's uncomprehending glance she elaborated, "Manuwai is the Peveril station, out on the coast north of here. The family settled there in the very early days. It's one of the few land grants still intact—an enormous place. Rafe found Gina and took her home with him, and his parents more or less adopted her. Rafe's an only child."

"Ah, I see." No wonder Gina and Rafe didn't share a surname.

And she'd been so sure the woman's sense of confidence had been born in her...

The woman leaned closer. "When I say his parents, it was his stepmother, really. His *birth* mother left him and his father when Rafe was about six. It was a great scandal—she divorced him and married a film star, then divorced him and married someone else—and it was rumoured the elder Mr Peveril paid millions of dollars to get rid of her."

Shocked, Marisa tried to cut her off, only to have the woman drop her voice even further. "She was very beautiful—always dashing off to Auckland and Australia and going on cruises and trips to Bali." Her tone made that exotic island paradise sound like one of the nether regions of hell.

Hoping to put an end to this, Marisa handed over the purchase in one of her specially designed bags. "Thank you," she said firmly.

But the woman was not to be deterred. "She didn't even look after Rafe—he had a nanny from the time he was born. His stepmother—the second Mrs Peveril—was very nice, but she couldn't have children, so Rafe is an only child. Such a shame…"

Her voice trailed away when another customer entered the shop. Intensely relieved, Marisa grabbed the opportunity. "I'm pretty certain your granddaughter will love this, but if she doesn't, come back with her and we'll find something she does like."

"That's very kind of you," the woman fluttered. "Thank you very much, my dear."

The rest of the day was too busy for Marisa to think about what she'd heard, and once she'd closed the shop she walked along the street to the local after-school centre. She'd chosen Tewaka to settle in for various reasons, but that excellent care centre had been the clincher.

Her heart swelled at the grin from her son. "Hello, darling. How's your day been?"

"Good," he told her, beaming as he always did. To five-year-old Keir every day was good. How had Rafe Peveril's days been after his mother had left?

Keir asked, "Did you have a good day too?"

She nodded. "Yes, a cruise ship—a really big one—came into the Bay of Islands, so I had plenty of customers." And most had bought something.

Fishing around in his bag, Keir asked, "Can I go to Andy's birthday party? Please," he added conscientiously. "He gave me this today." He handed over a somewhat crumpled envelope.

Taking it, she thought wryly that in a way it was a pity he'd settled so well. A sunny, confident boy, he'd made friends instantly and he was going to miss them when they left. "I'll read it when we get home, but I don't see any reason why not."

He beamed again, chattering almost nonstop while they shopped in the supermarket. Marisa's heart swelled, then contracted into a hard ball in her chest. Keir was her reason for living, the pivot of her life. His welfare was behind every decision she'd made since the day she'd realised she was pregnant.

No matter what it took, she'd make sure he had everything he needed to make him happy.

And that, she thought later after a tussle of wills had seen him into bed, included discipline.

Whatever else he missed out on, he had a mother who loved him. Which, if local gossip was anything to go by, was more than Rafe Peveril had had. He'd only been a year older than Keir when his mother had left.

She felt a huge compassion for the child he'd been. Had that first great desertion made him the tough, ruthless man he was now?

More than likely. But although the sad story gave her a whole new perspective on him, she'd be wise to remember she was dealing with the man he was now, not the small deserted boy he'd once been.

That night memories of his hard, speculative survey kept her awake. She hated to think of the way she'd been when she'd first met him—ground down into a grey shadow of a woman—and she'd been hugely relieved when he didn't recognise her.

Images sharpened by a primitive fear flooded back, clear and savagely painful. Two years of marriage to David had almost crushed her.

If it hadn't been for Rafe Peveril she'd probably still be on that lonely estancia in Mariposa, unable to summon the strength—or the courage, she thought with an involuntary tightening of her stomach muscles—to get away.

It had taken several years and a lot of effort to emerge from that dark world of depression and insecurity. Now she had the responsibility of her son, she'd never again trust herself to a man with an urge to dominate.

Twisting in her bed, she knew she wasn't going to sleep. She had no camomile tea, but a cup of the peppermint variety might soothe her enough.

Even as she stood in the darkened kitchen of the little, elderly cottage she rented, a mug of peppermint tea in hand, she knew it wasn't going to work. She grimaced as she gazed out into the summer night—one made for lovers, an evocation of all that was romantic, the moon's silver glamour spreading a shimmering veil of magic over the countryside.

Bewildered by an inchoate longing for something unknown, something *more*—something primal and consuming and intense—she was almost relieved when hot liquid sloshed on to her fingers, jerking her back into real life.

Hastily she set the mug on the bench and ran cold water over her hand until the mild stinging stopped.

"That's what you get for staring at the moon," she muttered and, picking up her mug again, turned away from the window.

Seeing Rafe Peveril again had set off a reckless energy, as though her body had sprung to life after a long sleep.

She should have expected it.

Her first sight of him at the estancia, climbing down from the old Jeep, had awakened a determination she'd thought she'd lost. His raw male vitality—forceful yet disciplined—had broken through her grey apathy.

From somewhere she'd summoned the initiative to tell him of her mother's illness and that she wasn't expected to live.

Then, when David had refused Rafe's offer to take her home, she'd gathered every ounce of courage and defied him.

She shivered. Thank heavens she was no longer that frail, damaged woman. Now, it seemed incredible she'd let herself get into such a state.

Instead of standing in the dark recalling the crash, she should be exulting, joyously relieved because the meeting she'd been dreading for the past two months had happened without disaster.

Oh, Rafe had noticed her, all right—but only with masculine interest.

So she'd passed the first big hurdle. *If only she could get rid of the nagging instinct that told her to run. Now—while she still could.*

What if he eventually worked out that she and Mary Brown were the same woman?

What if David was still working for him, and he told her ex-husband where she and Keir were?

What if he found out about the lie she'd told David— the lie that had finally and for ever freed her and her son?

Marisa took another deep breath and drained the mug

of lukewarm tea. That wasn't going to happen because her ex-husband didn't care about Keir.

Anyway, worrying was a waste of time and nervous energy. All she had to do was avoid Rafe Peveril, which shouldn't be difficult, even in a place as small as Tewaka—his vast empire kept him away for much of the time.

Closing the curtains on the sultry enchantment of the moon, she tried to feel reassured. While she kept out of his way she'd make plans for a future a long way from Tewaka.

Somewhere safe—where she could start again.

Start again...

She'd believed—hoped—she'd done that for the last time when she'd arrived in Tewaka. A soul-deep loneliness ached through her. Her life had been nothing but new starts.

Sternly she ordered herself not to wallow in self-pity. Before she decided to put down roots again, she'd check out the locals carefully.

Also, she thought ruefully, if she could manage it she'd buy some dull-brown contact lenses.

CHAPTER TWO

To SAVE money, Keir stayed at the shop after school two days each week. He enjoyed chatting to customers and playing with toys in the tiny office at the back.

Which was where he was when Marisa heard a deep, hard voice. Her heart thudded painfully in her chest.

Rafe Peveril. It had been almost a week since he'd bought the gift for his sister, and she'd just started to relax. *Please*, let him buy another one and then go away and never come back, she begged the universe.

In vain. Without preamble he asked, "Do you, by any chance, have a relative named Mary Brown?"

Panic froze her breath. Desperately she said the first thing that wasn't a lie, hoping he didn't recognise it for an evasion. "As far as I know I have no female relatives. Certainly not one called Mary Brown. Why?"

And allowed her gaze to drift enquiringly upwards from the stock she was checking. Something very close to terror hollowed out her stomach. He was watching her far too closely, the striking framework of his face very prominent, his gaze narrowed and unreadable.

From the corner of her eye she saw the office door slide open. Her heart stopped in her chest.

Keir, stay there, she begged silently.

But her son wandered out, his expression alert yet a

little wary as he stared up at the man beside his mother. "Mummy…" he began, not quite tentatively.

"Not now, darling." Marisa struggled to keep her voice steady and serene. "I'll be with you in a minute."

He sent her a resigned look, but turned to go back, stopping only when Rafe Peveril said in a voice edged by some emotion she couldn't discern, "I can wait." He looked down at Keir. "Hello, I'm Rafe Peveril. What's your name?"

"Keir," her son told him, always ready to talk to adults.

"Keir who?"

Keir's face crinkled into laughter. "Not Keir Who— I'm Keir Somerville—"

Abruptly, Marisa broke in. "Off you go, Keir."

But Rafe said, "He's all right. How old are you, Keir?"

"I'm five," Keir told him importantly. "I go to school now."

"Who is your teacher?"

"Mrs Harcourt," Keir said. "She's got a dog and a kitten, and yesterday she brought the kitty to school." He shot a glance at Marisa before fixing his gaze back on the compellingly handsome face of the man who watched him. "I want a puppy but Mum says not yet 'cause we'd have to leave him by himself and he'd be lonely all day, but another lady has a shop too, and she's got a little dog and her dog sleeps on a cushion in the shop with her and it's happy all day."

And then, thank heavens, another customer came in and Marisa said evenly, "Off you go, Keir."

With obvious reluctance Keir headed away, but not before giving Rafe a swift smile and saying, "Goodbye, Mr Pev'ril."

Rafe watched until he was out of hearing before transferring his gaze to Marisa's face. "A pleasant child."

"Thank you," she said automatically, still spooked by the speculation in his hard scrutiny. "Can I help you at all?"

"No, I just came in to tell you I'm now very high in my sister's favour. When I told her you had painted the picture she was surprised and wondered why you hadn't signed it. We could only make out your initials."

She couldn't tell him the last thing she wanted was her name where someone who knew her—or David— might see it. So she smiled and shrugged. "I don't really know—I just never have."

He appeared to take that at face value. "She asked me to tell you that she loves it and is over the moon."

Marisa relaxed a little. "That's great," she said. "Thank your sister from me, please."

"She'll probably come in and enthuse about it herself when she's next up, so I'll leave that to you." His matter-of-fact tone dismissed her, reinforced by his rapid glance at the clock at the back of the shop. "I have to go, but we'll meet again."

Not if I see you first, Marisa thought uneasily, but managed to say, "I'm sure we will."

Parrying another hard glance with her most limpid smile, she tried to ignore her jumping nerve-ends as she moved away to deal with another customer, who'd decided to begin Christmas shopping.

Surprisingly for an afternoon, a steady stream of shoppers kept her so busy she had no time to mull over Rafe's unexpected visit or the even more unexpected attention he'd paid to her son.

Or her reckless—and most unusual—response to

him. It had absolutely nothing to do with the fact that she'd slept entwined in his arms, heart to heart, her legs tangled in his, her skin warming him...

Get out of my head, she ordered the intrusive memories.

Later, after they'd got home, she hung out a load of washing, trying to convince herself that her apprehension was without foundation. A wistful pain jagged through her as she watched Keir tear around on the bicycle that had been her father's final gift to him.

It was foolish to be so alarmed by Rafe Peveril. He was no threat to her or—more important—to Keir.

Because even if her ex-husband was still working for the Peveril organisation, she no longer needed to fear David. Not for herself, anyway... She was a different woman from the green girl who'd married him. She'd suffered and been lost, and eventually realised that the only way she'd survive was to rescue herself.

And she'd done it. Now she had a life and the future she'd crafted for herself and her son. She'd let no one— certainly not Rafe Peveril—take that from her.

Yet for the rest of the day darkness clouded her thoughts, dragging with it old fear, old pain and memories of will-sapping despair at being trapped in a situation she'd been unable to escape.

Because there was the ugly matter of the lie—the one that had won her freedom and Keir's safety.

Unseeingly, Rafe frowned at the glorious view from his office window, remembering black-lashed eyes and silky skin—skin that had paled that afternoon when Marisa Somerville had looked up and seen him. Her hands, elegant, capable and undecorated by rings had stiffened for a few seconds, and then trembled slightly.

A nagging sense of familiarity taunted him, refusing to be dismissed. Yet it had to be just the random coincidence of eye colour and shape. Apart from those eyes, nothing connected Marisa Somerville to the drab nonentity who had been married to David Brown.

Marisa was everything poor Mary Brown wasn't.

He let his memory range from glossy hair the colour of dark honey to satiny skin with a subtle sheen, and a mouth that beckoned with generous sensuality.

A sleeping hunger stirred, one so fiercely male and sharply focused it refused to be dismissed.

So, Marisa Somerville was very attractive.

Hell, how inadequate was that? he thought with a cynical smile. His recollection of a body that even her restrained clothes hadn't been able to subdue prompted him to add *sexy* to *attractive*.

It hadn't been simple recognition that had shadowed that tilted, siren's gaze. His frown deepened. He considered himself an astute judge of reactions and in any other situation he'd have guessed Marisa's had come very close to fear...

Only for a second. She'd recovered fast, although a hint of tension had reappeared when her son had entered the shop.

Possibly what he'd seen in Marisa Somerville's face was nothing more than a feminine resistance to the basic, sexual pull between a fertile woman and a virile man—a matter of genes recognising a possible mate— a pull he'd also felt.

Still did, he realised, drily amused by his hardening body.

That certainly hadn't happened in Mariposa, when

he'd met Mary Brown. She'd looked at him with no expression, shaken his hand as though forced to and immediately faded into the background. What *had* lodged in his mind had been the dislocating contrast between fascinating eyes and the rest of her—thin, listless, her dragging voice, sallow skin and the lank hair of pure mouse scraped back from her face into a ponytail.

Rafe looked around his office, letting the warmth and practicality of the room soak into him.

This room represented the essence of his life; five generations of Peveril men and women had sat behind the huge kauri desk and worked to create the superbly productive empire that had expanded from a wilderness to encompass the world.

He hoped one day a son or daughter of his would occupy the same chair behind the same desk, with the same aim—to feed as many people as he could.

His father had set up an organisation to help the Mariposan government introduce modern farming practices, but after his death Rafe had discovered a chaotic state of affairs. That first, fact-finding trip to Mariposa had been the impetus to impose a proper chain of control, a process that involved total restructuring as well as hiring a workforce he could trust.

He made an impatient gesture and turned to the computer. He had more important things to think about than a possible—if unlikely—link between Marisa Somerville and the wife of one of his farm managers.

Yet he couldn't dislodge the memory of that flash of recognition and the fleeting, almost haunted expression in Marisa's eyes.

Although Rafe rarely had hunches, preferring to follow his logical brain, when they did occur he'd learned to stick with them. A self-derisive smile curving his mouth, he checked the time in Mariposa, then picked up the telephone.

His agent there was surprised at his question, but answered readily enough, "I was not part of this organisation then, you remember, but of course I do recall the circumstances. It was in the newspapers. Señor Brown burned down the machinery shed on that estancia. One of the farmhands almost died in the fire. I understand he was given the chance to leave or be handed over to the police. He left."

Brows drawing even closer together, Rafe demanded, "Why was I not told of this?"

"I do not know."

In fact, it was just another example of the previous agent's inefficiency. Mouth compressing into a thin line, Rafe said, "Of course you don't. Sorry. When did this sabotage happen?"

There was a pause, then the manager said a little stiffly, "I will need to check the exact date, you understand, but it was a few weeks after you and Mrs Brown left for New Zealand."

Rafe's gaze narrowed. The phrase probably indicated only that English wasn't his agent's first language. Technically true, but not in the way it seemed to indicate.

But if David Brown had thought...?

With a sardonic smile Rafe dismissed the idea.

However, it kept recurring during the following week as he hosted an overseas delegation, wining and dining them before intensive discussions that ended very satisfactorily.

He celebrated by taking an old flame out to dinner, tactfully declining her oblique suggestion they spend the night together. Although he was fond of her and they'd enjoyed a satisfying affair some years previously, he was no longer interested. And was irritated when a roving photographer snapped them together as they left the reception. New Zealand had nothing like the paparazzi overseas, but the photograph appeared in the social news of one of the Sunday papers the next day.

Back at Manuwai he found himself reaching for the telephone, only to realise that it was the weekend and he didn't know Marisa Somerville's number. It wasn't in the telephone book either.

And why did he want to ring her? Because she reminded him of another woman?

Grimly, he recalled what he could of the day he and Mary Brown had left the estancia, little more than irritating flashes and fragments—more sensation than sight—of the storm that had brought the plane down. Even after he'd woken in the hospital bed, fully aware once more, he'd remembered nothing of the aftermath.

He'd been told that Mary Brown had brought him to the hut, that she'd probably saved his life…

And without warning a flash of memory returned—a quiet voice, his gratitude at the warmth of arms around him…

That was all. Rafe swore and got to his feet, pacing across the room to stand at the window. He took a few deliberate breaths, willing his racing thoughts to slow. Why hadn't he remembered that before?

Had the sight of a pair of black-lashed green eyes prodded this elusive fragment from his reluctant brain?

After he'd been released from hospital both he and Mary Brown had travelled to New Zealand in a private jet with a nurse in attendance—a flight he barely re-

membered, though obviously it had set the gossips in
Mariposa buzzing.

Well, let them think what they liked. He never pur-
sued committed women, no matter how alluring.

Ignoring the flame of anticipation that licked through
him, Rafe shrugged. He'd find out whether Marisa
Somerville was in a relationship soon enough. Tewaka
also had gossips, and information inevitably found its
way to him.

Keir said fretfully, "Mummy, I don't want you to go
out." He thought a moment before adding, "I might
feel sick if you do."

At his mother's look he grinned. "Well, I *might*."

"You won't, my darling. I'll be here when you wake
up tomorrow morning and you'll be fine with Tracey.
And tomorrow is Saturday, so you can come into the
shop with me."

Keir knew when persistence could—occasionally—
be rewarded and also when to give up. The sigh he
heaved was heartfelt, but the prospect of an ice cream
muted its full force. "I like Tracey."

"I know. And here she comes now."

But Marisa couldn't repress a few motherly qualms
as she drove away. Although her landlord's daughter—
a seventeen-year-old with two younger brothers—was
both competent and practical, with her mother available only a couple of hundred metres along the road,
Marisa had never before gone out and left Keir to be
put to bed.

However, taking part in this weekly get-together
of local business people was something she'd been
promising herself. If nothing else it would expand

her circle of contacts and she needed to take every opportunity to make her shop a success.

Nevertheless, she felt a little tense when she walked into the room, and even more so when the bustling, middle-aged convener confided, "We're honoured tonight— normally we don't have speakers, but this afternoon I talked Rafe Peveril into giving us his ideas about how he sees the future of Northland and Tewaka."

"Oh, that should be interesting," Marisa said with a bright, false smile that hid, she hoped, her sudden urge to get out of there.

Ten days should have given her time to get over the impact of meeting him again, but it hadn't. Five minutes later she was producing that same smile as the convener began to introduce Rafe to her.

Smoothly he cut in, "Ms Somerville and I have already met."

"Oh, good," the convener said, not without an interested note in her voice.

Somehow Marisa found herself beside Rafe with her hard-won poise rapidly leaking away.

"I believe you're living in the Tanners' farm cottage," he said.

Of course anyone who was interested—and quite a few who weren't—would know. Marisa said briskly, "Yes, it's very convenient." And cheap.

"So who's looking after your son tonight?"

Slightly startled, she looked up, brows raised. "That's part of the convenience. Tracey—the Tanners' daughter—is more than happy to babysit. She and Keir get on well together."

He nodded, dark head inclining slightly towards her, grey eyes cool and assessing. A rebel response—heady and heated in the pit of her stomach—caught her by surprise.

"I hadn't realised this is the first time you've come to one of these meetings," he said.

"I've been intending to, but..." Shrugging, she let the words trail away.

"Point out the people you don't know."

Surprised again, she did so, wondering if he was using this method to politely move away. However, although he introduced her to everyone she indicated, he stayed beside her until it was time for him to speak.

Good manners, she thought stoutly, nothing more. Dragging her mind back to what he was saying, she realised that the quality of Rafe Peveril's mind shone through his incisive words and she liked the flashes of humour that added to both his talk and his answers to questions afterwards.

Reluctantly, she was impressed. Although his family had an assured position in the district, it was a long climb from New Zealand to Rafe's rarefied heights—a climb into the world arena that would have taken more than intelligence and a sense of humour to achieve. To get as far as he had he'd need uncompromising determination and a formidable ruthlessness.

In short, someone to be respected—and to avoid. Only too well did she understand the havoc a dominating man could cause.

The media lately had been full of him, from headlines about the signing of an important takeover to a photograph of him with a very beautiful woman in the gossip pages, but he'd soon be leaving Tewaka.

Hopefully to be away for another two months... That should give her time to stiffen her backbone and get over her disturbing awareness of the man.

* * *

When the meeting broke up—a little later than she expected—he caught up with her outside the library where the meeting had been held and asked, "Where's your car?"

Ignoring a suspicious warmth in the pit of her stomach, she indicated her elderly vehicle. "Right here. Goodnight." It was too abrupt, but she hid her expression by bending to open the door.

Their hands collided on the handle. The curbed strength Marisa sensed when his fingers closed momentarily over hers blitzed her with adrenalin. Before she could stop herself, she snatched her hand away as though she'd been stung.

And then it took every bit of composure she possessed to meet his focused, steel-sheened scrutiny without flinching.

Eyes narrowed, he pulled the door open and said coolly, "I rarely bite. Goodnight."

"Thank you." The words stumbled off her tongue and she hastily slid behind the wheel.

He closed the door on her and stood back.

Fingers shaking, she dumped her bag and the folder on the seat beside her and fumbled for the car keys. Why didn't he go away instead of standing on the pavement watching? Of course it took a while to find the key, but at last she finally stuffed it into the starter and turned.

Instead of the comforting purr of the engine, there was an ominous click, followed by an even more ominous silence.

CHAPTER THREE

"OH, NO." Swamped by a sickening feeling of impotence, Marisa jumped when the car door opened.

Rafe's voice, level and infuriatingly decisive, further fractured her composure. "Either your battery is flat or the starter motor's dead."

She fought an unnecessary panic, barely holding back the unladylike words that threatened to tumble out. Although she knew it to be useless, she couldn't stop herself from turning the key again, gritting her teeth when she was met with the same dead click.

"That's not going to help," Rafe told her, sounding almost amused. "It's the starter motor. If it had been the battery we'd have heard it try to fire."

Rebellion sparking a hot, barely contained resentment, she hauled the key out. It was all very well for him—*he* didn't have to worry about getting to and from work, or the cost of repairs. *He* could probably write out a cheque for whatever car he wanted, no matter how much it cost, and not even notice…

Rafe's voice broke into her tumbling, resentful thoughts. "This is an automatic, right?"

"Yes," she said numbly.

"So it's no use trying to push-start it. I'll ring someone to come and collect it and then I'll give you a lift home."

Marisa's lips parted, only for her to clamp them shut again before her protest made it out.

Wearing her one pair of high heels, it would take an hour—possibly longer—to walk back to the house. And she'd promised Tracey's mother the girl would be home at a reasonable time.

Then she had to get to work tomorrow. Marisa couldn't yet afford any help in the shop and weekend child care cost more than she could afford, so on Saturday mornings Keir came with her.

Rafe's voice brought her head up and indignantly she realised that while she'd been working through her options, Rafe had taken her assent for granted. He already had his cell phone out and was talking as though to an old friend.

"Patrick? Can you come to the library and pick up a car? Starter motor's gone. No, not mine." Without looking, he gave the name and model of Marisa's elderly vehicle. "OK, thanks, see you soon."

He cut the connection and said to Marisa, "He'll be here in a few minutes so you'd better clear anything you want from the car. I'll take out your son's car seat."

Marisa scotched her first foolish urge to tell him she could do it. Frostily, she said, "Thank you", and groped for her bag.

She'd vowed she would never let another man run her life.

So did she wear some subliminal sign on her forehead that said *Order me around—I'm good at obeying?*

Not any more.

Oh, lighten up, she told herself wryly as she got out. She was overreacting. Rafe was a local; he knew the right person to contact. Allowing him to organise this didn't put her in an inferior position.

But that clutch of cold foreboding, the dark taint of powerlessness, lingered through her while she waited.

Fortunately the mechanic arrived within minutes, a cheerful man around Rafe's age who clearly knew him well.

He checked the starter motor, nodded and said, "Yep, it's dead. We'll take it to the garage."

Surprised, Marisa watched Rafe help. He was an odd mixture—a sophisticated plutocrat on terms of friendship with a mechanic in a small town in New Zealand.

But what did she know of the man, really? He'd revealed impressive endurance and grim determination during their interminable trek through the Mariposan night and the rain. He'd made his mark in the cut-throat world of international business. Extremely popular with women, he'd been linked to some of the loveliest in the world.

It was oddly—dangerously—warming to see that he still held to his roots in this small town in the northern extremity of a small country on the edge of the world…

Once in Rafe's car and heading home, she broke what was developing into an uncomfortable silence. "Thank you very much for your help."

His sideways glance branded her face. "What's the matter?"

"Nothing," she said automatically, then tried for a smile. "Well, nothing except for major irritation at being let down by my car!"

Rafe asked, "How will you manage without it?"

"It won't be a problem." She hoped her briskness indicated her ability to deal with any situation. "As your friend Patrick seems fairly sure the car will be ready on Tuesday, I'll ring the taxi service when I get home and organise a pick-up for tomorrow and Monday."

It would be an added expense on top of the repairs, one she could ill afford, but she'd manage.

Rafe broke into her thoughts. "Can you drive with manual gears?"

Startled, she nodded. "Yes."

She'd learned to drive the tiny car her parents towed behind their house bus. And in Mariposa the only vehicle available to drive had been an ancient Jeep.

Although David had taken it out most days on to the estancia, and even when he didn't, the keys were never in evidence.

At first she'd believed he was concerned for her safety; Mariposan drivers could be pretty manic. Eventually she'd realised it was another way of exerting control.

Dismissing that bitter memory, she asked bluntly, "Why?"

"There's a spare car at home that might suit you." Rafe's tone was casual. Clearly he saw nothing odd in offering a replacement vehicle.

She gave him a startled look. The lights of an oncoming car revealed the austere framework of his face, a study in angles and planes. Even the curve of his mouth—disturbingly sexy with its full lower lip—didn't soften the overwhelming impression of force and power.

He looked exactly what he was—a ruler, born to authority...

A man to avoid. Yet every time she saw him—or thought of him—a forbidden, dangerous sensation darted through her. Fixing her eyes on the dark road ahead, she said firmly, "That's a kind offer, but it's not necessary."

"Think it over before you refuse. I know you open the shop tomorrow morning. Nine o'clock?"

"Yes."

"I'm coming into Tewaka just before then, so I could pick you up on the way. Then in the afternoon we could go out to my place and you can try the car."

"That's very kind of you…" she said warily, her voice trailing away as every instinct shouted a warning.

Dominant he might be, but it was ridiculous to think his offer meant he was trying to control her.

Ridiculous. Silently she said it again, with much more emphasis, while she searched for a valid reason to refuse.

"I can hear your *but* echoing around the car." The note of cool amusement in his voice brought colour to her skin. "Independence is a good thing, but reluctance to accept help is taking it a bit too far."

Crisply she returned, "Thank you, but there's no need for you to put yourself out at all."

His broad shoulders lifted in a negligent shrug. "If you're ready on time tomorrow morning, calling for you will add less than five minutes to my journey."

Marisa opened her mouth, but he cut in before she could speak, saying, "Small country towns—even tourist places like Tewaka—build strong communities where people can rely on each other when they need support. The car I'm offering used to belong to my grandmother. No one drives it now, but it's in good shape."

She rallied to say calmly, "I'll accept your lift tomorrow, but I really won't need to borrow a car. I can manage for a couple of days. And you don't even know if I'm a good driver."

Heat flared in the pit of her stomach when her eyes clashed with his sideways glance. There was altogether too much irony in the iron-grey depths—irony backed by a sensuous appreciation that appealed to some treacherous part of her.

She should be able to resist without even thinking about it.

Well, she *was* resisting—resisting like crazy.

Only she didn't want to.

And that was truly scary. Rafe Peveril was really bad news—danger wrapped in muscled elegance, in powerful grace, in unexpected kindness…

"How good *are* you?" he asked almost idly, his tone subtly challenging.

Marisa took a short, fortifying breath to steady her voice. "I think I'm a reasonably proficient driver, but everyone believes they're competent, don't they? It's very kind of you to offer the car—"

His mouth curved in a hard smile. "No more buts, please. And to set the record straight, I'm not particularly kind."

That made sense. Men who made it to the top of whatever field they entered usually didn't suffer from foolish generosity.

Remember that, she ordered the weak part of her that tempted her to—to what? Surrender? Accept being told what to do?

So stop that right now, she commanded abruptly, and squared her shoulders. She'd vowed never to allow herself to feel useless again and wasn't going to renege on that promise just because this formidable man was offering her the use of a car.

So she said, "If I needed the help I'd accept it with gratitude, but it's not necessary." She might not buy food for a couple of days, but the pantry held enough to tide them over and independence was worth it.

"Right." His tone changed, became brisk and businesslike as he turned the wheel to go up the short drive to the cottage. "However, the offer's still open."

Tracey met them at the door, her beam turning to blushing confusion when she saw who accompanied Marisa. Rafe knew how to deal with dazzled adolescents; his smile friendly, he offered the girl a ride back to the homestead.

Marisa watched the car go out of the gate and stood for a moment as another car came around the corner, slowed and then sped by. Shivering a little, she closed the door on the darkness, her thoughts tumbling and erratic.

Clearly Rafe Peveril was accustomed to getting his own way. And perhaps having grown up as son of the local big family, he felt some sort of feudal responsibility for the locals.

Well, he didn't need to. This new local was capable of looking after herself and her son.

She walked into Keir's room to check him. In the dim light of the hall lamp he looked angelic snuggled into the pillow, his face relaxed in sleep.

Her heart cramped. Whatever she did, she had to keep him safe.

But she stood watching him and wondered at the source of her unease. Rafe hadn't recognised her.

And even if he did remember who she was and where they'd met, would it matter so much...?

Pretending she'd never seen him before now seemed to be taking caution too far, her response based on a fear she thought she'd overcome. Thanks to the strength she'd developed, David was no longer a threat to her and no threat to Keir either.

But only while he still believed that lie…

She drew in a deep breath, wondering if the room was too hot. But Keir hadn't kicked off his bedclothes and a hand on his forehead revealed a normal temperature. Stooping, she dropped a light kiss on her son's cheek, waited as he stirred and half-smiled and then relapsed back into sleep, then left.

Back in her bedroom, she walked across to the dressing table and opened a drawer, looking down at a photo taken by her father a few days after she'd arrived back home. Reluctant even to touch it, she shivered again.

Never again, she swore with an intensity that reverberated through her. That pale wraith of a woman—hopeless, helpless—was gone for ever. Wiser and much stronger now, she'd allow no arrogant male to get close to her.

So although Rafe Peveril was gorgeous and exciting and far too sexy in a powerfully male way, she'd take care to avoid him.

She closed the drawer and turned away to get ready for bed. All she had to do was inform him she could deal with the situation and keep saying it until he got the message.

And avoid him as much she could.

But once she was in bed, thoughts of him kept intruding, until in the end she banished the disturbing effect he had on her by retracing the path that had turned her from a normal young woman to the wreck she'd been when she'd first seen him.

Loneliness, early pregnancy—and a husband who'd callously greeted that news by saying he didn't ever want children—had plunged her into a lethargy she couldn't shake off. A subsequent miscarriage had stripped her of any ability to cope. The shock of her mother's illness and David's flat refusal to let her go back to New Zealand had piled on more anguish than she could bear.

And then Rafe had arrived, tall and lithe and sinfully attractive, his intimidating authority somehow subtly diminishing David, and made his casual offer to take her home with him. By then she'd suspected she might be pregnant again and it was this, as well as her mother's illness, that had given her the courage to stand up to her husband.

Back in New Zealand and caring for her mother and a father whose grief-stricken bewilderment had rendered him almost helpless, she'd discovered that her pregnancy was a fact.

It had been another shock but a good one, giving her a glimpse of a future. With that responsibility to face, she'd contacted a counsellor.

Who'd told her not to be so harsh on herself. "A miscarriage, with the resultant grief and hormonal imbalance, can be traumatic enough to send some women into deep depression," she'd said firmly. "Stop blaming yourself. You needed help and you didn't get it. Now you're getting it and you'll be fine."

And during the years spent with her parents and looking after her son, she'd clawed her way back to the person she'd been before David. Her fierce determination to make sure Keir had everything he needed for a happy life had kept her going.

For him she had turned herself around. And because of him she would never marry again...

* * *

The next morning was busy, which was just as well. She'd been wound tightly, waiting for Rafe to call for her and Keir, but his pleasant aloofness almost convinced her that she had no reason to fear him. He might find her attractive, but a small-time shopkeeper was not his sort of woman. They tended to be tall and beautiful and well-connected, wear designer clothes and exquisite jewels, and be seen at the best parties all over the world.

In the afternoon she and Keir worked in the cottage garden; by the time she went to bed she was tired enough to fall asleep after only a few thoughts about Rafe Peveril.

She woke to Keir's call and a raw taint of smoke that brought her to her feet. Coughing, she shot into Keir's room and hauled him from bed, rushing him to the window and jerking back the bolt that held it in place.

Only to feel the old sash window resist her frantic upwards pressure. A jolt of visceral panic kicking her in the stomach, she struggled desperately, but it obstinately refused to move. Ignoring Keir's alarmed whimpers, she turned and grabbed the lamp from the table beside his bed, holding it high so she could smash one of the panes.

And then the window went up with a rush, hauled up by someone from outside.

Rafe, she realised on a great gulp of relief and wonder and fresh air.

He barked, "Keir, jump into my arms."

Gasping, her heart hammering in her ears, she thrust her son at him and turned, only to be stopped by another harsh command. "Get out, now! The verandah is already alight. The house will go any minute."

She scrambled over the sill and almost fell on to the grass beneath. A strong hand hauled her to her feet.

"Run," Rafe commanded and set off across the lawn and on to the drive, Keir safely held in his arms.

Half-sobbing, she watched as Keir was bundled into the back seat, then crawled in beside him as Rafe opened the driver's door and got in.

She had time only for a quick, hard hug before Rafe commanded abruptly, "Seat belts on. I need to get this car out of the way of the fire brigade."

So he must have called them. By the time Marisa had fastened the belts Rafe had the car purring quietly down the drive.

Rafe glanced briefly over his shoulder, his words cutting through the darkness. "All right?"

"Yes, thank you." Her voice sounded thin and wavery, and in spite of the warm summer night she was trying to stop herself from shivering in case it frightened Keir further.

"I've just come from the Tanners' place, so they'll still be up. I'll take you there."

Desperate to get Keir away from the sight of the burning building, she nodded. A few hundred metres down the road the fire engine tore past, siren wailing, lights flashing, followed by a stream of volunteers' cars.

Keir stared, fascinated. "Can we go back?" he asked eagerly. "I want to see them."

"No." She choked back a laugh that felt suspiciously like a sob. "The firemen need room to work and we'd only be in the way, darling."

"When I grow up," he told her importantly, "I'm going to be a fireman."

Her hand tightened around his. "When you grow up you can be anything you want to be."

The big car slowed, drew into the Tanners' gateway. All the house lights were on and Sandy Tanner came hurtling through the front door. He stopped, looked hard, then peered into the back as Rafe eased the car to a stop.

"Oh, thank God," he said hoarsely, wrenching the door open. "Come on, all of you, get into the house. Jo's got the kettle on."

Obeying, Keir and Marisa scrambled out and into the comfortable homestead, Keir with a wistful glance over his shoulder at the belt of trees that hid the cottage. "Our house is all smoky," he informed Jo Tanner, who gave him a swift hug.

"But you're here now and quite safe." She straightened and looked at Marisa.

Who asked steadily, "Could we put him down on a sofa somewhere under a blanket?"

"Of course we can. Come with me and we'll settle him."

Keir's hand clutched in hers, Marisa followed Jo into the big family room.

Briskly the older woman said, "You'll find the sleeping bags in that cupboard, with the sheets folded beside them. You'll want something else to wear too—I'll get Tracey's dressing gown. You and she are about the same size."

Still numb with shock, Marisa moved as if in a dream, spreading the sleeping bag on to the sofa and thanking the heavens that Keir still clutched his teddy bear. Like small boys the world over, Keir adored playing with his train and bulldozer, but Buster Bear went to sleep with him.

By the time Jo arrived with a summery, striped dressing gown she'd calmed Keir down enough to tuck him in and promise him she wouldn't go away. It was only when she pulled on Tracey's gown that she realised she was still wearing pyjamas.

OK, so the thin singlet top and boy-leg shorts would have revealed every line and curve of her body. Big deal, she thought trenchantly.

She had a lot more than that to worry about.

Everything she had was in the cottage, every precious memento—Keir's baby photographs, his wide grin showing his first tooth, her parents' wedding photo and the small silver-leaf brooch she'd loved to see her mother wear when she was a child...

Swallowing, she forced down the nausea that gripped her. She couldn't afford to break down. She had to be strong.

Nevertheless, when Keir dropped off to sleep, she had to force herself to get up and walk out of the room.

To her intense relief, the only person in the sitting room was Jo. She looked up and asked, "Has he dropped off?"

"Yes, it didn't take long. He rarely stirs, but I've left the door open and the light on just in case..."

Her voice trailed away and she blinked back stupid tears.

"He'll be fine," Jo said firmly. "Kids are surprisingly resilient. You're the one in shock, not him. I'll put the jug on—what would you like, tea or coffee?"

"It had better be coffee." She smiled weakly. "Jo, thanks so much—"

"Nonsense," Jo cut in firmly. "Don't worry, we've got everything organised. Rafe wanted you to go home with him, but I managed to convince him that Keir would be happier here for the night, where he knows us. The men are over at the cottage checking up, but they should be back soon, and then we'll know how badly the cottage has been damaged." She glanced at the clock and added more water to the electric jug.

Five minutes later a car pulled up outside. Nerves jumping, and acutely aware of the flimsiness of her clothes, Marisa leapt to her feet, bracing herself to meet Rafe's iron-grey gaze when he walked in. "What's happening? Is the cottage…?"

She couldn't finish, couldn't force herself to put it into words.

"Uninhabitable," Rafe said, not trying to soften it.

Marisa closed her eyes against his watchful scrutiny and dragged a painful breath into her lungs. "Did… Was it anything I'd done? I've been trying to work out whether I left anything on—the iron or…"

"Relax, it had nothing to do with you." Still in that level, dispassionate voice he went on, "It looks as though it was caused by someone flicking a cigarette butt out of a car window. The grass on the verge caught fire and the wind carried it up to the verandah. Once the balustrade caught it was pretty much all over."

"Was anything saved?"

This time Sandy answered, his voice sympathetic. "A good part of your stuff is all right, thanks to Rafe calling the brigade as soon as he saw the line of fire towards the house. The brigade killed the flames and Rafe and I helped them carry what was salvageable into the old garage there. It's smoke and water-stained, but it should be OK."

She dragged in a painful breath. "I'm so sorry, Sandy. Can you repair the place?"

"Not worth it," he told her bluntly. "It's an old house and once the fire got in it went up like a bomb. Bloody lucky Rafe happened to be passing and got you and young Keir out."

With an ironic smile Rafe said, "I had nothing to do with it, beyond yanking up the sash and catching the boy as Marisa pushed him through the window."

Foolishly, she wondered if meeting Rafe again had somehow set off some sort of tornado in her life, hurling all her careful plans into chaos…

She locked her fingers together to stop them shaking. Struggling to master her weakness, she blinked again, perilously close to collapsing into undignified tears as she recalled her frenzied terror when the window refused to open.

Rafe dropped one lean, strong hand over hers and squeezed. In a rock-steady voice he said, "Calm down. You saved yourself and your son, that's the most important thing right now. Everything else we can deal with."

We? Forget about that, she thought, and then felt surly, because he was being unexpectedly kind. "I haven't thanked you for opening the window," she said. "I was panicking, and Keir—"

He let her hand go and stepped back, waiting until she sank on to the sofa before continuing, "You were carrying something to break it—you'd have managed. Don't worry, Marisa, everything will be all right."

Conventional words, yet strangely they were of some comfort. When Rafe spoke in that coolly purposeful tone she couldn't imagine any power on earth gainsaying him.

Lifting her chin, she straightened her spine and asked with irony, "Is that a promise?"

Rafe smiled. "Only if you do as you're told."

And watched with interest as her delicate black

brows shot up at his blatant challenge. He was beginning to get some idea of her quality and admired that
quick recovery and the strength it showed. Shocked and
desperately worried, she was no weakling and her independence was bone-deep, as fierce and strong as the
maternal devotion that had seen her get the boy out.

Sure enough she said sweetly, "I gave that up years
ago."

He looked across at the two interested spectators and
asked, "Jo, is that coffee I can smell?"

"Oh—yes, of course it is!" Jo went into the kitchen.

Rafe left half an hour later, farewelling Marisa with an
order. "Make sure you've got the all clear from the fire
brigade before you go over to the cottage."

"Yes, sir," Marisa said, clearly too tired to think of
anything else. In her borrowed dressing gown she didn't
look much older than its owner.

He regarded her with a lurking smile, a smile she re-
turned. But before she turned away she said seriously,
"Thanks, Rafe. You're right, I'd have got him out, but—
I'm glad you arrived when you did."

Rafe almost managed to repress an image of her
clad in pyjamas so closely fitting they revealed every
curve of her delectable body and softly sheened skin.
His heartrate had careered off the chart.

The memory brought his body to full attention, so
much so that he knew it was time to leave. Laconically
he said, "If you're going to thank anyone, thank Jo and
Sandy. I'll see you tomorrow. Goodnight."

CHAPTER FOUR

MARISA'S decision to get up early and go over to the cottage by herself was stymied when she didn't wake until almost nine in the morning.

Through the door, she could hear voices and laughter, and a glance at the sofa revealed nothing but an empty sleeping bag and Buster Bear. After an incredulous look at her watch she leapt off the inflatable mattress on the floor.

At the door she hesitated, then went back and put on Tracey's dressing gown. For some reason she had to brace herself before opening the door.

But Rafe wasn't in the big living area of the farmhouse. Relief and a strange loneliness hit her as she saw Jo and her daughter washing dishes.

Jo looked around and smiled. "Well, you look as though you've had a good night's sleep! Keir's out the front, playing with the boys. Tracey and I are just working out what clothes she can lend you until we get some of yours washed and ready to wear."

"Do you mind if it's jeans and T-shirts?" Tracey asked a little worriedly.

Marisa hesitated, then said with a wry smile, "Of course I don't mind. I'm just finding it a bit odd being a refugee. If it's all right with you, I'll wear them over to the cottage to see what I can find in the garage that Keir and I can wear straight away." A thought struck her. "What's Keir got on now?"

"I fished out some of the twins' old clothes and I put him in them. They're a bit too big but he doesn't seem to mind." Jo said firmly, "And you're not going over there until you've had some breakfast and a cup of tea or coffee, whichever you like."

"Thank you," Marisa said a little starkly. "You've been absolutely wonderful."

But Jo brushed her thanks away. "Tracey will bring some clothes along to the room you slept in and you can see if they're decent on you."

They were a little tight, but they would do until she managed to wash some of her own—always providing, she thought wearily as she walked along the road to the cottage, she had any left. Jo had offered to go with her, but she'd refused. She needed to be alone.

But the sight of the cottage stopped her, and for a horrifying moment she had to fight an urge to turn and run, snatch Keir up and run away from it all...

She dragged in a slow, painful breath and blinked back tears. Although the flame-blackened walls still stood, the whole place stank of smoke. Her heart clamped painfully when she saw the charred sticks of what had been hibiscus bushes against the verandah balustrade, their wonderful silken blooms gone for ever.

Some members of the fire team were back, checking the place and damping down any hot spots. She gave her eyes a quick surreptitious dab as the fire chief came out to meet her.

He said, "I wish we could have done more for you. Don't go anywhere near the house—it's not entirely safe yet. The garage is OK, though. You might like to go and check on things." He paused before saying a little diffidently, "We couldn't save all your boy's toys and only a few of his books."

Regaining control, she said, "Thank you so much. Some is better than nothing."

She'd find some tangible way to thank them, but right then she could only stand in the doorway of the garage, nostrils wrinkling at the stench of smoke, and fight for composure.

Someone had hauled out the drawers from the dressing table and dumped them and their contents on the floor, along with what looked like clothes from the wardrobes, Keir's toy box and a handful of his books. A few pots and pans had made it, but nothing much else from the kitchen.

The pathetic remnants of her life made her swallow hard, but mourning could come later. Right now she needed to be strong.

After a deep breath she walked in, only to flinch when the first thing she saw was the photograph on the ground—the one she loathed yet couldn't bring herself to throw away.

Unmarked by smoke and free from water damage, that pale wraith of a woman haunted her. Never again, she vowed silently, and snatched it up, only just stopping herself from furtively glancing over her shoulder.

"Are you all right?"

Rafe's voice—too close—brought her heart into her throat, blocking her breathing and setting her pulse rate soaring. Her fingers shook as she crumpled the betraying paper, the tiny sound it made echoing in her ears like a small, suspicious explosion.

Had he seen it—that betraying photograph?

In a thin voice she lied, "I'm fine, thank you."

Don't break down, she commanded, her composure cracking. *Don't even think of it. You've coped with worse than this—you can deal with anything...*

Clearly he didn't believe her, but he said only, "I brought some plastic sacks. Do you want me to help you?"

After a swift desperate struggle to subdue her rioting apprehension, she forced herself to turn, hoping her face didn't show anything more than mild interest.

Rafe's trademark vitality was as potent as ever and he examined her face in a searching survey that sent shivers the length of her spine.

All she could trust herself to say was a quiet, "That was thoughtful of you. Thank you."

"It's not the end of the world," he said calmly and reached out his hand.

She stepped back, saw the infinitesimal narrowing of his eyes and said swiftly, harshly, "If you—anyone— touches me now I'll start to cry."

His mouth hardened. "Would that be so bad? It might be a good idea to release some emotion."

"Later, perhaps," she said bluntly, trying for a smile and failing badly. "There's enough water around without me adding to it."

Her breath huffed out in a long, silent sigh when he turned and walked out.

Like the lord of all creation, she thought ironically, watching the way the smoky sunlight kindled a lick of flame across his black head.

If he'd touched her she'd have crumbled, sagging into a humiliating heap of misery.

After another deep breath she hid the crushed photo in her handbag. She'd never be able to throw it away. It reminded her of how far she'd come and how strongly she refused to allow herself to revert.

So do something practical right now, she told herself, and after opening the big plastic sack, began to sort swiftly through the piles, grabbing the first clothes to hand. They stank of smoke and were damp, but a good wash would see them back in a wearable state.

Where could she go? At the most, she and Keir couldn't stay more than a couple of nights with the Tanners—it would be a total imposition after their kindness to her. So, even though she couldn't afford it, she'd have to book into a motel. Tewaka had several; at least one must have accommodation until she found somewhere more permanent.

Scarcely had the thought formed in her mind when she felt Rafe's presence behind her again and stood up, turning to face him.

He said, "All right?"

Jerkily she nodded.

He waited a moment, before saying calmly, "Where do you plan to stay?"

"I don't know yet," she said flatly, hating him for bringing her unspoken fears out into the open. Head held high, she tried to read his expression and failed.

Calmly he said, "Then I suggest you and young Keir move into my house until you find somewhere else to live."

Unable to believe he'd actually said what she'd heard, she stared at him, a swift rush of adrenalin surging through her.

One black brow climbed and his mouth quirked. "I'm pretty certain I haven't suddenly developed horns. It makes sense. Manuwai has enough bedrooms to billet a small army. If you think Keir needs reassurance at night, you could share the nursery suite, which has two bedrooms."

OK, so he didn't mean…what she thought he *might* have meant. Hot-cheeked yet relieved, Marisa recovered enough composure to say a little stiffly, "It's very kind of you, but I'm sure I can find somewhere—a motel, perhaps."

Amusement vanishing, he elaborated, "It's summer, this is a tourist area and the schools will be closing within weeks. Any chance of finding a motel unit— let alone a place to rent—is remote, possibly until the end of the holidays. Actually, you're not likely to get anything until after February because that's when people without schoolchildren take their holidays. I'm assuming you want a house within driving distance of Tewaka."

Numbly she nodded. "Yes."

Keir was very happy at school and she would *not* put him through the sort of upheaval she'd endured as a child. Nevertheless, the prospect of sharing a house with Rafe Peveril set every instinct jittering protectively.

Rafe went on, "Once summer is over you'll have a much better chance of finding a place."

His cool, reasonable tone grated her nerves. She blurted, "The end of summer is three months away."

The sound of her voice, sharp and almost accusing, stopped any further words. She drew a rapid breath and struggled for composure.

It took a lot of energy to steady herself and say with more than a hint of formality, "I'm grateful for the offer, but Keir and I can't possibly live in your house for that long."

"I knew there'd be a *but* in there somewhere," Rafe

said ironically. "So what will you do? Camp in the back of the shop?" He finished with a biting undernote, "Hardly a suitable place for a child."

Rallying, Marisa called on all her hard-won assurance to say briskly, "Please don't be offended. And, no, the shop is no solution. As my car appears to be unreliable, I'll see if I can find somewhere closer to town—preferably within walking distance—before I give you a definite answer."

There, that sounded sensible and practical and—her thoughts skidded to a noisy hum as Rafe nodded, a micro-flash of emotion in his eyes intensifying her unease.

"I'm not offended," he said coolly. "I'll ask around myself. Just don't be alarmed if nothing turns up." He gave a narrow smile. "And while you're looking around, the homestead is there. I'm heading overseas in a few days, so if me being there is a problem it needn't be."

The temptation to surrender to his calm assumption of authority was potent enough for her to pause before answering. Yet it fretted at something fragile and hardwon in her to accept Rafe's hospitality.

However, if she and Keir could find no other place to go, she'd grit her teeth and accept it for Keir's sake.

"I— No, of course it wouldn't be a problem. Thank you," she added lamely.

"Then I suggest you think seriously about it. Jo and Sandy will offer you beds, but it's not particularly convenient for them, or for you."

"No," she said swiftly. "I wouldn't dream of it…" Her voice trailed away as she desperately tried for some solution, only to realise she had no other options. That hard knot in her chest expanded, and she surrendered.

"Then—all right, I'll accept your very kind offer for a few days while I try to find a more permanent place."

Any place!

He didn't look pleased, merely nodded. "Fine. Thanks bore me, so let's have no more of them."

The urgent summons of her cell phone stopped him. She grabbed it and heard Tracey Tanner's agitated voice, and a background sound she recognised immediately. Keir—heartbroken.

"Can you come, please?" Tracey implored. "I've made him cry and he needs to see you're all right."

Marisa said, "We'll be there in a few moments", and switched off. Heading for Rafe's car, she told him over her shoulder what the girl had said.

At the Tanners' house a sobbing Keir ran into Marisa's arms and clung, while she looked her questions above his head.

Mrs Tanner frowned at her daughter. "I'm afraid he overheard Tracey talking to a friend about the fire and got it into his head that it was happening still, with you in danger."

Flushing, Tracey chimed in guiltily, "I'm really sorry—I should have checked to make sure he wasn't listening."

"Keir, it's all right. Stop crying now—Mummy's fine," Marisa soothed, aware of Rafe's hard face.

But his voice was cool, almost detached. "He'll get over it. Marisa is Keir's home base; now he knows she's safe he'll be fine. Won't you, Keir?"

Muffling his sobs in Marisa's breast, Keir nodded, but although he was manfully trying to control them, great half-choked sobs still shook his body.

Rafe went on, "And most of his toys are all right."

Acutely aware of an undercurrent of curiosity from the two Tanners, Marisa said briskly, "Keir, Mr Peveril helped me collect your clothes and your toys. What do you say to him?"

After a hiccup or two Keir emerged from her embrace to say, "Thank you. And my bulldozer?"

"Yes." Before he could run through a catalogue of his toys, she prompted, "And what do you say to Mr and Mrs Tanner and Tracy and the boys?"

Keir made his thanks, adding a codicil, "And thank you for the yummy chocolate, Tracey."

"Any time," Tracey said and ruffled his hair before exchanging a high five that dried the last of his tears and left him smiling. "See you later, alligator."

As they turned to go, Mrs Tanner asked in a worried voice, "Marisa, what are your plans? Is there anything I can do for you?"

Before Marisa had time to answer Rafe said smoothly, "She and Keir are free to stay at Manuwai until she finds somewhere else to live."

At Mrs Tanner's surprised look, Marisa inserted herself into the conversation. "Rafe has been very kind in offering us temporary refuge, but if you know of anyone who has a unit or a small place to rent, I'd be so grateful if you'd tell me."

"I'll ask around," Mrs Tanner said. She exchanged glances with Rafe and grimaced. "I'm afraid it won't be easy."

"Rafe's already warned me of that."

But the more people she had looking out for a place to rent, the more likely she was to find one. Tomorrow— no, as soon as they got to Manuwai—she'd call every estate agent in town to see if anything was available.

Once in the car Rafe glanced at Keir and said, "Straight home?"

Marisa nodded. "You took the words from my mouth. He's over-tired and overwrought. I'll do something about the rest of my stuff tomorrow."

Rafe nodded and started the engine and Marisa tried to relax, deliberately tightening and loosening muscles. It didn't seem to work. Every sense was alert and quivering, as though she felt an unknown danger.

In his car seat in the back, Keir was silent, but after several silent minutes he'd recovered enough to sing a song he'd learned at school, something about a car, only to stop halfway through with a cry that made her twist sharply.

"Look, Mummy! Camels!"

The car slowed and Marisa shook her head. "Not camels, although they're related. These are alpacas."

"Alpacas." He said the word with pleasure, then asked, "What does *related* mean?"

"Part of the same family," she said easily, aware of Rafe listening. "You're related to me."

"Like Nana and Poppa?"

"Yes."

"And like uncles and aunties like Tracey's Auntie Rose?"

"Just like that. Camels are cousins to alpacas."

While Keir digested this Rafe said, "They come from South America and they're bred for their wool."

From the back her son demanded, "Why don't I have any uncles or aunties or cousins, Mummy?"

Marisa said steadily, "Sometimes that happens in families, darling. The alpacas have wool that people use to make jerseys. I might go and see the people who own them to see if they make anything from them that we could sell in the shop."

As she'd hoped, that gave Keir something else to think about.

"Can I come too and pat the alpacas?" he asked.

"You can come, but they might not be tame enough to pat. Mr Peveril might know more about that than I do."

Rafe said, "I'm afraid I don't, but I can find out."

"No need," Marisa was quick to answer. "I'll do it."

Fortunately her words satisfied Keir and he settled back, humming to himself as he gazed out of the windows. Once more trying to relax, Marisa too looked out of the side window, her gaze skimming the hills and deep valleys of this part of Northland. On the very edge of her vision she could just discern a plume of smoke and had to swallow again.

Rafe asked, "Did you live in a city before you came here?"

Woodenly she answered, "Yes." Having to settle in one place had been a blow to her parents, but they'd needed to be close to the services available for her mother.

And she was being foolish to worry about the direction the conversation was taking. Rafe was merely making small talk, something to fill in the silence.

"In Auckland?"

"In the South Island," she said without elaboration. Right down in Invercargill, New Zealand's southernmost city, and about as far away from Auckland as you could get. Coolly she said, "I believe your property's on the coast."

Surely that was safe enough.

He inclined his head. "The house is almost on a beach."

An understatement, she realised when they arrived at Manuwai station. The homestead was a couple of kilometres from the road across paddocks that bore every sign of good farming. A thick, sheltering belt of kanuka trees separated the house from the working part of the station, the evocative, spicy perfume of their foliage permeating the warm air as the car moved into their shadow. From the feathery branches cicadas sent their high, shrill calls into the quivering sky.

A subtle, surprising delight filled Marisa and she leaned back in the seat. Ahead the drive bisected a large grassy paddock to head towards a far-from-modern house set in gardens that covered what seemed to be a peninsula.

She turned her head. Through the sheltering trees a basin-shaped inlet glittered blue against low, bush-clad cliffs. The point on which the homestead stood was its northern headland. In the opposite direction she glimpsed the long, silvery-pink sweep of a beach curving northwards.

"You're looking north to Ocean Beach and south to the cove," Rafe told her. "It's the only safe haven for about thirty miles and served as a refuge in bad weather for the scows that brought goods up and down the coast until the roads were developed."

"It's beautiful," Marisa responded inadequately.

A glitter caught her eye; she turned her head and glimpsed a helicopter parked just outside a hangar.

Well, *naturally*, she thought, mocking herself for her surprise. Of course Rafe Peveril would have a chopper on call. Did he fly the thing too?

Probably...

The big, orange-tiled house sprawled gracefully, its surrounding gardens melding imperceptibly into pohutukawa trees, their sombre foliage and twisted, heavy branches lightened by the silver reverse of each small leaf. Soon each ancient tree would glow scarlet and crimson and ruby, carpeting the beaches with brilliant blossoms like exploding Catherine wheels.

"This is the third house on the site—built in the 1920s," Rafe told her. "The family then had several very pretty daughters, so their father commissioned a house for entertaining. It's been modernised and added to down the years, but basically it's the same as it was then."

He spoke so matter-of-factly Marisa wondered if he took the house and its wonderful position for granted. A little wistfully, she tried to imagine what it must be like to know that your forefathers lived here, that for you there was always a base, a place you could call home...

The gates suited the mature opulence of the house, but were opened electronically, much to Keir's interest, and revealed a paved forecourt. Looking around, Marisa decided that the parking space was big enough to satisfy the social urges of a whole school of girls.

Rafe stopped outside the wide, welcoming front door and killed the engine. "You must both be hungry. I know I am."

"I am too," Keir piped up.

"I thought you probably would be," Rafe said, "so I phoned ahead to the housekeeper and warned her to have something ready that would please a boy." He lowered his voice. "And I wondered if you might like to go down to the beach afterwards."

But Keir's sharp ears picked up his words. Explosively

he said, "Yes, we do like to go to the beach!" and added, "Please, Mr Peveril, and thank you."

Tonelessly Marisa said, "That's very kind of you."

Rafe was too astute not to guess how she was feeling, but nothing of that knowledge showed in his face until they were out of the car and Keir had wandered a few steps away to gaze around.

Rafe looked quizzically down at her. "Sorry, I hadn't bargained for such good hearing on his part. It's been a while since I had anything to do with children. If today's not suitable, another day will be fine."

She tried for a casual smile. "We'd love to go to the beach today, wouldn't we, Keir?"

"Yes, please," he said with heartfelt fervour.

Rafe glanced at the opening door. "Ah, here's Nadine, who rules Manuwai with a rod of iron."

The housekeeper, a slim, brisk woman in her forties, smiled at both Marisa and Keir. "There's only one boss here and it isn't me. Lunch is ready if you'd like it now. I hope there are no allergies I should have taken into consideration."

"Not a one, thank you," Marisa told her. Keir enjoyed rude good health. She glanced down at him, sighed when she saw his hands and said ruefully, "But first we need to wash our hands."

CHAPTER FIVE

LUNCH was served in a sunny, pleasantly casual room where wide glass doors opened out on to a terrace over-looking lawns and the sea. Although Keir ate with his usual enthusiasm, his conversation revealed that his mind was bent on the beach rather than food.

After his second assertion that he wasn't hungry, Rafe pre-empted Marisa's response with a crisp, "We'll go to the beach when we've finished eating and after I've made a phone call, so it won't be for a little while yet."

Keir accepted this without protest. Uncomfortably—and not for the first time—Marisa wondered if she was depriving him of something vital by cutting his father out of his life.

Since her own father's death the previous year there had been no masculine influence on her son; watching him with Rafe now made her very conscious of Keir's simple pleasure in his presence.

As the years went by, that gap was likely to become a problem.

"Stop worrying," Rafe said.

Startled, she looked up, met a speculative gaze and felt her heart give a sudden leap. "I'm not," she told him, not quite truthfully.

"There's no need. Things will settle down."

His astuteness made her jumpy. It would be too easy to fall into the habit of relying on his strength.

On the way down a paved track to the curved stretch of sand at the base of the cliff, Rafe broke into her thoughts. "We've always called this the children's beach. It's very safe."

"And utterly beautiful." Mentally picturing the children who'd played here over the years, she looked around.

This exquisite boundary between land and sea—the brilliant sky, low red cliffs held together by the tenacious roots of the trees, salt and sand and the shrill calls of seabirds, a limitless ocean—this was the stuff of memories that made expatriate New Zealanders homesick.

And the unwavering self-sufficiency she sensed in Rafe, that deep inner confidence, was what she wanted—no, what she was *determined* to achieve for her son.

After some enthusiastic stamping and splashing in the tiny wavelets, Keir settled to build a large sandcastle, discussing the best way to construct it with Rafe in a very matey, man-to-man way that increased Marisa's tension.

If only there'd been an alternative to coming here. Not only was she far too aware of Rafe, but she didn't want Keir forming any sort of bond with him. Although he was surprisingly relaxed and easy with her son, there was no place for him in their lives.

And that was *not* maternal jealousy. As much as she could, she'd protect her child from any chance of future pain.

But she had to admit that Rafe was good with children. Possibly he'd had experience with them, although it didn't seem likely. What she'd read about him in the media indicated that most of the women who'd been linked to him were gorgeous creatures who flitted from party to party at all the "in" spots around the world. If any had children, no doubt nannies kept them well out of sight.

His world was very different from hers... Although Rafe might be attracted to her, she'd bet permanence was not his intention.

When he married he'd choose someone who'd fit into his world, not a nobody without a family.

Marriage? Stunned, she pushed the word away.

If—and it was an *if* so remote she couldn't ever see it happening—but if she ever again trusted a man sufficiently to consider marrying him, for Keir's sake any decision would have to be the right one, made with great care.

A decision that concentrated on good solid qualities rather than the impact of a glinting iron-grey gaze and seriously muscled elegance!

Rafe straightened up from a close examination of part of the sand fortification and glanced across to where she perched on a convenient rock. Her nerves tightened when he said something to Keir, who nodded and smiled and went back to his work as Rafe walked towards her.

Even in the casual shirt and trousers that had clearly been made for him, he looked like a model out of a photo shoot, one selling something magnificently masculine and expensive and powerful.

His first comment widened her eyes in shock.

"I gather Keir's father plays no part in his life."

Was he thinking of the mother who'd played no part in his?

"None," she said, her briefness making it clear she didn't want to discuss this.

His gaze narrowed slightly, but he nodded. "Or in yours."

"No."

After another level, penetrating look, he transferred his survey to the child. "Of the man's choice, or yours?"

Afraid to reveal too much of her nervous guilt, she monitored both her face and her tone. "Both."

"And you're happy with that?"

"Very." Her direct glance emphasised that he was trespassing.

But he was still watching Keir, his head turned to give her an excellent view of his profile. Her wary gaze skimmed arrogant nose and cheekbones and a jaw that epitomised formidable strength.

Handsome was too smooth a word to describe Rafe Peveril. *Commanding* sprang to mind, but even it didn't convey the essence of the man beside her.

It just didn't seem fair that any man should have everything. Except a mother, she reminded herself, and found herself hoping his stepmother had loved him.

Rafe turned his head, catching her eye. His gaze sharpened, darkened, ratcheting up her heart rate. "So is Keir the only man in your life?"

Very blunt. Why did he want to know?

Oh, don't be an idiot. You know the reason...

Her breath stopped in her throat. His open indication that he was as aware of her as she was of him fired a leaping, spontaneous excitement that took her by surprise.

Yet a cowardly impulse urged her to look him in

the eye and lie—or at least imply that she was in a relationship.

She couldn't do it. The lie that already involved him in her life without his knowledge still tasted bitter on her tongue.

And attraction—that heated, exciting tug at the senses, the disturbing, instinctive recognition of desire—meant very little. Perhaps Rafe was bored, looking for a diversion. He was free, and she was a novelty...

Whatever, he was dangerous.

"He's the only man in my life for the foreseeable future." Trying to ignore the odd husky note to the words, she added quickly, "He's heading for the water. I'll just go—"

"He's perfectly safe. Can he swim?"

"Not yet."

Rafe kept his gaze on the boy, the brilliant yellow plastic bucket Nadine had found clutched in his hand.

Marisa was being evasive. Her answers were straight enough and delivered with conviction, but a note of strain convinced him something was amiss.

He glanced at her. Face rigid, her posture tense, she was watching her son as though his life depended on it. Rafe felt a stab of compunction. She'd endured a gruelling twenty-four hours and he'd pushed her enough for the moment.

Quite apart from the possible mystery of her identity, she intrigued him. His initial flash of recognition had been accompanied by a primal, tantalisingly physical hunger, but that first mainly carnal awareness had been tempered by her stoic independence and her strength, and her love for the boy.

She'd come out to Manuwai only because she had
no other option. He still didn't know how she felt about
him—and that, he thought sardonically, made a rather
refreshing change from most of the other women he
met, who let him know they were very interested indeed, either in him, or his assets.

Crouching, Keir had proceeded to fill his bucket with
sand. Rafe commented, "He's already worked out that
wet sand holds its shape better than dry. He seems very
grounded."

His shrewd gaze noted the silent, small signs of re-
laxation in Marisa before she said, "I hope so. He has
his moments, of course, but he's mostly pretty placid."

"He doesn't mention any lack of a father?"

Tensing again, she kept her gaze fixed on her son
and answered in a coolly dismissive voice, "Not so far,
but I know it's inevitable."

"How do you plan to deal with it?"

Rafe watched her get gracefully to her feet, turning
away to tuck the shirt into the borrowed, slightly tight
trousers, and perhaps by accident giving him an excellent view of a swathe of taut, golden skin at her waist.
Deep inside him a feral anticipation woke and refused
to be leashed.

Dark lashes shuttered her green eyes and her voice
was remote when she answered, "I don't know. I'm hoping it won't be for a while yet."

Her tone made it clear that was all she intended to
say. And because he wasn't ready to take this any further right now he let her get away with it.

For the moment.

Always, he waited to move until he had every
available scrap of information. The photograph he'd

glimpsed in the garage had been enough to convince him she was Mary Brown.

What he needed to know was her reason for refusing to admit it.

The Mariposan agent's tone and words came back to him...*a few weeks after you and Mrs Brown left for New Zealand...*

In the hospital he'd been told they'd made it to a herder's hut, spent the night there and been found the next morning. He could—just—recall seeing the hut from the plane. After that there was a blank until he woke some days later in a hospital bed in the capital city.

How had they spent that lost night? Why had he never thought to ask? Because he had been too busy dealing with the mess that was the Mariposan agency, he decided mordantly.

He accepted that his cynicism had its roots in the knowledge that his mother had literally sold him to his father. It had been reinforced by the years he'd been a target for fortune-hunters. Was Marisa/Mary trying to set him up, and, if so, why?

You know, he thought sardonically, it would be for the usual reason—money.

She interrupted his thoughts, her gaze steady and unreadable. "I think Keir's been in the sun long enough." Her smile was set, her tone brisk and without emotion. "Besides, I need to wash the clothes I salvaged. We can't go on wearing the Tanner children's gear."

Rafe got to his feet. "Nadine will deal with them."

She glanced across at her son. Frowning, she pitched her voice too low for the boy to hear and said firmly, "Nadine is your housekeeper, not mine. I'm sure she's got enough to do looking after your lovely place without washing smoky clothes. I'll do it."

He said easily, "OK. Keir can stay here with me."

Brows lifting, she met his gaze, those cool green eyes unreadable, although her expression made it clear that he was, as his foster-sister would have told him, overstepping the mark.

"I wouldn't dream of it," she said cheerfully. "He doesn't know you well enough." She gave him a glimmering smile. "And I'm sure you've better things to do with your time than babysit."

He shrugged, matching irony with irony. "One of which is to make sure you try out my grandmother's car," he agreed smoothly.

She hesitated, then gave another smile, this one with wry but genuine humour. "OK, you win," she conceded. "But clothes first."

Keir's disappointment at being taken away from his construction work was plain, but he submitted with reasonably good grace to being brushed down and chatted cheerfully as they walked back up to the house.

As he'd expected, Nadine was instantly sympathetic. "Of course you'll want to deal with your own clothes. Just call out if you need any help."

Rafe said casually, "I'll bring in the sack." He looked at Keir. "Coming with me? You can help carry in the toys we found."

Keir was only too ready to go. Marisa said, "I'll come too. There are quite a few things to be brought in."

On the way out Rafe stopped outside a garage door and said, "You might as well check out that car now."

He opened the door and stood back to let Marisa look in, waiting with interest for her response.

After a moment of stunned silence, she laughed with genuine amusement. "*This* is your grandmother's car?"

"Indeed it is," he said drily, ignoring the swift stab of some unrecognisable emotion.

She sent him a flustered, half-accusing look. "I'd imagined a solid, sedate, *grandmotherly* car. This—" she indicated the sleek, low sports car in racing green "—is about as suitable for me as a motorbike would be. Keir's car seat won't fit into that tiny back seat, and where on earth would I put the groceries?"

"In the boot—it's very roomy," he told her laconically. "And if you look harder, you'll realise his car seat would fit."

After examining the space more closely, she gave a reluctant nod. "Well—yes, I suppose it would." She glanced down at her son who was inspecting the vehicle with absorbed fascination, then sent Rafe a straight, sparkling look. "It's gorgeous, but unfortunately it's just not suitable."

"How do you know? You haven't even sat in it," he pointed out. "It's in excellent condition—my grandmother used to drive very carefully, especially once she reached ninety."

"Kilometres or years?" she shot back, then stopped, a slight tinge of colour heating the skin above her cheekbones.

Rafe laughed. "Years. Keir and I will watch while you familiarise yourself with it."

Her reluctance was palpable, but after another long-lashed look at him she got in, her hands moving gracefully, confidently, over gear lever and wheel, checking the position of various instruments.

Hiding an odd impatience by talking to her son, Rafe waited. Finally she swung out, managing the exit with grace and style.

Smiling, her expression serene, she said, "It's a lovely

car and I wish I'd seen your grandmother in it. But it's really not necessary, and with the run of luck I'm having right now I'd be terrified I might drive it into a ditch. Thanks so much for offering it though."

Had she been composing that formal little speech while she sat in the car?

If his newfound need to know what really happened in those empty hours after the crash led him to a stone wall, he might feel slightly foolish, but at least he'd be free to find out whether the sensual promise of her fascinating eyes held true.

His silence brought Marisa's head up. A chill of foreboding ran through her when she met eyes of ice-grey.

That arctic survey heated when he smiled, a smile like an arrow to her heart, piercing and melting the armour she'd built around herself with such bleak determination.

That smile stayed with her, lodging in her brain like an alluring, far-too-dangerous irritant while she and Keir washed their clothes, hung them out in the fresh, flower-scented air and were shown into the nursery suite.

It was charming, with two bedrooms and a bathroom as well as a playroom that opened out on to a terrace and a garden. Closer inspection revealed that the garden was walled with timber slats and the only gate had a lock on it.

"Apparently I liked to explore," Rafe told her when he noticed her examining it. "The fence went up the day my mother found me down on the beach by myself." He glanced down at Keir, happily re-acquainting himself with his toys. "I was about half his age."

At her sharp breath he smiled without humour. "Exactly." He glanced at his watch. "I need to make a few calls but if you need anything, Nadine will help. I should be finished in an hour, so get settled in. You'll want Keir to eat when?"

"Six o'clock."

"Nadine can bring along a tray for him to eat here. When does he go to bed?"

"Seven o'clock." She knew she sounded abrupt, but a sudden wave of exhaustion was sweeping through her—not physical tiredness, more a soul-weariness that sapped her energy.

Too much had happened in too short a time; she felt her life slipping out of her control and didn't know how to regain it.

Rafe nodded. "Dinner is at seven-thirty. I'll come and collect you then."

She'd much rather have a tray on the small table in the nursery, but before she could say so, he continued coolly, "There's a monitor in the bedroom, so if he wakes or stirs someone will hear him."

After a slight pause she nodded. "Yes, fine. Th—" and stopped, warned by his sardonic expression to go no further with her thanks.

But over this at least she had some control. With her most dazzling smile she said, "I almost managed to hold back that time. I'll see you at seven-thirty."

Once he'd gone she stared around the room as though in a prison, before collecting herself. She couldn't crumple now. Yet Rafe's absence left behind an emptiness that startled her. He was…overwhelming, she thought, watching her son check out the bookshelf.

Idiot that she was, she'd not thought to bring his pathetic pile of books from the garage. Were his favourites a pile of ashes—the much-read tractor book and his favourite bedtime story about a cheeky dog, the bear tale she must have read a thousand times…?

Right then she could do nothing about them. And she didn't want to think of Rafe Peveril's disturbing impact, either. If his absence could make her feel this worrying emptiness, it was only because he was such a commanding presence, not because whenever she saw him her breath came faster and excitement sang through every cell.

Oh, she was fooling herself. His effect on her wasn't due to his height, nor the breadth of his shoulders or the lean strength that proclaimed his fitness. Or even to his harshly handsome face, its angles and bold features set off by a mouth hinting at a dynamic male sexuality.

It came from within the man, based on character and the formidable, concentrated self-discipline, along with his uncanny knack for reading the world's markets. Add a brilliant brain and he was a man to take very seriously.

She knew little about his rise to the top and not much more about his business empire, but she'd read an article in the business section of a newspaper praising his skilful governance for steering the organisation his father had left to its present prominence. The writer had also admired his firm control of it.

That had made her shiver. It still did. Control was something she understood only too well.

She banished him from her mind. "Keir, why don't you choose one of those books for me to read you later, then we can walk around the garden just to see what's there."

She had a son to settle in spite of a future that had developed a snarl of setbacks. Far better to bend her brain to ways of dealing with them, instead of mooning over a man who'd been surprisingly kind.

* * *

Although it took Keir a while to get off to sleep, Buster Bear eventually worked his nocturnal magic, allowing Marisa to scramble into the one respectable outfit she'd grabbed from the crumpled pile saved by the firemen.

It looked tragic—exactly what you'd expect from something rescued from a fire. Tomorrow night, when she had clean dry clothes, she'd feel more human.

But she bit her lip as she examined herself in the long mirror. What on earth was a woman expected to wear to dinner in the home of a mogul?

"Probably not a green fake-silk shirt and tan trousers," she informed her reflection, "but that's all you've got."

In spite of shaking them out and hanging them in the fresh sea-scented breeze from the window, their faint smoky aroma summoned alarming memories and not just of the previous night. Occasionally images of her sweaty terror as she dragged their luggage free of the plane wreckage still turned up in her dreams.

Squaring her shoulders, she turned away from the mirror and checked the baby monitor for the third time. Something too close to expectation fluttered in the pit of her stomach.

Of all the coincidences to be faced with, meeting Rafe had been the one she'd dreaded most—even more than seeing David again.

If this situation ever came to David's notice it would only add to Keir's safety. She couldn't—*wouldn't*—allow herself to regret the lie she'd flung at her husband when he'd demanded she return to Mariposa with him.

Marisa took a deep breath. She hadn't *cheated* Rafe—she'd just used his name and his reputation.

A knock on the door tightened every muscle, forcing her to take a couple of deep breaths before she opened it.

"Is he asleep?" Rafe asked.

Still stiff with tension, she nodded. "Yes."

Narrow-eyed, Rafe watched her close the door behind her. She looked tired, her exquisite skin paler than usual, those great eyes filled with shadows and mystery, and her lush mouth disciplined. Even so, erect and graceful, it was difficult to believe she was the woman he'd met in Mariposa.

So why didn't he challenge her directly, ask her what the hell this masquerade meant? He had no answer to that, because for once he preferred not to know.

He asked, "Did you have any problems settling him down?"

"Some," she admitted, "but I expected that, it's been quite a day. Buster Bear won in the end though." Her smile was slightly pinched, as though it was an effort. "He usually sleeps like a log, but I'm a bit concerned that he might have a nightmare."

"Does he have many?"

"Not many, but after hearing Tracey's account of the fire…" Her voice trailed away. She stiffened her shoulders and went on more briskly, "I'm glad there's a baby monitor."

Rafe opened the door into the small parlour. "Sit down and I'll pour you a drink. I remember you like white wine."

Would she realise that had been in Mariposa? She'd refused any of the red wine from the local wineries and her husband had said, "You'll have to excuse Mary—she only likes New Zealand sauvignon blanc."

And he'd given her some fruit concoction.

His words brought a faintly puzzled glance as she

accepted the glass, but he noted the fine tremor across the surface of the liquid.

Perhaps she did remember.

However her voice was light and without nuance. "Along with other wines. Perhaps you're confusing me with someone else?"

So she wasn't going to admit anything. He lifted his own glass, untouched until then. "Possibly. Here's to a pleasant stay for both you and the boy."

"Thank you." She sipped, then glanced down at her wineglass. "Would it be possible for me to have some fruit juice too? I'm rather thirsty and I might drink this too quickly."

A faint colour stained her cheekbones, but she met his eyes steadily.

Surprised by a swift impulse of protectiveness, Rafe told her, "A brandy would probably be the best thing for you, but perhaps not until you're ready for bed."

She gave a slight laugh. "Oh, I'll sleep well enough without it. But juice would be perfect, if you have any."

"Lime or orange?"

Not unexpectedly, she chose lime. At this time of the year juice from the oranges on his trees was almost cloyingly sweet.

He poured some for her and some for himself.

After a startled look at his glass, she said, "This is fresh, isn't it? Do you grow limes here?"

"Along with other citrus trees. We have a large orchard that provides enough fruit for the other houses as well as the homestead. In the early days when fruit and vegetables had to be home-grown in isolated districts, my forebears made sure there was enough to keep everyone on the station going."

"It was the same—" she stopped, an unidentifiable

emotion freezing her expression, and took another sip of
the lime juice before continuing "—everywhere, really.
I read about the early days on one of the high-country
settlers in the Southern Alps—amazing that their wives
managed."

She'd made a good recovery, but Rafe would have
bet on it not being what she'd intended to say. She'd almost referred to Mariposa.

She walked across to the windows to gaze out into
the warm summer garden. Gathering strength? It had
been a beast of a day for her, and she'd almost given
away the one thing she seemed determined to keep from
him.

When she turned it was to say quietly, "This is delicious. Thank you so much for asking us to stay. We
need to come to some arrangement about sharing costs."

Whatever he'd been expecting, it wasn't this. He returned brusquely, "I don't expect my guests to pay for
any hospitality they receive."

Black lashes drooped over her cool green gaze,
screening her thoughts. "Your guests are your friends.
Of course they don't expect to pay you—and they can
offer you hospitality in return. I can't do that." Her
lashes came up and she met his eyes steadily. "Rafe, I
don't need charity and I won't accept it."

"This is hospitality, not charity. Jo Tanner would
have offered you a bed if I hadn't."

Her body stiffened and her voice was brisk and no-
nonsense. "And I'd have paid my way there too if Keir
and I couldn't find anywhere else."

Something in her tone told him she'd already spent
some time trying to find alternative accommodation.
"No luck?" he asked, almost amused by the sharp
glance she gave him.

Shrugging, she said in a muted voice, "No luck at all. I didn't realise there were sailing championships this week at the yacht club, and I'd forgotten that next week the whole area has a country-music festival. Every bed-and-breakfast place I rang, every motel and hotel too, are booked out until well after the New Year."

Rafe said curtly, "Then forget about trying anything else—and forget about paying too." In his driest voice he added, "You may not realise this, but I can afford a couple of extra guests." When she looked up sharply he added, "Provided they don't eat too much, of course."

A wry, tantalising smile curved her mouth and quick laughter glimmered in the green depths of her eyes. "I'm not such a big eater," she returned, deadpan, "but Keir will probably amaze you with the amount he gets through."

"He looks as though he might grow into a big man." She'd know he was probing, even though he spoke in his most casual tone. "Is his father tall?"

After a taut moment of hesitation, she nodded. Rafe recalled David Brown—over six feet, and well-built—and felt an odd stab of something that was far too much like jealousy. Although he'd never expected virginity from his lovers, for some exasperating reason the thought of her making love to anyone roused an unsuspected resistance.

Experience told him she felt the same heated attraction he did. Which was possibly why she'd just tried to erect barriers with her suggestion of payment.

Setting boundaries on their relationship.

That stung. Periodically his sister accused him of being spoilt by too much feminine attention. Perhaps she was right, although Rafe hadn't been very old when he'd realised that many of the women who flirted with him were more attracted by his financial assets than his personality.

If he knew Marisa's reason for playing this odd game, he might find her reticence and refusal to cast lures in his path refreshing.

Impatience rode Rafe hard, knotting his gut. Once he had all the facts, he'd be better able to deal with the situation.

Her divorce from David Brown had been finalised just over two years after she'd left Mariposa. His PI had also discovered the boy's date of birth, almost exactly nine months after she'd got on to the plane for New Zealand.

Edgily aware of the saturnine cast to her host's expression, Marisa said, "You're going to get thanked in spades if we don't come to some arrangement about paying board. After all, I would have had to pay you for borrowing your grandmother's car."

"Borrowing doesn't require payment," he pointed out.

She stared at him, then summoned a lopsided smile. "It was a slip of the tongue."

"A Freudian one?" he enquired affably.

Her composure slipped a fraction. Heat warmed the skin across her cheekbones, but she kept her head up. "Freudian or not, it doesn't matter. I can't stay where I'm not allowed to pay my way."

He frowned, then lifted his broad shoulders in a dismissive gesture. "All right," he said crisply. "You'd better find out the going rate for board for one woman and a five-year-old child, plus the rental of a thirty-year-old car."

Suspicious, she stared at him and saw a gleam of amusement in the dense blue of his eyes. "I shall," she said stiffly. "And while Keir and I are staying here we'll keep out of your way as much as possible."

"Fortunately that won't be too difficult," he drawled and drained the rest of his glass. "The house is big enough for us to avoid each other quite successfully, but I expect to see you at dinner each night. Anything else—Keir's routine, for example—you'll have to organise with Nadine."

Privately Marisa considered the housekeeper had more than enough to do caring for this huge house without being bothered by the necessary changes a small child would make.

Staying here would only be a temporary measure. And Rafe was right. Not only was the homestead big enough for them to steer clear of each other, but by the time she left for work and came back again, the day would be gone.

Which left only the evenings…

Long evenings, as Keir was in bed by seven o'clock every night.

In spite of everything, the thought of dining each night with Rafe aroused a sneaky, unbidden sense of anticipation that startled her as much as it shamed her.

CHAPTER SIX

RAFE was a sophisticated, considerate host, making sure Marisa had what she wanted, talking about the district with the affection and insight of a resident, even making her laugh, yet his excellent manners didn't quite mask that subtle aloofness.

Until dinner was almost over, when he asked, "Is something wrong with your dessert?"

A note in his voice told her he knew very well that the poached pears and honey-flavoured crisp biscuits were utterly delicious.

Warning herself to control her expression more carefully, she said, "Absolutely nothing—Nadine is a superb cook. I was just thinking that once we've finished dinner I'll go and check Keir again. I don't want him to wake up in a strange place and not know where I am."

"Nadine would have let us know if he'd stirred. Eat up and we'll have coffee."

She said swiftly, "Would you mind if I didn't tonight? It's been quite a day…"

Rafe's mouth hardened, then relaxed. "Of course you can do what you want. As you say, it's been a difficult day for you." And he was perfectly polite when he escorted her to the nursery suite a few minutes later.

Yet every step she took beside him reinforced

Marisa's feeling of narrowly escaping something she didn't even recognise.

Tension had given her a slight headache. All she craved was a good night's sleep with no dreams about fire and no long, dark hours spent worrying over the future.

Keir of course was blissfully relaxed beneath the covers, with a parade of horse and unicorn posters looking down benignly from the walls. Smiling, Marisa picked up his bear and tucked it in beside him.

Keir was safe. That was all she cared about—all she could afford to care about.

As she always did, she bent and kissed his forehead, and as he always did he stirred and his mouth curved before he drifted off again.

Just as well someone was able to sleep, Marisa thought trenchantly some hours later, staring at the moon from her window. She felt like the only person left on earth. Usually a summer night brought some coolness with it, but not this one, and after discovering no night attire in the pile of clothes she'd scooped up from the garage, she'd gone to bed in a T-shirt and briefs.

Wryly she thought if she'd stripped off completely she might have stayed asleep instead of waking feeling sweaty and enervated. At least the air coming through the open windows was a little cooler than inside the room.

Breathing slowly, she gazed out into the night, a place of enchantment lit by the serene light of the moon. It was so still she could easily hear the soft whisper of wavelets on the sands of the children's beach and the long, lamenting cry of one of the waterbirds Waimanu was named for.

Where did Rafe sleep? Unbidden into her mind stole a picture of his lean, strong body sprawled out across a huge bed. Did he sleep naked? A sinful thrill warmed her. In Mariposa she'd been too exhausted and too worried to do more than accept his nakedness, but now she thought he'd be a brilliant lover...

On the other hand, why on earth should she imagine that just because he was a worldly success and had a very good body he'd be some—some super-Lothario?

Banishing the dangerous image, she left the curtains open, pulled off her T-shirt and went back to bed, where her plans for dealing with what had been saved from the fire were eventually overtaken by sleep.

An abrupt knock on the door brought her out of bed to race across the room, blinking sleep from her eyes.

Keir, she thought, panicking. She must have called his name, because through the door Rafe said urgently, "It's all right—he's fine."

"Then what—?" Marisa jerked the door open, then blinked again, staring at him in the glow of a dim light in the hall.

He'd obviously been in bed too, because all he was wearing was a pair of loose trousers, slung low on narrow hips. The soft hall light gilded bronze shoulders and he looked big and powerful and overwhelmingly masculine.

Marisa's pulse leapt into overdrive. After swallowing to ease a suddenly dry throat, she croaked, "What's going on?"

"I've just been rung by Sandy Tanner," he said, and grabbed her by the upper arms as she staggered. His voice harsh, he said, "It's not good news. The fire flared up again and burnt the garage down."

The words made sense, yet she couldn't process them. Dazedly she stared at him as he went on quietly, "With everything in it. By the time the brigade got back it was all gone."

It felt like a fatal blow to the heart. Every memory of her parents and every carefully preserved memento of Keir's life lost to her for ever...

Marisa sagged, but almost immediately tried to pull herself erect.

And then she was held in a strong embrace and Rafe said abruptly, "You don't have to take everything on the chin. You can allow yourself a tear or two."

"I c-can't...I can't..." she started to say, but got no further. Her eyes flooded.

When she choked on the next word Rafe said, "It's all right, I won't tell anyone," with a wryly amused note that finally broke through her resistance.

She couldn't stop weeping, not even when he picked her up and carried her back into the bedroom. Dimly she expected him to put her down and tried not to feel abandoned. Instead, he sat on the side of the bed and held her while she gave in to the tears she hadn't allowed herself since her father died.

Eventually it had to stop. She fought back the sobs and lifted her head, aware Rafe's broad shoulder was wet from her crying.

And that apart from a pair of briefs, she was naked, her breasts against his chest, one of his hands very close to them.

At a complete disadvantage, she muttered hoarsely, "I've got a handkerchief somewhere," and tried to pull away.

Rafe said, "I'll get some tissues from the box on the bedside table."

When he set her on to the side of the bed she shivered and hauled the sheet around her. His support had enfolded her, kept her safe and allowed her the luxury of grief—and threatened the life she was building for Keir.

She didn't dare let herself rely on any man—but oh, it had been immensely comforting to feel the steady driving beat of his heart against her cheek, his powerful arms shielding her from a world that seemed suddenly to have turned on her.

Comforting and—something else...

"Here," he said, handing her the box. He left her for the bathroom and came back shortly with a warm face flannel and a towel.

"I'm sorry," she whispered and hid her face in the warm, wet folds.

"Why are you sorry? For crying?" His voice was level and cool. "After the day you've had there'd have been something wrong with you if you hadn't released the tension somehow. And crying is a lot safer and better for you than getting drunk."

She shivered again and he said, "Where's your dressing gown?"

"Burnt by now," she said more steadily. "I'll have to call the insurance company. Again."

He sat down beside her and slung an arm around her shoulder in another sexless embrace. "Who are you insured with?"

She had to think; her mind seemed woolly and useless. When she told him he said, "Ah, yes, I know the local agent."

"I suppose you went to school with him." She moved away as far as the sheet would let, evading the too-confining weight of his arm about her shoulders.

Even in the darkness she could see the white gleam of his teeth as he smiled and got to his feet. In the dimness of the room he loomed like some primeval, godlike being. Every cell in her body quivered with delicious tension and she shivered with a sensuous, terrifying mixture of anticipation and apprehension.

It was the darkness, she thought wildly. If she turned on the bedside lamp everything would return to normal. Except that she was almost naked.

So what? It wasn't the first time she'd been almost naked in his arms. But he'd been unconscious then and they'd both slept heavily in the primitive comfort of their mutual warmth.

Now, standing so close to him, with the feel of his arms imprinted on her skin and the faint masculine scent still in her nostrils, she was seized by a sudden fierce longing for all the things she couldn't have—for support, for excitement, for love...

But most of all for Rafe.

Who had held her without the slightest sign of wanting her.

Keir, she thought desperately. Concentrate on Keir. And dealing with the fire.

"As it happens I didn't go to school with him," Rafe said, his voice amused, "but he's a decent chap and good at his job. I'll ring him tomorrow."

It would have been so easy to say thank you, to let him take over. He'd been kind when she needed it and she was grateful, but right now she had to fight this tantalising weakness that melted her bones and sapped her energy in a slow, smouldering heat.

"Thank you for offering, but I'll do it," she said unevenly.

He didn't object. "Will you be able to get back to sleep?"

What would he do if she said no?

"Yes," she blurted, so suddenly she made herself jump. "Goodnight, Rafe."

"Goodnight," he said, his voice level and uninflected.

She watched him walk out of the room, that reckless yearning she'd never felt before aching through her like sweet, debilitating poison.

Keir woke her the next morning, laughing as he tickled underneath her chin. She grabbed him and hauled him close for a kiss, then released his wriggling body to fling back the sheet and get up. The T-shirt she'd huddled into before she finally got off to sleep hung in loose folds.

And she remembered.

Remembered Rafe's arms around her, the powerful contours of his body against hers and the faint, subtle scent that was his alone—heat and virile male. Strange, but she'd always remembered it from the night after the crash, when she'd slept in his arms while rain hammered down on the grasslands...

Her skin burned and she said swiftly, "We have to get ready for work and school, darling." The previous night Rafe had told her he'd take her in and collect her and in the evening she could try out his grandmother's little car, and she'd agreed.

"Can we go to the beach?" Keir asked eagerly.

She glanced at her watch and blinked. "After work, perhaps."

The table on the terrace had been laid for breakfast and to her intense relief Rafe wasn't there.

"He's taking an overseas call," the housekeeper said

when Keir asked. She winked at Marisa and said, "I thought you might like to come and help me bring out the utensils, Keir." Keir's enthusiasm widened her smile. "If Mum agrees, of course."

Marisa laughed. "Of course I do. I'll come too."

"Stay where you are and enjoy the peace," Nadine advised. "Keir and I can do it."

I could get used to this, Marisa thought when they'd gone back inside, looking around at the garden and the trees, colourful and lush and beautiful.

And definitely not for her…

She bit her lip, forcing her mind away so she could concentrate on all she had to do. Get through the day first and then check to see what—if anything—could be salvaged in the burnt-out shed behind the cottage.

A shattering sense of futility gripped her, clouding her mind as she wrestled with a sense of obligation that was interrupted by a prickle of awareness between her shoulder blades.

After an uneasy moment she turned to look towards the house. Rafe was walking out through the French doors, moving towards her with the lithe silence she still found intimidating.

Colour burned up through her skin, accompanied by a pang of need so fierce it almost made her gasp. He looked at her keenly, but although her stomach knotted he didn't refer to her breakdown in his arms.

Instead, after greeting her, he said, "I've had news that will take me away from home for several days. I'll be leaving tomorrow afternoon, so after I've picked you up from work tonight we'll drop Keir off at the Tanners' and check out the garage at the cottage, then find out if you can drive the sports car."

* * *

"It's just like a toy car!" Bouncing with enthusiasm, Keir beamed at the sports car.

Rafe looked down at him. "It might look like a toy, but it's real enough," he said. "Let's strap your seat into the back and we'll see how your mother feels about driving us down to the road."

I'd feel a lot better if you weren't coming too. The moment the thought popped into her mind, Marisa looked guiltily away. He did seem to have a talent for reading her mind, but right then he was concentrating on getting the car seat into position according to Keir's instructions, delivered importantly and with pride.

She didn't want him to be so—so damned thoughtful. That afternoon he'd realised she was near breaking point when she'd seen the smouldering wreckage of the garage and he'd helped her control her shock and desolation by being coolly practical.

Nothing had been saved; the building and its contents were a twisted, blackened heap. Inwardly Marisa had wept at the loss. Yet after they'd collected Keir and driven home, in some odd, perverse way her grief had given way to a feeling of lightness, as though the fires had burned away the detritus of her past to allow her a freedom she'd never experienced before.

Wistfully, she watched Keir direct the attachment of his car seat, envying her son's confidence, his obvious enjoyment in helping Rafe. They could be father and son—both dark-haired and long-limbed...

Another thought to be firmly squelched. It brought with it an even heavier load of guilt.

"We're ready."

Rafe's voice startled her. She turned to see that the child seat had been fitted into the car and locked into place.

His smile was a little ironic. "Satisfied?"

"Yes." She looked down at her son. "In you get, young man."

He obeyed, but when she went to clip him in he said, "Mr Pev'ril can do it, Mum."

Something twisted in her heart. She said, "OK", and watched an amused Rafe follow more instructions, his hands deft and swift and sure as he slotted in the clip.

"There, that should do it," he said to her son's enthusiastic assent.

Marisa slid behind the wheel, fighting a difficult tangle of emotions. Love for her son mingled with fear that she was depriving him of a formative and necessary relationship by keeping him away from his father.

And then there was the confusing ache that had nothing to do with Keir.

She was so very aware of Rafe. Her body sang a rash, forbidden call whenever he was near, a call she didn't dare heed. If only he weren't so…well, so *nice* in his autocratic way. And Keir's pleasure in being with him was obvious from his confident, happy tone when he was chatting to Rafe.

Unfairly, she didn't want Rafe to be good with her son. Why wasn't he what she imagined a typical tycoon to be—dictatorial, overbearing and intolerant, puffed up with pride and a sense of privilege and entitlement?

Then she wouldn't feel this reckless attraction, this disturbing tangle of emotion and sensation that was changing from the initial strong, physical pull into something much more dangerous, an emotion with the power to change her life…

He lowered his long body into the front seat. Hastily she pretended to be studying the dials on the dashboard.

"Ready?" he asked.

Without looking at him, Marisa nodded and switched on the engine. "As ready as I'm likely to be. It's a good thing there's a long drive to practise on."

Although it had been some years since she'd used a manual gearbox, she soon remembered the technique as they set off slowly towards the road. From the back seat Keir chatted away, seeming not to mind that it was Rafe who answered his questions and pointed out various things he thought might interest her son.

At least concentrating on co-ordinating gear lever and clutch kept her from further obsessing about the man beside her.

And then they met the tractor. Not an ordinary tractor, but a behemoth, garish in colour and noisy.

"Stop here," Rafe ordered.

Marisa brought the car to a halt, smiling as she turned to look at her son when Rafe swung out of the car. Keir adored tractors and his attention was fixed on the vehicle and the man striding towards it.

After a brief discussion with the driver Rafe came back and bent to tell her, "The nearest gate is only about a hundred yards behind us, so back up and go into the paddock to let him past. Would you like me to do it?"

Powerfully tempted to surrender the wheel, Marisa set her jaw. Letting him take over would be a disintegrating reversion to the woman who'd allowed herself to become the wreck he'd seen at their first meeting.

In a clipped voice she said, "No, I'll be fine, thank you."

As though he'd expected her answer, he nodded. "Don't try to back through the gate. Reverse past it, then drive through. Once you're in the paddock you can turn around."

It wasn't exactly an order, but she had to conceal a bristling irritation as he straightened up again.

Go and talk to the tractor driver again, she urged silently.

Instead, he walked towards the gate, formidable and compelling, the sun gleaming red-black on his arrogant head.

A heady rush of adrenalin clamoured through Marisa, setting off tiny fires in every cell. Shocked by its force, she realised her hands were clammy on the wheel. As she dragged in a swift, shaky breath she ordered herself to be sensible, an injunction that did nothing to calm her twanging nerves.

Concentrate, she told herself fiercely. *Reversing is not one of your strongest skills, but for heaven's sake, this is dead flat and perfectly straight—you can do it. Just don't scrape the side of the car as you go through...*

How she hoped the mechanic would have her car fixed on Tuesday! And that she could find a place of her own soon—before Rafe returned from wherever he was going.

Tuning out Keir's chatter, she set the car in motion. Rafe stood beside the opened gate, watching her. Acutely conscious of him, she slowly reversed the car down the drive.

"I like Mr Pev'ril," Keir said from the back, waving at Rafe, who lifted his hand in response. "Do you like him, Mum?"

"Yes," she said colourlessly, because what else could she say?

Like? What a pallid, wishy-washy word. She didn't like Rafe Peveril—she wanted him.

There, she'd admitted it. *She wanted him.* Whenever he was nearby her treacherous body did its best to weaken her will. Even though every instinct whispered that he was a dangerous man with the power to cause her huge grief, she thrilled to the sight of him.

To Keir's enthusiastic commentary, she drove carefully into the paddock and turned the car to face the drive. The tractor thundered by, stopping a few metres beyond the gate and the driver swung down to speak to Rafe. Carefully she eased the car on to the drive again before stopping and glanced in the rear-vision mirror.

Something about Rafe's stance caught her attention. Whatever he was being told had made him angry. He spoke briefly and curtly, then strode towards the car.

"Here he comes!" Keir announced superfluously.

Marisa's hands clenched on the wheel. She took a huge breath and turned her head as Rafe got in, meeting eyes as cold and deadly as the moon.

Her stomach knotted and for a moment she froze in a familiar, dreaded fear. Whenever David had been angry with her he'd go silent, refusing to give her a reason and ignoring her tentative efforts to find out what she'd done wrong. Periodically he'd walked out, sometimes for days, leaving her alone without knowing where he was or whether he was ever coming back.

Involuntarily she asked, "Is something wrong?"

And stopped, angry with herself for reverting so rapidly. Rafe wasn't David and she was no longer a depressed girl rendered helpless by those long silences.

"Possibly." He paused, then continued in a level voice, "The driver's been clearing some gorse along the riverbank and noticed some suspicious plants on the other side."

"Suspicious pl—*oh*!" She stared at him. "Does that mean what I think it means?"

"Yes."

"On your property?"

"Yes." In a lethal tone that sent icy shivers down her spine, he finished deliberately, "Which could indicate that someone from Manuwai put them there."

Marisa blinked, then glanced in the rear-vision mirror. Clearly not listening, Keir had twisted around and was watching the tractor drive away.

She said, "They'd have to be awfully stupid, wouldn't they, because your workers would be the first suspects. Is the plot easily accessible from the sea?"

"In an inflatable it's reasonably easy to get at. And I don't for a moment think it's someone from the station. In fact, I have a pretty good idea who it might be."

Marisa switched on the engine and put the car in gear. Choosing her words with care, she said, "Let's remember there's a third party present."

Frowning, Rafe nodded and Marisa eased the car along the drive, asking, "So what are you going to do?"

"Call the authorities." His icy composure was far more intimidating than David's silences had ever been. "No one does that on my land and gets away with it."

CHAPTER SEVEN

BACK at Manuwai Marisa parked the car carefully in the garage and held out the keys.

"Keep them," Rafe told her negligently. "Use this car until you've got your own back."

"I… Thank you." It was on the tip of her tongue to ask when he'd be returning from his trip, but she restrained herself in time. It would have sounded far too personal—as though she had some right to know.

He said to Keir, "Look after your mum while I'm away, young man. She's had a tough day."

Keir managed the difficult task of registering both pride and dismay. "Yes, but when are you coming home?" he asked.

"Probably after six more sleeps."

Watching Keir struggle with disappointment, Marisa winced. It was one thing to wonder if her son needed more male influence in his life; that he was fast fixing on Rafe as that influence was something else entirely. She didn't want Keir to become attached to him, only to find he had no place in Rafe's life.

She fought back a tide of weariness and put Keir to bed, where he dropped off immediately.

When she found that Nadine had ironed their smoke-stained clothes, weak tears sprang to her eyes as she stammered thanks.

"You're worn out and no wonder," Nadine said briskly. "I'll make you a cup of tea."

Marisa straightened. "I'd love that, but I need a shower more, and then shall we sit down and work out a system? I know our being here is making extra work for you, but I'll make sure it's as little as possible."

The housekeeper smiled. "I enjoy having people around and it's lovely to have a child in the house again. Makes it a home, somehow."

Which warmed Marisa, but once she'd drunk the cup of tea she rang around the various estate agents.

And got the same answer—nothing to rent.

Still she kept trying, spurred on every morning by Keir's eager query, "Is Mr Peveril coming home today?" Rafe had departed in the chopper, which he *did* fly to and from the local airport, to Keir's complete entrancement, but every morning when either Marisa or Nadine said, "No, not today," his face fell.

Marisa understood his feelings. Lovely as Manuwai homestead was, the place seemed empty without its driving force, the man who owned it.

She missed Rafe like an ache for something she'd never attain, a hunger that could never be satisfied.

Yet it was too easy to settle, to relax, to let the big house embrace them. She and Nadine worked out their system and enjoyed each other's company, she met several of the farm workers, and Keir demanded to be allowed to travel in the school bus with his new best friend, the son of one couple.

"No, darling, we can't do that," she said at first.

Thrusting out his lower lip, he produced something

too close to a whine. "Why? Manu said his mum said it was all right and she'd take me with him when she takes him and the other kids on the bus down to the gate."

She thought for a moment. "Here's what we could do. I'll talk to Manu's mother and if she's happy to take you down you could go in the morning, but after school Nadine is too busy to look after you. And it's not her job. So in the afternoon you'd still have to go to the day-care centre and the shop."

He wavered, then gave a reluctant nod.

Manu's mother laughed when she rang. "I've been waiting for your call," she said cheerfully. "My little scamp told me all about this plan he and Keir dreamed up. Of course I'll pick Keir up in the mornings—it'll be no bother."

So the next morning Marisa watched Keir climb into Ngaire Sinclair's car, feeling rather as she had on his first day at school.

On the third day Patrick the mechanic rang to say her own car was fixed.

"But it's going to need more work done soon," he warned her when she arrived to pick it up.

Anxiously Marisa asked, "Expensive work?"

He grimaced. "Yeah, 'fraid so. Rafe told me to give it a good going-over so I took it for a drive and your transmission's slipping."

"What does that mean?"

He answered soberly, "Basically it means you'll be driving it one day and it'll stop. And then it will cost you."

Marisa drew a deep, impeded breath and drove carefully home, anxiously trying to work out how she could afford to pay for any future repairs. Renewed efforts to find somewhere to live close to town still met without success. That and dealing with her insurance claim kept her busy, and the Christmas buying frenzy was slowly starting.

A week after Rafe had left, she tucked Keir into bed, then walked along to the small parlour where she'd joined Rafe that first night. She pushed open the door and took two steps inside before she realised she wasn't alone. Her heart stopped, then began thudding in an irregular tattoo as an incredulous, terrifying delight filled her.

"How— I didn't hear the chopper," she said a little indignantly.

"I came out by car."

Rafe felt a swift jab of something too close to compunction. She looked tired, and although her face was impassive, she held herself stiffly, as though ready to stand her ground and fight.

At their first meeting in Tewaka he'd recognised the brittleness beneath the bright confidence, but now— now he knew exactly what caused it.

He should despise her. He did despise her, yet whenever he saw her his body sprang to life, reacting with hot, sexually charged arousal...

Marisa met his gaze with what could almost have been defiance, but her voice was unsteady as she went on, "You're back early."

"I've done what I had to do." He poured a glass of wine and held it out to her. "You seem startled."

Her smile looked genuine, but no amusement showed in her eyes and again he sensed that tight control.

"Thank you," she said and sipped an infinitesimal amount, red lips curved against the glass. "Not startled, just a bit surprised. I didn't think Nadine was expecting you for another couple of days."

The sensation in his gut expanded into lust, like an arrow from some malicious god. *Not now,* he thought grimly, silently cursing his unruly body.

His voice sounded harsh when he said, "Nadine expects me when she sees me."

After another fleeting glance, she hurried into speech. "I've called social services, so I know how much I should be paying you for board." Her voice was almost challenging as she gave him a figure.

Rafe nodded. The amount meant nothing—he'd already decided to put the money into a bank account for her son. But her immediate mention of it meant she was still trying to set barriers between them, reduce everything to a commercial basis.

And if he was going to see this thing through, he needed to follow her example and ignore the fact that the pulsating awareness between them was not only mutual, but unlike anything he'd ever experienced before. The situation was too complex, muddied by other considerations, other concerns.

They had a lot more to deal with than this unforeseen and extremely disruptive physical reaction.

Although, he thought ironically, it could work in his favour...

And cursed again at the leap of hunger in his blood.

As though she sensed it Marisa took a step back and said jerkily, "What a lovely, serene room this is."

"It was my mother's favourite," he told her. "I think the women of the house have always used it for their refuge."

She seemed to be interested. "It must be very..." she stopped a moment or two, finally producing with a slight grimace "...*grounding*, I suppose is the word I'm looking for—to grow up in a house where your family has lived for generations. Unusual too in New Zealand."

"Not so very unusual—plenty of families still live where their ancestors settled. There have been three houses here, actually. My several-times-great-grandfather and his wife camped in a canvas tent until the local tribe showed them how to make a more permanent structure—a *whare* with a frame of manuka poles thatched with the fronds of nikau palms."

He noticed her face go rigid for a fleeting moment, then the long lashes swept down. When they came up again the green eyes were blank and shallow as glass.

So many damned secrets. Why? And the need to know every last one of them was becoming intolerable.

But her words surprised him. "His wife must have been so lonely here."

"You'd think so, but it wasn't long before she had children to look after, and she was an ardent gardener."

"I suppose she had to be."

He nodded. "She became friends with quite a few of the women of the tribe here. In fact, her oldest son—who took over Manuwai when his father died young—eloped to Australia with the daughter of the chief. She was a great beauty."

Her eyes widened. "Goodness, what happened?"

"The girl's parents were furious," he told her drily. "She'd been promised to a chief from the Waikato region so it caused quite a scandal. But once the babies started to arrive all was forgiven."

Marisa stiffened again, but forced herself to relax. "That usually happens, doesn't it?" she said neutrally. "Children have a habit of winding their way into people's hearts."

Although his gaze was far too keen for comfort, his voice was casual. "Where did you grow up?"

For a second she hesitated, then said smoothly and quickly, "Everywhere."

At his raised brows, she managed to produce a smile. "Quite literally. My parents were gypsies—not real ones, but they travelled all over the country."

"In a caravan?"

"No, a house bus."

"An interesting childhood," he observed noncommittally, his gaze never leaving her face.

It was like being targeted by lasers. Shrugging, Marisa said, "I'm afraid I didn't appreciate it as I probably should have. I wanted to be like other kids and stay in one place."

"Why?"

"Herd instinct, I suppose." Before he could put any more questions she asked, "Did you ever hanker for a different life?"

"There was enough here to keep me happily occupied while I was at primary school. But I spent my secondary years away at boarding school and by the time I left I knew I didn't want to come back here and farm the place as most Peverils before me had. So I went to university and did a couple of degrees before setting off to make my fortune."

There had been problems about that decision, she deduced from the raw undernote to his words.

Rafe went on in a coolly judicious tone, "But Waimanu has always been my home, so your choice of word was apt. Grounded is exactly how the place makes me feel. What did your parents do to earn a living?"

"My mother was a fantastic knitter and embroiderer, and my dad made gorgeous wooden toys. Between them they earned enough for us to keep travelling. They loved the life."

So much that she wondered if the illness that forced her mother to stay in one place had worn away their will to live.

She scotched that thought with a rapid, twisted smile. "I'm afraid I was born without their wanderlust, or their manual skills."

"You can paint," he said crisply. "Gina is a connoisseur and she rates your oil very highly."

His words surprised and warmed her. "I have a small talent, that's all. I'm delighted she likes the picture, but I hope she's not expecting it to increase in value much over the years."

Painting was another thing she'd had to surrender in the mockery that had been her marriage. David had considered it a frivolous waste of time. At first she'd thought he didn't understand the pleasure she got from it, but soon she'd realised he understood too well—he saw it as competition, something that took her attention away from him. Without making a decision to give it up, she'd found it impossible to keep going when somehow her materials had disappeared and new ones never arrived.

Bad memories. She dismissed them and sipped some more wine, trying to think of a way to steer the conversation back to Rafe.

"Perhaps you don't fully appreciate the talents that were developed through your unconventional life with your parents. And surely growing up in that sort of milieu must have given you the knowledge and the skills to choose your stock when you set up the shop?"

Marisa gave him a swift, surprised look. "I suppose it did," she said quietly. "Tell me, how big is Manuwai?"

The acreage he gave startled her. "That's huge," she said involuntarily.

He shrugged. "We don't give up what's ours," he said.

A note in his voice sent an involuntary shiver through her.

He went on, "Have you worked out a schedule with Nadine?"

Marisa's smile probably showed too many teeth. Or perhaps it was the saccharine sweetness of her tone when she said, "Yes, sir", that hardened his gaze.

"Did that sound like an order?"

"Very much," she told him coolly.

His smile was a little taunting. "And you don't respond well to them?"

"I tend not to respond to orders at all."

She hoped her voice was a lot more confident than she felt. Periodically the old Mary Brown emerged from beneath the carefully confident shell she'd built around herself, but no one was ever going to control her again.

Not even a man whose efficiency in running a worldwide organisation earned him general respect and admiration.

"Indeed, why should you?" he said negligently. "However, I didn't intend to bark out commands."

Marisa shrugged. "As it happens, Nadine and I work very well together."

"Good," he said, but absently as he checked his watch. "And if we're to avoid her sternest face, we'd better get ourselves to the table. It's such a pleasant evening we're eating out on the terrace."

Once outside, he said, "I assume Keir's already asleep."

"Well and truly. They had swimming sports at school today."

"How did he do?"

"He told me he came third in the dog paddle. That was clearly a big deal." She smiled a little at the memory of his innocent delight. "He informed me that next year he's going to win."

"You didn't go?"

"No. I had to look after the shop."

He gave her a keen glance but made no comment, possibly guessing that she'd spent quite a bit of the two hours allotted to the sports wishing she could be there.

She said sturdily, "And thanks very much for the loan of your grandmother's car. It's been fun driving it. Your friend Patrick told me that you'd asked him to give my car a good going-over."

"Did he?" He looked amused.

She wanted to tell him to step back from her, keep out of her business, but it seemed churlish. "Thank you," she said woodenly, and looked around. "How lovely it is out here."

The terrace garden always reminded Marisa of photographs she'd seen of tropical resorts, usually in glossy magazines filled with impossibly beautiful people. But tonight everything seemed brighter, more sweetly scented, more—well, just *more*.

Because Rafe was here…

After sitting down she kept her gaze fixed on the circle of lawn bordered by plants with dramatic leaves and bold flowers.

"The light's not too bright?" Rafe asked.

"Not a bit." A canopy sheltered them as the sun sank towards the west and a little breeze sighed past, carrying the fresh, green scent of foliage and flowers, the tang of salt.

Some people, Marisa thought almost enviously, had all the luck.

No, luck was for lottery winners. Rafe's life might be based on the hard work of the generations who'd lived at Waimanu before him, but his own efforts had propelled him further than they had gone.

And he was an excellent host. Over the meal she engaged in a spirited discussion that had her forgetting—almost—her very equivocal situation.

What she couldn't ignore was the swift build of excitement, the intoxication of exchanging views with a man whose incisive brain stimulated hers—and the more subtle stimulation of green eyes meeting grey, the deep timbre of his voice, the way a stray sunbeam lingered across his head, kindling a red-black flame before dying as the sun went down and twilight descended upon them.

He was dynamite, his potent masculinity adding to the impact of his powerful personality.

"Don't you like that wine?" Rafe asked.

"It's lovely, but I've had enough, thank you," she said swiftly.

She didn't need wine. This rare excitement that throbbed through her, exhilarating and heady, came from her heart's response to the man who watched her across the table.

He leaned back in his chair and looked at her, his gaze intent yet oddly chilling. Without preamble, he said in a voice that held no expression at all, "I've just flown back from Mariposa."

Her heart stopped. Literally.

Then it started up again, hammering so loudly she couldn't hear the silken song of the waves as they kissed the beach. She felt the colour drain from her skin, leaving it cold and taut. For a horrifying moment she thought she might faint.

Not now, she thought frantically, her gaze locked on to the cold grey of his. She dragged in a deep breath and forced her spinning, shocked brain into action.

"How interesting," she finally got out.

And closed her mouth against any further words in case her voice broke and she shattered with it into a million pieces.

He didn't move. "Is that all you have to say?"

Her skin tightened in a primitive urge to flee, to grab Keir and run as though the hounds of hell were after them. She resisted the urge to swallow and managed to speak. "What do you think I should say?"

"You might start," he said, his tone so level it sounded like a judge's delivery of a verdict, "by telling me exactly who fathered your son."

CHAPTER EIGHT

MARISA dragged a shaky breath into airless lungs. Silence stretched between them as she desperately searched for something—anything—to say. Her voice sounded limp and strained when she finally said, "I have no idea what business that is of yours. Why do you ask me?"

Rafe was still leaning back in his chair, watching her like a predator about to strike the killing blow. "In Mariposa I discovered that when we were found after the crash both of us were in bed together. Naked." His gaze narrowed into iron-hard intimidation. "Did we make love?"

Colour flooded her skin. "No!"

Too late she realised her explosive denial had betrayed her identity. Dismay and a kind of fear paralysed her.

Not a muscle moved in Rafe's hard, handsome face. Without apparent interest he asked, "So why were we naked?"

Abandoning hope of keeping up the pretence, she summoned every ounce of willpower to keep her voice steady. "You were naked—I was not. We crashed in a rainstorm. By the time we reached the hut we were both drenched and you—you looked like death. You were shivering, and I couldn't—"

Marisa stopped, recalling her helpless terror as she'd tried to work out what to do.

"Go on," he said tonelessly.

She bit her lip, then forced herself to continue in a flat voice. "There was a sort of bed—a hammock, really, made of cowhide nailed to a wooden frame. At first I thought we could use the frame to make a fire, but there were no matches. It was freezing…" She took another breath and finished rapidly, "And the only covering was another cowhide. It had no warmth to it. So I went back to the plane and retrieved our luggage."

He said quietly, "In the rain?"

"It hadn't stopped." Terrified the plane might somehow explode, and ashamed of her primitive, anguished fear of the dead pilot, two things had kept her going— fear Rafe might die if she couldn't warm him and the need to collect her passport, her only hope of freedom.

By the time she returned to the hut she was so tired she'd ached as though she'd been beaten, but worse than her exhaustion was seeing Rafe collapsed on the sorry excuse for a bed, his indomitable will finally conquered by the injury.

For a shattering moment she'd thought he was dead.

All emotion drained from her voice she went on, "When I got back I had to shake you awake, but I could tell you had no idea what was happening. I managed to persuade you out of your wet clothes, but after that you relapsed into unconsciousness again, so I couldn't get you into anything dry."

Not that their clothes had been dry exactly, but damp had been an improvement on sodden.

Something of the cold dismay that had overtaken

her then swept through her now. She steadied her voice and said, "I took all the clothes from both our cases and spread them over you and put the skin over them, but you didn't stop shivering. You were cold—so cold—and I thought you might die before anyone came."

Nothing showed in his face, nothing but harsh control. "And you?"

She stared at him.

He said crisply, "I assume you were wet too, and just as exhausted."

Surprised, she said, "I hadn't been hurt. You probably don't remember, but you pushed my head down just before impact and all I got were a few bruises. I was soaked and cold, so I stripped off everything except my bra and pants and got in beside you and held you, and after a while we both warmed up and went to sleep."

His arms had closed around her as though he was accustomed to holding a woman in his bed. That firm, confident embrace had somehow reassured her that he'd survive until rescuers arrived.

"And that's how they found us," he said, but not as though it were any revelation.

His steady, remorseless gaze searched her face. Marisa forced herself to master her chaotic emotions and the choppy, disconnected thoughts racing through her mind.

"The noise of the chopper woke me. I managed to haul on some clothes, but you...you couldn't." He'd been breathing and he was warm, but that time she hadn't been able to wake him.

"In Mariposa," he said, his voice deliberate, "the general opinion is that we made love."

Head held high, Marisa met his unreadable scrutiny

with a steady one of her own. "We didn't," she said bluntly. "Neither of us was in any fit state, believe me."

"So why does your husband believe I am Keir's father?"

Oh, God, how did he know that? She closed her eyes, then forced them open again to meet his coldly implacable gaze. Tension knotted her nerves, scraped her voice raw, but she owed him an explanation. "Because I told him you were. It was a lie."

Still his expression didn't change, and now—too late—she understood the hard power of the man. The ruthless determination that had got him out of that plane and supported him to the hut was as much a part of him as his brilliance and the splendid bone structure of his face.

Still in that cold, uncompromising tone he asked, "Why?"

Her throat was dry. This must be how a person on trial felt. "Because it was the only thing I could think of that would keep my child safe."

"What do you mean—safe?" The question came hard and fast as he straightened. "Did he beat you?"

She shook her head. "He never hit me." And couldn't say anything more.

Because in spite of David's rigid self-control, the threat of his leashed violence had been ever present, eventually dominating her life. Strangely, Rafe's anger didn't frighten her; he was truly formidable, but she couldn't imagine him ever losing that iron discipline.

Not even now, when he had every reason to be both disgusted and furious.

An inner caution taunted her, *How do you know that? How can you be so sure?*

She'd been so wrong before—could she be equally wrong about Rafe?

His regard for her and Keir had almost convinced her that he had no taint of her ex-husband's desire to control. Yet it could be because he'd wondered if Keir might be his own…

Rafe stayed silent, waiting. She took a deep breath and tried to explain. "David wants—*needs* to control. I think it must be a compulsion. That's why he took the job in Mariposa, away from everyone we knew. The people there were lovely—so hospitable—but David wouldn't join in the district's social life. And he didn't want me to, either."

"You can drive," Rafe said, frowning. "What stopped you from going out on your own?"

"We didn't have a car."

His brows rose. "There was one on the estancia—a Jeep."

"It was usually needed—David took it with him."

Rafe's frown deepened. "And when it wasn't?"

She flushed, angry with herself for being so embarrassed after all this time. "When he didn't need it he read the odometer before he left the house and again after he came home." Once, early on and feeling mutinous, she'd driven into the nearest town, a mere village, but the resultant inquisition had been such a fraught experience she'd never repeated it.

She glanced at Rafe's hard face and said flatly, "It happened. It will *never* happen to me again."

"You're implying that he kept you a prisoner on the estancia."

"Yes," she said, unsurprised by his attitude.

Rafe said, "The contrast between you now, and the

woman I saw in Mariposa, is almost unbelievable. I'm
trying to understand how it happened."

"I was barely nineteen when I married and we went
straight to Mariposa after the wedding," she returned
in her crispest tone. "Apart from David, I knew no one
for thousands of miles and I didn't speak Spanish."

David had had some small knowledge of the
language—enough, she discovered later, to turn down
all invitations from the warmly hospitable Mariposans
in the district.

She went on doggedly, "I couldn't walk anywhere—
the distances are too great."

"Your parents? The estancia has a computer. Were
you in contact with them?"

"They didn't have a computer and I couldn't ring—
the telephone system was chancy at the best."

And what could her parents have done? Even if she'd
appealed to them they didn't have the money to pay for
her to go home.

Her upwards glance clashed with Rafe's burnished,
metallic survey. In that cool, judicial voice he stated,
"And I don't suppose you had any money."

Words froze on her tongue and she had to swallow to
ease her parched throat. "No," she admitted. "I was far
too young—too unsophisticated—to deal with it. My
parents adored each other—and David said he loved
me and wanted to keep me safe. I knew something was
wrong, but I had no weapons to fight him."

"What were your parents thinking of to let you get
married so young?"

She shrugged. "They married young and it worked
for them. But I was the one who insisted on it. I wanted
a home, somewhere to call my own, where I could make
a place for myself. Each year my parents chose a place

to stay over the winter, so I had time to make friends and enjoy going to school instead of doing correspondence lessons. Then in the spring we'd leave. My friends and I would promise to keep in touch, but eventually the letters would stop and I'd have to start all over again. So I married the first man who offered me a settled life."

"Did you love him?"

Her smile was wry. "I was sure I did. My parents really liked David and they thought Mariposa was a wonderful idea, that at last I was showing some adventurous spirit. And it seemed so romantic." She allowed herself a small, cynical smile. "For the right man and the right woman, it could be. For me the estancia was literally a prison. I was so lonely. When I made him angry David would disappear for days and days, and I'd be left in silence and isolation. I didn't know how to deal with it."

A cool breath from the sea made her shiver. Rafe said abruptly, "We'll go inside."

"No, I'd rather stay here." Where she could breathe. After a few seconds' pause, she resumed quietly, "Then I got pregnant. David didn't want the baby. I lost it in the first trimester, and he said it was a relief—he was happy with the way things were. He didn't ever want children."

For a moment she thought Rafe was going to speak, but when she glanced at him his face was carved in stone.

Marisa stiffened her spine, squared her shoulders. Her voice was sombre and harsh with memories. "That was when I realised that I'd never have anyone to love— no child to love me. It was the last straw. I slid into depression and when he made it impossible for me to go home after my mother became ill I was too numb to even fight any longer. I just wanted to die."

Silence, heavy with unspoken thoughts, stretched between them. She looked down at her hands, so tightly clasped together that the knuckles were white, and forced herself to drop them into her lap. "But then you came and I saw an opportunity."

His arrival had cut through the stifling oblivion of her days, offering a tantalising, life-saving chance of freedom. "Besides, I thought I might be pregnant again, so I knew I had to take any chance I could to get away."

"You said David wasn't violent, so why do you believe he'd have harmed his own child?"

"He wouldn't have hurt him physically," she said quickly, then paused. She met his gaze without flinching. "At least, I don't think so. But there are different ways to hurt. Children don't flourish in a dictatorship."

"So you told him we'd slept together and the child was mine."

His voice was neutral, but the icy depths of his eyes told her he was holding himself on a tight rein.

"I couldn't think of anything else to do," she admitted bleakly. "About a month after I'd got back to New Zealand he rang and demanded I go back to him. By then I knew for certain I was pregnant. I was—desperate. My parents needed me and the thought of returning to Mariposa filled me with a kind of terror. I did the only thing I could think of to make sure David would never want to claim my baby. I used you and it worked."

She hesitated, then confessed on a spurt of raw honesty, "I wish I could say I regret it, but I don't. I'd do it again in a blink to keep Keir safe."

Rafe's face remained emotionless—an arrogant study carved in granite.

Nerves jumping, she finished, "Rafe, I am so sorry I involved you. But it shouldn't be a problem—no one else knows…"

Her voice trailed away as she recalled his statement that in Mariposa people assumed she had slept with him.

He said without inflection, "No one else is sure, but it seems to be accepted that he left Mariposa because you and I had an affair."

"He's left Mariposa?" Her voice shook and she jumped to her feet, staring at him in shock. "When?"

"About six months after you did." He stood too, a formidable silhouette in the dimness of the terrace. Relentlessly he demanded, "Why are you so afraid? If he doesn't want children, then surely Keir is safe enough even if Brown does find out the boy is his."

Fear hollowing her stomach, Marisa gathered her thoughts, trying to adjust to the news. A gull cried in the distance, harshly distinctive, and she shivered.

"I think he saw me as some kind of chattel," she said after several silent moments. "Love for him meant—*means*—ownership, not respect. He grew up in a foster home where he had to fight to keep anything. I'm afraid that if he ever finds out that Keir is his he'll want to own him too."

Rafe's survey was keen and hard to bear, but his thoughtful answer made her hope he was beginning to understand. "That seems rather melodramatic."

She shrugged. "I don't pretend to understand him. What I'm certain of is that men like David don't make good husbands or fathers. You know Keir—he's a bright, happy, confident child. You must remember what I was like after just two years spent with David. Although, to be fair," she added with unsparing candour, "that wasn't entirely his fault."

Rafe's brows lifted again. "No?"

"No. When I got back to New Zealand my mother insisted I see her doctor. He sent me off for tests and they finally decided that a mixture of depression and chaotic hormones after the miscarriage had dragged me down. Medication and a good therapist fixed me."

"With some effort from you," he said quietly.

She nodded. "Lots of effort," she agreed.

"Tell me one thing."

The almost casual tone was so much at variance with his hard scrutiny that she tensed. "What?"

"How did Marisa turn into Mary—the name change, I mean, not the emotional disintegration?"

She flushed, but said coolly enough, "David thought Marisa was a silly, pretentious name, so he chose another one." Like renaming a pet...

Rafe nodded, as though the answer had confirmed something for him. He didn't comment, however, but moved on. "Before we finish this, I'd like to know why you came to Tewaka."

It wasn't exactly an order, but she owed him an answer to that too. At least this one was easy, she thought mordantly.

"I've always loved Northland. Having parents who made a living by catering to people's tastes gave me a feeling for what sells and what doesn't, and the shop seemed like a missed opportunity."

"In what way?"

"Poor buying," she explained. "I researched Tewaka and found it has a six-month season of cruise-ship visits as well as a year-long tourist trade, and the district is prosperous. Small shops like mine can't compete with the big chain retailers, so they need to cater for a different market. Which was what my parents did with their handmade stuff." She gave him a taut, glittering smile. "One thing I did *not* learn from my research was that you lived here."

One black brow shot up. "Would that have killed the deal?"

"Yes. I felt—still feel—guilty about using you. When my father died last year I decided to leave the south. It holds bad memories. David is from there, my parents died there and I wanted to find a place where no one would know me. Where I could make a new beginning."

"I can understand that," he said unexpectedly.

Disconcerted, Marisa looked at him and then hastily away again. While they'd been talking dusk had given way to night. Soon the moon would rise, but for now the velvet sky was spangled with stars. Her dark-attuned eyes clearly made out the arrogant bone structure of Rafe's face, the width of his shoulders against the fall of white blooms from a creeper along the wall. Something stirred deep inside her, a slow, sensuous melting, as though a resistance she'd hadn't known existed was being smoothed away.

Steadying her voice, she went on, "I wanted to settle before Keir started school. And once I started the process, everything just fell into place—it was so simple I got the feeling it was meant to be, you know?"

Only to fall spectacularly apart as soon as she'd learned he lived here.

With a twist to his mouth he said, "I'm always suspicious of deals that seem to come together perfectly. Usually it's because someone's manipulating things to their own advantage."

"Not in this case." She gave him a rueful smile. "I'd been here several weeks before I found out you lived here and my first instinct was to get the hell out of town. But Keir loves the school here and the shop is going so well." And she'd been told Rafe was rarely at home. Quickly she went on, "Anyway, I was pretty sure I could carry off my new identity. What made you recognise me? I hope there's very little resemblance between poor Mary Brown and me."

"It seems that the poor Mary Brown you refer to so disparagingly could well have saved my life. For which I'm grateful."

The tone in which he drawled the final sentence jolted her senses to overstretched alertness. Was this the only reason he'd been so helpful towards her?

A pang of disappointment shocked her with its intensity.

If he'd gone to Mariposa to find out what had happened after the crash, something she'd said or done must have aroused his suspicion.

Banishing that entirely inappropriate chagrin, she said on a note of humour, "I'll make a bargain with you. I'll stop thanking you if you stop thanking me."

"Done!" He held out his hand, and she put hers in it, ready for the sizzle of response that ran through her whenever he touched her.

It happened, but this time she didn't jerk away.

As their hands parted he said, "Although offering you a refuge is hardly recompense for saving my life. It never occurred to you to leave me in the wreckage of the plane?"

Amazed, she stared at him. "No. It wasn't an option. You sort of came to while I was checking the pilot and you muttered something about fire, and then I smelt petrol—"

"Avgas," he corrected with a half-smile.

"Whatever. It smelt like an explosion to me. You were set on getting out and it seemed a really good idea. Do you remember any of that?"

"No," he said briefly. "Finding the hut in the storm must have been difficult."

She recalled it only too vividly. "It wasn't easy. I was afraid the effort would be bad for you, but although you were obviously in pain you were so determined to get to the hut I realised you'd set off by yourself if I didn't come with you."

"Apart from the blow to my head I had no injuries," he said shortly.

"I thought the hut would be a better bet than staying in a plane that might explode." She returned to her question. "You barely saw me in Mariposa and most of the time you did you were more or less unconscious. How did you recognise me?"

"Your eyes," he said succinctly. He reached out and traced an eyebrow, his lean forefinger leaving a trail of fire on her skin. His voice deepened. "Such a strong, true green is unusual enough, but the way they tilt—and the way your brows follow that tilt—that's both exotic and unforgettable."

His touch transformed that insidious melting sensation into swift heat that ricocheted from nerve-end to nerve-end right throughout her body, sending signals to every cell.

"I have my grandmother's eyes," she said inanely.

The way he looked at her built that inner, shameless heat into a fire. Desperate to quench it, she blurted, "How did you find out about the lie I told David?"

"You told me."

Bewildered, Marisa stared at him. "But you knew before then, surely?"

His mouth curved in a sardonic smile. "I knew what he—and most of Mariposa, apparently—believes. I was intrigued by your attitude—a mixture of forthrightness and extreme caution and reserve. And I couldn't work out why the hell you'd pretend to be someone else, if that's what you were doing, unless you were afraid or had something to hide."

"So you had me investigated." She tried to sound angry, but her tone was resigned.

Hooded eyes never leaving her face, he nodded. "And discovered you'd given no name for his father on Keir's birth certificate. I wondered why."

She said nothing and after a few seconds he resumed, "Keir was born two weeks short of nine months after the night you and I spent together in the hut, so he could have been the result of one night of amnesiac passion on my part."

"No," she said decisively.

"In Mariposa I found out that we'd been naked—"

Hot-cheeked, she corrected, "*You* were naked."

"The general opinion seems to be that of course we slept together. Such a life-affirming activity is quite natural—even normal—after a fatal crash."

His words were delivered in a silky voice that froze Marisa. But only for a moment. The shock of his knowing had receded and she asked angrily, "What I'd like to know is how everyone—*everyone* meaning everyone in your circle, I assume—knew that."

"The people who rescued us talked, of course," he said caustically. "That's why your ex-husband believed you."

Anger dying, she absorbed that, then said quietly, "Keir is David's son."

"I believe you." He reached out and took her hand again. Frowning, he closed his fingers around hers. "Why didn't you tell me you were cold?"

And to her astonishment he pulled her into his arms and held her against the heat of his powerful body. "It's all right," he said evenly, his voice reverberating against her ear. "I'm sorry to take you through this inquisition, but I needed to know what was going on."

She couldn't think, couldn't tease out a sensible answer. A fierce desire clamoured through her, weakening her so that her words were husky and hesitant when she finally blurted, "I'm not cold—just...shocked, I suppose."

"Too much has happened to you lately."

His arms contracted and she looked up, eyes widening as she met the focused gleam in his. She shivered again.

He bent his head and said against lips that ached for some unknown pressure, "After the crash you risked your life to warm me. I wonder if I can warm you up this time."

The kiss rekindled the fires, setting her alight with the passion she'd been fighting ever since she'd seen him again. Sighing, she surrendered to a sharp excitement, a reckless need that came roaring up out of nowhere, summoned by Rafe's touch, his arms, his lips...

Summoned by Rafe.

Desire burnt through her, his mouth on hers causing a conflagration, a violent force that swept away everything but hunger and the ruthless, wildfire longing. Stunned by its intensity, a flash of insight made Marisa face the truth—this heady clamour was what had broken through her inertia in Mariposa. Involuntarily her body had reacted to Rafe's compelling magnetism, stimulating her into the action that had finally freed her.

She wanted more of it... She opened her mouth beneath his insistent demand and he took immediate advantage of the silent plea. The deep kiss that followed caused a peak of sensation, robbing her of all thought, all emotion, except a voluptuous craving unlike anything she'd ever experienced.

She almost cried out when he lifted his head.

"I'm sorry," he said harshly, and let her go, stepping back several paces as though he needed to put space between them.

"Sorry? *Sorry?*" She said unsteadily, "Why—why did you stop?"

CHAPTER NINE

RAFE bit back an oath. *Way to go, you fool*, he thought grimly, looking down at her, the soft lips trembling, her eyes wide and dazed.

The last thing you should be doing is kissing her like some lust-crazed idiot after she's just relived as nasty a case of emotional abuse as you've ever heard.

His voice harsh, he said, "Now is not the time. You've been through hell—"

Marisa crossed the space between them, reached up and put her hand across his mouth. "You're the first man who's touched me since I left Mariposa." She gave a twisted smile. "I used you, lied about you. I'm not going to lie again. I want you too."

Other women had come on to Rafe, some with disconcerting directness, most with considerably more subtlety, but none had made him feel like this. Marisa's touch, her words, sent desire pouring through him so that he had to grit his teeth to stop himself from losing control.

"Are you sure?" he demanded, his voice low and feral.

She dropped her hand. "Sure that I want you? Completely." Her voice shook and heat swept along her perfect cheekbones, but her gaze was honest.

"Why?" And why the hell was he probing? In his previous affairs all he'd expected was mutual desire. Now he wanted more—without knowing what that *more* would be.

The question shocked Marisa like a bucket of water in the face, jolting her out of her sensuous haze.

Panicked, she thought, *However much I want to, I can't do this.* Whatever Rafe was offering, it wouldn't be permanence… She was not only gambling with her life, she was gambling with Keir's.

Yet a flicker of subversive regret made her wonder if she was going to remain celibate until her son grew up.

Ashamed, colour flaring up through her skin, she said awkwardly, "I wish you hadn't asked that—but I'm glad you did. I don't have just myself to think about. Keir is becoming fond of you and it's going to hurt him when we leave." Desperation tinged her voice. "I have to find somewhere else to live!"

Rafe's intent, probing gaze, colder than an Antarctic sky in winter, seemed to pierce the façade she'd manufactured with such effort and patience. Shaking with the need to surrender, she watched him re-impose control and wished forlornly that it could be as easy for her.

"In that case," he said coolly, "I'll stay away as much as I can while you're here."

She firmed her mouth, knowing it was the best thing he could do. "Yes," she said colourlessly. "Thank you."

She looked up and met his level, iron-grey gaze. Deep inside her something contracted, almost banishing her tiredness in a surge of heat.

"Goodnight," she said and shot through the door, closing it behind her and leaning back against it, her heart pounding so noisily in her chest she could hear nothing else.

Of course Keir's welfare was the most important factor in her life. Yet for a moment she wondered what it would be like to be able to dream of something else, something for herself...

Sleep refused to come. Restlessly she tossed beneath the sheet, turning questions over in her mind.

What did she know about Rafe? Not enough to trust him. Oh, he was not only respected in Tewaka, he was liked—but no man could reach the heights he'd achieved without a strong streak of ruthlessness.

Why was she attracted to dominant men? She'd vowed never to allow that to happen to her again.

Yet she wanted Rafe. And he knew it. The minutes spent responding to his kisses with such passionate abandon had given her away completely.

Wildly successful, magnetic, brilliant, worldly—she could probably spend the rest of what promised to be a long and sleepless night thinking up words to describe him, but they all meant the same thing.

The good fairies around his cradle had showered him with more gifts than necessary. He could have any woman in the world.

Which was probably why he'd pulled back when she'd turned to jelly in his arms.

It was so...so *unlikely* that he'd want someone like her, not only scarred emotionally, but so very ordinary.

Unless he still wondered if Keir might be his son? Perhaps that was why he'd invited them to stay at Manuwai?

That thought made her feel sick, but it had to be faced.

She went over the conversation, testing everything Rafe had said. It was possible he did wonder...

Where was David now? Hot and sticky, she turned her pillow over and kicked off the sheet. Outside the little owl the Maori had named *ruru* was calling from a nearby tree. *Morepork, morepork*—a lonely, familiar sound, one she'd heard all over New Zealand, yet in the pleasant bedroom Marisa shivered.

Tomorrow she'd have plenty to face; right now she needed sleep.

Eventually it came.

Keir woke her, saying urgently, "Mum, it's late. You better get up now. The sun has got his smiley face on."

She bolted upright, checked the clock and said something under her breath, then huffed out a sigh and relaxed. "Today's Sunday, you horrible boy," she said affectionately. "It's a holiday. No shop and no school."

He grinned. "We can go down to the beach and swim all day," he suggested eagerly. "After we have pancakes for breakfast with lemon juice and brown sugar?"

Laughing, she threw back the sheet and swung out of bed, ruffling his hair as she went past him. "First I have to shower and get dressed."

At least, she thought a few minutes later, she didn't have to worry too much about what she would wear to face Rafe again. Jeans and a well-worn T-shirt that echoed the colour of her eyes would have to do.

Not too long afterwards she and Keir walked into the kitchen. Rafe looked around from the counter, where he was setting up the coffee machine.

"Good morning," he said, that perceptive gaze going from Marisa's guarded face to Keir's delighted one.

Keir ran across the room, his pleasure so patent it wrung Marisa's heart.

"I didn't know you were here," he said exuberantly. "Did you come home on the helicopter last night? Did you fly it?"

"No and no," Rafe said calmly. "The chopper's having a check-up so I came home by car after you were asleep. How have you been? Has your car arrived back with a new starter motor?"

"Yes, but I liked your grandma's car better, only Mum says we have to drive our own one again."

As she busied herself making pancake batter, Marisa listened to the two of them talking and thought miserably that if only she and Rafe had made love on that wreck of a bed in the hut…

A voluptuous need coiled through her, seductive as the original serpent. *Don't go there*, she thought feverishly.

But if Keir were Rafe's son, his future would be assured.

If only she didn't feel this scary, primal attraction… Every time she saw Rafe her brain went mushy, tempting her in so many dangerous ways.

She switched on the gas, coated a pan with butter and waited for it to sizzle before ladling in the batter.

"Pancakes?" Rafe said thoughtfully. "They're one of my favourite breakfasts."

Ever helpful, Keir said, "Then Mummy can make some for you."

Marisa looked up, saw a glint in Rafe's eyes and smiled, a dangerous expectation scintillating through her like diamond dust in her blood. "I made enough batter for us all," she told him.

Rafe cocked a sardonic brow, but remained silent.

The faint shadows beneath Marisa's eyes were more than enough evidence of a wakeful night.

His gut tightened as he thought of another way she could have spent those hours of darkness—a much more satisfactory way for both of them. The kisses he'd exchanged with her had left him hungry and frustrated in the most basic way, killing sleep until late.

He was a sophisticated man—not promiscuous, and normal in his appetites. He liked rare steak, a good wine, the refreshment of a cool shower after exertion, the softness and passion of women. He expected to marry—some time. His parents' disastrous marriage had convinced him that a steady, safe, completely reliable affection was the best basis for a lifelong relationship.

What he'd never anticipated was this smouldering hunger that wouldn't leave him alone.

Had the situation been normal, Marisa would have spent last night in his bed, in his arms. His body tightened, but he ignored it. Her revelation about her marriage complicated everything. Rafe killed a primitive urge to make David Brown pay for the emotional pain he'd inflicted.

Any further advance in their mutual attraction would have to be on Marisa's terms, not his. And she'd made it very clear that for her, young Keir's welfare came before everything else.

They ate out on the terrace, the sun beaming down on them like a benediction, and the motionless branches of the pohutukawa trees spangled with blue-green glimpses of the sea behind.

* * *

After breakfast Rafe headed off to his study. Mariposa's time zone was fifteen hours behind New Zealand's—if his luck was in, he'd get an instant answer.

Sure enough, the manager emailed back within ten minutes. Rafe's frown grew darker as he read the answer. *You may remember he lit a fire in the machinery shed. When questioned, he said it was to make a point, but that he didn't intend to harm anyone. The previous agent believed this.*

Rafe could almost feel the agent's curiosity smoking off the screen, but contented himself with a terse note of thanks. An odd sensation of foreboding gripping him, he left the computer and walked across to the huge kauri desk his father had worked at, like his forefathers before him. Making up his mind, he lifted the telephone and punched in a number.

He listened to what his private investigator had to say with a gathering grimness.

After a short conversation he put down the phone and strode across to the window to stare unseeingly out.

His strong sense that something was wrong had stood him in good stead before. He'd learned to pay careful attention to it.

He found Marisa with Keir in the garden. "We need to talk," he told her and switched his gaze to Keir, absorbed in examining a large, jazzily striped Monarch butterfly caterpillar on the swan plant. "I've asked Ngaire Sinclair to come across with young Manu around ten; she's happy to keep the boys down on the beach until midday."

Marisa opened her mouth to object, then closed it again. If they needed to talk, it would have to be without any chance of Keir overhearing. But her stomach clamped at the thought of what lay ahead. She'd desperately wanted a peaceful day to recharge her batteries.

"All right," she agreed.

From the terrace off the small parlour Marisa watched the boys frolic around Ngaire like two puppies across the lawn and disappear down the cliff path to the children's beach. Turning, she tried to relax taut muscles. Colour stung her skin when she realised Rafe was watching her, his grey eyes coolly speculative.

Heart jumping, she said, "Something's happened. What is it?"

"Your ex-husband is somewhere in New Zealand."

She flinched as though struck by a blow. Rafe had to rein in a fierce, intemperate anger. The man might not have hit her, but she was actively afraid of him.

"How—?" She stopped, cleared her throat and firmed her lush mouth into a straight line. "How do you know?" she demanded.

He frowned, "Come inside. You're shivering."

Silently she accompanied him into the house. Once inside one look at her convinced him this was hugely unpleasant news. Her eyes were blank in her white face, but as he watched she gave herself a little shake and some colour came back into her skin.

Tight-lipped, he said, "I thought you knew that. You divorced him a couple of years after he left Mariposa."

"That was done through lawyers," she shot back. "He had a lawyer in Invercargill. I certainly didn't know he was here in New Zealand."

"He went to Australia first," Rafe said, watching her closely.

Her relief was patent, but it didn't last long. She

looked up at him. "When did he come back to New Zealand?"

"When you moved north to Tewaka."

The little colour in her skin leached away and she sent an involuntary glance towards the beach as though she thought her ex-husband might be there, threatening their son.

Once more Rafe watched her get a grip on her fears. "How do you know all this?" she asked in a quiet voice very much at variance with that first moment of panic.

"Sit down," he ordered.

She gave him a speaking glance, but sat down in the chair. "I'll be back in a moment," he said and strode through to the other room.

Marisa was sitting very erect when he came back, but there was an emptiness in the green eyes he recognised, and her soft mouth was held in firm restraint. No woman should ever look like that. He reined in his anger and handed her the glass.

She took it automatically, and sipped, then choked. "Ugh!" she spluttered. "What *is* this?"

"Brandy. Drink at least some of it. You've had a shock and it will help."

"Not to keep a clear head, it won't," she said, and put it down. She fixed him with a determined stare. "You didn't answer my question. How do you know all this?"

"I employ an extremely experienced firm of private investigators to check up on anything I need to know," he said, half-amused by her attempt to wrest control of the situation from him.

Half-amused, impressed—and secretly frustrated as hell.

Because his body still thrummed with a ruthless

need. But that wildfire hunger was backed by a strong urge to protect her and the boy.

She frowned, her lips easing into a faint, humourless smile. "Yes, of course you do. Are they so good you know where David is now?"

"Not that good," he acknowledged drily. "In Australia he was working on a cattle station in the Outback. He flew to New Zealand about a month ago, landing in Christchurch. Since then, nothing."

Which possibly meant he was travelling under an assumed name.

She drew in a sharp breath. "I could try his lawyer."

"Even if they're still in touch, his solicitor isn't likely to tell you unless you can give a damned good reason. Like the fact that Brown is Keir's father..." Deliberately he let the words trail off.

"That's never going to happen," she asserted fiercely.

"In that case, stay away from his solicitor."

Narrow black brows met for a moment and then she agreed, "You're right, I'd be stupid to make any contact."

Her hands clenched together in her lap. She raised her dark green gaze to meet his and said bleakly, "It's all right. I'll work something out."

His voice raw, he said, "Hell! You're not just afraid of him, you're terrified."

Marisa looked away, but he caught her chin in a firm grip and turned her face towards him. The heat faded from her skin. Unable to answer, she nervously swallowed and he let her go.

"Yes," he said, as if somehow she'd confirmed it. "Why? He has no power over you now."

Buffeted by his formidable determination, she couldn't assemble any coherent answer from the disconnected fragments of thought that tumbled and jostled through her mind. When she did find her voice it sounded weak and ineffectual. "If he ever finds out that Keir is his, he'd fight me for him." She glanced up at him, eyes shadowy and troubled. "Rafe, this is not your battle, even though I involved you in it."

"I want to know why you're so afraid of this man," he stated, not giving an inch. "Have you told me everything? You're a strong woman—yet you're terrified of him. Even if he does discover that Keir is his son and gain access, you'd be able to monitor the situation."

Surrendering, she dragged in a breath. "I suppose I'm as much afraid of myself as I am of him," she said, her voice rough. "I married him as a normal nineteen-year-old and within two years I was a wreck. Loneliness was a big part of it. But there were other things—little things…"

Her voice died away.

"Go on," Rafe said steadily.

She summoned her courage. "One of the men brought me a parrot—a little gold-and-blue bird that lives in the trees by the streams and can be taught to talk. It had fallen out of the nest somehow and I nursed it back to health, but almost as soon as it started to repeat the words I was teaching it, it died. He wouldn't let me see the body. He just told me about it and then he buried it. I didn't think anything of it. Then there was a kitten. It was fine one day, playing at my feet, but it died overnight too."

Although she paused, Rafe remained silent, the only sign of any reaction the thinning of his mouth. So she went on, "He promised me a puppy to replace it, but it never arrived…"

She glanced up, saw him frown and went on starkly,

"And painting—he referred to it as a hobby, but as the months went by it became my lifeline. When I ran out of paints he said he'd ordered more, but none ever came. I wish I could explain just how empty I felt with nothing to do except housework, nobody to talk to except him. There were no books and he didn't see any reason for a garden…" Her voice tailed away.

Rafe said, "Go on."

"I wanted to learn Spanish; he thought—or said he thought—it would be a good idea. He was learning quite a bit from the men, but he was always too tired to teach me and he didn't want me talking to the men. He used to read my parents' letters, so I couldn't say anything to them." She made a swift gesture of despair. "It sounds petty and foolish—"

"It sounds like a reign of terror," Rafe said grimly. "What about his parents? Were you in contact with them?"

"Oh, no. David never knew his birth parents—he was given up for adoption as a baby. But something happened when he was seven—I don't know what—and he spent the rest of his childhood in foster homes. Some were good, but he never stayed long enough in one to really find a home."

"Why?"

She shrugged. "I don't know. He didn't like talking about it. He told me he had to be tough; when he was hurt he didn't rest until he'd paid people back, punishing them, because that way they left him alone. And if—if he still feels that way, what better way to punish me than try to take Keir away?"

Recounting this took all of her courage, but she owed Rafe. She finished, "Keir is starting to look more and more like him. If he forced me to allow Keir to be DNA tested he'd discover the truth." She lifted her gaze at Rafe, searching his hard, arrogant face for some sign of understanding. "You called it a reign of terror. That's what I'm afraid of—the damage he might be able to do to Keir's peace of mind, his lovely, sunny personality..." She blinked back tears and said fiercely, "I'll do anything I can to make sure it doesn't happen."

"I see now why you don't want him in Keir's life, but if he did apply, he'd almost certainly get access." Rafe spoke objectively, clearly weighing the information. "Your lies would put you in an unfavourable position."

Bleakly she admitted, "I know. Do you think I don't worry about what I've done? I do. That lie has weighed on my shoulders ever since I told it." She caught her breath and held her head high, meeting his eyes with a defiance based on fear. "But I'd do it again. Is it too much to want Keir to have a serene childhood, one where he can grow up and be happy and not be burdened with adult problems? You know him—does he seem to be missing anything?"

"Not obviously, no." Rafe paced across to the window, big and lithe and predatory. Once there he swung around and surveyed her, his expression closed. "But that could change. Children are said to need a stable male figure in their lives. If it did come to a custody dispute, you'd be in a much stronger position if there was a man in your life, someone Keir liked and respected." He paused, before saying calmly, "The simplest way to ensure that would be for us to get engaged."

Marisa stared at him, his words dancing crazily through her head. It took every ounce of self-control to say, "No, no, that's not necessary."

"It makes sense," he said coolly, his mouth twisting

as he took in her patent shock. "If it does nothing else, it will reinforce the idea that the boy is mine."

"Yes, but there's absolutely no reason for you to be involved—"

"You involved me when you came up with that lie," he told her uncompromisingly.

Colour burned her skin, then faded. She couldn't refute that.

Before she could come up with a reply, he said, "You can't admit to the lie without possibly jeopardising Keir's well-being, so you might as well make use of it again."

Marisa shook her head, swamped by bone-deep exhaustion.

Rafe touched her shoulder, then dropped his hand. "You're exhausted and no wonder. Drink some more brandy." His tone was remote and decisive, as though working out some strategy.

Nerves jumping in a complex mixture of tension and dismay—and something deeper, more basic, that she wasn't prepared to explore—she tried to match his judicial tone. "I don't need brandy, thanks. And I can't believe that being engaged to you would sway a family court."

"You'd be surprised," he said cynically, adding in a gentler voice, "Marisa, try not to worry. We don't know that Brown is interested in establishing contact with Keir. We'll discuss this further when you've had time to think things over."

Not if she could prevent it. All she wanted to do was crawl into some hole, pull the door shut behind her and stay there until this whole thing went away.

If it ever did…

But Rafe's use of *we* comforted her.

The sound of children's voices dragged her gaze towards the garden. Surely it wasn't lunchtime—no, Ngaire was piggybacking young Manu.

Galvanised, she said, "Something's happened to Manu, I think."

"Probably a cut from a shell. I'll get the first-aid kit."

Before he left she said in a muted voice, "Rafe, when you told me David was back in New Zealand I panicked. All this time I'd presumed he was still in Mariposa, you see, which is why I didn't—*couldn't*—tell you who I was."

"I understand that your son's welfare is the most important thing in your life."

He sounded completely in command, as though it was quite ordinary to propose a fake engagement with a woman he barely knew to safeguard a child who wasn't his own.

CHAPTER TEN

THE children were so disappointed by the early cessation of their stay on the beach that Ngaire said, "Look, why don't you let Keir come home with us? Quite frankly, it would be a good thing. Manu's going to have to keep off that heel for the rest of the day, so he and Keir can watch a DVD together. I'll drop Keir off around four?"

At Keir's exuberant little jump, Marisa laughed. "You have your answer. Thanks very much, he'd love to come."

Which left her alone in the house with Rafe. However, he retired to his office, emerging for lunch with an abstracted air and returning immediately afterwards. She told herself she was relieved. Feeling awkward was irritating and she refused to accept that she had any reason for it.

The problem was it wouldn't go away.

When he walked out and found her bringing in a load of washing from the line, he asked, "Surely Nadine can do that?"

"These are our sheets," she said firmly. "And our clothes." She folded one of Keir's small shirts and put it over the top of a lacy bra.

A smile curved Rafe's mouth, but he said, "Have you made up your mind yet? Are we engaged or not?"

At the sardonic note in his voice her stomach went into free fall. "Oh, don't be silly," she blurted, then could have kicked herself for coming up with such an unsophisticated retort. "You know it's not at all necessary."

"I'm beginning to feel it's very necessary," he said curtly, eyes never leaving her face.

Eyes widening, she stared at him, a torrent of thoughts cascading through her mind. "You've heard where he is," she breathed.

He shook his black head. "No." Then paused, as though weighing his words.

His tone was level, perfectly steady, yet when she looked at him an emotion close to fear chilled her.

"But I've just been talking to the chief of the local fire brigade."

"You don't need to tell me—you went to school with him," she said brightly, sensing he was about to tell her something she didn't want to hear.

His smile was brief and unamused. "As it happens, yes, I did. He said the first fire—the cottage—was probably caused by a cigarette thrown from a car. The long grass at the fence line caught and it got to the house. The garage might be arson."

She blinked and felt her muscles sag. When he took a step towards her she stiffened, straightening her spine and warding him off with a rapid, involuntary gesture. He stopped a pace away.

"Kids?" she hazarded tautly. "Bored teenagers?"

"Possibly." He paused, then said, "Your ex-husband was sacked from the estancia because he burned down the machinery shed shortly after you told him I was

Keir's father. He didn't intend to harm anyone, but one of the farmhands had a narrow escape."

Marisa could feel the colour drain from her skin, leaving her cold and shaken. "Who?" she breathed, her mind ranging over the farmhands.

He looked surprised. "I don't know—whoever it was got out just in time. As far as I know he wasn't hurt."

Before she could say anything he continued, "One of the Tanner boys looked out the night the garage burned down and saw a vehicle parked by it. He thought it was another volunteer checking the cottage. However, the brigade had left, convinced there was no further chance of the place catching fire."

"And you think…" Marisa searched for words, but could only shake her head.

His gaze still on her face, Rafe went on, "You told me Brown rang you about a month after you'd come back to New Zealand to be with your parents."

"Yes."

"And that was when you told him you'd slept with me and that the baby you were having was mine?"

His coolly judicial voice steadied her.

"Yes," she repeated numbly.

"He lit the fire five weeks after you'd left him."

Marisa's teeth clamped down on her bottom lip. "Oh, heavens," she whispered. "Rafe, I'm so sorry."

He shrugged. "It's not your fault. I assume he tried to pay me back in the only way he could—by destroying something of mine. If he set the garage alight, he'd be punishing you by destroying something of yours."

"But we don't know… I can't believe…" Her incredulous voice trailed away, because it made a hideous sort of sense.

"I think you do," Rafe said, mercilessly refusing to

offer any sort of comfort. "Why else would you be so afraid he might find out Keir is his child? You sensed he was capable of violence."

"I didn't—" She stopped, met his dispassionate gaze and expelled a long, sobbing breath, facing the truth at last. "Yes. Yes, of course I did. But I can't believe he'd try to *kill* anyone."

"Whoever lit these fires didn't intend to kill," he said crisply. "The danger comes when a fire gets out of control. Or when people aren't where arsonists expect them to be—as happened in Mariposa."

A pause made it obvious he expected a reply, but Marisa remained silent, grappling with the implications of this. From somewhere close by a seagull called, its screech a threat and a warning. She shivered, and hugged herself, rubbing her hands over her suddenly cold arms.

After a few seconds Rafe continued, "Of course this is all supposition. We don't have a single fact to go on beyond that he admitted to lighting a fire in the machine shed in Mariposa. But your instincts are good. You recognised something about him that convinced you he'd never be a good father."

She nodded. "What…what I'm trying to work out is how I can deal with this."

"*We* are going to become engaged," he said deliberately, emphasising the first word. "Then, if it's necessary, I can protect you and Keir."

"That's outrageously noble of you," she fired back, so tempted to surrender it was difficult to get the words out. "But nobody gets engaged for such quixotic reasons."

Rafe's smile curled her toes. "I can be as foolish as

the next man," he drawled and took the shirt she'd just unpegged and tossed it into the clothes basket.

He drew her towards him, but although she longed for his mouth on hers, his arms didn't tighten around her and he said above her head, "If it is arson, and if it is your ex, an engagement to me is likely to be as good a protection for young Keir and you as anything else."

Better, she thought, trying to resist the powerful, honey-and-flame rush of desire she'd been longing for through the night.

And not just last night.

Without realising it, she'd spent the past five years missing the primal security she'd once felt in Rafe's arms. Locked against his lean, strong body while the rain hammered down outside the hut, she'd inhaled the faint, unmistakably masculine perfume of his skin, listened to his regular breathing, been reassured by the steady beat of his heart. And in those long hours, some essential, unknown part of her had surrendered.

Yet it was more than a simple longing for a safe haven...

He'd roused a sleeping hunger in her, an appetite both erotic and emotional—something she'd refused to admit even to herself. Only when she'd seen him again had that forbidden yearning prompted her to wonder what it would be like to share the burden, give her a chance to be more than Keir's mother and protector—to be Rafe's lover.

Now, in this perilous moment, she was given a glimpse of paradise. Rafe's embrace extinguished sanity in a surge of sensual craving, and she barely had time to think, *I mustn't let this happen*, before he tilted her head and examined her face. Heat kindled in his iron-grey eyes and that dangerous, voluptuous yearning overwhelmed her as he took her mouth.

Last night their kisses had been measured, almost experimental. Rafe had explored her lips with assurance and sensuous, erotically charged skill, but she'd been wary, unable to resist, yet not ready to yield to headstrong temptation.

This was different. This time when he kissed her a surge of reckless delight persuaded her to open her lips, to savour his taste as though she'd hungered for it all her life.

His reaction was instantaneous, close to ruthless. With their bodies sealed together as though nothing could ever separate them again, Marisa dug her fingers into the hard muscles of his back with an abandon that felt so good, so completely right.

When at last he lifted his head, her knees buckled and she had to cling desperately.

He held her effortlessly and said on a harsh, raw note, "Marisa."

She looked up into grey eyes, stormy as the clouds that lashed Mariposa in the rainy season. They locked on to hers, probing through to her soul.

Fiercely pleased, she said, "What is it?"

"What you do to me," he muttered and lowered his head again.

She shivered with desperate delight when he kissed her throat and the silky, sensuous spot below her ear, a soft kiss that sent rills of voluptuous anticipation aching through her. Deep in the pit of her stomach a deeper, more primitive sensation tightened into hunger.

His hand slid down to cup her breast. Instantly the rills turned to torrents that drowned her in acute, almost painful anticipation, contracted every pleading muscle with the need to find—to find a place where she could give in to the desire that consumed her with reckless, compelling power.

It would be so easy to stop thinking, to give in to the heady clamour of her body—to make love with Rafe...

Keir, she thought desperately.

Shocked, shamed by her easy surrender, she tried to wrench herself away. Rafe's arms tightened instinctively, but after only a second he let her go. He didn't move; when she took an uncertain, wavering step back his hand shot out to steady her.

"What is it?" he demanded forcefully.

"No," she gabbled, searching the harsh, beautiful contours of his face. "No, we can't do this. It's...it's..." She searched for the correct word, finally blurting, "It's dangerous."

"Not in my book."

His voice was hard and arrogant. It should have frozen her desire, but when she saw her own need echoed in the dark intensity of his gaze she shivered again, fighting herself and the impetuous demands of her body.

"And what is dangerous?" he demanded. "Making love? Or becoming engaged?"

"Both," she flung at him, closing her eyes against his face in case it torpedoed her resolution. "But especially getting engaged. Too many things could go wrong."

"Name one."

She seized on the most painful. "Keir. He's already learning to love you. When we leave I know now he'll be upset, but he knows—I've told him several times— that we're just on holiday here, not going to stay. If he thinks there's a chance we might live here with you all the time, he'll be heartbroken. I don't want him to end up like a child from a broken home."

"He's already from a broken home," he said curtly.

Marisa closed her eyes against this blunt, cruel statement and pulled air into her lungs by sheer force of will. "Until I saw him with you I didn't realise how much he's been missing a father. To find one in you, then to be torn away from you—I couldn't put him through that again."

"Again?" he asked sharply.

She nodded. "He grieved for my mother after her death, but he was heartbroken when Dad went—he'd been Dad's little mate."

He stepped away, leaving her suddenly cold, his expression closed against her. Quickly, before he could say anything, she blurted, "And you could meet someone and fall in love with her."

Only to have him dismiss it with quick, cold assurance. "I keep my promises."

Shocked by a lightning flash of insight, Marisa clenched her teeth on something too close to a sob. If Rafe ever loved another woman it would hurt—so much.

But it would be even worse to be engaged to him and know it was only his unsparing integrity that kept him beside her.

An acute, panicky sense of vulnerability stopped her from speaking. She'd already endured one barren relationship; she was not going to let herself be seduced into another.

Was this love...?

No. She didn't even know what love was. Whatever she'd felt for David had been false, based on her need for security. This too might be the same...

She gave him a hunted look. "Do you think I—any

woman—would be happy knowing only a promise was keeping a man beside her?"

Rafe's brows rose. "I hope that your complete lack of sense is due to raging passion," he murmured lazily, "rather than a sudden loss of brain cells. Relax—it's not going to happen. If it makes you feel any better, I'm not at all sure that I'm capable of the sort of love poets celebrate. But I can assure you I don't deliberately hurt people…and I think we have more than enough going to enjoy a very satisfactory relationship."

And he ran a forefinger from her chin down the slender column of her throat to the far-from-sexy neckline of her polo shirt.

Shivering, stunned by her body's sensuous response to that sure, sensitively judged caress, she concentrated on marshalling her thoughts into a coherent argument. "R-Rafe, this is serious. We can't play with lives like that—not Keir's, not our own. And we don't even know if getting engaged will keep David away."

His finger stilled before he lifted it to tilt her chin so that he could search her face. "I am not in the habit of playing with lives." Each word was clipped and decisive, as though her words had touched a nerve. "And if an engagement isn't likely to keep your ex-husband away, a marriage certainly would."

Marisa had to lock her knees to keep herself upright. Eyes widening, she stared at him as though he'd threatened her with a gun.

"Are you mad?" she asked faintly, managing to take one wobbly step away from him.

"I suspect I am," he said, something like humour glinting in his eyes. It disappeared quickly and in a crisp, judicial voice he said, "You have two options. You can run again and hope Brown never finds you and

Keir, or you can stay and fight this out once and for all. Hiding in New Zealand is pretty near impossible. It's too small, with too few people. Even in huge countries with large populations, it's difficult to stay hidden. If you meet him face to face, you'll feel safer with some protection. I can give you that."

"Why?" she asked starkly. "You don't really want to marry me—you don't even *know* me…"

"I know you saved my life," he said austerely. "I can imagine how hard it was for you to get me out of that plane, then support me to the hut."

He waited, but her quick brain let her down and a more primitive part adjured her to remain silent.

Crisply Rafe said, "I know you'd gladly sacrifice your life for your son. I also know loyalty like that is hard to earn and probably even harder to keep."

"Any mother would do the same," she returned with stubborn determination.

"Not all. My mother took a pay-off of ten million dollars and left without a backwards glance," he told her with savage emphasis. "I was six. I stood in the gateway and watched her drive away, knowing she'd never come back."

Mutely she nodded.

He didn't reach out to her, but his intention was as palpable as though he'd stroked her. "*I* know I want you and that the wanting grows every time I see you."

"Yes, but is that enough?" she asked impulsively, then stopped, dismayed. Her skin heated again when she met his glinting scrutiny.

Damn, she thought urgently. Oh, damn and double damn—she'd just admitted she was every bit as hungry for him as he was for her.

Not that it mattered. Rafe was a sophisticated man

and according to the media he'd enjoyed the charms of some very sophisticated women. He'd have recognised the drumming heat of carnality between them the first time they'd kissed.

"For me, yes." He shrugged. "My father fell in love with my mother and married her out of hand. It was a disaster. His second wife he chose more carefully. They built a very strong marriage and were happy."

Marisa tried to ignore the treacherous inner part of her that was ignoring all the caveats and cautions to whisper seductively *Why not...?*

Swiftly she said, "I've already made one really bad decision when I married David. Now I have to think of Keir. If things fall to pieces one day it's he who will really suffer."

Rafe said calmly, "I agree. I'm not proposing an immediate marriage. An engagement will give us time to know each other better. It will also give you time to discover whether or not you'll be happy here." Clearly he discerned her fears, because he added, "And to find out whether you've made the same mistake with me as you did before."

"I don't think so," she admitted quietly. Rafe was even more dangerous to her than David—in an entirely different way. "But what's in it for you?"

And saw with wry amusement that her directness startled him.

But only for a second. It was soon chased away by a smile that held both amusement and a certain irony. "Apart from anything else, the pleasure of knowing that no matter how much I learn about you, you're always able to surprise me."

She blinked. "I don't set out to."

"I know. That's why I enjoy it. As for the other—"

He reached for her, letting his hands rest lightly on her shoulders before pulling her slowly into his arms, giving her time to step away. "I foresee that I would enjoy being married to you very much."

Her heart thudded to a stop, then lurched into uneven overdrive.

Eyes darkening, she froze. She couldn't say anything, nor did she struggle when he turned her face up towards him.

"And I intend for you to enjoy it very much too," he said with a narrowed, dangerous look that dared her to object.

And kissed her. Lost in the magic of his touch, his mouth, she spun out completely, but a tiny shred of self-control lingered, enough for her to say shakily when he lifted his head, "I d-don't think this is a good idea."

"Why?" he said, his mouth curving.

She dragged a breath into starving lungs, compelling her dazed, dreamy mind to concentrate. Soon, she thought hazily, soon she'd pull away, free herself from the heady exhilaration that drugged her.

"Because," she breathed helplessly.

Rafe's laughter was underlined by a raw note that emphasised the hardening of his body against her. He closed her eyes with quick kisses, then lowered his head and dropped more kisses on her throat.

A sensuous groan tore through Marisa, partly protest but caused by the most intense pleasure—like nothing she'd ever felt before.

It was enough to make her jerk backwards. For a heartbeat he resisted, then let her go, his expression hardening when he inspected her clouding face.

She burst into speech, trying to clear that sensuous haze from her mind. "You're not the sort of man to marry just to help someone out. And don't give me that guff about saving your life, either—you're rich enough to give me a million dollars and not even notice it had gone. That way you could salve any feelings of gratitude without tying yourself to me and another man's child. So what's in it for you?"

"Is that what you'd rather have—a million dollars?" he asked with a mirthless, cynical smile.

"If you gave me a million dollars," she told him, parrying his hooded gaze, "I'd hand the lot to a refuge for battered women."

He flung his head back and laughed. "I suspect you would and without a second thought."

"Count on it," she told him, adding with a twisted smile, "although I can't guarantee not to give it a second thought, or even a third one. But I've learned how to live without relying on anyone else and I plan to keep on doing that. I don't want your money."

"Good, because I don't plan to give it to you. I learned the lesson my father had to learn the hard way—don't pay people off." He added on a deeper, more harsh note, "As for what's in it for me..."

He reached out for her.

Marisa's heart began to pound again. He didn't try to kiss her—he didn't even hold her tightly, yet her body ached with sweet delight at his nearness and she had to stop herself from sinking against him.

"I think you know what's in it for me," he said quietly. "And whatever it is, you feel it too."

"Lust," she said, the word stark with an obscure disappointment. What had she expected—a protestation of undying love?

It would never come from Rafe. Dared she accept his

proposition—follow this fierce longing down whatever path it led her? Dared she risk Keir's happiness?

Stupid questions. Common sense and everything she'd learned told her to refuse his proposition and walk away before she got hurt again.

Yet still she hesitated, so tempted to take a rash chance without putting her son first that she had to clench her jaw to stop the impetuous words tumbling out.

Was it too selfish to want something for herself?

Because she wanted Rafe with an intensity that made her dizzy, setting her body alight and scrambling her brain—and threatening her principles.

At least there would be honesty. Rafe had laid down his terms and she knew exactly what sort of marriage they'd have. One that was convenient for both of them. One that would provide a safe haven for Keir.

"What are you thinking?" Rafe asked.

She said, "That I need something—"

His brows rose. "What?"

Was there a hint of cynicism in his tone? Marisa thought furiously for a few seconds, then snapped her head up. "I want to make a condition. Two, actually."

CHAPTER ELEVEN

RAFE released her. Something in his expression chilled Marisa, but she went on, "I'll understand if you refuse them. I want a promise—a *written* promise—that if you fall in love with anyone else our engagement will finish. And I want you to promise me that when we part, you'll keep in touch with Keir. Seeing him with you has taught me that he needs a man in his life. One he can rely on. I know it's asking a lot—"

He said nothing, and she made a gesture of negation. "Forget about it. It's not worth the risk. We shouldn't let this— I can't let this…this—"

"The word *written* made me wonder if you've learned anything about me at all," he said on an odd note.

His mouth crushed her answer to nothingness and the words fled from her mind. Desire was a primal need in her, a longing that brooked no restraint, a potent force that grew as their lips clung and his body hardened against her.

When he lifted his head, he said harshly, "Lust, desire, passion, hunger—who cares what name we give it?" He released her, dark eyes narrowing as he scanned her face. "It's there and we both feel it."

"Yes," she said, the word a husky sigh.

It was surrender and he knew it. His gaze hardened,

heated, sending erotic shivers through her. "I agree to your conditions. So we'll go ahead with an engagement."

Bemused, her heart hammering so loudly in her chest she was sure he had to hear it, she nodded. A strange mixture of emotions coursed through her as she waited for him to pull her into his arms again with an expectancy that was as much foreboding as hope, as much fear as love.

But he made no move towards her and the heat from his kisses faded, leaving her cold from her heart out.

Rafe didn't ask for love, nor did he promise it. She honoured him for that. Perhaps this fake engagement would enable them to trust each other. They might even forge a bond—a relationship something like his father's second marriage, solid and long-lasting, only without the commitment or the sex...

And Keir would be as safe as she could make him.

In a muted voice she said, "Thank you."

Rafe's gaze narrowed. "I don't ever want to hear that again. If I do, I'll have to thank you in return for saving my life. It could get boring."

Feeling oddly disconnected, Marisa forced a smile and retreated into the new Marisa, the one who could deal with anything. "We can't have that. Anyway, it's untrue. You were utterly determined to get out of that plane."

Her world had suddenly been shaken vigorously and turned upside down. The irony of it, she realised later in the day, was that David might not be anywhere near Tewaka so there was no need for her to put her heart in such jeopardy...

She spent the rest of the afternoon making lists of

things to do, things to buy—the most important and necessary being clothes for Keir and herself. The pile she'd brought home before the garage burned down was pathetically small.

She was also called by the insurance agent, presumably on Rafe's instructions. It was a relief to talk to him of practicalities, although the loss of her small store of treasures and mementoes was still too painful to face.

And she ironed the clothes she'd brought in, the domestic routine almost soothing her. Nadine had the day off but she always made sure there was food prepared, so after organising dinner Marisa put Keir to bed, and then, heart thumping erratically, surveyed her scanty wardrobe. In the end she chose a light shirt in a bittersweet red that somehow gave her skin a honey-coloured sheen, teeming it with a narrow pair of trousers.

"You look like a sunset," she said aloud.

For a few moments she hesitated in front of the mirror, nerves taut, then swung around and headed for the small parlour. Rafe was standing at the window, looking out over the lawn, still spring-green and lush. He turned and the banked fires in her blazed up when he smiled.

"All well?"

"Yes, he's sound asleep." She covered her strange nervousness by glancing at her watch. "Dinner should be ready in half an hour."

He indicated a tray. "Champagne is definitely appropriate for tonight. Do you like it?"

"Of course." Watching him ease the cork free, she found herself wondering dismally how often he'd done this—and for how many women.

The thought alarmed her. She'd never indulged in jealousy and she wasn't going to start now.

And the champagne was delicious.

"It comes from a vineyard I own in the South Island," he said. "Now, I have a toast."

She didn't know what to expect, smiling when he said, "To us—you, Keir and me."

Moved by the simplicity of his words, she repeated them.

Once again they ate dinner out on the terrace. Dusk fell silently and the Southern Cross emerged, diamonds on black velvet. Rafe told her more about Manuwai's fascinating history, indulging her curiosity about the place.

Marisa wondered if he knew that as each minute passed a delicious tension was building inside her.

Eventually they came inside where Rafe said calmly, "You need a ring. There's family jewellery if you'd like that, but I'll also get a jeweller to come up with a selection. I doubt if it's necessary to announce it in any newspapers—"

"Oh, no!" She went a little pale. "No, that hadn't occurred to me."

"It's possibly going to finish up in the media, just the same." Observing her dismay, he said a little tersely, "Expect some interest—and speculation—from the gossip writers, though I'll do what I can to dampen it down."

Slightly relieved, she nodded. David wouldn't read gossip columns. But when she said, "I don't need a ring", Rafe frowned.

"You do."

A note in his voice told her that need it or not, she was going to get one. After a wavering second, she decided this wasn't worth drawing a line in the sand, but she directed a challenging look at him. "Why?"

"An engagement ring means it's serious, not just a case of living together. To satisfy everyone, including your ex-husband, we need all the trimmings. And we need to do some entertaining. My friends will expect to meet you."

She tensed. "Do you think that's necessary?"

"Yes." He observed her a moment. "I hope you like them. Have you met Hani and Kelt Crysander-Gillen?"

The sudden change of subject threw her for a moment, but she shook her head. "I know of them," she said cautiously. "He's some sort of royal, isn't he, from an island in the Mediterranean?"

"No, *she*'s some sort of royal from an island in the Indian Ocean," he said with a glimmer of a smile. "Kelt's some sort of royal from a country in the Balkans, but he doesn't use his title. They live down the coast here on Kelt's station. I've known him since I was a kid. They're both extremely good company, and perfectly normal."

"Except for being royal," she said with a slight snap.

"Don't worry, they won't expect you to curtsy." When she gave a strained smile he said crisply, "You didn't have any such fears about my friend Patrick, the garage owner who fixed your car. I choose my friends for their own sakes, not because they happen to have titles. I've been called plenty of things in my time, but never a snob."

"I know you're not," she said immediately, feeling rather small. She couldn't tell him she was fighting a private battle against becoming too entrenched in his life, and that meeting his friends somehow made their agreement too personal.

His hard gaze warmed. "I'll give them a call and see if they'll come up to dinner shortly."

Marisa said politely, "That would be lovely. Do you want me to be hostess?"

Her refusal to take anything for granted irked him, but she was skittish enough without calling her on it. "Of course." He examined her face, his body tightening when his gaze skimmed the softly full contours of her mouth.

Soon he'd take her to bed and scotch any chance of second thoughts by making her his in the most basic and simple way of all.

She might have agreed to this engagement to protect young Keir, but she'd made no attempt to deny that the attraction between them was mutual.

Rafe sometimes thought he'd been born a cynic. If he had, it had been reinforced by his mother's abandonment. Certainly he doubted that love—the romantic, transcendent passion poets eulogised—really existed. He suspected it was a temporary madness and one he'd long ago accepted he wasn't likely to succumb to.

Desire he understood, and friendship. He felt both for Marisa and, as well, he recognised and respected her protectiveness towards her son—perhaps because of the mother who'd sold him for ten million dollars.

Marisa's kisses told him she'd be a willing and responsive lover. As well, she was a stimulating companion and she'd settled easily into life at Tewaka.

She broke into his thoughts with a coolly delivered statement. "You look like a lion eyeing up an antelope— anticipatory yet satisfied, because the lion knows its prey hasn't got a hope of getting away. And that makes me nervous."

Rafe threw back his head and laughed. He wasn't going to tell her she'd nailed exactly how he was feeling.

"I wasn't thinking in terms of predator and prey,"

he said, "and certainly not of killing anything. On the contrary, my thoughts and emotions are bordering on the lustful."

A surge of colour burned through Marisa's skin, and with it, a bold impulse. "Then why don't—?" Mortified at what she'd almost said, she clamped down on the rest.

But she couldn't pull her gaze away. Fascinated, she watched his gaze kindle as it swept her face, echoing the heat that flamed into life inside her, surging through her like a forest fire...

Fires destroy, she reminded herself and tried to breathe. But forest fires allow new life to flourish in their aftermath.

A little roughly he asked, "Are you indicating I'm being too noble by giving you time?"

Lips clamped tightly together in case she made an even greater fool of herself, she hesitated. He didn't move. Marisa's breath locked in her throat as she wavered on the brink of a momentous decision, one she couldn't take back or flee from.

If she made the wrong decision she'd regret it for the rest of her life.

If only she knew which *was* the wrong decision...

This was one thing she had to decide for herself, yet it took all her courage to follow her heart and give a swift, shy nod.

Rafe covered the distance between them in one rapid stride. He looked down and this time she met his gaze with no hint of challenge.

"Marisa?" He said it steadily, still not reaching out to her.

Why didn't he touch her? She dragged a breath into starving lungs. "What?"

"Say yes," he commanded almost harshly. At her nod, he tipped her chin. "*Say* it—but only if you feel it."

And suddenly it was all right. He did want her—as much as she wanted him.

Yet, like him, she needed the words. "I feel it. Do you?"

"Hell, *yes*," he said fiercely and at last caught her to him and held her there, burying his face in her hair as his grip strengthened and his body became hard against her.

She made a muffled noise in her throat and turned her face up in invitation—one he had no hesitation in accepting.

This time there was no holding back. Rafe kissed her as though he'd been starving for her since they'd first met. The thought flashed across Marisa's mind, only to be immediately banished by the force of his passion, powerful and demanding and everything she wanted.

His arms tightened around her, bringing her against his hips. Responding instantly to their blatant thrust, she gasped his name as he lifted his head and looked down at her, his narrowed gaze intent and gleaming.

"I know how to shut that quick mouth of yours now," he said on a raw note.

"Don't you dare—"

Rafe laughed so deeply she felt it reverberate through her and realised with shock that nothing like this had happened before to her.

"I like to see those green eyes light up like smouldering emeralds," he murmured, his sensuous mouth an inch from hers. "What am I not to dare?"

She had to think, reassemble her thoughts from passionate confusion. "Kissing me might stop me talking, but only while it lasts," she said clumsily, pursuing this because something told her it was important.

His eyes narrowed even further. "I know that," he said quietly. "I am not your ex-husband, Marisa. I value you for the person you are."

Value. A cold, unemotional word compared to love, yet to have Rafe value her was precious. She stiffened.

Love? Stunned, she realised what she wanted.

Rafe's love…for ever.

Because somewhere, sometime, she'd fallen in love with him. How had it happened so quickly, sneaking up on her like a silent-footed predator?

Ambushed by love, she thought half-hysterically. And this was no fly-by-night passion.

Yes, she wanted Rafe, but she loved him for other things—his surprising kindness, the unyielding determination that had got them to the hut, even his intimidating authority.

Her newfound love burned deep inside her, a steady flame that would stay alive for the rest of her life. And one day, perhaps, Rafe might learn to love her. If he didn't…

For a moment she quailed, but forced herself to face the chance of a future without Rafe.

"Get that damned man out of your head," he commanded, the words hard and short.

Marisa rallied. If he didn't learn to love her, she'd cope.

But it would hurt some secret, essential part of her for the rest of her life.

Her uplifted glance told her he expected an answer. Revealing her love for him would be a humiliation she didn't think she could bear, yet she had to bite back the words. They were going into this as equals and she wanted it to stay that way. Confessing to a hopeless love might well wreck their relationship; certainly it would alter the balance of power and put her in an inferior position.

See, you don't really trust him, something cowardly and treacherous whispered at the back of her mind.

"He's not there. I value you too," she said helplessly.

He nodded, but she sensed a subtle withdrawal, an aloofness that fled when he kissed her again and that rapturous fire took her over, mind and body.

Looking around, he said, "We can't make love here. I refuse to make love to you on a sofa."

Marisa laughed huskily and tried to cover her total surrender by muttering, "I feel like a secondary-school kid in a car."

"Not my style, even then."

She wavered, feeling uncommonly like a guilty schoolgirl. He looked down at her and laughed again, and she relaxed and smiled at him. "Nor mine," she said.

"My room."

Rafe's bedroom was huge. And beautiful.

Even living amidst the gracious beauty that was Manuwai, she hadn't expected this. The house was filled with delightful things chosen over the years by people whose wealth was restrained by discernment and taste. There was no striving to impress, no overt opulence or display emphasising wealth and power.

Rafe's room was different, although she couldn't quite put a finger on it. It breathed sophistication from the huge French sleigh bed on a shallow dais, its frame glowing with the polish and loving care of at least a century, to the massive armoire on one wall and the opulent curtains and silk bedcover.

Yet it was oddly impersonal and so far from her experience she hesitated, then stopped.

"It's overwhelming, I know."

She flinched at Rafe's accurate deduction.

He continued, "Apart from the bed, my mother— my birth mother, that is—had it redecorated when she married my father. When she left he moved out, but I like the outlook so I took it over when I was eighteen or so."

Marisa swallowed. "It's very lovely."

His hand light on her arm, he turned her around so the huge bed no longer dominated her field of vision and surveyed her with an expression she couldn't read, his boldly chiselled features impassive. "I hear another *but* coming and you're right. It's expensive and over the top—like my mother, I believe."

"I love that bed," she said swiftly. "And the armoire."

"Are you having second thoughts?"

"Not about you," she said, then stopped, furious with herself. She'd vowed never to be vulnerable to another man, yet here she was, blushing like a virgin.

She swallowed and started again, trying hard to be cool and confident. "Are you and your mother in contact?"

His face could have won him a fortune at poker. "I haven't seen her since she walked out," he said distantly. "A few years ago she got in touch through a lawyer; she'd run through the money she sold me for and needed more."

Marisa opened her mouth, then cut short the impulsive words.

He answered her unspoken question. "I made her an allowance." His mouth twisted. "As much as she needs, not as much as she wanted."

Marisa thought of the boy—barely older then Keir—whose mother had walked away from him and turned into his arms, impulsively hugging him. "Do you hate her?"

"In a way it's worse—I feel nothing for her," he said levelly, pulling her closer. "I saw very little of her even when she lived here. When my father remarried several years later Jane was far more of a mother to me than the one who actually bore me." He shrugged. "You won't have to worry about a mother-in-law. Believe me, she isn't ever likely to want to establish contact."

The last word was a caress against her lips and then his mouth took hers, warmly seductive and very persuasive. Marisa went under—lost in pleasure, in excitement, in the security and sensuality of his powerful body against her.

On fire, she luxuriated in her own response as he explored her mouth and then the warm length of her throat, one hand deftly flicking open the buttons of her shirt to cup a breast. Her heart thundered in her ears, each drumbeat marking another step in her surrender.

Delight shot through her at the sinuous stroke of his fingers across the alerted tips of her breast. Like honey-eyed lightning, pleasure crackled across every cell in her body, mingling crazily with an erotic frustration that urged her to tug his shirt free.

More than anything she wanted to feel his skin against her palms, but the shirt refused to move.

Rafe kissed her again, a snatched, urgent kiss that was cut short when he straightened and in one smooth movement pulled the garment over his head.

He was magnificent—skin sheened coppery-gold over corded muscles as he tossed the shirt on to a chair and turned to face her again. Silken scrolls of hair joined in the middle of his chest, forming a line that plunged downwards. Dumbstruck, Marisa devoured the sight of him, then reached out a tentative finger and followed that line to the waistline of his trousers.

Mouth compressed, he froze. Clumsily, Marisa wrenched off her shirt and tossed it after his. Rafe's eyes narrowed and the ache in her became a demand, an insistence.

And then cold caution forced her to shut her eyes against him. She dragged in a breath too close to a sob and opened them again. "Rafe, we can't. I'm sorry—I didn't think. I'm not protected."

"I have protection," he said curtly. "Do you trust me to use it?"

"Yes." Her voice shook, but she held his eyes steadily.

"You make me feel a hundred metres tall."

Startled, she asked, "Why?"

"You forgot about it until now," he said and gave her a wry smile, "and although it might be arrogant of me, I can only assume you forgot it for the same reason I did."

Because she was too absorbed in the erotic enchantment of his love-making...

Nodding, she waited impatiently, but he didn't take the small step that separated them.

He was waiting for her to make the first move.

What should she do? Colour burned up through her skin, heated her face. She just didn't have what it took to stand there and strip off in front of him.

Silently he turned her with a light touch. She shivered at the feel of his fingers against her skin while he made short work of the clip before twisting her to face him again.

When she met his eyes it was all she could do to hide

a gasp. They blazed, fiercely hungry in a face that was all harshness, its bold planes and angles in high relief.

In a voice that told her how much restraint he was using, he said, "You are beautiful."

"I have stretch marks," she blurted.

He flung back his head and laughed, and before she had a chance to do more than bitterly regret her inane remark he swept her close to him and held her tight, one hand sweeping down to hold her against his aroused loins.

Headstrong hunger took her over. She shuddered at the power of it and even more when he slid his other hand between them, taking with it the zip on her trousers.

"I don't care about stretch marks," he said and kissed her again.

Sinking into pleasure she'd never before experienced, Marisa believed him.

He lifted her and carried her across to that huge bed, easing her down on to it and somehow managing to rid her of her last garments so that she lay naked on the silken cover. Still embarrassed, feeling far too much like some harem girl brought in for her master's pleasure, she closed her eyes under his scorching survey.

Until Rafe's voice caused them to fly open again.

"Look at me," he commanded. "There's no one else in this room but you and me, and I want you." He dropped his trousers and stood straight, splendid as a bronze statue of some ancient athlete. "Do you want me?"

"Yes," she said instantly, her voice sure and direct.

"Then there's no reason for you to worry about anything else," he said and came down beside her and kissed her, one clever, experienced hand slipping the length of her body to show her just how erotically disturbing this potent hunger could be.

Later she'd allow herself the voluptuous luxury of remembering how skilfully he'd coaxed her into wildness, caressing her skin and then covering it with kisses until an agony of need brought a muffled cry from her lips.

But while she experienced his lovemaking, she had no words to use, could only surrender to a raw passion that met and matched his until he said something short and terse beneath his breath and slid over her and into her, and then stopped, every muscle locked while she convulsed beneath and around him, her body in thrall to such transcendent ecstasy she almost sobbed as each wave took her further and further into satiation.

Until finally it shattered and she came down in the safety of his arms, gasping as she dragged air into her lungs.

When she looked up she whispered, "I'm so sorry…"

He frowned. "Why?"

"Because you haven't… I…" She exhaled and said, "I didn't know it could happen so fast." Or at all…

Not to her, anyway.

"Now I feel two hundred metres tall," he said and kissed her, this time with something like tenderness.

To Marisa's stunned astonishment his kiss summoned fire from the embers. She welcomed the slow backwards-and-forwards friction that gently, sensuously, stirred her into life once more. And this time she soared even higher, drowning in a tide of bliss, and almost immediately he followed her, his proud head flung up, skin gleaming as he took his pleasure in her.

When it was finished he held her close as she sank down to something approaching normalcy, her whole being lulled by a kind of radiance that almost made her weep, while their heartbeats slowed and synchronised.

Eventually Rafe said, "I wish you didn't have to leave, but I suppose sharing a bed with me is something we'll have to introduce Keir to slowly."

"Yes," she said, a little jolted at being recalled to real life again.

Would Rafe get tired of always having to consider her son? It should be reassuring to know that although love didn't come into this equation, he enjoyed sex with her.

The question nagged sufficiently for her to ask him.

He didn't hand her an automatic reply, but said after a moment's pause, "I've always had to consider other people—my sister, and the workers here and at the various interests I have around the world. I'm growing fond of Keir—he's a good kid." He moved slightly so he could see her face. "I won't resent him—because that's really what you're asking."

His perception was brutal but accurate. "Yes, I suppose so," she said with a rueful smile. "I'm glad."

"I'll be spending far more time at home than I have in the past," he said, still watching her.

Rafe rather prided himself on his ability to read faces, but Marisa's hid far more than it revealed.

However, he was sure of one thing. She'd enjoyed their lovemaking. Neither orgasm had been faked, not even the second one. His body stirred at the memory and he pushed back the tumble of honey-gold hair from her face and kissed her again.

She responded with gratifying enthusiasm, but he curbed his instinctive urge to take things further. Her shocked delight at her own capacity for passion hadn't escaped him, but he wasn't prepared to jeopardise her fragile trust by exhausting her.

Soon the news would get around and that could well flush David Brown out of whatever rat hole he was hiding in. Tomorrow he'd ginger up his investigator.

CHAPTER TWELVE

THE next day Marisa and Rafe told Keir that he was going to live at Waimanu for a while. Warily, Marisa watched her son absorb this, dark eyes going from one to the other.

Eventually he asked a little tentatively, "Will you be my dad then?"

"I'll always be your friend if you want me to be," Rafe said.

His words and the calm tone were perfect. Marisa let out a silent breath of relief when Keir flushed and beamed.

"Yes," he said exuberantly, adding with automatic politeness, "Please."

He gave another huge grin and high-fived— something he'd learned from his schoolmates. As Rafe bent to clap palms with him, relief gave Marisa's smile a buoyancy she hadn't felt for a long time.

"Yes, I do want to be your friend," Keir said positively. "Like Manu. He gave me half his banana the other day at school and he said I could come and play with him after school one day." He looked at his mother.

Marisa said, "One day, certainly." She didn't expect everything to be so simple, but his acceptance of the

situation delighted her—overwhelming for a few minutes her fear that Keir would be hurt.

When he'd gone off to tell an already informed
Nadine, Rafe looked at her. "Don't worry about him.
Or his father. Even if he turns up, you and Keir will
both be perfectly safe."

"How are you going to manage that?" she asked
starkly.

"I have ways. By the way, I've warned the school,"
he said.

Marisa's head came up, and she stared indignantly
at him. "I saw the principal in the street today."

"I see. I wish you had discussed it with me first."

"I should have," he agreed urbanely. "It won't happen again."

He reached for her, holding her in a grip that was
firm and infinitely exciting.

"Relax," he said. "I know how independent you
are—I admire you for that immensely—but let me deal
with this, all right?"

Trying to relax, she said, "I'll let you get away with
that this time, but don't think it will work every time."

He laughed and kissed her, and for a few precious
moments she could forget everything.

Until Keir's voice intruded. "Manu said his parents
kiss all the time," he announced from behind them. "Are
you going to too?"

Marisa jerked, but Rafe held her in a firm grip.
"Quite a lot," he said. "Why?"

Wrinkling his nose, Keir said, "'Cause it looks
funny." He switched his gaze to Rafe. "Manu said you
can ride like the best jockey in the world. Can you show
me so I can ride too? Manu said you still have the horse
that showed you how to ride."

"I have," Rafe said, releasing an intensely relieved Marisa.

Clearly her son was going to use Manu's parents as an exemplar for their relationship. Nothing of possessiveness had showed in his voice and her spirits soared.

"Sammy is too old for anyone to ride now," Rafe continued. "I'll put you up on another horse. Then if you still want to learn to ride, we can see about finding a pony for you."

While Marisa was warily digesting this, Keir bounced with excitement. "Now?"

The telephone rang and Rafe said easily, "No, not now. This is an important call and I'll take this in my office."

As he left the room Keir grumbled, "I don't like that telephone. I want to ride."

"You heard Rafe. He'll take you for a ride when he can. Let's go and see if any birds have found the feeder we made yesterday yet."

But as they went out Marisa felt a cold finger of foreboding down her spine.

It took three days for Rafe to be able to fulfil his promise, and neither he nor Marisa had been allowed to forget it.

Marisa was surprised at how well it went. That afternoon Keir had been allowed to come home on the school bus with Manu and play at his house. She'd collected him after shutting up the shop and he was still buzzing about it. However, he obeyed instantly when Rafe warned him to speak quietly because it might spook the little brown mare.

Watching a little anxiously, Marisa was impressed by Rafe's patience and expertise.

"I should know what I'm doing," he said coolly when she commented on it. "My father put me up on a horse before I could walk and I watched him teach Gina to ride."

"I have to say the horse is extremely patient." They had made love the previous night and she had not been patient at all during the two other nights. Although she tried to convince herself she was imagining things, that odd sense of disconnection was still between them, as though he was building a wall against her.

"That's why I chose her," he said. "She's very sweet-tempered."

Keir was clearly enjoying himself, frowning with concentration as he listened, and instantly obeying each of Rafe's instructions.

"He has good balance and no fear," Rafe observed when the ten minutes he'd allotted for the first lesson was over. He looked at Marisa. "Do you ride?"

"This is probably the closest I've ever been to a horse."

Rafe asked, "Are you afraid of them?"

"Only in as much as they're a lot bigger than I am and I have no idea how they think."

"If you like," he said casually, "I'll take you on as a pupil too."

It was said lightly enough, but something in his tone alerted her, adding to her creeping apprehension.

Something had definitely changed. It was too subtle for her to put a finger on, but every sense was on full alert, stretched so tight she felt light-headed. He seemed to have withdrawn, revealing nothing but the most superficial of feelings and making polite chitchat as though she were a visitor, not the woman with whom he'd made wild and uninhibited love the previous night.

Her cheeks grew warm at the memory. Now she knew just how reckless she could be, how her body could sing under his skilful hands and turn to fire...

"Marisa?"

"Oh," she said, startled. Her colour deepened and she said swiftly, "Yes, I think I would like it, thank you."

When she looked up his gaze kindled, was shielded by thick black lashes, but he said merely, "Fine. But if Keir's to have his dinner on time, it's time to go."

Later, when Keir had been put to bed, she walked along to the terrace where they normally had dinner. Rafe wasn't there, and that elusive apprehension abraded her nerves once more.

The housekeeper came in. "Ah, there you are. Rafe said to tell you he's riding and he'll be later than usual tonight. Shall I get you a drink?"

"No, thanks." Marisa paused before asking, "Where does he ride?"

"He's gone along the beach. Usually that means he needs to think through something. If you walk out to the summerhouse you'll probably see him coming back." Nadine smiled affectionately. "I think he misses playing polo. He had to give it up after his father died because he was so busy."

The summerhouse was placed to take in a view of the long sweep of the ocean beach. Cicadas shrilled their high-pitched wooing calls—like miniature buzz-saws, Marisa thought as she took up the binoculars kept there and focused them on the horse and rider in the distance. Her heart thudded when she noted great clumps of wet sand flying from the big gelding's hooves.

It couldn't be as dangerous as it looked.

And Rafe was obviously a superb horseman, moving as one with the animal. When they came closer she could see his face, purposeful and set as though he'd made a difficult decision.

She waited until horse and rider left the beach, then ambled back to the house, enjoying the scents and sounds of summer. A stray bee buzzed around her head before zooming off like a golden bullet in the sunlight towards a bush humming with other nectar-seekers.

She loved this garden. *Face it, you love everything about Manuwai—the house, the beaches, even the workers you've met so far...*

And she'd give it all up if the man who owned it decided he no longer wanted to live here.

She'd been told love was all-encompassing, and during the short time since Rafe had entered her life again, she'd learned that it was true, there were no limits to it.

How long she walked in the muted light of early evening she didn't know. Questions—most of them unanswerable—beat her bluntly like physical blows.

Was Rafe regretting their engagement? Pierced by pain, she faltered. Whatever happened, she'd deal with it. But she'd never be the same again.

And coping seemed a dreary way to spend the rest of her life.

You'd have Keir...

It hurt to admit it, but her son was no longer enough. She was a woman and Rafe had woken her to her full potential.

She stopped beside the vivid flowers of a tropical rhododendron, so blazingly golden they were incandescent in the soft light. They dazzled her eyes and brought tears to them.

Was that all it was? Sex?

No, she loved Rafe for what he was, not just because he made her feel a rapturous certainty in his arms.

And she'd had this conversation with herself before. She had to stop going obsessively over and over the same worries, the same concerns.

A sixth sense lifted the hair on the back of her neck. She swivelled and saw him watching her. Something she saw in his face brought an icy wave of fear.

"You'd better tell me," she said harshly.

If anything, his face hardened even more. "Walk with me to the summerhouse."

Once there, she met unreadable eyes, burnished and brutal as the barrel of a gun. Voice shaking, she demanded, "What is it?"

"David Brown is dead."

The words fell like bombs into the still, salt-fragrant air. *"W-what?"* she stammered, her legs shaking so much he caught her.

Only for a moment. As though he no longer wanted to touch her, he lowered her into one of the chairs and stepped back, turning slightly to look out to sea before he spoke.

"He died this afternoon on the road here." No emotion was evident in his cool, judicial tone. "You know that steep patch through bush just before you come out on to the coast? He was driving too fast to take the corner. He drove straight over the edge on to the rocks below. He'd have died instantly."

She flinched, imagining the fall—the terror and the pain. And then oblivion...

Tears burned behind her eyes. Whatever she had feared, she had never wanted this. "Thank heaven for that at least," she said unevenly. "I'm glad he didn't suffer. It's horrible to be so—so relieved, but I d-didn't want him to die. But—he was coming here?"

"No, speeding away. It looks as though he was waiting for Keir to come home in the school bus with Manu." He paused as she dragged in a sharp breath and turned blindly towards the house. Roughly he said, "It's all right, Marisa. He's still in bed, still asleep. I've just checked."

That stopped her. After a short hesitation she turned back to him and said harshly, "How do you know this?"

"I had someone keeping an eye on both you and Keir." He saw her blink at that, but she said nothing, and he went on, "Yesterday she noticed a man in a car who seemed very interested in the children leaving school. When she phoned the details through she found the vehicle had been bought by Brown in Auckland a month ago."

Struggling to control her distress, she asked, "But how did David know Keir would be on the bus today?"

Rafe quelled an instinctive desire to comfort her. Better to get the ugly truth done with first. "He was there again today, watching Keir get on to the bus with Manu. He left then and my investigator stayed with the bus, following it. When they reached Waimanu he was waiting, but as soon as he saw her drive up he took off. She followed and he took the corner too fast and went over on to the rocks."

He restrained himself from telling her that his investigator had unearthed enough information for him to be very concerned about the reappearance of David Brown.

White-faced, she stared at him, absorbing the implications. "No, that won't fit. He didn't know Keir was his son. Even if he had been, he wouldn't have been interested…" Her voice trailed away and her gaze narrowed, became accusing. "You know more than you're telling me."

She had to know sooner or later. It might as well be sooner. "The garage at the Tanners' place *was* deliberately set on fire and his car was seen on the road close by that night."

"But if he was following Keir, he must have had plans for him too," she said thinly.

"We'll never know. Possibly he was finding out where I lived so he could set fire to something else."

She refused to accept his false comfort. "But you don't believe that."

He shook his head. "I don't know. Nobody will ever know. Leave it at that."

Visibly gathering strength, Marisa straightened her shoulders. Sombrely she said, "I suppose when he found out I'd moved to Tewaka, he'd have thought I'd chosen it because you live here."

"Almost certainly." When she shivered, he said brusquely, "You realise that his death has freed you from any need to be concerned about Keir's future?"

She stared at him, her eyes too darkly shadowed for him to guess at her thoughts.

So that was it.

Marisa tried to speak but her throat was too dry. He was telling her she could go. She had to swallow before she could say, "Yes, I do." Moving carefully, like an old woman, she got to her feet. "Then I have to thank you for…for everything. Keir and I will move out as soon as I can organise it."

Stone-faced, he said, "You don't have to." He paused, then added curtly, "I'd like you to stay. But if you want to go, then of course you must."

Marisa looked away, pride fighting a losing battle with need. *Tell him*, she urged herself. *Tell him you don't want to go—then at least you'll know...*

But cowardice kept her silent.

Almost aggressively Rafe asked, "Do you want to go, Marisa?"

She stiffened her spine and looked directly at him, and took the biggest gamble of her life. "No, I do not. I want to stay here and marry you and have your children—if—"

Her voice broke on a sob.

After one short, explicit word under his breath, he grabbed her—*grabbed* her, her cool Rafe, always so self-sufficient, so confident—and hauled her against him as though he would never let her go.

"I knew I loved you when you made those conditions for our engagement," he said unsteadily.

Joy burst through her, a nova of delight and relief and pleasure. Trembling, she asked, "Why? I thought they'd put you off."

He didn't kiss her. Instead his arms clamped around her and he said unsteadily in a raw, formidable voice, "You were prepared to set me free without any recriminations if I met someone I could love and I thought, *I've already met her.* Before that I wanted you—your eyes caught my attention in Mariposa and when I saw you again I got a shock of recognition, as though I've been marking time since then, waiting for you."

"I know," she whispered, filled with a joy so palpable she felt she could fly. "Oh, yes, I know exactly how you felt—it was just like that for me too."

Eyes kindling, he looked down into her face. "But I had no idea how *much* I loved you until I heard of Brown's death. I've been through hell, afraid you'd leave once you knew any danger to Keir was over." He took in a sharp, impeded breath. "Damn it, Marisa, how do you feel about me? I need the words."

"I love you, of course. Surely you must know that?" she cried. "I think I must have started to love you when we met in Mariposa—before then I'd been that drab, miserable shell of a woman, but you arrived like a storm—like rain after drought. I'd been so passive, so—so *useless*—and somehow—by just being *you*— you forced me to realise that if I wanted to get away, I had to fight for it. And I did. I told David that I was going home whether he wanted me to or not."

"And you did," he said with immense satisfaction and at long last bent his head and kissed her.

Later that night, lying in Rafe's arms, she thought dreamily that she was where she belonged. Her parents had loved her, but they'd wanted a daughter like them, a gypsy at heart, and David had tried to force her to become whatever he'd wanted…

She hoped he'd found peace at last.

As she had. Along with passion and laughter and the sweet torment of love, she had found a home. Rafe was everything she'd wanted without even realising it and he accepted her as she was; with him she could be her true self.

"Going to sleep?" His voice was rough and tender at the same time. "When are you going to marry me?"

She yawned and turned over and kissed his shoulder. "How soon can we get married?" she murmured.

Rafe laughed, the low, triumphant laugh of a lover. "We can probably get married within a month." He paused, and then said in a voice she'd never heard before, "I've been so sure I could never lose my head over a woman, that I simply didn't have it in me to fall in love, and then you moved in and I fell before I understood what the hell had hit me."

"You and me both," she told him with love and a sense of utter commitment, and ran her hand down his chest.

"I love you," he said deeply. "I'll love you for the rest of my life."

"And I love you and always will."

Their wedding would come in time, but both knew those words marked their pledge to each other.

Rafe kissed her, murmuring against her mouth, "Tired?"

"I thought I was," she purred, running her hand across his chest, "but I seem to have new lease of life…"

He smiled. "Me too."

And together, confidently, they embarked on their future.

* * * * *

LET'S TALK
Romance

For exclusive extracts, competitions
and special offers, find us online:

[f] facebook.com/millsandboon

[twitter] @MillsandBoon

[instagram] @MillsandBoonUK

Get in touch on 01413 063232

For all the latest titles coming soon, visit
millsandboon.co.uk/nextmonth

MILLS & BOON
A ROMANCE FOR EVERY READER

- **FREE** delivery direct to your door

- **EXCLUSIVE** offers every month

- **SAVE** up to 25% on pre-paid subscriptions

SUBSCRIBE AND SAVE

millsandboon.co.uk/Subscribe

WANT EVEN MORE

ROMANCE?

SUBSCRIBE AND SAVE TODAY!

'Mills & Boon books, the perfect way to escape for an hour or so.'

MISS W. DYER

'Excellent service, promptly delivered and very good subscription choices.'

MISS A. PEARSON

'You get fantastic special offers and the chance to get books before they hit the shops.'

MRS V. HALL

Visit millsandboon.co.uk/Subscribe and save on brand new books.

JOIN THE
MILLS & BOON
BOOKCLUB

* **FREE** delivery direct to your door

* **EXCLUSIVE** offers every month

* **EXCITING** rewards programme

50% OFF
YOUR FIRST
PARCEL

Join today at
Millsandboon.co.uk/Bookclub

MILLS & BOON

THE HEART OF ROMANCE

A ROMANCE FOR EVERY READER

MODERN

Prepare to be swept off your feet by sophisticated, sexy and seductive heroes, in some of the world's most glamourous and romantic locations, where power and passion collide.

HISTORICAL

Escape with historical heroes from time gone by. Whether your passion is for wicked Regency Rakes, muscled Vikings or rugged Highlanders, awak the romance of the past.

MEDICAL

Set your pulse racing with dedicated, delectable doctors in the high-pressure world of medicine, where emotions run high and passion, comfort ar love are the best medicine.

True Love

Celebrate true love with tender stories of heartfelt romance, from the rush of falling in love to the joy a new baby can bring, and a focus on the emotional heart of a relationship.

Desire

Indulge in secrets and scandal, intense drama and plenty of sizzling hot action with powerful and passionate heroes who have it all: wealth, status, good looks…everything but the right woman.

HEROES

Experience all the excitement of a gripping thriller, with an intense romance at its heart. Resourceful, true-to-life women and strong, fearless me face danger and desire - a killer combination!

To see which titles are coming soon, please visit

millsandboon.co.uk/nextmonth

JOIN US ON SOCIAL MEDIA!

Stay up to date with our latest releases, author news and gossip, special offers and discounts, and all the behind-the-scenes action from Mills & Boon...

 millsandboon

 millsandboonuk

 millsandboon

It might just be true love...

GET YOUR ROMANCE FIX!

MILLS & BOON
blog

Get the latest romance news, exclusive author interviews, story extracts and much more!

blog.millsandboon.co.uk

MILLS & BOON

MODERN

Power and Passion

Prepare to be swept off your feet by sophisticated, sexy and seductive heroes, in some of the world's most glamourous and romantic locations, where power and passion collide.

...ight Modern stories published every month, find them all at:

millsandboon.co.uk/Modern

MILLS & BOON
True Love
Romance from the Heart

Celebrate true love with tender stories of heartfelt romance, from the rush of falling in love to the joy a new baby can bring, and a focus on the emotional heart of a relationship.

Four True Love stories published every month, find them all at:
millsandboon.co.uk/TrueLove

MILLS & BOON

Desire

Indulge in secrets and scandal, intense drama and plenty of sizzling hot action with powerful and passionate heroes who have it all: wealth, status, good looks…everything but the right woman.

Four Desire stories published every month, find them all at:

millsandboon.co.uk